BALLINA STORIES AND POEMS

BALLINA STORIES AND POEMS

AUBREY MALONE

First published January 2019

ISBN 978-0-244-14560-6

Cover: St Muredach's cathedral Ballina

PENNILESS PRESS PUBLICATIONS
Website :www. pennilesspress. co. uk/books

Some of these stories originally appeared in a different form in *The Sunday Tribune, The Irish Press, The Evening News,The Connacht Tribun* and *Mature Living.*

Some of them were also published in *Penultimate* (Citron Press), *Flight* (Cillenna Press), and four books from Chipmunka Publishing: *A Window to the World, I Was an Elvis Impersonator, A Life at the Bar* and *The Foggy Ruins of Time.*

Some of the poems appeared originally in two books from Lapwing Publications: *Idle Time* and *Mature Student.*

CONTENTS

A Life Less Ordinary

I was born in Ballina. There were five in my family. I was the youngest. That's the kind of detail Freudians have a field day with. To them it would mean I was the 'special one'. I had two older brothers and sisters.

My mother was too busy rearing us to worry about who might have received special treatment. She told me once that she never wanted to get married. After my father fell for her he demanded that she got to the altar with him.

Neither did she ever want children. That made it all the more strange that she ended up having five of us.

She was pregnant more often than not. Money was so tight, the only holidays she got was when she was in hospital having babies.

My father had a dream of putting his sons through college. Daughters, in those days, were generally not thought of in that way.

My older siblings left home before I got into my teens. Being on my own gave me a lot of independence.

I spent a lot of time in my own world. Every weekend I cycled to Enniscrone, the beach eight miles away from us. When I got there I just sat down looking out at the sea.

I was never a mixer. Because of that I developed an empathy with outsiders. One of my best friends at school was from a broken home. Sometimes he came in with marks on his body. Things like this weren't followed up on in those days. His father was a drinker. He beat him when he was in a bad mood, which was most of the time.

My father was a labourer in an engineering firm. We all knew he'd never get a promotion because he allowed people use him as a doormat. My mother said this kind of thinking was foolish, that people were the same to you regardless of what you did or didn't do for them. But he had this intense craving to be liked and it came against him.

He was a humble man even in his own house. He always sat in the same seat in the corner of the kitchen beside the stove. Most times you'd hardly know he was there at all. He came home at four o'clock every day and hung his coat on a nail on the back of the door. My mother gave him a cup of tea that he drank almost in a gulp. After he swallowed it he'd light his pipe and look out the window. That seemed to be all he wanted in life. If anyone asked him a question about politics or anything outside his personal orbit he'd get tongue-tied.

I never knew if my mother was happy or not. She was like a sphinx. Sometimes she cried if we were sick but she didn't talk much, either to us or to my father, unless there was something practical to be sorted out.

I hated school. Sometimes I feigned sickness to get out of going, My father usually fell for it but my mother would do her best to get me to go. A good education, she felt, could get us out of the poverty trap. I told her I'd be just as happy selling nails as being a university lecturer, something she could never understand.

My father had different ideas about how he'd come into money. He was forever buying tickets for raffles, forever filling in coupons in the paper. Every Sunday night he did the Spot-the-Ball competition in the *People*. That was an English newspaper. My mother didn't like it because it had pictures of women with hardly any clothes on them.

One year he won the Spot-the-Ball competition but so did half of the country. When the money was divided he only got a pittance. After that the whole idea of winning anything became a farce. We laughed about it as we sat around the fire but my father wasn't amused. It was as if his pitch for glory had passed him by.

I loved him but I couldn't help being ashamed of the fact that he never did anything with his life. At night in bed I used to dream that I was secretly the son of a king, that one day my true identity would be discovered like in the fairytales.

As I grew older I started to feel ashamed of being ashamed. I knew he was doing the best for us, and for himself. Everyone had the right to whatever life they lived. Most of us really had very few choices in that. The people at the top and the people at the bottom were all just responding to what they were given.

One day I asked my mother why she had so many children when we were poor. 'Ask your father,' she said laughing. How was it, I wondered, that the people with large families often didn't seem to want them. And then there were all these people who would have loved children but couldn't have any, for one reason or another.

Being the youngest made me look up to my brothers and sisters, to put them on pedestals. It was only years later, when their problems caught up with them, that I realised we were all really the same. Nobody had any answers.

I grew up confused. Being in my own world, I wasn't aware of a lot of things that were going on around me. I daydreamed through most of my youth. When teachers were telling me things I rarely heard them. I'd see their lips moving as a deaf person might. One day a priest threw a stick of chalk at me for not listening. When it happened a second time he threw a duster.

'One of these days,' he snarled, 'You might deign to give us the pleasure of your company.'

The other people in the class seemed to know things I didn't, even things outside education. They knew when a free day was coming up, for instance, or a half day. They knew things like the price of houses or where their classmates were living. Joseph Timmons used to collect car magazines. He had a fascination for Skodas. I just saw cars as cars. They were things to get from A to B.

One night there was a debate in the college on the subject

of milk. I was told I'd have to speak about it and I panicked. How could anyone have anything to say about milk except that it came from cows? I didn't know anything about Bord Bainne or government grants to farmers and any of the other subjects we were supposed to talk about.

In the end I didn't go. I got beaten the next day because of my non-attendance but it was worth it.

My father brought us to the cinema a lot. That fed into my daydream world. I knew James Stewart better than the man who lived across the road. That was because I was interested in him. We remember what excites us.

I found school a struggle because of all this. Why could I not master things that came so easily to others? Or did I really want to?

In a little notebook I jotted down facts that might come in useful to me sometime but my scrawls were often illegible. At exam time I often couldn't read my own writing.

I didn't know what I was going to do in life but then I rarely thought of the future. Getting through each day was enough for me. None of the teachers saw much potential in me. The general thinking was that I'd drift through things without making too much of an impact on anything. I generally acceded to that view, having little confidence in myself. I considered following my father's path and getting some job that would mean I didn't starve. Beyond that anything was up for grabs.

Many of the teachers were cruel to us. We got beaten often and accepted it as our lot. It was no big deal. We were all in the same boat. One year a priest with red hair came to the college. He said he was doing away with the stick. He said he wanted to get to know us 'as people.' I wasn't sure what that meant. I wasn't even sure if I was a person. Nobody had told me I was up to this.

He got us to read books that weren't on the course. He also played table tennis with us after school and told us jokes. This was a revelation to me. I began to think life could be fun after all.

That priest brought me out of myself. He took an interest in me, in my differentness from the other pupils. He asked me questions about myself. Nobody outside my family had ever asked me questions about myself before him. He made me feel I belonged to something.

He asked me what hobbies I had. I couldn't think of any for a while but then I said, 'I like the guitar.' He encouraged me to take up lessons on it.

There were classes one year for it so I decided to go down to them. It was the first thing I ever joined. I wasn't much good at it but I enjoyed trying to find the chords. My fingers burned with the pain but even that was fun.

When we play music we're more interested in listening to it and that happened to me. I got into singers like Gilbert O'Sullivan, groups like Fairport Convention.

Music also gave me confidence with girls. People always liked a guy with a guitar at a party. It was like cachet. One night I started talking to Breda Lally, a girl I liked from the convent. I was like a machine, I couldn't stop. Before that the cat always bit my tongue.

When I was seventeen I fell into the local river and was almost drowned. Sean Cadden pulled me out. He was the biggest boy in our class. He cycled in every morning from his farm in the country. He developed legs as big as tree trunks as a result.

The experience haunted me for years afterwards. I couldn't forget the sensation of the water gurgling around me as I went down. I blocked out the memory of it for years afterwards. It was too painful to think of.

My mother was traumatised by the event. Coming so near to losing me made her cling to me. That affected her relationship to my father and also my relationship to him. I didn't want her to be like that but I couldn't stop her. I felt he resented the extra attention she gave me.

I tried to stay away from home to help things between them. I was finishing school now, and thinking about leaving the town for good.

Some of my friends were going to Dublin. I thought of joining them but in the end I settled for a local job.

I worked with a farmer whose son had been in my class. He actually used to sit beside me. I never thought of us as friends and now he did this for me. I couldn't believe it. Work became therapy. It also brought in money, something school never did. The days flew by.

In the evenings I started to mix around with girls more. Some of the ones I went out with liked me. Others thought I was wired to the moon. I came on strong with some of them but then just as soon turned off. I couldn't explain why, either to them or myself.

Our frames of reference were wildly contrasting. If we went to a bar I knew little about tipping barmen or even ordering drinks. And I was useless at getting taxis. Somebody always seemed to jump the queue on me.

I talked to them about what I wanted to do in life but they tended to focus on more practical things like the clothes I was wearing.

Would I ever be suited to marriage? I doubted it. One girl I went out with told me she wouldn't see me any more until I got a car. This amused me. How could I get a car when I could hardly afford a bicycle? I was giving half my earnings to my mother by this time.

I left the farm after a while. I knew it wasn't for me. I was a 'townie.' I preferred buildings to grass.

I drifted between jobs, my concentration span being as low outside the college as it was inside it. I got interested in things but then the interest waned. I felt as if I was continually shedding invisible skins.

I was accused of being irresponsible by some of the

bosses I worked for. That was because I lacked passion for my work. I only did it for the money. I wasn't interested in being promoted. I certainly didn't bring my work home with me like some of the more ambitious ones. In a way I felt sorry for these people. I thought they'd wake up one day and find they hadn't lived. Then it would be too late to do anything about it.

When I talked like this to my mother she looked at me as if I was from some foreign planet. My father would just say, 'He's finding himself.'

It was more to satisfy my mother than for any other reason that I decided to become a Primary teacher. The other jobs were going nowhere. For some reason she got the impression I was a bookworm.

I crash-landed in teaching due to a lack of alternatives. I re-did the Leaving Cert to get a better result than the first time. I'd only scraped through it then and that wasn't good enough for becoming a trainee teacher.

I got four honours in the repeats. When I wanted something I could always work for it. The problem up to now was lack of motivation.

Afterwards we moved to Dublin. I studied at St. Patrick's Training College in Drumcondra. It wasn't too bad. I was bored by the lectures but I made some friends at them. Most of the students were salt-of-the-earth types. In my own way I felt superior to them, even though I was shy. A lot of them were simple Joes.

I did well in my exams but I was aware that most of the stuff I was writing down was nonsense. Still, you had to do it. Would I make a good teacher? I liked children but knew nothing about them. Being the youngest of a family meant I had little or no involvement with them up to this.

I drank too much at this time of my life but in drinking I discovered new sides to myself. People who are quiet in their childhood often over-compensate when they grow up and that happened to me. I usually became a bore when I had too much taken but of course you never realise this when you're drunk. Other people have to point it out to you, and even then you don't believe it. Or maybe you get into a fight with someone, or an accident. Both things happened to me more than once.

The years in Pat's went by like a breeze. One day I was a rookie and the next a qualified teacher. I found it hard to believe. There was no chalk in my blood, as the expression went, so it was new ground for me. I approached my future with a mixture of nervousness and excitement.

I got a job easily enough. There was a shortage of men in the profession so I had an automatic advantage at interviews. This was unfair, I felt, because I always believed women were better teachers than men.

I worked in a school outside Dublin and managed to get myself a flat near it. It was a country school and the children were very well-behaved. I spoiled them for the most part. They liked me because I didn't act like an adult with them. How could I? I wasn't one.

My father died shortly after I got the job. Maybe he felt his work was done now, that the youngest was set up and he could step aside. He'd never spent a day in hospital since the day he was born.

My mother accepted his death stoically. I couldn't be like that. I wanted to get maggoty drunk, to rail against the heavens for taking him from us. My personality meant I blew hot and cold. I always felt things intensely, both my loves and my hates. She was the polar opposite of that, placidity personified.

Whenever I visited her in the following months she didn't want to talk about him. She did her crying silently behind closed doors. Whenever I broached the subject, all she said was, 'His time came.'

Afterwards she usually turned the conversation around to

me, asking me how the school was going. I told her some funny stories but she always looked behind them to what was really going on. She knew I was bored a lot of the time. She had a quiet intelligence that was much more impressive than a lot of big mouths I knew.

I did my teaching on auto-pilot and tried not to miss home. The other members of the family were coming and going all the time but I drifted away, trying to connect with a hidden side of myself. I went off in a different direction to them.

One year I joined a drama society. Afterwards I started to write poems. Some of them were printed in magazines. I also did the occasional film review for the papers. Acting in plays helped me forget my boredom and so did going to films. But writing the reviews brought it back.

Writing didn't come easy to me but I enjoyed the activity of it. I remembered the panic I felt when the debate about milk was so much a threat to me that night in the college. I may not have been able to talk about milk but the poems came from my own head. That was all the difference I needed.

I also wrote a book of short stories. I noticed people changing their attitude towards me after that, especially at work. They weren't spontaneous with me anymore. It was as if they thought I was sizing them up or something. Maybe that happened to all writers. It wasn't the same as being a plumber or an electrician. When you wrote something it was like putting a sign above your head saying, 'I did this and you didn't,' as if you were somehow better than them, and they resented that.

The sixties were meant to be an exciting decade but I found them dull. Even in music they were dull. Elvis went soft. Little Richard found religion. Buddy Holly died in a plane crash. I couldn't get into The Beatles like most of the people around me, finding their lyrics mushy. When I listened to 'I Want to Hold Your Hand' I almost threw up.

As the years went on my mother kept asking me if I was 'going steady' with anyone. I knew she wanted me to. She felt it would cool me down and get rid of all the nonsense in my head that was making me write these books she could never understand.

I went on dates without conviction. I didn't let myself fall for anyone for fear of how they might uproot my life. I'm sure my indifference rubbed off on whoever was unlucky enough to be interested in me as a potential husband. If I fell headlong for someone that would have been all right but I wasn't interested in getting married for the sake of it. There was so little passion in the job now, I needed it somewhere else.

There was one exception, a girl called Caroline. She seemed like the answer to my dreams for a time. We met at a club in the city centre one Saturday night, both of us the worse for wear. She was dancing with herself at the other end of the bar and I was fascinated looking at her. Her hair was mussed and she had a slit down one side of her dress. Where was she getting all her energy from, I wondered.

I asked her to go for a drink with me and she agreed. We bonded immediately. She was just after coming out of a messy divorce, she told me. I reciprocated by telling her about myself, maybe too much about myself. We started meeting every week and then I moved in with her. After a few months it was as if we knew each other forever. She had that easy way about her.

For a while I thought we could make a go of it but then my old restlessness started to fester in me. The more dependent she became on me, the more nervous I got. I deluded myself into thinking we were compatible but deep down I knew we were searching for different things. It just took me a long time to admit that to myself.

After we split up she went back to her husband. I was

glad for her, for both of them. Some things could be recovered. It all boiled down to what you wanted.

'The best way to get over a woman,' one of the teachers said to me in the staff room, 'is to get under another one.' He was a prude but he concealed it under witticisms like this. How was it everyone was so clever about other people's problems and crap at solving their own ones?

Unfortunately, for me there was no other woman. I drew a line in the sand with Caroline. After she went out of my life I reverted to my customary reclusiveness. I became too fond of my own company, of my dull routines. I told myself she encroached too much on my space, caused too many variables to enter my life. What was it T. S. Eliot's Prufrock said? 'I have measured out my life in coffee spoons.' I didn't like complications in my life, or traps. There were too many of both with marriage. (Maybe that's why they called it wed*lock*).

I ended up being the only bachelor in the family. The others all traipsed up the aisle as fast as their feet could carry them and then started to breed like rabbits. Sometimes I babysat for them. Seeing their little routines gave me a porthole into what married life might have been like. Some parts of it I liked, but only in small doses. More often than not I was content to stay as I was. Children were fine to mind for a few hours or to teach from nine till two but I wasn't sure I could cope with them all day long.

Wives were another question.

'Would you not give us a day out?' my sister said to me, 'We're waiting, you know.'

'I'm afraid you're going to have to continue to wait,' I told her.

Not having children of my own, I continued to spoil the ones in my care. I didn't come down heavy on them if they hadn't their lessons done and I let them give me a bit of backchat during classes as well. I thought it relieved the monotony.

Sometimes I gave them tips if they did messages for me.

'My God,' a colleague said to me one day when she heard I'd given an over-generous amount to a child for an errand, 'I wouldn't give one of mine that for their week's pocket money.' There was a perception that I was ruining the pupils, that I didn't know what was what because I was outside the loop as a bachelor.

My fondness for the arts cemented this view. I brought in poetry to them a lot – not my own, needless to say – to get their reactions to it. This was frowned on as being slightly pretentious.

'Just teach them enough to put their autographs on cheque books,' the principal advised, 'We don't need to see them flying off to Mount Olympus on wings of poesy.'

In the eighties my brain went to sleep. It was a boring decade, a decade of self-serving people boring us all to tears in my view. After the excitement of the sixties and relative excitement of the seventies it was a decade of anti-climax. I didn't find many good films to go to or many good books to read. Even the politicians bored me. I yawned as I watched the news on TV every night. There were strikes and tribunals, unemployment and walk-outs. If the seventies was like a hangover of the sixties, the eighties made the seventies positively alluring.

It was also was the decade of Margaret Thatcher and Ronald Reagan, two people who thought they had the answer to the world's economic ills and were intent on lecturing the rest of us about it. Their intolerance of left-wing concerns floored me. Somebody coined the term 'Reaganomics. ' I had a phrase that suited me better: 'I hate Ronald Reagan.' (Or as I called him, Ronald RayGun).

I gave out about the Terrible Two in the staff-room at almost every day. I found myself despising the way the world was being policed by such figures. They seemed to act as fronts for all sorts of self-righteousness, 'the brash dash for cash' that was epitomised by Michael Douglas in the film *Wall Street.*

The people in the school weren't too bothered about issues like this. They were too busy just getting through their days. Whenever I sounded off about them they'd say things like, 'I'm more worried about Maria McCarthy not being able to spell "cat" with the exams just around the corner. How is she going to get by in life?' I knew Maria McCarthy would survive. I knew she'd probably buy and sell the rest of us. That was the thing about teachers. If we knew as much as we liked to think, why weren't we out there running the world instead of just blabbering on about it?

I grew apart from my colleagues as a result, paddling my own canoe. They thought I was a bighead but I wasn't. I was just angry.

'Why don't you get more involved with the politics in this country instead of the U. S.?' one of them asked me. I didn't have an answer for that. I always felt America was like an extension of Ireland. I remembered a statement our Maths teacher made one day when I was a young boy in the college, 'When America blows its nose, Ireland reaches for its handkerchief.'

One day we had a discussion about Reagan's bloodthirstiness in the staff-room and I got quite worked up about it. The principal came in at the tail end of it and I could see by his face that he wasn't too pleased. When the other teachers were gone back to their classes he said to me, 'I'm not sure if it's a good idea to be getting so worked up about things like that. By the way, did you give me your plan for your classes this month?'

I was floored. Reagan was trying to blow up the world and here was this gobdaw banging on about a class plan. My blood boiled. I told one of the other teachers I was outraged by his attitude but she just shrugged her shoulders. 'Whose bread I eat,' she said morosely, 'his song I sing.'

It was bad enough the principal being a philistine but now they were joining in. After that I grew more and more distant from them. Sometimes I didn't even join them at the coffee breaks, staying in my room instead. I started to see them as parasites.

George Bernard Shaw once described a teacher as 'A man among children, a child among men.' He was right. We deluded ourselves that we mattered in the greater scheme of things but we were really just running away from life. Maybe that's why I overdid things in the evenings.

It wasn't just the teachers, I came to realise as I got older, it was everyone.

My neighbours talked about putting the bins out, paying the ESB bills, joining Neighbourhood Watch. They wanted me to be that soldier. So did my mother. I was, after all, a teacher, a so-called pillar of the establishment. But in my mind I felt more like Samson. I wanted to tear down the pillars, to rent the temple in twain.

Most of the people I worked with were elated to be in the job they were in, elated to be dictating to their underlings from the top of the classroom. They thought I'd be the same, having crawled out from the blue collar world of my father into this holy grail of pedagogy, forming the minds of a generation.

I couldn't see it like that. I didn't feel superior to the boy in the back seat who couldn't spell his name. For me we were all equals. I hated their self-congratulatory airs, their sense of being the 'in' set. I always hated the 'in' set, right back to when I made a friend of the boy from the broken home at my own school.

One of the teachers told us he ordered a kettle in his house to be quiet one night. It was when he was correcting copies. He was making a cup of tea for himself. The kettle reached boiling point. When it started to whistle he said, 'Shut up!' It was a voluntary reflex, the result of saying that for so many years to a roomful of people whenever he heard them talking among themselves.

That was what teaching did to you. You felt like God. You hated noise, or anybody doing anything different to everyone else. I was terrified I'd turn into that kind of person one day. I hoped I got out before then. I knew I wasn't cut out for the job. How could I fashion the minds of a generation when I couldn't even make up my own mind about anything? Or was that an asset?

'To be perfect is to have changed often,' said G. K. Chesterton. Bob Dylan gave the idea a more modern slant when he wrote, 'He who's not busy being born is busy dying.'

It didn't go down too well when I quoted these people in the staff-room. Everyone thought I was trying to upset the applecart of their cosy little bureaucracy. Indecision didn't look good for a teacher. We weren't supposed to have changed often or to be busy being born. In training we were told never to say, 'I don't know. ' (The lecturers were wrong about most other things too).

I told myself I'd always fight the good fight for the underdog but as the years gained on me I started to tire, both physically and in my mind. I stopped talking about politics because it was doing my head in. I was getting no back-up and it started to drain me. If RayGun pressed the button, where would we be then with our class plans?

The thing that saved me from ending up in a funny farm was the summer holidays. That was the time I got back my personality. The two months was long enough for me to be able to forget my stresses, or at least pretend to.

The point was, teaching made us all schizoid, giving us the opportunity to live two lives. For half the time we were authorities. Then the bell rang for the end of the day and we went back to being so many fucked-up human beings trying to sound sorted.

Most of the other teachers went to far-flung places for the summers but I just went back down to Ballina. I knew I needed to touch base with my roots. I went on these endless walks, walks where I never knew what lay around the next corner. That was how I liked it.

Sometimes on my sojourns I ran into farmers. I used to spend ages talking to them. You didn't have to account for yourself to a farmer. You didn't even have to introduce yourself to them. They were people for whom the modern world hadn't happened, the few genuine people left in the country who hadn't been taken over by technology.

At night I drank neat whiskies in the pubs. If I had enough ingested I made a fool of myself with women. That kept me sane – even if it drove them *insane*. In their absence I wrote poems trying to explain myself to myself. I imagined myself as W. B. Yeats without Maud Gonne MacBride. Or Gone Mad MacBride.

The job, meanwhile, went on, for better or worse. Or maybe both. I wasn't getting any younger but the pupils stayed the same age year after year even if their faces were different. That was the thing about teaching. It got harder as they years went on, unlike most jobs where you could put your feet up a bit more. They were also good psychologists. They sussed it when you were even the least bit under par. If they smelled blood they went for you.

I got too involved with them for the first few years and when I tried to step back they weren't having it. I became their prisoner. If I told them a joke they wanted to tell me ten. The actor in me enjoyed the performance aspect of the job but I was playing to an audience that wanted to take over the stage.

The other teachers might have got better results than me with some of their pupils but I had a talent for spotting qualities in them that they missed. I knew how to draw them out. But sometimes I drew them out too much. I made them into performers too.

We attended seminars on the theme of trying to motivate kids. I suggested we should have a seminar for my bunch that focussed on *de*-motivating them. They were like balls of energy, so many laughing hyenas let loose in a menagerie called my classroom. Sometimes at the end of a day I said a silent prayer of thanks that I survived.

The principal said to me, 'Once the toothpaste is out of the tube it's difficult to get it back in.' The problem with my tube of toothpaste was that it was all over the floor.

Most of the teachers thought I lived in cloud cuckoo land. I felt like the Greek character Thales. Thales fell into a gutter when he was looking at the stars. There was a moral there somewhere – one I usually preferred to ignore.

When I started to write poetry they thought I was gone off the deep end entirely. It didn't fit the profile of Primary Teacher for some reason. They'd probably have preferred if I was writing football reports, or grocery lists.

The principal said to me, 'I don't mind you being Seamus Heaney as long as you don't start composing when you're trying to teach Irish verbs.' There was no danger of that. Teaching Irish was the time I got my daily nervous breakdown. It just didn't float their boat. My pupils despised Irish and as a result so did I. I wanted to get back to the time we were under British rule and it was prohibited. That would have been a more relaxing time to be a teacher – even in a hedge school.

Sometimes I read my poems to my mother. Sadly, they meant nothing to her. I might as well have been composing bus timetables

'We're on different wavelengths,' she said.

That was one of her favourite expressions. It summed the situation up. She just wasn't 'into' poetry. I didn't want to be snobbish about it because she was ten times the person I was but I was frustrated about the fact that we drifted apart a bit as a result of that.

We were also poles apart on politics. She regarded America as the country that had saved us from Hitler during the war. For me it was an imperialist power looking for oil in war-torn regions while carrying on the pose of The Great White Saviour.

She died at the end of the eighties. Her death affected me differently than that of my father. I wasn't as emotional this time, probably because I was that much older. Maybe I was expecting it, I don't know. She was there one day and gone the next. That was the only way I could view it.

I failed to grieve properly for her. In her later years I'd seen her less and less. I felt guilty about that after she died. I had no excuse for not spending more time with her. Maybe I felt I'd get too dependent on her if I did. I was afraid of loving her more than I was afraid of loving my father. It was a different kind of love. I feared it would drag me down with its power as I got older.

When the nineties came in I found age catching up on me. I had periods of fatigue that seemed like occupational hazards for teachers facing burn-out from their hyperactive pupils.

I was beginning to cop on to the direction my life was taking. Not only was I not going to change the world anymore, I wasn't even able to get little Johnny in the back seat to change his dirty socks. All occasions were informing against me and I wanted this oh-too-solid flesh to melt.

The louder I shouted in the classroom, the less they listened. I knew the secret was to whisper and carry a big stick, as someone wisely put it, but when I whispered nobody listened and the stick was outlawed by the Department of Education. The pupils were the new tyrants. They'd finally got their revenge for a generation of abuse from emotionally-disturbed teachers. (I was now becoming one of these).

Thatcher and RayGun disappeared from power, thankfully, but my own country started turning ugly. The crime statistics went off the scale. Each day I woke up and turned on the news there seemed to be a new murder, some drug baron shot in the head in a pub somewhere or dumped in the canal. 'As long as they're bumping each other off I don't mind,' one of the teachers said to me. This was fine but I felt it was only a matter of time before it went further than that. There was also speculation about a serial killer on the loose when a number of women went missing. It was a pity he couldn't have come into my classroom and put manners on a few of the headbangers there.

And then there was the even crazier stuff: More parents killed their children one year than in the decade beforehand. What was going on? It was a long way from De Valera's comely maidens dancing at the crossroads.

In the staff-room I found myself listening to a lot of stories about clerical paedophilia. It gave a whole new meaning to the term 'Suffer the little children to come unto me.' Suddenly what Eamon Casey did with Annie Murphy seemed almost tame. At least it wasn't against the law. Someone said he'd invented a new form of chess: 'Bishop jumps everything.'

I think it was Thoreau who said most men lead lives of quiet desperation. Mine was more noisy. I talked to the other teachers about the inequality of society but nobody was listening to me anymore. How many times could a man turn his head and pretend that he just doesn't see? Bob Dylan could get away with saying it but not me.

Every school had a grump and I was our one, trying to prick people's consciences by taking the high moral ground. I became just a scratchy old record to them, the local schoolroom crackpot. I retreated from their company to lick my wounds in the classroom. At least there was still some innocence left there.

I thought of the line from *Hamlet*: 'There was a kind of fighting inside me that would not let me sleep. ' Every night I ticked off the days to the end of term when I'd be able to head west to recharge my batteries. As soon as I crossed the Shannon I felt rejuvenated. Nobody understood how much it meant to me, what it did to me. Waking up to its dawns, sampling its clear blue waters, its brilliant skies.

Sometimes I stopped in Ballina on the way down. I had a complicated relationship to the town. I was drawn to it but critical of it too. The people who lived there still talked about things I found trivial – parking charges, new buildings going up, the revamping of the Market Square. I tried to be patient with them, to tell myself that most people probably spent most of their lives talking about trivial things. Including myself.

I was so long out of the place it was less threatening to me than when I'd been a pupil there. I tried to remember the good things about it: playing with a train in the snow on my eighth birthday, robbing apples from the local orchard as the owner chased after us with his rifle, listening to myself singing on an old tape recorder donated to us from my aunt, the spools as big as dinner plates.

I met some people I knew from the good old days – or the bad old days. We traded stories about having the lard beaten out of us by teachers who compensated for their inability to teach by becoming trainee Sonny Listons or Al Capones. It was more comical than anything else now.

I visited my *alma mater* one day out of a kind of vague curiosity. I was no sooner inside than two teachers passed me by with querulous expressions on their faces. I was almost past them before I realised one was our old Latin teacher. He recognised me. I'd run into him once or twice in the town in recent years so it wasn't that big of a deal.

'What are you doing here?' he said, 'Did you not have enough of us as a pupil?'

'A murderer always returns to the scene of the crime.'

'Murderer? I thought you were the victim.'

'I used to be. I've become one of you now.'

'You couldn't wait to get out of the classroom when I knew you.'

'I still can't.'

We chatted about the difficulties of the job, of trying to teach children who were addicted to television.

'I had to move with the times,' he informed me, 'It's not talk-and-chalk anymore. You have to have all these bloody audio-visual aids.'

I found it hard to imagine Latin with audio-visual aids. (A slide of Caesar throwing a bridge across a river?)

We parted like old friends. We were, after all, colleagues now, twin members of The Most Respectable Profession In The World.

As I approached retirement I tried to keep a lower profile in the school. The numbers dropped. There was a need for us all to pull together to keep the ship afloat. Suddenly it wasn't about fashioning minds anymore; it was about holding onto our jobs. We were all feeling the pinch.

I drank more to blot out the fact that I wasn't doing what was expected of me. A glass of whiskey would always tell you that you were as good as Montessori, or Mister Chips – even if you'd had them.

Over time my car started to get noticed outside the local pub. It was there almost as much as the ones belonging to the bartenders. I was told I should take out shares in the place.

The principal said to me, 'Don't shit on your own doorstep.' It was good advice. After that I moved my business elsewhere. Now I could stumble home unnoticed. But it was hard to teach with a hangover. (It was hard even without one).

The days became longer, the evenings shorter. I fantasised about the holidays like a prisoner waiting to be released from jail. Maybe that happened in all jobs with time. For me it was a return to my youth, to the time when I saw schools as forbidding institutions, laboratories churning out dead fossils.

My dreams were dying. I needed to be high all the time, high on life. But life was letting me down. It was turning into something prosaic. It was nothing more than setting the alarm for work, correcting exercises, smiling sweetly at parents as you went into a room for twenty hours a week to prop up a bland *status quo*. Where was my next illusion going to come from?

I transferred my priorities to my home life. The school only owned my body, not my mind. I wrote poetry into the small hours, dredging up old sonnets I'd written in the seventies and abandoned. I blew the dust off them now and tried to re-work them.

A lot of midnight oil was burned as I sought inspiration from somewhere to give me a reason to get up in the mornings. I listened to the songs of Jim Morrison in the middle of the night, drowning myself in his hypnotic rhythms. When my energy flagged I revived it with beer and coffee. Before I knew where I was it was morning. The birds sang in the trees and I was revived, rejuvenated.

I started to attend film festivals. Most of the people I met at these were more interested in being seen than in studying anything that was on a screen. They were little more than social occasions for them, opportunities to trade platitudes with the chattering classes about surrealism or the *nouvelle vague*. They ate finger food and tuna fish sandwiches. They held their little fingers crooked as they sipped cocktails. They bored me to death with their banter.

My enthusiasm for American politics was re-ignited

when Bill Clinton was elected president of the U. S. He became the Great White Hope for a number of years before Monica Lewinsky tarnished his legacy. Was she a Republican plant? Anything was possible. Republicans always knew they could bring a Democrat down with a woman. If John F. Kennedy was living now he wouldn't have needed to be assassinated. By all reports, Clinton was a monk in contrast to him.

Clinton inhabited the *interregnum* between the two Bushes. One of them was as bad as the other for me.

When the Twin Towers went down in 2001, people now had a new fall guy for all the evils of the world: Osama bin Laden. I was as horrified by the carnage as the next man but you had to look behind it to what caused it – our old friend American imperialism.

In the staff room I found myself speaking up for an Arabian terrorist fighting the bureaucracy that had empowered him. This was a bridge too far for the principal. He worried about what kinds of things I was filling my pupil's heads with in the Civics classes. It was as if he wanted George Bush to ride over the hill with the Seventh Cavalry behind him – or maybe John Wayne from the film *The Green Berets*. I tried to teach them that life wasn't like a John Wayne movie. In life the good guys didn't always win. (In fact they didn't even win in John Wayne movies. John Wayne did).

One of the teachers said to me, 'I hope you're not going to join the Al-Queda. ' I didn't appreciate jokes like that. Or was it a joke?

George Bush came on the Sky TV with his homespun wisdom. He promised to quell the fears of a society that seemed to believe every time something went bump in the night it was Bin Laden at the door with an AK47 and an armload of Semtex.

'We'll smoke him out dead or alive,' he said with his

merry little eyes twinkling, 'He can't hide forever.' I knew Bush and his henchmen had been responsible for more people dying in Afghanistan than were burned to death in the Twin Towers. How many Sky broadcasters were going to publicise that?

Who was the real terrorist. - a man who dressed in a sheet and lived in a cave or a smoothie in a smart suit blackening the skies of Kandahar with his B52s?

I made these points in the staff-room but guess what? Nobody cared. They were still more worried about Jimmy McCarthy not having his sums done. I knew this was one war I couldn't win: a war of words. So I gave up. The odds were stacked against me.

I continued to do my work like a robot. Left, right, left, right. *Attenshun!*' Pretend you're in the army. About turn. At ease, soldier.

On Sundays I drove to Howth to chill out. I parked the car at the top of the hill and savoured the peace. Sometimes I walked until I got lost. Afterwards I usually went into the bar at the bottom of the cliff. More often than not it was full of 'pierees'. That was the name I gave to the people who walked up and down the pier to keep in touch with nature. I couldn't imagine them out on the wild seas. In fact I couldn't imagine them doing anything more dangerous than having an ice cream on the benches as they discussed their next game of bridge.

Sometimes I played pool with these people. They'd be dressed in polo necked jumpers or smart suits. A lot of them played golf in the club up the road. They struck me as the type who always played the percentage game, either on the table and off it. To annoy them I'd smash the balls all over the table, occasionally knocking them off it altogether.

'Why do you hit them so hard?' they'd ask me.

'It gets rid of my tension,' I'd reply.

The next day at school I'd only be half there, vacantly scratching symbols on the blackboard as visions of mountain tracks filled my head.

I tried to make my classes as interesting as I could. At times I felt like a performing seal. The pupils looked at me as if I had two heads. Sometimes I felt I had.

'They won't thank you for it in the end,' the principal said to me one day. He'd come into the room unannounced and saw them dressed up in medieval garb to act out a Yeats poem I was teaching them.

'What's this,' he snorted, 'The Abbey Theatre?'

'What do you mean by that?'

'All this dramatisation of the curriculum you go on with. It's only useful up to a point. Sooner or later they're going to have to get down to learning things off. There's no substitute for hard work.'

'I'm trying to expand the children's minds,' I said.

'You're a teacher, not a social reformer. They're hardly old enough to walk to school on their own. Are you trying to brainwash them?'

'No,' I said, 'but you are. We're in the 21st century, not the Stone Ages. You make me feel like Gradgrind.'

'Who's he?'

'A character out of Charles Dickens.'

'Dump him.'

'Have you never heard of the child-centred curriculum?'

'I've heard of it all right, and you obviously have too, but this is an old-fashioned school. We like the pupils to know the three Rs. They'll hardly learn them in those ridiculous costumes you have on them'

I felt like throwing a punch at him. Was this what he wanted? Was he trying to work me up enough so I might go for him?

'A lot of them have low concentration spans,' I said, 'The only thing they benefit from is when they act something out.'

'They'd benefit a lot more from a clip on the ear,' he shot back, turning on his heel.

I knew I was in the wrong school. I needed a progressive headmaster. I was seething for the rest of the day. But when I thought about it, what did I care? I had to be myself. As Jim Morrison said, 'Once you make your peace with authority, you become authority.'

I went down to my doctor. I asked him if I was going barmy because I seemed to be on a different wavelength to everyone else.

'You're the most sane person I ever met,' he said, 'You're just going through a period of stress at the moment. I'll give you a prescription for some tranquillisers.'

I didn't think that was the answer. What tranquilliser could get rid of the principal? Or the small-minded teachers I had to face at coffee break every day who were doing my head in with their tunnel vision?

One night I went to a Woody Allen film where he told a joke about a man who thought he was a chicken. The doctor said, 'Why don't you get rid of the chicken?' The man replied, 'I can't. I need the eggs.'

That was the way I felt. The world was crazy but it was the only one we had so we might as well make the best of it. Maybe we all thought we were chickens in our different ways. The real chickens were the cowards who refused to be themselves.

Seeing the film changed my attitude. Suddenly I didn't care about being uptight any more, didn't care about being out of step with the world.

I threw away the tranquillisers and didn't go to the doctor anymore. The following month the children were acting out a poem one day in the class when the principal came in unexpectedly. One of them was standing against the door and he got bounced across the room.

'What's going on here?' he roared.

'You caused that!' I roared back.

The pupils were behind me. They applauded. The boy who was bounced stood up. He looked in a lot of pain. The principal got worried. Would he sue? What would he tell his parents?

'This is unacceptable,' he said, 'I want to see you in my office. ' He was using attack as the best means of defence but I wasn't having any of it.

'You can take your job and shove it,' I said. Again the pupils applauded. The principal looked as if he was getting a heart attack. I barged out of the room and straight into my car.

I never went back to the job. Instead I decided to become a professional poet. I applied for a scholarship to Annaghmakerrig, a place where I could hone my skills in comfort without philistines trying to drag me down to their level.

At the moment I'm working on an epic that starts in prehistoric times and comes up to the present, drawing a connection between the caveman and modern technology. It's going to knock the socks off *Poetry Ireland* when I send them a draft.

I miss the kids in the class but I got fed up trying to be Superman to them. You can't buck the system. I know that now. The pen is mightier than the sword. Maybe when the people of Ireland read *Odyssey of the Caveman* they'll see that.

One day I met the principal on the street. He was dressed in his inevitable duffle coat. What a loser, I thought. His face looked like a stick of chalk.

'You were a brilliant teacher,' he said, 'Why did you leave? The profession needs free spirits like you.'

'Less of the *plámás*,' I said, 'It's a pity you didn't say that to me when it might have meant something.'

I told him the system sucked. I'd had my bellyful of trying to take on the big guns. Let someone else stand in the firing-line for a change. Why should I have been delegated as the new Messiah? The kids were going to grow up the way they were going to grow up. If they wanted to go out into the world with iron in their souls without the salving potion of poetry that was their problem, not mine.

'The only mistake I made,' I told him, 'was that it took me so long to see the light.'

Often the biggest solutions to our problems are the most obvious ones. We obsess too much about nothing, getting ourselves into bad health by sweating the small stuff.

No more, not for me anyway. If I can't bring down the educational system at least I can hammer my points home to the few poetry-lovers left in this damn world of ours who might be interested in listening. If they're not listening, sod them.

Anytime someone asks me now why I'm not seeing life the same way they do, I just smile. I say back to them, 'It's simple. I've become a chicken. I need the eggs.'

The Defence Rests

We lost our father.
Alive we took him for granted;
dead he became a legend.
Now, middle-aged ourselves
the age he was
when we imagined him ancient,
we spend our nights
embellishing the anecdotes
we turned a deaf ear to
when he walked among us.

Stories told in Tony Crane's pub
after midnight
to fellow members of the bar
– the other one –
became verbal gold
as we remembered him
standing up to a judge
or regaling fellow tilted wigs
with wit and wisdom,
drunk on Guinness, drunk on life.

These were the nights
that he became a god to me
a king in his domain
even if that domain was a street
few people had ever heard of
in a town like any other
in an isolated country
on the edge of Europe.

When the Celtic Tiger roared
it was rediscovered

for however brief a time.
The past became more real than the present
and some of us
turned into him, falling a little
 in love with our childhoods
on that street
with the old school, the cinema,
the fire station, the garage
and Syron's chip shop.

'Why didn't we listen to him more?'
we asked ourselves, 'Why didn't
we remember more of his stories?'
No longer demonised as a drinker
no longer trivialised
as a snob
we revere him now
from the safe distance of posterity
as an era of blandness
pays lip service to eccentricity.

He gave his body to science
so no flowers grow on his grave,
no headstone celebrates his life.
There's nowhere to visit him now
except in our memory

but that's enough.

Santy and Benny Walkin

I was going to Mass with my father. A group of people in front of us sang 'Adeste Fideles.' 'Aren't they great?' he said. They were collecting money for charity. One of them rattled a box at us. He put some coins in it. I asked him what 'Adeste Fideles' meant but he just laughed at me.

We crossed the bridge. The Moy was flowing freely. Two fishermen were up to their knees in waders. A saw a trout jump up and catch a fly.

We went into St. Muredach's, the cathedral that crowned the town. The bells were ringing. They made a very loud sound, so loud I thought people would be able to hear it in Foxford.

They'd been broken until recently. My cousin paid for them to be repaired. He was from Bunree. I used to see him driving around the town in his car. He was always giving money to the church.

We sat into a pew. The bells were still ringing. 'They make me feel sad,' I said to my father. He said, 'Cheer up. Christmas is coming.' I didn't like to tell him Christmas made me feel sad too. It was like the end of something.

I knelt down. My hands were cold on the rail. It had a brass panel screwed onto it. It said, 'Pray for the Donor.' All the seats said that. I never knew who The Donor was. Was he a priest? Was he some man who died?

The Mass started. Fr Harte told us we should all be feeling holy because of the time of year that was in it. He was facing us. In the old days, my father told me, the priest used to face the altar instead. He preferred it that way.

Fr Harte said the Mass was being said for Mrs Foody. She'd died recently. She was from out near Attymas. We all started praying. I tried to feel sad for Mrs Foody. I said the words but I didn't know what they meant. I looked at the stained glass on the windows to try and help me.

Every few minutes we sat back in our seats. Then you had to kneel again. I followed whatever everyone else was doing. Some of the prayers were in Latin. I didn't know what they meant.

When we got to the gospel my father said, 'I'll be back in a minute.' He went out to the sacristy. He was always doing that. It was why he liked sitting at the back.

He tried to light a cigarette. Someone opened the door and the match went out. He had to try again. The second match worked. He was smoking Boston. They were very small cigarettes.

The gospel ended. He came back in. Fr Harte went into the pulpit. It was half way down the church. '2000 years ago,' he said, 'a child was born.' He started talking about Jesus.

I looked across at the side altar. There was a crib there. The sheep and cows were huge in it. I loved the side altar. I often saw my aunt Mary in there. She was my father's sister. Some people said she lived in the church. She was always going up and down saying the stations.

I tried to listen to Fr Harte talking about Jesus but my mind wandered. I looked across at Mrs Geraghty. She had a new coat on her. John Hanley was sitting on his hat. A baby cried.

Fr Harte said we needed to put Christ back into Christmas. He said it was getting too commercialised. I didn't know what commercialised meant. Fr Harte was always using big words. So was my father. He had a dictionary in his office. He used it when he had to write an important letter somewhere.

'What does commercialised mean?' I asked him.

He said, 'It's when you're always looking for things.'

This Christmas I was looking for an aeroplane. I'd seen one in the window of Benny Walkin's toy shop. It was huge. It had a blue stripe on the side of it. It made a ringing sound when you wound it up. It sounded louder than the church bells.

Santy was going to bring me one just like it, at least if I was good. That was what my mother said. Nobody wanted to be on Santy's bad list. If you were on the bad list you got nothing.

The sermon ended. Fr Harte turned his back on us. He said some more prayers. John Hanley's hat fell onto the floor when he knelt down. Fr Harte held up the host. We all bent our heads. You weren't supposed to look at it.

My father and myself went up to Communion. I clasped my hands. Fr Harte said 'The body of Christ' in a wavering voice as he put the host into my mouth. I tried to keep it from my tongue. It was a sin if it touched it. You had to swallow it fast or it stuck to the roof of your mouth. It felt like eating paper.

I tried to feel holy but I couldn't stop thinking about my aeroplane. Finally Fr Harte said, 'Go forth in peace.'

I always liked when he said that. It meant the Mass was over. I didn't say that to my father. I knew it was the wrong way to think.

We filed out of the church. Everyone suddenly started talking to one another in excited voices. A few people shook hands with my father. They wished him a happy Christmas. One man I kind of knew gave me a hard look. He said to my father, 'He's getting very big.' My father said, 'Soon he'll be outgrowing me.' The man patted me on the head and went off.

Nobody ever talked to me directly. They always spoke about me as if I wasn't there. That was because I was young. One day I'd be grown up and they'd talk to me directly. It would be strange to be grown up. You'd be part of the world then.

The night was windy. We walked across the bridge. The fishermen were gone home. So were the carol singers. I asked my father if we could go up to Benny Walkin's shop to see my aeroplane. He said, 'Of course.'

I pulled my coat up tight as we fought the wind. We got to the shop. I looked all over the window but I couldn't see the plane anywhere. It was gone. That gave me a fright. 'Where is it?' I asked my father. 'Santy must have taken it,' he said. I didn't know what he meant. Was he not going to bring me his own one from the North Pole?

We walked past Queenan's shoe shop. A group of boys from Lord Edward Street were standing at the corner. They usually stood there after being in the pub. It was like the centre of the town. They were laughing about something. One of them tipped his hat to my father. 'Nice night, sir,' he said. My father nodded.

We turned into King Street. It was cold going up the hill against the wind. We passed Moylett's shop. We used to bring strawberries there that we picked in my cousin's house in Bunree. Mr Moylett paid us money for them. I thought if I got enough money I'd be able to buy the plane but then my mother said I could ask for it for Christmas. I spent the money on marbles instead.

Gaughan's pub was half way up the hill. There was a smell of drink from it. I hated that. People always drank more at Christmas. I wondered if my father wanted to go in. He looked in the window but it was only to see who was in there.

We turned into Bury Street. Mr Burns lived there. He had a big guest house. My father knew him from work. He knew his wife too. They used to go out together once, before he met my mother.

We got to the font at the top of Teeling Street. People flooded out of the Estoria. They were all talking about the film they'd just seen. It was called *Miracle on 34th Street*. I'd seen it advertised in the *Western People*. There was a poster of it in a glass case outside the cinema. It had an Irish actress in it. Her name was Maureen O'Hara. She'd gone to Hollywood and become famous. She was in another film called *The Quiet Man* that was made nearby. John Wayne was in it with her. He was one of the most famous actors in Hollywood.

When we got to the house I saw my brother outside. He winked at my father. I didn't know what that was about. He handed him a key. It looked like the one for the front room.

My mother was standing in the hall. She gave my father a kiss. We went into the kitchen. She said she'd be going to midnight Mass later on with my brother.

She opened the oven. There was a sizzling sound. I smelled the turkey. She took it out and cut a piece of it. I tasted it. It was delicious. 'No more now until tomorrow,' she said.

She told me to go to bed. I wanted to watch television but she said 'No, not tonight.' I had to be asleep early or Santy wouldn't come. He only came to people when they were asleep.

I said goodnight to her and to my father. I went upstairs. Why did I have to go to bed? I hated being the youngest in the family. It meant you were second in everything. Why wasn't I born the oldest? Then I could have gone anytime I liked, or even stayed up all night talking about what was on in the Estoria.

I got into my bedroom. It looked sad. I took off my clothes and lay down. People were laughing on the street outside. Downstairs I heard my parents laughing with my brother. People always laughed around Christmas time. They laughed about stupid things.

I kept thinking about the key of the front room. Why had my brother handed it to my father? It was nearly always left open.

After a while I nodded off. I slept for a few hours and then I woke up. I heard the sound of a bell. I looked at the clock. It was coming up to midnight.

Who could be calling on us at this time? It couldn't be Santy. He'd be coming down the chimney. That was where I left my letter for him asking for the aeroplane. I knew he hadn't come yet because it wasn't beside the bed. That was where he always left the presents for me every year. Last year I'd got a cowboy suit.

The bell kept ringing. I decided to answer it. I went down the stairs. I opened the front door but there was nobody there. I closed it again.

The ringing sound continued. I realised it was coming from the front room. When I opened the door I saw dozens of toys on the table. There were a few toys and a transistor my brother was getting.

In the middle of them was my aeroplane. My father was winding it up. That was what was making the noise.

'What are you doing up?' he said. He looked very upset. I told him the bell woke me. I thought there was someone at the door.

'Where did all the toys come from?' I asked him.

'Santy left them,' he said, 'Go back to bed. If you don't go to sleep Santy won't come to you.'

He led me out. The door closed behind me. behind me. As I went upstairs I heard him locking it.

I got back to my room and lay down. What was going on? Why had Santy left the toys in the front room instead of at the foot of the bed? That never happened before. And why was the aeroplane gone from Benny Walkin's window? Was Benny Walkin Santy?

I couldn't sleep. I heard the church bells again. My mother and my brother would be just going into the church now. They'd hear Fr Harte saying all the prayers my father and myself heard him saying. They'd hear him giving the same sermon about Jesus being born 2000 years ago and how we had to put the Christ back into Christmas.

I started crying. I didn't know what I was crying for, whether it was for myself or someone else or everything. Why had I seen the aeroplane when Christmas hadn't come and why was it in the wrong room? I knew when I fell asleep they'd bring it up and put it at the foot of my bed but it wouldn't be the same. My mother would come in to me in the morning with a big beam on her face and say, 'Look what Santy brought,' but it would be no good.

I saw it too soon. Everything had happened too soon and in the wrong way. It wasn't like Christmas anymore. The sound of the bell had spoiled everything for me.

Alma Mater

Brando telling us piningly
that he could have been a contender
or Shane squaring up to Wilson
in the final reel in Grafton's saloon

were heroes that shaped me
much more than those of 1916 or 1798.
Dolores Sheridan waltzing down Bury Street
in her Convent of Mercy gabardine

was an infinitely more enticing figure
than our Blessed Lady or Joan of Arc,
and Pythagoras' square on the hypotenuse
was nothing beside our own Market Square

where pitched battles were held nightly
and we rattled Silvie McConn's gate
with a thousand and one mis-taken penalties.
We didn't have a Parthenon or an Acropolis

but we had Moyne Abbey and St. Patrick's Well.
We were told that Jesus saved the world
but Audie Murphy looked more durable
from my velvet seat in the Estoria

as he fended off Geronimo.
We read about the Pass of Thermopylae
and the brave 300 Spartans
but John Wayne at the Alamo

spoke more to us about strength.
As we thrilled to Ben-Hur

the crucifixion was an anti-climax
to Charlton Heston's chariot forays.

When we read *Paradise Lost*
we might have rooted for God to win
but our hearts lay with the doomed Lucifer.
The Estoria was our Bel Air,

the posters on the stairs
our gateway to the Gods
When we were beaten at school
we wanted to be Pretty Boy Floyd

or Babyface Nelson, anything
to challenge the old order.
At the Saturday matinees we told ourselves
we would create our own Dead End Kids

our own angels with dirty faces
to dethrone the cane-wielding life-deniers
holding court at the blackboards,
their canes like swords.

When I go back to that old college now
and walk through the deserted rooms
where once I felt terror
at the punishments dished out

for failing to memorize some history date
I feel strangely grateful.
The padres gave me a rebel's cause
like Brando's dumb longshoreman

with the mobster bosses.
They woke me from a sleep

that could have lasted all my life
were it not for their scabbard strife.

My family life was too edenic
to blood me for the challenges
that lay down those mean streets
far from the bosom of cinema

where real Johnny Friendlys lurked,
only some of them wearing soutanes.
Education, they say, prepares us for life.
Not because of book learning, I think

but something more cerebral and dark.
What little academic lore
I took into this limp brain
has long deserted me,

replaced now by the sights and smells
of a past I cherish
every passing year
for its negativity, and fears.

On the Quay Road

He hadn't seen her since the Christmas party.

'How is your mother?' he asked.

'Bearing up,' she said. 'It's good for her that I'm around all the time now. She's a bit funny on her feet.'

She'd come back from Galway after her father died of a heart attack. She was working in a secretarial office but they gave her compassionate leave because of the tragedy.

'You were great to come back for her,' he said.

'What else could I do? You only have one mother. How could I reuse her?'

'I don't know. People get caught up in things.'

They walked down by the river. Fishermen were taking in salmon, hitting them on the heads with their truncheons as they wriggled in the nets.

They sat on a bench and looked out at the Ox mountains in the distance. The sun was speckling the fields, dancing in and out of the shadows. He felt sick anticipating what might happen or not happen. A cold mist was blowing in from the sea.

'Does this change anything between us?' he said, 'I mean you being here again.'

'I can't think about things like that at the moment. Don't push me. I still haven't recovered from my father.'

'Don't worry, I'm not getting any ideas. I just like seeing you.'

He'd put an engagement ring on her finger at the Christmas party in Grogan's bar and drunkenly proposed marriage to her. It was only a joke one from a Halloween barmbrack but he felt she knew he meant business. He'd been crazy about her since the first day he set eyes on her but he'd never expressed his feelings till then. He wouldn't have had the courage to give her a real ring but the way she accepted the pretend one made him think he might have a chance with her after all.

They watched the fishermen loading the salmon into their boxes.

'I heard you met Keelin,' he said.

She paused, 'Is that a problem for you?'

He wanted to say, 'If you're that cut-up about your father why are you seeing him?' But he couldn't. Instead he just said, 'Of course not. I'm just mentioning it.'

'You're jealous of him, aren't you?' she said.

'Not jealous, just a little bit nervous.'

She's been going steady with Keelin for two years until he went off to Dublin with a nurse from Pontoon. They were supposed to get married but then they broke up and now he seemed to be on the loose again.

'You probably think I'm seeing you on the rebound,' she said.

'I didn't say that.'

'No, but I bet you thought it.'

They got up from the bench. The wind was knifing through them. They walked down past the college. It stood out in front of them like a proud man sticking his chest out.

They soaked their feet in the swimming pool. It felt good. Afterwards they went down the Quay Road. They were headed for Crocketts, the new pub that had opened during last year's festival.

The sun was low in the sky as they went in.

'This place has really been jazzed up,' he said.

'Yeah,' she agreed, sounding bored.

He wanted to say a hundred things to her but he knew if he started she'd fly off the handle and he'd lose her. Instead he just talked about all the day-to-day things that had been happening since the party.

'Would you like something to eat?' he said when he'd exhausted his news. She looked gorgeous in the fading light, her ringlets curling slightly in the breeze that clipped her dress up around her waist.

'If you want, but wouldn't a drink be better?'

He was glad she said that. He wanted a drink because he felt high seeing her but he was also afraid that if he got drunk he'd say something stupid and kill off any chance he had with her. The alternative was not to drink and maybe say nothing at all, which would probably kill off his chances in another way. Drunk or sober he felt beaten.

'Okay. Are you still on the Guinness?'

'Does the Pope pray?'

They went into the bar. He ordered a half-pint of Guinness for her and a pint of Smithwicks for himself.

'You can have eet *al fresco* if you like,' the barman said. He was Italian.

'I beg your pardon?' he said.

'A*l fresco*. You know, outside. '

'I don't think so. It's a bit nippy out there.'

He paid for the drinks and went back to the table.

'Did you hear that?' he said to her when he sat down, 'We could have had it *al fresco*.'

'It's far from *al fresco* I was reared.'

He came over with the drinks.

'*Gratias*,' he said as he put them down.

'Bloody foreigners,' she said when he was out of earshot, 'When are they going to give our country back to us?'

They were sitting under a photo of Humphrey Bogart kissing Ingrid Bergman from *Casablanca*. On the wall across the way there was another one of Marilyn Monroe with her dress blowing up over her thighs from a hot air vent.

'I love those old photographs,' she said, 'Don't you? They really conjure up the time.'

He remembered bringing her to *Casablanca* one night years ago in the Estoria. She'd probably forgotten that, and all the other films too. There were so many men in her life he felt he was just another statistic.

'So Keelin is gone back to Dublin,' he said.

'Jesus,' she said, 'If you mention him again I'll scream. So what if he is?'

'I'm sorry, it's just that people were talking.'

'I'm not surprised. We live in the valley of the squinting windows. If you go out with someone twice in this shithole you're engaged to be married to them.'

'I was just asking.'

She sipped at her Guinness. Outside he could hear the waves slushing against the wall of the quay. When he looked out the window he saw a fisherman cycling by with his waders.

'How long do you have off?' she asked him.

He'd been working at the sawmills in Ballyhaunis but he had a breakdown when she went off with Keelin and had to give in his notice. He hadn't told her that.

'There's a question mark over the mills,' he said, 'It might be closing down with the recession.' It was a lie but there was no way she could know that.

'Crikey, that sounds bad.'

'It's happening everywhere.'

'I know but it's different when it hits yourself. Are you really serious?'

'Oh I don't care too much. I'll get another job if I have to pack that one in. If you're willing to roll the sleeves up there's always something.'

'Of course. And you've got all your credentials now.'

'I suppose so.'

He wasn't sure if she was being sarcastic or not. The piece of paper he got from UCG was hardly worth blowing your nose with.

'So you've got an indefinite leave of absence?' she pressed, furrowing her brow as she quizzed him.

'Kind of. I'm waiting on word for my next move.'

'Does Mrs Finnerty mind you being there so long?'

'She doesn't seem to. At least she said nothing.'

Mrs Finnerty was a friend of his family who went back to the old days. When he'd sold his house and moved to Dublin she said he was welcome back any time and he took her up on the offer.

'What a woman. I wish I knew people like that. It would be great not to have to think about money.'

'Why do you need to worry? Your mother's house is coming to you, isn't it?'

'You mean when she dies? Jesus, don't say things like that.'

'I'm sorry. I hope she lives forever. I didn't mean it in the way you thought.'

'It's okay. You don't have to apologise.'

'It came out the wrong way.'

'Don't worry about it. I'm probably just a bit jumpy.'

The evening wasn't going the way he'd expected. He didn't want to be talking about morbid things like jobs folding up or how long people might live. He wanted to ask her what were her feelings for him, if he had any chance with her or if she was still carrying a torch for Keelin.

'We should be getting back,' she said.

'Are you serious?'

'Mam wants me to go to the chemist for some pills.'

'I thought they stayed open till around nine or ten.'

'Yeah, but she worries when I'm out late. She's a bag of nerves since Dad died. I'm sorry. Maybe we can stay longer the next time.'

'All right,' he said taking a gulp of his drink. He still had a half glass left but he was starting to feel tipsy. Sometimes one drink made him feel drunker than ten. Or was it her presence that was doing it?

53

'Can I see you again tomorrow?' he asked as he put his coat on. The courage of the drink, coupled with her urgency to move, made him more direct than he might otherwise have been.

'Maybe we should wait till next week, especially now that you're going to be here for a while.'

'Whatever you say, but I could be called back anytime.'

It was another lie but there was no way she could know that.

'Look,' she said, 'I really like you but –'

She paused. His face fell.

'But what?'

'Nothing. Forget it.'

'But not enough,' he said, 'Isn't that what you were going to say?'

'Don't put words into my mouth. We've both been through a tough time recently. Can we not just take things slow for a while?'

'Of course. It's just that – '

He didn't know how to finish it either.

'Just that *what*?'

She was being as good as him, making him feel awkward for not being able to put his thoughts into words. He wanted to say he heard a rumour that Keelin was on the prowl again, that people were saying he intended to come back to the town the following day after a game of football in Crossmolina. But of course he couldn't. She'd only fly off the handle again.

'I don't know. Forget I said anything. 'I'm fine about next week. We'll play it slow if that's the way you want it.'

'That's good of you. My feelings are all knotted up at the moment with all the business with Mammy and everything.

'You don't have to explain yourself. I'm like that a lot of the time myself too.'

'You're so understanding.'

He started to put his arms around her but she drew herself away. His desire for her was growing with the drink but what was the point when it wasn't reciprocated?

He could bring her here seven days a week and she could promise him the earth but he'd be tortured not knowing how she felt about him, tortured by the knowledge that she mightn't didn't even know herself. Was she waiting for Keelin to decide either way before she'd consider an alternative to him?

As he got up to leave he found himself wobbling on his feet.

'My God,' she said, 'Don't say you're getting tipsy on one drink. '

He tried to make light of it.

'It's not the drink, I just stood up the wrong way.'

'Sure, any my granny's in the Merchant Navy.'

'I'm serious, Maybe the floor is uneven.'

'If this continues,' she said, 'We'll save a fortune on nights out.'

She laughed at her own joke. He wanted the ground to swallow him up in his embarrassment and she was laughing. She obviously thought he was a wimp because he couldn't handle his drink. Whatever tiny chance he had with her was probably gone now. He knew what her values were. Keelin Gormley wouldn't have wobbled after one drink, or twenty-one. Neither would he have blamed the floor if he did, or the way he stood up.

He thought back to the Christmas party. Everything seemed so simple then. He was genuinely drunk that night and so was she. Everyone was singing patriotic songs. They had Santa hats on their heads. When he presented her with the ring it was as if everything was suddenly possible: a life together with a barrel-load of kids and her getting the job she'd always wanted at the secretarial college in Galway.

But now it all seemed to be nothing more than a pipedream, like all the pipedreams he'd had about her. She'd always be looking over her shoulder at someone else, either Keelin or one of the other Keelins that had come and gone in her life since that first day he'd seen her mending a puncture on a bicycle outside her house.

He saw his future sharp and clear. She didn't want him and she'd never want him. She'd use him and then discard him, like all women did when they were finished with you. It was almost like a law. She'd disappear out of his life as everything else that was important to him had disappeared out of it. probably because of some kink in himself that didn't seem to be able to hold on to things. How did other people manage it? What was their secret?

They walked up by the Moy again. At the bridge they turned left. They might have been any couple taking an evening stroll. She was oblivious to the way he was feeling and that made it worse for him. Or was she just pretending to be oblivious?

As they went up the town a car honked. A woman with a fuzzy hairstyle stuck her head out the window and started shouting greetings. She waved back at her playfully.

The car screeched off around the corner.

'That was Orla,' she said, 'I used to work with her.'

'Oh,' he said blankly. He didn't know who Orla was and he didn't care either.

Why was she torturing him like this? He wanted her to tell him either to be gone from her or to stay but not be left in this eternal limbo, this agony of waiting.

Would she one day condescend to take him seriously when her looks faded and her other possibilities dried up? These were the things he wanted to know, not who bloody Orla was.

'It's a pity she didn't stop,' she said, 'she's certifiably insane. You'd love her.'

They walked up King Street past the grocer's and the sweet shop. His heart quickened as they passed Grogan's, the pub where it all began. It brought the party back to him. He thought of the stupid hats and the even stupider proposal. She'd probably forgotten it by now.

She tapped on the window, spotting someone she knew inside.

'Get the fuck out,' she shouted at a group of men, 'You're all barred.'

They looked up from the table they were sitting at. One of them started to laugh.

'Those guys,' she said, 'Alcoholics. All of them. Wouldn't do a day's work to save their lives.'

And yet he felt she'd have preferred to be inside guzzling pints with them than outside with him.

They turned into Connolly Street. That was where her house was.

'I'm sorry if I came across as being too solemn in the pub,' he said to her.

'Don't be stupid,' she said, 'That's one of the things I like about you. Most of the men I know are shallow. I know you'd walk across water for me.'

He thanked her for the compliment but he knew that was part of the problem. He cared too much.

The ones who didn't care always got the women. That was how life worked. Maybe they weren't able to hold on to them but at least they got them and had their time with them, however short a time that was, as opposed to his own desolate longing.

'I'd walk on land for you too,' he said. Again she laughed.

'You know what?' she said, 'Some of the stuff you come out with just cracks me up. You should be on the television or something.'

'I don't want to be on television. I want to be going out with you.'

'Oh Christ. Don't let's get back on that one again.'

'I know I'm too possessive. That's the main problem, isn't it?'

She didn't reply to this.

'If you agreed to come out with me,' he said, 'I wouldn't be this intense. I wouldn't be plaguing you with phone calls or any of that stuff.'

'I know,' she said.

'So can we...'

She gave him a sad smile. He stopped talking. It was hopeless. There was nothing left to say.

They walked towards her house. He knew his time was running out. He started to panic. What if she went in and he never saw her again? He wouldn't be able to live with that.

As they got close to it he tried to slow his step so they wouldn't get to it too soon but before he knew it they were there.

How often had he stood outside it, he thought, either when she was inside or wasn't? How often had he walked up and down her street in the vain hope that she'd pass him by and exchange even a few words with him?

'Well,' she said, taking her key out of her handbag, 'Home sweet home.'

'I suppose that's it then,' he said.

'Don't think I take you for granted,' she said, 'You're a sweet man.'

'Thanks,' he said, even though it felt like an insult. She might have been someone patting a little boy on the head. Women never called their men sweet if they were interested in them. A bastard had a better chance with a woman than a sweet man.

She put her key in the door. It opened onto a hallway.

'Did you mean it about next week?' he said, his voice trembling.

'Scout's honour,' she said, putting her two fingers up in a V sign.

As she walked in, her mother appeared at an upstairs window. She was calling down to her about something.

'Oh shit,' she said, 'I forgot the bloody pills. Now she's going to have my guts for garters.'

He tried to kiss her but she was already moving away from him into the hallway.

'Are you not going to give me a goodnight kiss?' he asked desperately.

'I'd love to,' she said as she closed the door on him, 'but she's always like a divil when I'm out late. If it goes past midnight I'll be shot.'

A Small Step

August nineteen sixty nine.
I've just got off the train
at Heuston Station.
My mother has been diagnosed with cancer.
My father is a patient
in a hospital in Dublin 8.

An astronaut has stepped on the moon.
A woman has died in Edward Kennedy's car.
The words Chappaquiddick
and Mary Jo Kopechne
are on everybody's lips,
making tragedy almost exotic.

I'm about to go into a new college,
a new house.
Cars whirl around me
as I blink in the haze,
trying to dodge them like on a merry-go-round.
I walk like a ghost
my footsteps barely touching the ground.

I've left Ballina for Dublin,
been whisked from it
much sooner than I expected
the family move
taking me from a town I love
and a college I hate.

I try to acclimatize to my surroundings
to a redbrick house in Cabra Park
that you reach through a lane.

My brother puts his arms around me,
Welcoming me into his little empire.
He's wearing a crumpled suit
and an awkward smile.
On the window-sill is the statue
of a falcon.

Later in the night
I'm in another house
at a party
where I know nobody.
I can't see faces,
only shadows on the wall.
People talk to me and I respond
merry with a drink I've been given.

The things that are happening to me
seem to be happening to someone else.
I submit to them,
a willing victim.
Someone asks me if I feel disoriented
when I knock over a glass.

People are talking about the Sorbonne riots,
the murder of Sharon Tate.
It is the end of a decade,
or more than that.
I feel a part of some unnamed revolution,
sucking at sensations
like a character from a play
I've either written or performed in
but still don't feel a part of.

A woman puts her lips on mine
and I taste the smell of her breath.

She seems to know who I am
but I don't know her.
Who are all these people
and why are they making for me?
I feel I'm at the still centre
of an avalanche.
I try to remember Ballina but I can't.
Already it's gone,
replaced by another illusion.

I watch the evening skyline,
the grey bricks of Belvedere College,
a picture of the new family home.
There's a mahogany table shining at me,
the placid smile of a priest in a college.
This is where I'm going now.
I have a foot in both camps and neither,
my mind neutral.

My father speaks to me in slurred words,
sleepy from the drugs he's on
in St. Patrick's Hospital.
In a different hospital in another suburb
my mother says, 'Are you minding yourself?'
She wants to know about food, clothing,
how things are going in the flat
in Cabra Park.

I walk down a steel staircase
into the Cosmo snooker hall.
A man knocks over a fruit machine beside me.
Another man is sleeping
under one of the tables.
I leave the dark vault,

the night sky almost touching me as I emerge.

The Astor Cinema is showing *The Razor's Edge*.
On O'Connell Bridge
a neon sign lights up the sky.
It shows a man flicking sausages
onto a pan
in glittering colour.
I watch the page of a newspaper
blowing over the Liffey,
drink in the coffee stench.

My past has abandoned me
I feel like I'm on a train track
that keeps narrowing but going nowhere.
The lights on the street go
green, yellow, red,
green, yellow, red
like in a dream.

A beggar approaches me.
He's telling me the story
of a woman who left him.
He tries to cry.
I take my coat off, sit on a bench.
A blue light falls on the river.
1'm engulfed by the tall buildings around me,
engulfed by sadness.

There's an airlock in the radiator
of the hospital my mother is in.
It clacks like a drumbeat.
I bend down to kiss her,
her skin like folded parchment.
She's locked into a machine

that kills the bad cells
and the good ones.

The papers are full of the moon landing,
the safe return of the astronauts.
A journalist asks: 'Will science fact
spell the end of science fiction?'

Excavators are digging up the city.
I walk for the sake of walking.
The streets trap me, exhale their magic.
I hear the sound of Fairport Convention
from a doorway
like an invitation.

There's a palm tree in the garden
of the house we're going to.
It reminds me of American films I've seen.
When I enter it I see
there's no furniture in the rooms.
My footsteps resound on the wooden floors.

The phone rings
and a strange voice talks to me.
I can't remember what I say.
I hear static,
an engaged tone.
Images flicker on a television set.
It's a black and white programme
with Peter Lawford in it.
In slow motion the lights on the street still go
green, yellow, red
green, yellow, red.

The leaves in the trees are fluttering.

In the distance a dog barks
like an incantation.

A hippie waves at me.
The phone rings again.
My mother is getting better.
Where's my father?
Will he be all right?
I don't recognize him anymore,
don't recognize anybody,
not even my face in the mirror.
Will the night ever end?
Will any night?
And where will my future lie?

Nineteen sixty nine,
the year everything changed for me.
One life ending,
another beginning
and I'm not sure if I'm a boy or a man.

The Hibs

It's not much fun cycling down to Muredach's every day. I'm not any good at school. You usually get beaten anyway, even when you know your lessons. There are a few nice priests but they're the exception rather than the rule. Mainly you go because you have to. Afterwards you try to forget it as quick as you can. Life really begins when you come home. I'm from a fairly big family so there's usually a lot of stuff going on. We usually cycle down to Enniscrone for the day if the weather is fine. We go to the pictures if it isn't.

If I'm not going anywhere I walk down to the lane at the end of Arthur Street and have a game of football with Michael. He's two classes behind me at school. We see a lot of one another on account of living so close together. His house is just across the road. There's a gate beside it that we use for a goal. Other times we just kick the ball up and down the street and in between the cars. Or else we might stay in our house playing cards.

In 1963, when I'm ten, I start playing a lot of snooker with Michael. I'm not that good at it but it passes the time. The place we play is The Hiberninan Hall but we refer to it as The Hibs. It's a huge building across the road from the Post Office. They do boxing on the top floor. We can hear them breathing hard as they punch one another. Sometimes when you're playing a shot the ceiling vibrates. If they pound hard on the floor sometimes, the sawdust comes down through it and lands on the table, making the balls move crookedly across the cloth. You can also hear the thunk of the punches. Sometimes the boxers come down for a game with us afterwards if they have nothing else to do. Jodie Melia is the best at snooker. He made a break of 57 once.

The boxers push us off the table when they come down. If that happens, we just sit and watch the games instead of playing ourselves.

There's a man called George who's a genius of sorts. He can play an in-off the red up to twenty times in a row. He has no time for snooker, which he regards as a children's game. He just wants to play a billiard shot all day. He puts a red on the pink spot and the white in the D and keeps going in off it, time after time. I could watch him forever at that, especially the way the white spins round in a banana shape as soon as it hits the red. His expression never changes as he plays the shot.

In the Hibs I feel unwatched and unmonitored. The dark figures I consort with here are like my extended family. Their language is that of nudges and winks, of petty crime and the hint of it. The bravado is forced but it's still a haven for me from the robotic nullity of the college, or even the cosy cushion of my own home. I look at the cue ball lurch across a field of green and its movement becomes a world to me, a world I might one day turn into smalltown glory if I ever get good at the game. It's a skill that's frowned on by my family. That's another reason I like it.

The chalk is always extra hard on the cold evenings. I dig a penny down into it and keep swirling it around until I make a bowl effect in the square. That makes it easier to apply to the cue. There are rips in the cloth near some of the pockets which means that you can hit the ball off-line and it could still curl in. Knowing things like this wouldn't win you world finals but it can be pretty effective here when you're playing the local grease-ball for a shilling you can't afford to lose.

My father, who's a solicitor, doesn't like me coming to the Hibs. He says you'll only meet the riff-raff of the town there. He wants me to play in the Moy Club instead. That's where the rugby crowd go. I don't have much time for rugby or the rugby crowd.

Besides, they only have one table down there. Sometimes when I'm going down to my cousin in Bunree I pass by the Moy Club. I look in the window and see some old codgers lurching around the table. They always look bored. Now and again my cousin lets me play a game in his house. He has a full-sized table in it. He had to have the roof gelignited to get it to fit in because it wouldn't go in the door. It's a beautiful table but as I say, I only get to play on it now and again. Most of the time I play bagattelle in an outhouse he has. Bagatelle isn't much fun. There are lots of holes on the table, and things that look like plastic mushrooms beside them. You have to get the balls into the holes without knocking the mushrooms over.

When I'm not in The Hibs I usually play table tennis with Michael in our house. It's also my father's office. We have a mahogany table that he puts all his files on. When he's not busy I put them in the shelves along the wall and have a game. It's one of those tables that can be reduced in size when you fold it over. There's a crack in the wood where the fold is. When the ball hits this it bounces straight up into the air, leaving the other player an easy slam. We always laugh when that happens.

Even though we can play table tennis all day without paying, I think I prefer snooker. Michael and myself don't stop playing even after the frame is over. We keep setting the balls up again and again until someone comes in and makes us stop. If there's nobody there we play with the lights off but if the caretaker is around we put sixpence in the slot. That gets you half an hour's light.

The Hibs is empty in the middle of the day except for a few old men playing cards in the corner. They play a game called 110, which is like an extended form of 25. Every trick you get is worth five points. You try to work your way up to

110. If there are a group playing, they band together against the man with the most tricks. Sometimes I join this game when I'm waiting for my turn on the snooker table but if my name is called I give someone else my cards.

It's now 1966 and I'm 13 years of age. At this point of their careers the world class players are probably making their first centuries. I've never got near this. I think 31 is my biggest break and even that had a fluked shot in it. Despite that, I refuse to give it up. Michael is almost as enthusiastic. We play until we're drunk with it and only then go home. Then we come back and become drunk with it again.

Every day it's the same routine. Down to Michael's house to collect him, then up past Syron's, Cottrell's petrol pumps, the place where they make headstones, the old school, the Estoria. We know every crack in the pavement. We turn left at the font and then go down past Dr. Igoe's, Benny Walkin's, the offices of Bourke, Carrig and Loftus, Dolores McHale's house – she goes to the convent with my sisters – past the post office where the film projectionist works and across the road to the Hibs. After we go in we become vampires, lords of our domain. It's just as much of an escape from reality as the Estoria is.

Each evening after playing for four or five hours we vow we'll never enter the hall again but then after a while the bug bites again and we go back, trying to whirl the white ball around on an imaginary string.

One day we're supreme, the next 'cat,' as Michael puts it. (I think that's short for 'catastrophic' but I'm too young to know that word. He calls some films in the Estoria 'cat' as well). There's no in-between. It's like a lottery. The memory of even one good shot is the drug. It fires you up like any junkie craving another fix on the green baize.

The inspired moments you keep going through all the abysmal hours when nothing goes in. The memory of even one good pot is enough to inject you all for the hours of nothing, when you play the game like someone who's just taken it up yesterday even though you've been at it for four years now, four years that seem like twenty four.

They call me the 'Fifteen Minute Playerr.' I can perform okay for that amount of time but then I usually go to pieces. I often go for mad pots, sometimes knocking the balls off the table in the process.

'A cue should be handled like a woman,' Bill O'Hara tells me, 'with delicacy.' Bill is one of the regulars. He has his own cue in a case on the wall. Only the really serious players have their own cues. The rest of us just take what's provided by the hall. Some of them are warped.

I'm also called The Olympic Player. That's because I play so much. The Olympics are just about to take place in Mexico. Some of the other people in the club ask me when I'm packing my bags for that particular location. (They call it 'Mehico'). There's no snooker in the Olympics but that's beside the point.

The fact that I never come off the table creates some problems for the other players. Sometimes they physically remove me from it. One day I had a cue broken over my back for overstaying my welcome at the table. Such are the minor occupational hazards of being an addict.

The only other thing I don't like about The Hibs is the amount of mice in it. Sometimes I think it has more mice than people. I almost end up being on first name terms with them in time. They're not afraid of us. Usually they just sit there watching us. 'Maybe they're trying to get tips on how to play better,' Bill O'Hara jokes. Maybe they have their own mini-tables behind the woodwork too. Maybe they practise there into the wee hours.

There are a lot of 'characters' in this mouse-infested club. There are also a lot of characters in it. Not many of them have much talent except George but to themselves, and to those of us watching them, they're legends.

There's one man I refer to as The Memory. He's always telling you about the great games he played as a youth. Most of his stories are made up but over time he comes to believe his lies and so does everyone else. He probably never won a game in his life.

Another one of the players is always talking about what he's going to do instead of just getting down and playing the shot. He'll tell you the 54 things that were on his mind which caused him to mess up his shot. If there's any way to misplay a shot, this man will find it. A red could be on the lip of the pocket and he'll hit it so that it'll stay out. Or maybe the white will follow it in. It takes a certain genius to be this bad. And yet I believe his analyses. I'm too young to see through anyone, and gladly so. Ignorance is bliss. Such are the petty mythologies of these mad nights.

Nobody is unduly bothered about the rules of this strange game in the Hibs. Usually they're honoured more in the breach than the observance. If you can't reach a ball you simply jump up on the table. Or else you bring it back to where you're standing to make it easier to hit.

There are two tables in the hall, the Good one and the Bad one. The Good one only has a few holes in the cloth so it's by far the more desirable. This is the table the 'real' players play on, the ones who know all the angles.

The Bad one has something that only passes for a cloth. It's many years now since it has been green. It looks more like a frayed carpet, or scorched grass. The cushions are like elastic bands. If you hit the cue ball with any strength it zooms up and down the table about twenty times. You could go out to Clarke's café around the corner for a cup of tea and when you came back it would probably still be moving. Sometimes if I get bored waiting for it to stop rolling I stop it with my hand. Otherwise the half-hour's electricity would expire without me getting a chance to attempt a pot.

In a funny way I like this table more than the Good one. Over the years I've got to know its curves and its rolls. But when the Olympics are over they put a new cloth on it and it's not the same anymore. It's just like the Good table. That means I have no advantage over strangers. The new cloth is the leveller. We're all in the same boat now. Now I can't even beat the Out-Of-Towners on it.

The loyalty of the people in the Hibs is matched only by the revulsion they have for someone who comes in that they don't know. Even before he strikes a ball he'll immediately be deemed a shark. If he plays for money, even if he plays well, he'll probably lose, because the regulars will hustle him out of it. He'll either be talked out of a game or they'll find some other way to unnerve him. Maybe he'll be given one of the crooked cues. Or someone will dummy up the scoreboard when he's not looking.

If he's not too good a player, it's probably easy enough to beat him honestly. The secret is to bottle him up, to make him nervous about his game, to never praise his shots. Your own man, on the contrary, will get cheers to raise the roof, even for pots it's practically impossible to miss. 'Good on ye' they'll resound, 'Ye boy ye.' Sometimes I think we could give strangers a thirty point lead in a game and still win.

Everyone goes quiet when these people come into the hall. It's like in a cowboy film when a gunslinger goes into a saloon. After he leaves, the tension goes away again and everything goes back to normal. Tongues are loosened, post mortems conducted, shots embellished out of all proportion. To celebrate, maybe another money match will be held. Here a different kind of tension will creep in, one without hostility, but there'll be less chat than usual. You'll hear nothing but the purring of the air vent and the gentle pock of the balls off one another.

The players in the Hibs make no apologies for the fact that the hugeness of the world is reduced to this twelve foot by six foot mass of cloth. This is reality, a reality greater than the one we all return to when the lights go out for the last time, when we stroll home to the people who care about us or don't, who sympathise with us or beat us, who ask us what we were doing for the evening. I go home to a comfortable home in Arthur Street but most of the other players are from Lord Edward Street, a rougher area of Ballina that we call Guntown. I get on better with these people than with my neighbours. I can be myself more with them. I don't have to play a role, or say things that sound impressive or important. It's classless.

The important thing is to be a good loser, to shake hands with the man who beats you even if you're cursing him inside yourself, for you'll be beaten more often than you win and it's important to come to terms with that fact, even though you'll dwell on all your missed pots in the privacy of your room later. I said to a player once, 'You learn more from defeat than success.' He replied, 'In that case you must be very fucking educated.'

Defeat is good therapy for your next match. It's a good steeling device against making a fool of yourself again. The next time out you're more crafty, resisting any adventurous shots, making the other man at least work for his victory rather than presenting it to him on a plate.

Nobody mentions the professional players much in the Hibs. Television hasn't yet popularised the game, nor are the professionals very attractive anyway. Joe Davis is a name you hear now and again. So is Ray Reardon, and Patsy Houlihan. Alex Higgins is, as yet, only a giant in the Jampot. Steve Davis is in short pants. Jimmy White isn't long out of nappies.

Showing a lack of interest in the professional game gives you more of a sense of importance in your own one. I'm glad I don't see snooker on television because the skills on display would intimidate me. I'm happier in my own bubble where we're our own gods, even if some days I can't hit a ball out of my way to save my life.

I particularly seize up at the competitions that are run every now and then, rarely, if ever, getting within an asses roar of the final. My hands tighten up and I start to sweat. The fact that people are watching. I get nervous in the silence and usually end up being beaten by players even worse than myself. This bugs me, the knowledge that I've beaten myself. Or that I've been psyched out of it.

The elderly players know the best way to beat me is to tie me up in knots. They know I have a flash-bang style riddled with holes. They don't mind me getting the odd dynamic pot so long as they win the game. They often knock the black safe, keep the cluster of reds together, or stick the cue ball up against the cushion as often as they can. They know sooner or later I'll be tempted to break the pack. Sooner or later I'll stick them on easy reds and they'll dish up. It will be just a matter of tapping them in; they'll be hanging on the edges of the pockets.

Or else they play snookers on me. 'It's the name of the game,' George said to me once, by way of an excuse. I'm okay at getting out of snookers but I invariably leave a ball on afterwards.

I keep thinking that the next competition will somehow be different, that one day would be my night, that in some strange way everything will come right at the same time. But it never does. I never have the smell of success. My opponents hustle their way to the finals of these competitions where they meet fellow grinders and the matches go on so long you feel you could grow a beard watching them if you were old enough. Like golfers they size up every possibility and then in the end do nothing but knock a ball safe.

As the sixties draws to a close, my father starts to talk of retiring and moving to Dublin. That will mean I'll have to leave the Hibs. I know if that happens I'll miss it more than anywhere else in the town, maybe even more than the town itself. But changes are already happening in it. New types of players have started to come in, more 'respectable' ones. Some of them have motorbikes and dress like the Beatles. I prefer the old people at the 110 table than these.

The Hibs is starting to lose its atmosphere. Maybe one day the mice will even desert it. Then where will I be?

By now snooker is losing its image of being the sign of a mis-spent youth, but to me it's the hours outside the club I feel are mis-spent. I know I'll miss the dirt and the grime, the players who live on the edge of crime or poverty, the ones who are here to escape life, who are like the people in that Kris Kristofferson song, searching 'for anything they can to keep from going home.'

I've met these people, I've played with them for hours on end, I've lied for them when their girlfriends or wives have appeared at the door to try and find out if they're inside. The person they're looking for might be hiding under the table, or upstairs where the boxers train. He might pay the caretaker, or me, to tell the white lie. The ball and chain can wait. The balls and triangle can't.

Shortly before we leave Ballina a table soccer machine is installed in the Hibs and for me this spells the beginning of the end. As time goes on, people seem to spend more time at it than they do at snooker. The cues are now used more for sword-fighting than playing snooker.

Then another hall opens in the town. It's not far from the Savoy cinema. It's less exclusive than the Moy Club but better kept than the Hibs. It's a place with plants and video machines, a place where they sell coffee and salad sandwiches. Snooker halls, it seems, are no longer places you go to when you're bunking off school. They're places that would suit you for an evening out, somewhere to bring your girlfriend.

Would cheese-and-wine parties be next, I wonder, or formal dress like at the official competitions in England?

Pool, the poor man's snooker, has also started to sprout, and it takes a quick hold on people. They like it because it's instant, and because even if they're not particularly accurate in their aim they're still able to clear the table relatively quickly, thus forming some idea of talent within themselves. Pool is also cheap. And you can play it with a pint in your hands.

By now I'm in Dublin and pining for the old days. A show called 'Pot Black' has also started up on television, and coverage of some of the other professional tournaments. Everything, it appears, has been tidied up. No longer does my father disapprove of me playing this subversive game. No longer does he fear I'll fall into bad company with it. It isn't people on the dole that inhabit snooker halls anymore, he knows, but 'decent' people with jobs.

The only problem is that the decent people bore me. Modern snooker bores me. I want to get back to the stink of the streets.

Te Absolve

There was never anything to equal
the purification you felt
on Saturday nights
coming across the bridge
at St. Muredach's Cathedral
after being forgiven in confession
for taking pleasure in salivating over
Gina Lollobrigida's alluring breasts
in *Solomon and Sheba*.

The old man behind the grill
looked too decrepit even to know
what you were talking about
when you told him
about your enchantment,
especially when he said
'Say a prayer for me, my child'
after giving you absolution.

There was nothing to compare
to the near-ecstatic relief
you felt when the wind hit you
crossing the Moy.
You knew you would feel pure
the following day
when the priest at Mass
who asked you to pray for him
would now be praying for you.

At the time you thought him saintly,
the perfect contrast
to your adolescent self

but in later years,
as the clerical scandals unfolded,
you wondered if his request
hid a secret.

Maybe you were better off not to know
in those feckless days
when priests were sinless
and to be genuflected to
when you passed them
on the street
or when they forgave you
for your sins
in that dark box,
whitening your soul
like a detergent.

You thought of it
as a safety deposit box in your stomach
that lost credit
every time you thought about
Gina Lollobrigida
or Claudia Cardinale
or Brigitte Bardot
or Marilyn Monroe,
likening them to those temptresses
from the Bible
who did wild dances
and called for heads on a plate.

If you passed by the Savoy
and stopped to look again
at the poster of Gina Lollobrigida
with her breasts hanging out
of a Biblical dress

you told yourself she was unavailable
to you
except from your cinema seat
unless you wanted to endure
the wrath of the old priest
or God.

You were about to finish school.
Your boring future
was about to start
and you were called upon
to contemplate more pressing things,
than the plunging neckline
of an unattainable Jezebel
6000 miles away in geography
and 2000 in history
as you walked the road
to Damascus
in your hungry heart.

Fantasies of the Estoria

Keith was my oldest brother. He would have been the first to admit he practically grew up in the Estoria Cinema, which was across the road from where we lived. My father brought him to the latest attractions there almost as soon as he was able to walk (and quite possibly before).

The first thing Keith did after coming home from Muredach's was look up the *Western People* to see what would be showing the following week. If it was a Cagney or a Bogart, that was 'magic time.' After seeing the films he'd recite practically the entire scripts to the rest of the family, taking the parts of all the characters in them. This meant moving from one side of the room to the other to imitate the different voices and poses.

The big one was *Shane*. This was our second Bible, 'the Daddy of them all.' The poster said, 'There never was a film like *Shane,*' and we grew up believing that. Most of us still do. Keith acted out the saloon scene where Shane takes on Ryker as if he was living it. When he said, 'Your kind of days are over, Ryker,' you believed it.

Gone with the Wind was another favourite of his. He could do Clark Gable's voice even better than Alan Ladd's. 'We could have made a go of it when Bonnie was alive,' he'd say, imitating Rhett Butler talking about his ill-fated daughter to Scarlett O'Hara, talking as if his mouth was full of pebbles just like Gable did. When he acted out *Double Indemnity* he did Fred MacMurray and Edward G. Robinson equally well. If you closed your eyes you were back in the Estoria again. It was Keith's extra showing in the comfort of your own home. These were the people who made him live. Reality was the illusion.

Most of the films in the Estoria only ran for two nights but big budget ones might play for a week. If a film was 'Retained' that was even better. That happened with films like *The Guns of Navarone* and *The Big Country*. There was no limit to the amount of times Keith was capable of going to one of these releases. He loved the 'small' pictures as well. I never heard him mentioning an actor or actress he didn't like. He was incapable of it.

I was only two when he left Ballina so I didn't know him well as a child, seeing him only when he came home from Dublin on holidays. From that point of view he was more like an uncle to me than a brother. But he left a library of film books behind him that made it seem as if he was there himself. There were three main books as far as I remember, all about as heavy as a bale of briquettes. One of them was called *Silent Movies*. Another was called *TheTalkies*. I can't remember the name of the third one, only that it had a red cover.

I spent many days of my youth poring over the pages of these books and learning off the names of the people who were in them. There was very little writing in them. They were mostly comprised of photographs. Some pages had up to twenty photos on them, all thumbnail portraits of more stars than you could shake a stick at. You'd have to squint your eyes up to see some of them. Keith had a photographic memory and could identify even the most minor of them. If someone had a bit part in a Shakespeare play he'd probably have known his name – and what he ate for breakfast.

Once or twice I asked him if he'd like to have met his movie heroes. He didn't seem to express too much enthusiasm about this. I knew Cagney had been in Ireland to make *Shake Hands with the Devil*, and John Wayne, another hero of his, to film *The Quiet Man*. My father was rumoured to have met Wayne in Cong during the filming of it.

Keith wasn't too interested in things like that. It was as if the person would spoil the illusion of the character being portrayed in the film. Cody Jarrett from *White Heat* was more important to him than James Cagney. So was Ethan Edwards from *The Searchers* than John Wayne.

Even though all the family grew up in Ballina, Keith was actually born in Dublin. It was when my parents were living in Greystones shortly after they got married. He used to boast about that. I could never understand why because he loved Ballina to the core. He never lost his country accent when he moved to Dublin and if Mayo were playing Dublin in a football match you didn't have to guess who he'd be rooting for.

Keith went to UCD after leaving Muredach's. He did two degrees at once, Arts and Commerce. I never knew the reason for that but it made me aware he had a business side to him that was just as strong as his artistic one. He took a lot out of himself studying all the different subjects and when he graduated he felt more or less burned out. He came home to Ballina to recharge his batteries and try to figure out what job to go into. He wasn't wildly enthusiastic about any of the ones suggested to him. I remember him sitting in the kitchen picking his lip. His feet would be up against the stove like Henry Fonda in *My Darling Clementine*.

He still went to the Estoria, and occasionally the Savoy, the other cinema near us, if there was something good on there, and he still acted out the part of the characters when he came home, but he was a bit more serious now. Life had intruded upon his 'ballroom of romance.' Why did people have to get jobs, he wondered. Could they not spend their whole lives watching films?

He went over to England and worked in Walls ice cream factory for a while to decide on what he wanted to do for his future. If they had a good cinema over there he'd probably have stayed. Afterwards he went to Dublin to live, getting a job in a factory in Finglas called Unidare where he worked as a cost accountant.

He hated every minute of this. He was living in a rented house in Phibsboro at the time with another brother of mine who was studying Engineering in UCD and a sister who was working in the American Embassy. It was a tiny house in a long street with dozens of similar ones, all of them clustered together like sardines. I visited him now and again in the summer holidays. It was so different to our house in Ballina where you had all the space in the world. Here you felt you could almost touch all four walls of any room if you stood in the centre of them with your arms spread out.

In 1969 my father retired and the rest of the family moved to Dublin as well. By now Keith had married a girl called Jacqueline who'd grown up in England. Her mother was from Limerick and her father from Wales. They lived in Artane, where I would eventually end up living myself.

No matter how devoted Keith was to his work, which was a lot because he took everything he did very seriously, it always came secondary to his love of films. He went to the Dublin cinemas – the Carlton and the Corinthian, the Adelphi and the Regent, etc. – with the same dedication as he'd patronised the Ballina ones in the decades before. When videos came in, Jacqueline would record old movies that were showing on television and they'd watch them together that night. It was like having the Estoria back again, in miniature this time in his own home.

Sometimes he invited the rest of the family over for a showing, as if he was a Hollywood director doing a test screening. You almost expected to have your ticket halved at the door on evenings like this. When the film began, an almost sacred silence had to be observed. You weren't allowed talk when it was running and if you left the room to go to the toilet or to get yourself something to eat, it would be paused until you came back.

Keith's favourite decade was the forties so most of the films he recorded were from that time. They were usually films he'd first seen in Ballina and was now watching again with the same reverence. If he liked something enough, he never tired of watching it, even if he could quote the script off by heart. Or maybe especially if that was the case. Afterwards there'd be a discussion of what went on in the film, or who gave the best performance. Keith's answer to the second question was usually, 'Everyone.' If you said the dialogue was corny or the plot stilted you got a stern stare. You felt you mightn't be invited to the next showing as a result of your arrogance.

I tried to get him to watch some of the new films when I came to Dublin as these were the ones I grew up on just as he grew up on James Cagney and Humphrey Bogart. It was an uphill battle. I brought him to *The Deer Hunter* one night. He admitted it was well made but it didn't really work for him. In his world, Robert de Niro would never have got the girl in the last reel in the same way Bogie would.

His favourite Bogart film was *Casablanca*. He knew all the lines of this by heart too and quoted them to anyone who'd care to listen. If there was a get-together in his house, this was usually his partypiece. He'd hoist his trousers up the way Bogart did and put on his gravelly voice as he got ready to deliver the scene at the end where Bogart gives up Ingrid Bergman to Paul Henreid for The Cause:

'Last night we said a great many things. You said I was to do the thinking for both of us. Well I've done a lot of it and it all adds up to the one thing. You're getting on that plane. Inside of us we both know you belong to Victor. You're part of his work, the thing that keeps him going. If that plane leaves the ground and you're not on it you'll regret it, maybe not today or tomorrow but soon, and for the rest of your life. I'm no good at being noble but it doesn't take much to see that the problems of three little people don't amount to a hill of beans in this crazy world. Some day you'll understand that.'

I sometimes go back to Ballina and think of Keith full of excitement as he went up Arthur Street to the Estoria, or down Garden Street to the Savoy, immersing himself in the worlds of people who lived in circumstances so far removed from his as to almost resemble people from another planet. And yet these were the people who made life treasurable for him. They were the people who helped him get through Muredach's, and later Unidare.

When anything went wrong with his life he was able to retreat to their worlds and make them his own. He became Dorothy from *The Wizard of Oz* or Norma Desmond from *Sunset Boulevard*. After an injection of their fantasy he would be himself again. He'd be ready to make an onslaught of a world that failed to measure up to theirs on any number of levels.

Keith retired young to write a book on Hollywood screenwriters. He spent the last twenty years of his life at it. It became just as much a passion for him writing about films as seeing them had been for him as a younger man. Every morning he'd add some new item of information on one of his writers to his ever-growing file, dipping in and out of the innumerable tomes in his ever-growing library. Otherwise times he spent the day travelling between bookshops to find more material to suit his theme. I often asked him if he was sending sample chapters from his book to publishers to see if they might be interested in it but that was never really on his radar.

I'd had some books published myself by this time and had been 'bitten by the bug' of writing. As a result I found it difficult to understand his attitude of nonchalance. It was only later I realised that publication, in his eyes, seemed to sully the act of composition. It brought it from the sanctum of his house into the marketplace. He reminded me of the Chinese poet Li Po who was said to burn his poems after writing them, his thinking being that the writing was the thing, not the fact of them being seen by anyone.

Keith contracted Parkinson's Disease in his later years but it didn't dent his enthusiasm for his *magnum opus*. He still had movie showings at his house and we still attended them with the same zeal. I didn't have the patience of other members of the family for the more long-winded ones, and I point-blank refused to watch *They Died With Their Boots On,* having something of an aversion to Errol Flynn, so I stayed away on nights like this, but when he was showing classics like *The Big Heat* or *Build My Gallows High* I loved soaking myself in the atmosphere he created. I loved to see his face as he mouthed the dialogue with the actors, raising the volume on his remote during the really dramatic scenes (or when we dared to talk).

I used to run into him every now and then in town when he'd be ferreting through an old film encyclopaedia in some old second-hand store off one of the main streets in the city centre which stocked only rare movie memorabilia. Most people in our lives begin conversations by asking how we are but Keith's ones always started with talk about films. You could have had a quadruple bypass the day before and he'd greet you with something like, 'Do you think James M. Cain was over-rated? I've always preferred Raymond Chandler myself – especially the early stuff.'

On one of the last times I saw him in a bookshop he was riffling through a biography of Frank Capra looking for some previously unpublished photographs of him. He was especially looking for photos of him with screenwriters, thinking they might be suitable for his book. The idea was that the reader would recognise Capra and be induced to read about the screenwriter beside him. In this way they would 'educate' themselves about a lesser-known figure. It sounded good in theory but Keith was never practical enough to realise that photographs like these were usually privately owned and had to be bought, often at huge prices, or sought out by contacting the person who took them, who might be either dead or uncontactable.

I told him I wasn't really that interested in Capra, being of the opinion that his films were too sweet, even his most famous one, *It's a Wonderful Life*. I said I'd seen this so many times over the years, particularly at Christmas, that whatever allure it once held had slowly worn off. His face fell when I said that.

'What's wrong with being sweet?' he asked me. I said that all too often 'sweet' meant 'saccharine', which was probably why the term 'Capracorn' had been coined, to refer to Capra's more shallow efforts.

I then said I was working on a book about the dark side of Hollywood, the world of drink and drugs that plagued so many actor's lives and ended so many of them prematurely, including those of his heroes Humphrey Bogart through cancer and Alan Ladd from a lethal cocktail of drink and drugs. I told him I thought that would make a better book than one on the sugar-coated world of Capra.

Again his face fell, but I was on a roll now and I couldn't stop. I told him the book I really wanted to write was one on John Huston's film *The Misfits*, which spelt the end of the careers of three movie icons: Marilyn Monroe, Montgomery Clift and his hero Clark Gable. Monroe was in bits with her nerves when she made it and Clift an alcoholic. Gable died soon after filming from a heart attack that was brought on by his exertions on the set.

By now Keith had had enough. 'You're always writing about misfits, aren't you?' he said, what's so wrong about people who *fit*?' I realise now that he was right, that films shouldn't be about people who trawl society's underbelly. They should be a release for us from our problems, they should take us on journeys that transport us away from 'the whips and scorns of time' to some other level, for however brief a time. As T. S. Eliot once said, 'Humankind cannot bear too much reality.'

Keith died before his book was finished and maybe that was fitting. Maybe he should have been buried with it too. It was as much a part of him as the clothes he wore. It was his other self, his Siamese twin.

When I think of him now I see him rummaging through one of his filing cabinets for a new photograph of someone like Capra or Hitchcock or one of those screenwriters he treasured like De Witt Bodeen, his eyes dancing in his head with rapture as he managed to fit the image to the chapter or the word to the theme. If I say he never fully grew up I mean that in the best possible sense. Even in his seventies it was impossible to see him as anything but the Ballina boy in short pants buying his sweets in the foyer of the Estoria as he sucked in his breath in anticipation of some Arabian Nights fantasy.

The problems of three little people might not amount to a hill of beans in this crazy world but for Keith they were what made it go round.

'You're getting on that plane,' Bogart told Bergman in *Casablanca*. But Keith didn't get on the plane. That would have been too banal. Instead he stayed on the ground with Claude Rains, walking away into the sunset with his old buddy as it sailed off into the sky. It was the beginning of a beautiful friendship.

Farmer

The sun is bleeding yellow in the sky,
a sheep spilling her lamb
onto the scorched earth.
The dead entrails of all lives
come back to haunt us
at moments like this.
The heather is blazing
but the hills are dead,
the lights of the surrounding houses
bespeaking no lives or loves inside,
only the silence
of another failed harvest.

Creeper

Fergie lost most of his money during the recession but he still had the shell of affluence about him. Eithne, his wife, had been my former girlfriend. She still acted too friendly with me when I was in their company but Fergie seemed to enjoy this. I'd introduced them to each other when Eithne and myself broke up and they married soon afterwards.

'Too soon afterwards,' as Eithne often reminded me.

We were after coming from Creeper's funeral in Leigue cemetery. He was a priest who terrorised everyone who was ever taught by him in Muredach's before shuffling off the mortal coil at 83 and we were celebrating him, if that's the word, in Fergie's upmarket semi-d in Bohernasup. There was a huge turn-out, unusual for such a savage. Fergie said he was only there to make sure the old bastard was safely down.

He wasn't long in the door before he started laying into the neat whiskeys. Every glass he drank seemed to drive him further away from Eithne - and her closer to me. We watched him like two conspirators in a crime we didn't even know we were going to commit as his eyes became sleepy and he rocked unsteadily on his feet.

'Remember the day we fecked his cane into the Moy?' he said, standing out on the balcony of the house as the night came down. I knew it would lead into the story of poaching salmon down by Bunree, or lifting Helen Ruddy's skirt up one night at a hop, or spiking the Convent of Mercy girls' tea with whiskey in Cafolla's when we were lucky enough to get them in there during their free classes.

'Go easy in the hard stuff, Fergie,' I said, 'it'll destroy your brain cells.'

'I never had any in the first place,' he snapped back at me, 'That's your department, Einstein.'

'Well it'll rot your liver then.'

'Don't waste your breath,' Eithne said to me, 'You should know by now that it only encourages him.'

'You might have something there,' he said, and then, winking at me as he gave Eithne a side eye, 'One of these days she'll realise she's only married to an old lush and jump ship.'

The prospect didn't seem to bother him. Maybe there was someone else already lined up to fill her shoes, one of those flirty little things he specialised in hiring in his building firm in Gurteens - and then firing as soon as they spurned his advances.

He liked to refer to himself as an alcoholic. He said it with such formality that it almost sounded like a religion.

'Who cares about my liver anyway?' he roared, lighting up a slim panatella, 'You only get one spin on the merry-go-round in this lousy life. Make it last. We'll all be down with Creeper sooner or later.'

Eithne muttered 'Sooner, sooner' under her breath but he didn't hear her. I looked at his huge bulk silhouetted on the balcony and thought: If cirrhosis of the liver doesn't get him, lung cancer will. It was a delightful prospect with which to greet his forthcoming fortieth birthday.

'You're coming to my bash, aren't you?' he asked then, as if reading my thoughts, 'I'll put you sitting next to Etty. The pair of you can canoodle away to your heart's content as I drink myself stupid.'

She blushed slightly as he spoke. 'You'll have a short one before you go, won't you?' she said to change the subject but I told her if I had any more I'd explode. At Irish funerals, I knew, people tended to imbibe even more alcohol than at Irish weddings.

'I have to be away,' I said, apprehensive about the fact that Fergie was warming up for some more mischief. 'Away' was my fashionable bedsit in Bachelor's Walk where I passed the time between preparing company reports and dreaming of something better than the air-conditioned nightmare of factory furnaces and bone-headed accountants grooming me for grandeur on society's top storey - if boredom didn't kill me first.

'Sing us a song before you go,' Fergie implored, 'You were always a great man for Big Tom, weren't you?' Before I could say anything he started singing himself, one of the insufferable ditties we used to do in the Aran Islands on those 'educational' holidays we were sent on from Muredach's way back when, which invariably turned into excuses to get plastered.

I started to yawn when he got to the 13th verse. He paused briefly as Eithne put her hand up, having heard a noise coming from upstairs. 'You bloody eejit,' she said, throwing her eyes to heaven, 'You know he cries at the drop of a hat.'

'I'll give you that,' he allowed. 'I thought it might act as a lullaby. Maybe I'm not Caruso after all.'

She beckoned me to go up with her and I was relaxed in her presence I went. As we walked up the stairs together I looked around at all the ornate furnishings. I thought of John Updike's statement: 'The first thrill of adultery is entering the house. Everything has been paid for by the other man.'

As we went into the bedroom I became seduced by her perfume. She went over to the child and felt its brow. For a moment I envisaged myself as her husband, her life as my life. I was a part of this room, this child, the whole package. Could it still happen? Did she want it to?

I listened to a mobile tinkling above the pram. The stars were like a sea in the sky. Downstairs I listened to the gentle snores of Fergie. 'He's probably asleep in a stump,' she laughed, 'cradling a naggin of whiskey by his side.' (Or, as was more likely, sleeping in a sea of it, having spilt it all over himself).

After the baby fell asleep she looked at me with the kind of tenderness we shared when we were planning to marry. Neither of us seemed to know why we didn't, or still couldn't. We parted for no better reason than geography, her job taking her in one direction and mine in another. But now, sitting on the bed beside her and wanting her again, it was as if the past was here again and marriage to Fergie had never happened.

I put my arm on her shoulder and she cried into my arms. She was speaking too, but I couldn't hear her words. All I knew was that this was inevitable. It was what the last few months had been leading to, it was what I wanted and what she wanted, it was the culmination of all the conversations I'd had with her any time she rang me to tell me he was killing himself, or sleeping with another woman, or making her sick with his language. Getting back with her now seemed to be as inevitable as the fact that he would soon self-destruct and she would be his free and beautiful widow.

She was speaking to me but I was too dreamy to hear her words. She was saying something to me like, 'He's nothing, it was always you, you know that, don't you?' and I was nodding my head in half-agreement as I wondered what might happen next.

I held her away from me for a second and then didn't.

We fell onto the bed together, a bed that smelt of after-shave and cheap wine. The drink from the funeral suddenly seemed to hit me. The room swam and when I jumped up to steady myself I seemed to sober up. In front of me on the mantelpiece was their wedding photograph.

'What are you looking at?' she said, trying to pull me back down with her.

It was frayed at the edges. Fergie was in a three-piece suit. He had a handlebar moustache and long hippie-style hair. Eithne was even more beautiful than I'd imagined her. She was looking at the camera with pleading eyes. Even then she seemed to know that a life with him could only hold the worst kind of surprises.

I don't remember how long I slept. When I woke up she was gone. It was morning. I was madly thirsty and still drunk. A cold dawn sneaked across Nephin.

Downstairs I smelt cooking. I was in the room on my own, still in my clothes, feeling vaguely ashamed.

I stumbled down the stairs and into the kitchen. She was dandling the baby on her knee, reciting some kind of nursery rhyme to it. 'The dead arose and appeared to many,' she said. And then, 'You won't believe this but he's gone to the office.'

I thought she was joking at first but when I thought about it I realised it wasn't the first time he'd rallied like this. He was like a rubber ball that kept beagling back to the grindstone no matter how many glasses of rotgut he poured into himself the night before. It was why he was rich. He worked as hard as he played. Sometimes it seemed as if he didn't know the difference

'What about me?' I asked.

'What about you?'

'Does he know I stayed the night?'

'Well he hardly thinks you called for breakfast, you idiot. Your car is parked out front- or had you forgotten?'

'Jesus,' I said.

'Don't worry, he doesn't mind. He'd trust you with me in a jacuzzi even if both of us were buck naked.'

Why was it, I wondered, that women were always more earthy in the morning and more subdued at night? With men it was the opposite. The dawn made us timid. Was this what people meant when they said men were from Mars and women from Venus?

The baby started to prattle. As she tended to it I got a glimpse of what her average day must have been like, the things women did that men took for granted, thriving on motherhood as if it was the one residue of normality still available to her with her speculator spouse.

'I better go,' I said, the day already drifting away from me even as she relaxed into it.

'Sit down there and shut your mouth,' she said, 'Did your mother never tell you breakfast was the most important meal of the day?'

I thought of what I was going back to in Bachelor's Walk, the grinding repetitiveness versus this oasis of peace that I always half-embraced and then rejected as if I was somehow afraid of the happiness it afforded me.

'Go on so,' I said, 'Spoil me with an old-fashioned fry-up.'

As the sausages sizzled in the pan she imitated Fergie singing his stage-Irish ditty, right down to falling onto the sofa in a stupor. She laughed so much she made the baby cry. I went over and sat beside her. She looked into my eyes and said, 'Why can't it always be like this?'

I looked out at Nephin. There was a thin layer of snow covering it. Above it the clouds gathered. The sky was grey with a kind of metallic emptiness.

All of a sudden an unexplainable sadness came over me, for Fergie and myself and all of us.

Could I say that I was any less a victim of circumstance than he was? Was I any less culpable? The fact that we were both the same age seemed to involve us in some kind of communion, to make us part of an irresponsible society where we could misbehave and then forgive one another's lapses over and over again. Because we'd gone to school together, because we knew Creeper, because we graduated together and got married around the same time, all these things meant we were meshed into some kind of blood brotherhood that made us immune to blame or contumely either from one another or anyone else. For better or for worse we were bonded like criminals.

Yes, I thought, I would go to his fortieth birthday party. I would sit beside Eithne and listen to his crude jokes. I would drink his stale whiskey and ache for her as he stood at the top table and called on me to sing a Big Tom number. Meanwhile he would eye the young talent, this 40 year old man with the 20 year old mind and the 80 year old liver, swaying on his feet as his gaggle of Gurteen groupies egged him on to more riotousness. My soulmate, my surrogate brother, larger than life but also broken by it as I was, emerging from whatever dark tunnel of the mind he inhabited to tussle with those who hovered on the edge of experiences like Creeper, the first man who denied both of us life before his own non-life ended.

'I'll see you at the weekend,' I said as I got up to go, my words lingering in the air. She put her fingers to her lips to tell me not to speak too loud because the baby was nodding off again.

I blew her a kiss at the doorstep and walked towards my car. I wasn't sure if it was the first morning of my new life or the last of my old one. I sat inside and gunned the engine, inching slowly forward as I thought about the road not taken and the one I might yet one day have the guts to take.

Mature Student

His father was a self-made man
and he lived in his shadow.
His mother spoiled him rotten.
I know nothing of his childhood.
His story began for me
in TCD
where he spent some time studying
in between parties.

He graduated by default at 33.
Marriage by elopement followed,
and then a brace of children
that arrived almost by rote
until work, that fearsome word,
was sandwiched between parties
and the friends he imagined
he'd left behind when he substituted books
for the clearer knowledge of intuition.

Insecurity warred with bravado
as his thirties slipped by,
the haze of cigar smoke and whiskey
replaced by the genial enquiries of judges,
guardians of the peace, and his conscience.
Through the thin veil of laughter
he negotiated a trajectory of industriousness,
knuckling down to support
his novena of children
in Arthur Street
as the debt-collecting buzzards gathered
to dent that fragile sensibility.

He blamed his father for his frailties.
His mother too,
though she refused to threaten.
Together this strange, unrelated pair
formed the pincer-jaws of his gaiety,
their cruelties and indulgences
the fodder that savaged his head
as he faced down
the gun-barrel of commitment
year after year
until exhaustion and disenchantment
devoured the boyishness he wore
like a second skin.

When his office was burned down
he worked from home.
It was the excuse he needed to retire,
His wife filling in for him so well
They said she should take silk.
She'd always been the power in the marriage
but it gave her no delight
to see him play the secondary role.

The last ten years of his life
he spent mostly in bed.
For some that might have been a cop-out
but for him it was a celebration,
giving him more time to pontificate
on a world gone mad at the core.

Ireland needed a benign dictator,
he said. Hitler would have done,
or Salazar, even Franco.

He sang 'God Save the Queen'
in front of IRA men in pubs
and had a knife put to his face one night
when merriment got the better of him.

There were times he laughed so hard
as he told one of his oft-repeated yarns,
the ribbons on his pyjamas came loose,
making them fall halfway down his legs.

I saw him setting the mattress on fire once
as he attempted to light his pipe
and then calling casually to my mother
to douse the flame
as he continued to read the paper.

It was usually full of scandal.
'Good news is no news,' he'd say,
tearing out a page
that might inspire him
for the anger he unleashed
in his diatribes to editor
of the Western
who said he was the last
real personality left in the town.

He hated the new church
with guitars on the altar
and nuns tumbling the wildcat
between the pews.
'Rome hath spoken'
was the way it was in his day;
now it was afraid to whisper.

The paedophilia scandals
hadn't reared their head
as he weakened with age
and the world still a simpler place
despite his own complexity
so maybe it was for the best
that a row with a coalman
on an uneventful Friday
in February 1977
caused that big heart
to finally give out.

Killala

The phalanx of cottages lay cosseted in the hollows of the plateau, spindly webs of smoke wafting upwards from the chimneys like fabricated genies. The old farmers of the neighbourhood lurched homewards in the gathering dusk, so many shadows worming their way up the pebble-dashed walls that surrounded them, their paltry frames silhouetted against the pallor of the evening. All around him were the stone walls that divided one man's property from another, the endless mosaics that served as firm reminders of where one man's property ended and another's began.

He walked to the cliffs as he did every evening now. There was a dull moon being rocked to sleep on the billows of the sea below, the waves nibbling greedily at the edges of time-blackened rocks, then sinking backwards into the depths of the sea with a gurgling sound.

It was four months now since they'd tumbled over his father after he fell from the cliff. They seemed to re-enact the event each time he watched the foam splashing violently under the watchful gaze of the moon, then dwindling into coy curtsies as the wind died down and everything took on the carapace of stability.

It seemed only yesterday since he'd sat hurdled in the cottage waiting for news, old women whispering aspirations and slipping their rosary-beads through their fingers until Thomas came barging through the door. 'He didn't make it,' he barked out hoarsely, 'Dessie McDonnell saw it happen. They haven't found the body. It was washed out to sea.'

There didn't seem to be much shock about it in the area. It was almost as if everyone sensed what would happen even as his father had slammed the door and set off on his own across the fields, as deaf to the howling of the wind as his wife calling 'You fool,' after him until he disappeared. And all for a cow that wouldn't have paid for the shirt on his back.

Maybe it was true what the neighbours said, that he'd gone willingly into the danger. They said nobody who wasn't anxious to die would have ventured out that wild night, especially towards the cliffs. Even after he'd fallen, even then he would have made some attempt to struggle or swim with his seafaring background. But Dessie McDonnell had seen him seeming to ignore the lifebelt sent out from a currach that was near him.

Was it true that his life had reached a standstill in recent times? People said he carried a sense of tragedy about with him. Or was it simply that he couldn't allow himself to be bested by a recalcitrant brute? But there was no point in questioning now: he'd died with his secret.

Philip was hysterical when he got the news but the train of events seemed almost farcical to him now, the frantic search ending in frustration and then, most absurdly of all, the missing cow returning peacefully to pasture the nest morning.

His father's death had changed everything for him. There was no life here for him now. Tomorrow he was going to Dublin on the bus and from there he was going to Boston where his uncle Finbar had set him up in a job. He didn't know much about America except what he saw in television shows. He had visions of skyscrapers, of people wandering around in multi-coloured clothes. Thomas said it was a sick country poisoned by wealth That was the general consensus in the neighbourhood but the farmers all queued up for free drinks from Finbar in McGonagles pub whenever he was home. Maybe they were jealous.

His mother made fun of Finbar, claiming he's lost his Irish accent about five minutes after he had set foot on American soil. She said she'd never had much time for him because he bought all his friends. But he was worth keeping in with for the rainy day. Now her opportunism had reaped a benefit. She contacted him after the tragedy and asked him if he'd have Philip over. 'You remember him, don't you?' she said over the phone, 'the skinny lad.' Thomas was the stronger son. Philip felt she favoured him for that. He was a thinker, a reader. But Thomas 'got things done.'

Philip wasn't going away out of any particular devotion to either Finbar or America but simply because he had to. He knew farm work wasn't for him. A few months ago he'd had dreams of a university degree but after his father died Thomas told him he was putting paid to such notions.

'University my arse,' he said, 'I heard of a Ph. D. fella the other day that's sellin' hubcaps to make ends meet.'

The application forms for college were binned. Instead a letter went to Finbar to see if he could help them out. He said there was a furniture firm near his house and that he knew the manager. It was worth a try. It wouldn't bring in much money but it might lead to better things in the future. 'It's better than shovellin' muck,' Thomas said, 'which is all you're fit for otherwise.'

He decided not to think about what it might lead to, not to think about anything.

The die was cast. There was no going back now. All he could do was hope for something better than the stasis of the past four months, months he'd mostly spent brooding. 'There's Hamlet,' Thomas would say if he saw him with his head in a book.

The night came down on him like a light being switched off. Clouds bundled themselves over the shoulder of the mountain as though mustering themselves for a storm.

He turned for home. Here and there along the road the harvesters threw straw at him playfully. He found himself becoming jealous of their camaraderie. Some of the older men stopped to enquire about his family; others just nodded curtly as if he were a stranger. He had the odour of death about him still, he thought: most families in the area had family members who were drowned. They didn't like to be reminded of the fact.

He reached the house. Thomas and his mother were sitting in the shadows inside. They were as silent as ever. It was a silence of complicity, an easy comfort with one another.She was knitting a jumper under the Sacred Heart lamp. Thomas sat with his wellingtons up on the stove. He was reading the paper and nursing a bottle of Guinness, his nightly indulgence. .

They could sit for hours like this and then just as casually fall into conversation. In an hour or so Thomas would go to the pub with his friends and repeat there the glib wisdom of the political editorials. The farm had been the cornerstone of his life but since his father's death he'd blossomed into a social entity. He was the man of the house now, the inheritor of the soil. He wore the robes of his new office well.

Philip stepped into the room with his head down. He felt apologetic when they looked at him; they made him feel he was guilty of some unstated crime. It had always been the way. It was too late to change now. The friction between them had become intensified since his father's death, the centre of power having shifted to Thomas since then. He had always fought with his father, not physically but with words, arguing with him over the smallest detail about the running of the farm. Now he had it his own way.

Philip, in contrast, had been the pet. If his mother had died first, Thomas would have been the one to suffer. It would have been the buildings in Kilburn for him if that happened instead of some seedy furniture firm in downtown Boston for his brother.

'Where have you been all evening?' his mother said as he sat down, her eyes bulging threateningly.

'I went for a walk.'

'Oh is that the way now? Well that's a fine thing all right. Have you any sense in your head at all? Do you think it's off to the fair in Ballina you're going tomorrow? Do you know how long I've been waiting for you to pack your things?'

'No.'

'All the blessed evening, that's how long. It'd be just like you to be rummaging round the kitchen at 5 a. m. tomorrow and the tail end of the bus disappearing off down the road without you.'

She ruffled his hair playfully.

'That'd be him all right,' Thomas put in, 'Paddy last.'

'I'm going upstairs now to pack the last of your luggage. The fairies won't do it, you know.'

When she left the room Thomas looked at him impishly.

'Well, Phil me lad,' he said, 'Did you write any more masterpieces today?'

It was the old barb, a reference to a poem he'd had in a local paper some months back. It was an endless source of merriment to Thomas and his cronies whenever they met at a mart.

'I tell you, boy,' he said, 'you'll soon forget poetry when you get your hands dirty in the U. S of A. Or at least you'd better. It wasn't through scribblin' I got these.'

He turned his palms outwards to display his calluses. Maybe they were his proudest assets.

'You haven't worked up many a sweat in your time but maybe you're about to start so you should get used to the idea. The days of being protected by the old lad are gone. Do you realise that?' He seemed to be psyching himself up to a pitch, the muscles quivering on his face,

'I realise it,' Philip said. He didn't want to give him any ammunition for his anger by talking back.

'Well that's good. That's damn fuckin' good. Because otherwise you'll be on the next plane home. You'll be back to diggin' spuds. The insulatin' tape is gone now. It's sink or swim for you.'

He went silent for a moment, anticipating a reaction. When he didn't get one he stared at Philip intensely, trying to achieve with an expression what he hadn't with his words.

The poem he'd published was on a cabinet. Thomas went over and took it up in his hands, reading it to himself and nodding in mock-appreciation. Then he tore it in half.

That didn't get a reaction either so he went one further. He opened the stove and threw the paper in.

'Nothin' but ashes now. Do you understand? Because that's all it's worth. There are no nancyboys in Amerikay, me lad, none at all. They won't thank you for yappin' on about flowers and birds and walks in that country. They go for hard graft over there. It's graft that gets a man a farm like this.'

His pulse quickened with anger.

'You got it because my father died,' he said, 'No other reason.'

Thomas' face changed from surprise to amusement. He'd never been stood up to before.

'Oh is that right?' he said. 'So you have a voice after all. It must be the visa that gave it to you.'

He squared up to him. Then he hit him.

'Don't be lippy with me, you little cunt or I'll sort you out. By fuckin' Jaysus I will.'

His mother came down the stairs.

'What's going on?' she said, 'I heard a noise.'

'I had to give him a thump,' Thomas said, taking a swig from his Guinness, 'he was giving me lip.'

'Go easy on him, Tom,' she said, 'Tonight is his Irish wake, after all. We wouldn't want him to go across the pond with bitter memories of us now, would we?'

She went over to Philip and examined him.

106

'Are you all right, love? Did he hurt you?'

'No.'

Thomas took another drink. The anger went out of him now that the blow had been delivered.

'Say you're sorry,' his mother chided.

He stretched his big frame and yawned.

'What? Oh yeah, sorry,' he said vacantly.

'There now,' she beamed, 'We're not so bad after all, are we, Phil? He says he's sorry for giving you a puck.'

'I may be sorry,' he said, 'but I don't believe in sparin' the rod, unlike the old lad.'

'What kind of a family have I reared at all?' she said, 'The pair of you are like chalk and cheese. But you should go to bed, Phil, before he gets worse. You have a big day ahead of you tomorrow.'

'I feel like staying up,' he said.

It was unusual for him to make even this slight protest against her. She looked surprised.

'That wouldn't be a good idea. You might sleep it out.'

'I'll take that chance.'

'Well let it be on your own head then. But I'm not having you down here wasting the night on me. Go upstairs now and see if you have all your stuff. I don't want Finbar on the blower to me tomorrow night asking me to send you on your trousers.'

He went upstairs. His possessions were scattered on the bed, most of the things of any value he owed thrown together in a heap. She hadn't bothered to tidy them. He checked his passport and plane ticket, feeling gone from the place in every way but with his body.

He listened to his mother pottering around the kitchen. He wondered if she'd come up to him for a chat before he went to bed. He hoped she wouldn't. It might force him into an intimacy he didn't want, a showiness that would embarrass both of them with its artificiality.

She'd changed towards him when his father died. She became even more aggressive than before. It was as if the Thomas side of her took over, as if she'd buried whatever small vestiges of gentleness she had with her husband. Sometimes he didn't think she'd ever loved him. She grieved very little after he died, what little emotion she showed usually being when there were lots of people present, the more to milk it.

He wondered if she'd marry again. She'd preserved her beauty and there were many men in the village who would have been proud to have her as their wife. But she didn't seem interested. Maybe she was too independent for any man. Even if she didn't remarry, he felt, she wouldn't be left alone. He knew Thomas would stay with her until she died even if it was more out of need than love.

He'd never been able to square her attachment to Thomas with her indifference to his father. Maybe one even caused the other, like two sides of the one coin. In some ways she showed more anger than grief at the funeral, anger at the fact that fate should have the audacity to upset the steady rhythm of her life. In the weeks afterwards, though, when she immersed herself in her routines again, she snapped out of it. It was almost as if it hadn't happened. And yet it would have been unfair to call her hypocritical. She was a creature of the moment. She couldn't see beyond that or didn't want to. Maybe she'd married too young, before she'd properly lived life. There was still time for her to do that now if she wanted.

But her bitterness would kill whatever adventurous spirit remained.

Philip lay down on the bed. As he did so he found his head flooded with memories of his father, the casual grace he exuded, his elemental sense of mystery. He had a nobility about him, he thought, which was unusual in someone who never dressed in anything but overalls. He had an authority that resounded even when he was knee-deep in grime. Each room he went into he seemed to command even without speaking, but people resented this. Maybe that was why there was so little sadness in the village when he died, why people started to invent the theory of the suicide to protect themselves from his memory.

He thought about Thomas, what way his life might go in the years ahead now that he'd taken on his mantle, or at least appeared to. He wondered if he'd continue to play the role of the bully in the way he'd done since the drowning or whether with time he'd revert back to the person he'd been before it, someone who seemed more fulfilled on the farm than in the bar, a man who fretted over crop rotation and the vagaries of the North Atlantic Drift, the casual interludes of fate on a discardable existence.

He could imagine him going out less and less as the years went on, probably becoming more frustrated as his mother grew older. When she died the loneliness might drive him to marriage, to a drunken proposal some night in McGonagles with the Dutch courage of badly brewed Guinness, thereafter living out his life not with a mother but someone who doubled for one, and raising a moderately sized family who'd learn early not to give cheek to their parents and to appreciate the simple things in life.

He looked out at the night light and felt himself getting sleepy. There were so many things to think about. Would he like America? Could he come back if it didn't work out? Was there a third option?

There was no point working himself up with speculation. For now he was getting out of a prison and he welcomed that. Anything across the water had to be a bonus.

His mother didn't come up to him. Neither did Thomas, though they slept in the same room. He listened to them talking until well after midnight and then went to bed. He fell asleep almost instantly.

He woke at dawn. It was perhaps the one thing of the farmer about him. He got out of bed and looked around him. Thomas was snoring. The day looked clear. When he looked at the clock he saw it said 6.15. The alarm wasn't due to go off for an hour yet but he decided to get up anyway.

He wanted to savour the remainder of his time here. He walked in and out of rooms, looked out at a landscape he might or might not miss. Cows chewed the cud. It started to rain. He listened to the silence of the morning. Time always stood still at this time.

He came back to his room and zipped up his travelling case. In the bed beside him Thomas was still snoring, his huge frame rising and falling like the sea. When he went into his mother's room he saw she was asleep too. The alarm hadn't gone off despite all her talk. He decided to leave her that way.

This time tomorrow he'd be in Boston, either suffering from jet lag or culture shock. He wondered how Finbar would receive him, if he'd have the same personality as his mother or if they might be able to build a relationship from scratch.

Before he left the house he looked out at the rugged cliff-face once again. The sea was tame today, as though absolving itself of complicity in his father's drowning, covering over the tracks of his grave. On the beach beside it the currachs lay inverted like so many beetles. A tepid sun glared down on them.

He'd miss the farm, if not its inhabitants. Would Boston be a release or just a different form of imprisonment? He didn't know. Either way it would be a change, a possibility for him to become a man instead of the pretence at manhood his brother had branded him with.

A pang of guilt gnawed at him over his refusal to say goodbye to either of them. Maybe they wouldn't have wanted him to. I owe them nothing, he told himself. They had one another for solace. All he had was a smudged address in an alien suburb in a country he knew precious little about. It would be lonely where he was going. And that much lonelier for being the only place he *could* go.

He took his case and walked out onto the road. The fields looked burned. A raw wind was blowing the stalks. In the distance he heard a tractor. Tomorrow that sound would probably be replaced by the honk of a yellow cab.

He walked to the crossroads where the bus was due to stop. His stomach felt hollow as he looked down at the farm. He wondered if Thomas had woken yet. The punch was his last violence against him. Such a thought seemed to drive its pain away.

The bus approached him, its cheery cream jarring with the green spread beyond, a symptom maybe of where he was headed. He hailed it and it stopped. As he entered it he imagined his mother cursing him for his early departure.

He felt no anger towards her now, only an overwhelming pity. He felt no anger towards Thomas either. Now that he was gone they'd have nobody to take their own anger out on. He wondered if it would affect their relationship with one another.

He sat into his seat and the bus started to move. The land receded behind him. The farmhouse looked minute between the mountains as he looked back at it a last time, the wisps of smoke that rose from the chimney puncturing the sky like auguries of another death.

Vespers

It was strange, he thought, how quickly things could change, how suddenly you could turn from a hero into an embarrassment. When he first attended Muredach's – it was an unofficial recruitment college for seminaries – it was with high ideals. The day the missionary priest called and gave a lecture about the important work he could do in America if he went there after being ordained, it sounded even better. He always had a messianic side to him and now, after all the years of study and over three decades serving in a parish in Lahardaun, it was finished.

There would be no more visitations, no more homilies, no more responsible duties – just menial tasks performed in Philadelphia to make him feel he belonged. Visits with old ladies on wet Sundays, maybe, or saying Mass on side altars when half the congregation was asleep. In the evenings, he was informed, there would be cards.

It was strange too how you could forget rituals that had once been your life before a woman turned it upside down. The fact that he didn't brood on it wasn't surprising; it was his formula for survival. At first anyway. Afterwards he found it almost automatic to deny her, to invent himself anew.

Was he really reinvented though? Or was this something he told himself to make the departure bearable?

The morning arrived. He watched the sun filtering through the windows and thought of where he was going. He'd already said his goodbyes to everyone in Lahardaun. Some people had wished him well but more had blanked him.

Would there be friendship in Philadelphia or would he be a pariah there too? Maybe it didn't matter.

'I know what you did,' a twelve year old boy had said to him two days before, tugging at his cassock as he finished saying Mass. '*What you did.*' As if it blotted out everything else from the previous three decades.

He went down to the kitchen.

'Top of the mornin' to ye!' said Des. He was the priest he worked and lived with. What secret had he that he was always in good form?

'Are you going to see the bishop later?' he asked.

'Don't remind me. Just say a prayer he doesn't chop my head off.'

'That I will,' he laughed, 'Actually I happen to know he thinks very highly of you.'

'He has a strange way of showing it.'

They ate breakfast. It became a morning like any other. Des was going off to a hurling match, to the familiar pock of ash on ash, to swear words and thick ankles and locker room banter afterwards. He had been that soldier once himself. Before - what was the expression they used? – 'the temptations of the flesh' - assailed him. Now he was a spoiled priest.

'You could never give all of yourself to a woman,' she accused the last night he saw her, which was probably true. She looked poignant in the moonlight, fidgeting with a dress strap. He could have fallen for her again in a second if he let himself.

'Are you still going?' she asked him, as if there was some other alternative.

'What else can you suggest?'

'Nobody has to do anything if they don't want to. Is the bishop chasing after you with his crozier?'

He didn't want to argue with her. What could it achieve? Either he was leaving the church or he wasn't. He had nothing to gain by trying to score points. She wouldn't change her view and neither would he. The die was cast.

He broke the rules. That was all that needed to be said. 'Thou Shalt Not Commit Adultery.' There was a time he might have had the courage to give it all up for her but he knew now the other calling was stronger. It had, after all, been his first one.

The parishioners couldn't forgive him; that was what made it hurt the most.

'Don't be too much of a father figure to them,' the bishop had warned him when he first arrived in the parish, 'It will work against you in the end.'

'I don't see how that could happen,' he replied, 'Are you telling me to be distant?'

'All I'm saying is to beware of aligning yourself too much with them. If you lie down with the dogs you get up with the fleas.'

It was a poor parish. He'd viewed them like that because they came from the wrong side of the tracks.

'They haven't had the opportunities in life that we've had,' he said, 'You'd be better off trying to bring them up to our level rather than descending to theirs.'

'I see them as superior to me for having gone without,' he said, 'not inferior.'

When he said that the bishop grunted. It was his first gesture of rebellion against him. The beginning of the end maybe.

'Do you really think you can wander freely between all your little worlds like a child in a fairytale?' he said then. 'I've lived in this parish all my life. I've seen the squalor and the depravity. I feel no guilt over not sharing it. I know I'm respected for what I am, that I'd lose their respect if I became one of them. So don't lecture me about deprivation. You've not "gone without," as you put it, either, my good man. You sit on a luxurious sofa every night. You watch television with a fire burning behind you.'

He was right, of course. His commitment to them was half-baked. He could never totally inhabit their lives.

He christened them, he taught them in school, he married them and then he buried them. They came crying to him in the confessional and he dispensed advice. He put the holy wafers on their mouths to exorcise them. When they were sick he said prayers over them to make the badness go away. Sometimes it did and sometimes it didn't. That was where faith came in. How much of this had he left? Not much in himself anyway.

Maybe hope was more what he had. Or charity. To who, though? Himself? Or was there still something in him that could actually help people live better lives? He wondered if it was true after all that his destiny was to be a listener, a witness. You couldn't change society. All you could do was try to live in it. But he couldn't do that anymore. Catherine had made it impossible.

The fact that he could fall for a woman after so many years being away from women seemed absurd. Or was that the very reason he did? He'd known her even before he entered. He was attracted to her; they'd even dated a few times. But then she got married. He thought he'd put her out of his mind afterwards. It was only when her marriage broke up that she came back into his life.

Her child was reared, her husband gone. She'd come to him for counselling and one thing led to another. After they became intimate he realised that nothing ever really went away, no matter how many years passed. She'd thought she loved her husband, at least until he was unfaithful. That ended everything. Their split was acrimonious.

He had no real advice to give her; he just guided her through her heartache. It was during that guidance that she confessed her feelings for him.

He told her not to be ridiculous at first. Then he realised he was starting to reciprocate them.

'I never stopped caring for you,' she said to him, 'even when I was married.'

'You only think that,' he said. He tried to talk her out of it, tried to talk himself out of it. Was she using him? Was the counselling merely a cover to lure him into her web? That was what the bishop thought, what Des thought. He believed them for a while but then he turned against them, cottoning on to the fact that they were misogynists.

'I'm leaving the priesthood,' he told Des one night after a sodality, 'I'm in love with Catherine.'

'You only think you are,' Des replied, 'We all go through these phases.'

'It's not a phase,' he said, 'not after thirty years.'

The bishop saw it as a crisis of faith, a kind of dark night of the soul. He wanted him to apply for counselling himself. He said it would get her out of his system. The way he said that, she might have been an illness, a disease. Maybe he was right. Maybe love *was* a disease.

A disease he was going to embrace.

But when it came to it he couldn't take the plunge. His habits were too ingrained. He thought of things like shopping, going on walks together, the 'ordinary' things all other men did. He spent so many years not doing them they wouldn't be ordinary to him. They would be anomalous. He would be clumsy at them, a fish out of water.

Even if he hadn't been a priest, he told himself, he would probably have been a bachelor. The vocation, or so-called vocation, wasn't really about religion. It was a lifestyle choice. It just *suited* him. But how could he tell her that? How could he face the fact that he'd wasted almost a year of her life with his false promises, his false bravado? He was taking the coward's way out. He would receive a belt of the crozier and crawl to Philadelphia with his tail between his legs until the powers-that-be saw fit to return him to his fold. It was a yellow card rather than a red one as Des put it. A transatlantic sin bin.

He thought back to his last night with her. It was rich with the promise of her body. He'd had some thoughts about leaving even before then but had banished them, like some medieval monk being tempted by a Jezebel.

'You can still change your mind,' she said, 'Don't let them tell you something is wrong if you don't believe it yourself.'

He'd been like a boy caught in a guilty act, stealing coins from his mother's handbag.

'Do you love me'?' she had asked him. It was a simple question and he answered it equally simply.

'How could I not?'

'But not enough to stay with me.'

'I feel guilty.'

'About me or yourself?'

'About not being able to be with you all the time. About having other things going on.'

'You told me once that I was the only significant thing that had ever happened in your life.'

'Yes, and I meant it.'

'Then for God's sake don't go.'

'You don't understand. It's out of my hands now.'

She gazed out over his shoulder. The sun threw itself down over the horizon.

'So I'm to be the *femme fatale* then. The fallen woman. I'll serve as a warning to your new flock some night after a sodality in Philadelphia.'

'Stop it. I told you how I feel about you.'

How could he trade her for the death in life that was his new parish, this glorified sacking dressed up as promotion? Paedophile priests had even been treated better.

He'd fallen in love with a woman, the ultimate sin. Sex with a child might have been easier to hide. 'The church hates women,' she said to him once, 'all the way from Eve onwards. By giving in to them you're becoming a part of that.'

Maybe she was right but how could he change his plans now? Religion was in his blood. He couldn't trust himself to stay with her longer than with it. If Philadelphia didn't work out maybe he could go back to her. If she'd have him. But it couldn't work the other way around.

'*I know what you did.*'

The words echoed in his ears again, the sediment of backyard chatter by his ex-pupils behind the bicycle shed. The three decades of his ministering to them blotted out by his momentary aberration. 'The world will forgive you eventually,' Des had said to him, 'but will you forgive yourself?' That was the 64-marker.

He'd always wanted to be a priest; there seemed to be no alternative to it. An altar boy in Muredach's as a youth, it was a natural progression for him. His mother's saintliness had helped too. She didn't push religion on him, it was just a part of her, like an inner light. She didn't chew the altar rails, as the expression went, but she still lived it - all day every day. *Laborare est orare.* After that came the dream of being on the missions, of carrying an ideal to a foreign shore. The years in Clonliffe had fulfilled that dream. He had no distractions then, fulfilled totally within walls where he debated heatedly on issues of theology, epistemology, social ills.

When he got close to ordination he moved out more into the world. He got his feet wet in parishes, discussed grittier issues with those in deprived regions where religion came only in the form of pragmatic help. *Peregrinatios* more than *triduums*. First grub, as Brecht had put it, then ethics.

Occasionally he'd been tempted by women even then, his head wrecked with the tension of it all. He used to talk about it to his colleagues in the seminary. Many of them had temp-

118

tations too. One or two of them were even gay. That term wasn't in existence then. They were just queers.

'Don't worry about it,' he was always informed, 'It's just God testing you. You wouldn't be normal if you didn't think like that. It will make your vocation stronger if you conquer it.'

Sometimes it went away and sometimes it didn't. He sweated at midnight with his needs, praying for them to go away. If he had one night with a woman, he thought, that might take away such needs. Or would it make them worse? He didn't know. Maybe he was better off not knowing. When you had a taste of something you might want more. How many priests were virgins? If they were, how could they understand anything about sexual sins?

He'd heard stories about women in marriage who were told by their doctors that if they conceived again they could die. Their husbands came home to them demanding their sex and their supper. Such women succumbed to their advances in an age before contraception became fashionable, before Vatican Two caused so many women to turn their backs on an ideology they once held dear.

The years went on. He sublimated his desire in work but it didn't go away, lying inside him like a tumour.

Then he was ordained. It was meant to be his happiest day but it turned out to be his most miserable one.

Every doubt he'd had since a child became magnified a hundredfold as he took his final vows. He felt like a groom walking down the aisle realising he'd just made a terrible mistake. He told himself it was all in his imagination, in the drama of the occasion. It would go away like all his other fears went away – the fear of not being confident enough to give a sermon, not confident enough to socialise with his parishioners, not confident enough to tell them what was good for them when he hardly knew what was good for himself.

His parents cried when they saw him, not because of what he was going through but because he looked so perfect in his soutane. They compared him to actors like John Gavin and Tom Tryon.

Tryon had been in a film called *The Cardinal*. Maybe he'd even be a cardinal himself one day. Was such pride lodged inside him? Was this what was behind his so-called vocation? *Hubris*.

'You'll break a lot of women's hearts with that dog collar around your neck,' one of the guests at the reception said to him. It was the last thing he wanted to hear. Good looks made being a priest all the worse. It might mean women would come on to him. Ugliness would be a kind of protection against that. Did men go into seminaries because they were ugly? Or women into nunneries because they were plain? How much of our life choices were based on the way we looked? Was faith even a part of this?

In subsequent years he blotted out his confusions through work. He joined the Charismatic Renewal Movement, the thing to do in the seventies. It was trendy. He visited the poor on his bicycle rounds and used big words to them, words like 'holistic' and 'ecumenical.' They looked up to him like an icon then. He felt as much a part of his ministry as he ever dreamed. All the fears of yore fell away. People opened up to him; they told him he was a breath of fresh air to the parish, a dose of young blood. That was all he needed, an endorsement.

But then, just as he started to feel all his old worries were gone, Catherine came into his life. A real woman this time, not just a Biblical symbol or a midnight fantasy. He fought his desire for her but that seemed to make it greater, to make it ultimately irresistible. He tried to convince himself it was just physical, that he wasn't falling in love with her. That would have been easier to handle. But he continued to see her behind the backs of the parishioners. In time she became so much a part of him that she blotted out everything else he'd ever done there.

Then one night he found himself telling her he wanted to marry her. She didn't know what to think because he'd been giving her mixed signals up until that point. She didn't try to encourage him either way but that made it worse too, her understanding of his confusion. If she'd been selfish it might have been easier to walk away from her.

He wanted her and didn't want her. She knew that. She hated his doubt. 'I'd have to share you with God,' she said, 'It would be a hard one to win.'

He would have preferred to make his mind up one way or the other before it became public. When it did, the situation was taken out of their hands. It wasn't an an emotional issue any more now; it was one of politics, image, his possible defrocking. What a terrible word. It made priests seem like women. Was she not the one who wore the frock?

His cowardice drove him away from her in the end but she was too kind to put it like that. 'Do what you have to do,' she said, the words sounding to him like nails on his coffin.

And now what? Capitulation? Compromise? The denial of everything that made him live?

After Des went off to his game he walked to the bishop's house. His heart was pounding. He didn't respect him and yet he feared him. He'd spent his whole life locked in this pincer-jaw of confusion. It was why he was destined to be forever unfulfilled.

He thought of turning back more than once, turning away from the hallowed ground and making his way to her tiny apartment. They could talk, thrash it out again. But he knew if he did that they would come up with the same answers. Or non-answers. So he forged on.

When he got there he took a deep breath. He stood on the threshold. He was trying to build himself for what he was going to say. All the arrangements had been made. He'd got his passports and his shots. All that remained was to seal the deal.

He knocked on the door, its stained glass making him feel he was at a church. The housekeeper came out after a few moments.

'Oh,' she said as if she wasn't expecting him. She glared at him, which made him suspect she knew everything. Then he heard a voice coming from the main room.

'Let him in, Peggy,' it said.

He went inside. Peggy took his coat. The bishop came out and shook his hand.

'Let's go into my room,' he said, 'Nice night, isn't it?'

'A bit cold maybe.'

He followed him down the corridor toward his room, their shoes squeaking on the shining parquet floor.

When they got inside, the air conditioning almost knocked him out. He looked around him at the oak-panelled library, the religious artefacts. It smelled like incense.

He wrung his hands.

'This shouldn't take long,' he said nervously, 'I have a letter of introduction for you here. You can read it on the plane. There's nothing new on it.'

'Thank you,' he said, putting it into his pocket.

'Would you like a drink?' he asked.

'No thank you. I'd prefer to keep a clear head for the flight.'

'Good thinking. Well let's get straight down to business. I want you to know I'm sorry this business got to where it is but there's no point going into that now. Would you like to sit down?'

'It's all right. I'm fine standing.'

'Well I'll sit if you don't mind. Arthritis in the knees, you know.'

'It's a terrible curse. I have a bit of it myself.'

He sat down.

'God take pity on us.'

He had a glass of port beside him. He took a drink of it. As he did so, he sucked in his breath.

'I'll be brief and to the point,' he said. 'I've spoken to the priests in Philadelphia and they're delighted you're going to be with them. They know a little about you and they feel you'll fit in wonderfully. I feel that too. Needless to say, it will take you a little while to find your feet but when you do it will be more or less the same as Lahardaun.'

'How long will I be there?'

'That depends. It could be anything from a year to five. As you know, it's all about the reaction here. It may blow over. Sometimes people have short memories. Absence might make the heart grow fonder. Let's hope and pray they forget about this woman. We'll bring you back when they do. The people in Lahardaun like you here, they respect you. The situation is just too hot to handle at the moment.'

'So there's no way I can stay.'

He knew it was a pointless question but he had to ask it anyway.

'Sadly, no. You've given me no alternative but to move you. And I'm sure you want to be away from the woman too, for obvious reasons. Out of sight, out of mind.'

'Of course,' he had said, not knowing whether he agreed or not.

Then came the dagger thrust.

'You can't ever see her again, though. You know that, don't you?' He'd never once said her name. That would have made her too human, too real.

He nodded like a child.

'If you did, we'd all be rightly sunk. It would bring it all back to you. Or she might talk.'

There was a knock on the door.

'Is that you, Peggy?' he called out.

She came in with a tray. It had a cup of tea on it.

'Isn't she very good?' he said. 'You'll have to take a seat now. Peggy doesn't take no for an answer, do you, Peggy?'

She smiled shyly as he sat down. She brought a table over to him and put the tea on it. It looked more like water than tea.

'Thank you,' he said.

'You're welcome.'

She gave a little bow to the bishop before going out.

As he sat sipping it he was reminded of the first day he'd been in the room. It was shortly after he'd decided to be a priest. He was high on the promise of his new life then. They'd been drinking the same weak tea in the same cup in the same dead silence.

'What are you thinking about, Father,' he asked him. He took another sip of his port.

'Not very much, I'm afraid.'

'Don't worry about anything. I can understand how you would be apprehensive after so long being here but it does us good to have change in our lives, even change we have no control over.'

'I suppose you're right.'

'And I know you're an adaptable sort of man. I expect you'll shine over there once you find your bearings. '

'I hope so.'

He stood up.

'Very well then. I think that's everything. I know your heart is in the right place, and of course how difficult this has all been for you. But believe me, you'll be a better priest for it in time.'

He nodded vaguely.

'You have everything you need, I take it?' he said then.

'Everything.'

'If there's anything else, you know where to reach me.'

'I appreciate everything you've done.'

124

'It was nothing. There's nobody else I'd prefer to have done it for.'

They shook hands.

'And now may I take this opportunity of thanking you for all the work you've done in the parish over the years. You've put us on the map, you know, with your ideas. And the way you've bonded so much with the young.' The way he said it, they might have been a foreign species.

'Thank you.'

He wanted to say something negative to him, to make a cutting remark to take the clean look off everything. It had always been a part of him, this need to puncture something that had been done and dusted, that was wrapped too neatly in pink ribbons. He was being packaged like meat from a processing plant, having had the address label adjusted for a new clientele.

'I'm sure you'll enjoy it in Philly,' he said finally, 'at least once you settle in. It's quite a picturesque little parish, you know, though I imagine a little too conservative for you.'

'I doubt that will be a problem for me. We all get more conservative as the years gain on us. I'm sure I have too.'

It was as if he was toying with him now.

'You? Oh come, now.' He gave a little laugh. 'That'll be the day. Everyone knows you're something of a radical in your thinking.'

'We all compromise sooner or later, though, don't we?'

Either he failed to see the irony or he failed to acknowledge it.

'Well anyway I wish you well in your new life. Good luck to you. And may God bless you.'

'And you too, Your Grace.'

'I hope you won't forget us now. When this situation blows over I want to get you back here. ASAP. Keep your head down and it will be as if it never happened. We'll keep the pulpit warm for you. If things work out, maybe we might even become friends one day - at least if you could abide a stodgy old fusspot like me.'

'Stranger things have happened,' he said.

Maybe the old man wasn't so bad after all, he thought. Maybe he was just a victim of his time.

They shook hands again. Suddenly there was nothing more to be said. They both stood awkwardly in the silence, the ticking clock the only noise in the room.

'So that's it then,' he said again, slapping his hands together. 'Peggy will let you out.'

He walked to the door. As he did so, it opened from the other side as if she'd been listening. She gave him a watery smile.

'Goodbye, your Grace,' he said.

'Goodbye, Father, and mind yourself.'

Peggy led him down the corridor. When they got to the door she handed him his coat. He thanked her as he put it on. He looked back towards the bishop's room but the door was already closed.

'*Bon voyage*,' Peggy said.

'Thank you.'

She gave him a half-wave as she closed the door behind him. He walked down the avenue and out onto the road.

On the way back to the house he wondered what lay in store for him. His plane was taking off at nine o'clock. It was seven now. He had to be there an hour before the departure to check in. That wouldn't be a problem. He had all his things packed and a taxi ordered.

He tried not to think about how things were going to go. People always told him he was adaptable, as the bishop said. He'd make new friends in Philadelphia, impose himself on the parish. The other priests there would no doubt have been informed of his history but it wouldn't be talked about. It would be brushed under the carpet the way the authorities brushed everything under the carpet once the arrangements were made.

'If the girl doesn't become pregnant we can bury this,' the bishop had said when it first came to light. His words sounded brutal. He could discuss the nuances of scripture in one breath and then, almost seamlessly, divert himself into the expediency of such earthly matters.

Des was reading his breviary when he got back to the house. He envied him his simplicity. He could never be bothered by the complexities of theology, by the doubts that plagued most other priests at some time in their lives. His life ran on well-oiled wheels, the daily Mass followed by a few local house calls and then maybe a walk in the park. In his diary he mapped out the weddings and funerals that provided some slight diversion from these daily routines. Des would never have to worry about whether a woman he knew might be pregnant, or how to ingratiate himself with a group of strangers in a parish 3000 miles away who may or may not have known he'd blotted his copybook back in the old sod.

'Did you enjoy the match?' he asked him.

'It was so-so. More arguing than playing, I'm afraid.'

'At least you had a bit of fun anyway.'

'How did it go with head-the-ball?' he asked, the nickname a kind of camouflage for the reverence in which he held him.

'It wasn't as bad as I expected.'

'Good, good. So he wished you well then?'

'Indeed he did.'

'And you kissed his ring?'

He smiled.

'Not quite.'

'He's not too bad, you know. Like the rest of us he's struggling.'

'I know. He doesn't bother me as much as he used to. In any case it's done now.'

'The church is going through a bad time at the minute and he has to take the brunt of a lot of that. It's not like the old days where people took everything you said as gospel.'

'Even the gospel,' he said.

'Indeed! You never lost your sense of humour. It will be a good asset to you in America.'

'I hope so.'

'Will you be seeing her before you go?'

In all the months he'd never mentioned her name either, just like the bishop. It was as if she was an abstract concept of evil rather than a person. She was the poisoned apple in the Garden of Eden, the dancing Salomé, the destroyer of Samson's strength.

'I promised him I wouldn't. I might phone her from the airport to say goodbye. That will be all.'

As he'd walked away from the bishop's house he thought he might disobey him one last time and see her but he talked himself out of it. He knew it wouldn't have been a good idea to do so even if he was allowed to. She would be bitter. An argument might develop. She might even try to change his mind again. She might even succeed. He had his mind set on a course of action now and he couldn't let her interfere with that. It wouldn't have been fair to her. Or to himself.

The taxi-man knocked on the door. He went over to where his case was.

'Well,' he said, 'This is it. I won't be dramatic but I hope you'll keep in touch.'

'Of course I will. I'll be anxious to hear how things go.'

'You'll be the first person I'll write to.'

'I'll be watching for the postman.'

They hugged. He picked up his case and moved to the door.

'Can I help you with that?' Des asked him.

'I think I can manage it.'

'I hope you'll be happy. You deserve it.'

'Thanks, Des. You're a good friend.'

'I'll miss you. And don't forget that letter.'

'I won't. As long as you keep me up to date about how Mayo are doing in the football.'

'I'll do that too. I'll even tell you if the curse is lifted.'

It was a joke between them, a curse that was supposed to go back to 1951, the last year Mayo had won the All-Ireland, put on the team by a priest who thought they didn't show proper respect for a funeral on their way home from victory in Croke Park.

He walked down the driveway towards the taxi. The taxi driver took his case from him and put it into the boot. He sat into the car and waved goodbye to Des.

Night was coming down but the sun was still strong. They drove down the street past the church, its steeple spearing the heavens like a knife.

Keeper of the Flame

You could set your watch by him
as he cycled down by the Moy
on his crock of a bike
and over the bridge to the cathedral.
Paddy the sacristan,
holier than the Pope
in our minds,
never took a drink
or dated a girl
or smoked a cigarette,
nursing his mother till she was 81
and then crying buckets
on the side altar
when she finally died.

Afterwards he had no need for company.
You'd see him in country lanes sometimes
looking lost,
a prayer book clenched in his fist,
dog-eared at the Feast Day pages,
limping with his arthritis
from the ivy-clad house
that saw a family of thirteen
grow up in it,
all of them dead in their fifties
and only Paddy left
the Last of the Mohicans
a lover of cowboy films,
giving out Communion
and talking about Gene Autry
at the same time,
the penny catechism faith keeping him going.

When I heard he died
I cried,
though I never really knew
what made him tick.
I remembered
his wrinkled face excited
at the altar as he waited
for his chance to light the candles
like an overgrown child.
Later at the shops
he would be edgy,
slow to talk
if you asked him
anything about himself.
He couldn't take a compliment
and reddened if you gave him one,
allergic to praise.

But Paddy we're missing you,
at least the few of us who know you're gone.
The church looks empty without you
and your shy smile
and your fifth-hand suit
with the bicycle clips
sticking out of your pockets
as you doused the last of the candles
and pulled a trenchcoat up
over your shoulders
to get ready
for the long spin
back to Attymas
in the rain.

From Ballina to Dublin

We used to live two doors away from the Town Hall so most nights I went to sleep listening to music – The Everly Brothers, Elvis, Petula Clark, Acker Bilk and Buddy Holly singing 'Everyday' in that hiccupy voice he had. Sometimes they had live bands that played old time waltzes. Our local singer was a man called Jack Ruane. He had a band that went around the country playing gigs. He used to learn off the latest hits and sing them to the younger jivers. I could almost feel the reverberations of the floorboards when couples danced on them.

As the nights wound to a close I started to hear other sounds – drunks fighting on the street-corners, taxis picking up people to bring them down to Belleek and Bohernasup, over-enthusiastic men trying to make dates with the girls they danced with. Sometimes I looked out the window of my bedroom and saw couples kissing at Fahy's corner, or lone figures slinking away in the dark if the night hadn't worked out the way they wanted.

The O'Reillys lived between us and the Town Hall but my father said they were rough and we weren't to play with them. Paudy O'Reilly used to eat worms. He always laughed when he picked one up. He'd say, 'Look what I've gott' with a big grin on his face. He had protruding teeth so we called him Goofy. We didn't say this to his face because we knew we'd get beaten up by him if he heard us.

The Connollys lived across the street. They'd come from England originally. Sorcha was the beauty of the family. She'd made a record once called 'Doonaree.' Whenever she sang it everyone went quiet. It had a haunting quality about it and so had she. I was always too shy to talk to her but I'd see her at the door of her house going in and out after school or bringing in messages to her mother. Her father owned a garage and sometimes I used to see her at the pumps taking money from the drivers for petrol. She looked like the film star Jeanette McDonald. She was a pure spirit that reminded me of an angel on earth. Any man that was lucky enough to marry her, I thought, could never want anything else in his life.

I went to the pictures a lot of nights. The Estoria was just up the road from us. My father knew the manager and he got us free passes for it. Sometimes I went to see the same film over and over just to use them up. I remember seeing *The Dirty Dozen* four times one week, going in at different times every night just for the fun of it.

We knew the projectionist as well. His name was Frank Foody. He was obsessed with football. Sometimes he cut the films short if he had to get home early to watch a match on the television. I always hoped he didn't want to get home early if there was a cowboy film on. Once or twice he left the window of the projection room open. By some trick of the light you could see the moving images reflected on the wall of the building opposite. That was almost as exciting to us as being in the cinema.

When we weren't at the pictures we played football non-stop. Sometimes we went down to Belleek for games but mostly we just played on the street. This was our main pitch. We didn't think of things like goalposts or winning games, we just kicked the ball wherever we liked when it came to us. Sometimes it got stuck under the cars that were parked on it or between the footpath and one of the tyres. That always delayed the game. There were often cats under the cars as well. They squawked when the ball hit them, or maybe just squawked anyway.

Another game we played was 'Three to get in.' That was up against Padraic Gallagher's gate. He'd painted it green years ago but it was all flaked off from the ball ramming against it. He used to give out stink to us if he saw us but he was away a lot so that wasn't much. He was a commercial traveller who brought shirts and other clothing products to Castlebar. You'd see them in the back of his car on hangers, dozens of shirts that were all exactly the same just sitting there. At tea-time our mothers appeared at various doors and called us in. Usually we didn't go. Some of us had to, the ones who'd get beaten if they didn't, but I wasn't one of these.

My parents were gentle people. My mother came from a hunting family in Roscommon. We had the walls of our house painted black and yellow, her riding colours.

My father liked to drink but most people's fathers seemed to do that as far as I could see. It was an accepted fault. He was a solicitor who worked from home after his office burned down in Bridge Street. His new office was really just the dining-room. He had a big hole put in the wall between this and the kitchen. My mother used to put cups of tea into it when he was seeing clients. We called it The Hatch. I used to be able to fit my whole body into it when I was young if I crouched over but then I got too big and I couldn't do that anymore

As well as a solicitor, my father was a Commissioner for Oaths. There was a sign outside the door saying that. I never knew what it meant. I used to think it was something to do with oats, or farmers. People often came to the house to have things signed and he came in with the Bible and had them swear over it. He usually dressed in pinstriped trousers and a black jacket with a grey waistcoat underneath it. He wore studs in his shirt and he had a garter on his elbow. He had a special knife that he used for opening envelopes.

If he was going out for a night he always wore a white scarf even if the weather was warm. He often brought me to the Estoria. There was a red velvet cushion kept especially for me there. I was too small to see the screen without it. Mr. Mulligan used to put it on the seat for me, winking at my father as he did so.

His favourite actor was Edward G. Robinson. He called him Edward Robinson, without the G. He often wore a white scarf in his films, especially when he was playing a gangster. My father had the same build as him. Maybe he was trying to be like him with the white scarf.

Sometimes there were priests from the college at the films. They didn't like us to be out late at night but if I was with my father, which I usually was, they didn't say much. They were always nice to me when he was there but they'd be different the next day at school, telling me it was wrong e to be out late at night instead of doing my homework.

I hated school. I went down to the college every morning expecting to get beaten for little or nothing. I always had a knot in my stomach cycling down the Killala Road and across the bridge. The chain had a habit of coming off and I used to get oil on my hands trying to fix it. I had a cloth I kept in my pocket to dry them because you'd get slapped if your hands were dirty going into class.

There was a big hill up to the college. If I was tired from being at a film the night before I'd get off the bike and walk up to the top of it. Then I'd park the bike at a rack where you could slide the front tyre in.

Gerry Gilmartin was usually there before me. Gerry liked to smoke. 'Here,' he'd say, 'Have a puff.' I didn't like smoking but I couldn't say that to him or he'd make fun of me. I tried not to cough as I inhaled because that would have given the game away.

In the classroom you'd get hit for not knowing history dates or irregular Irish verbs. One of the teachers had a set on me. We called him Punk. He pulled my locks and threw chalk at me, and sometimes the duster. He didn't like me because I was a townie. He preferred the country boys, boys who cycled in from Attymas or Bohola with shit on their shoes after being up at 6 a. m. to milk the cows on their farms.

Punk was our geography teacher. He had a globe that he plugged into an electric socket. When he did that it lit up from the inside. I loved looking at it but I didn't know any of the countries on it except for Ireland. Geography was my worst subject. If Punk asked me where the Ox mountains were I'd hardly have been able to tell him, even though you could see the peak of them from one of the school windows. I had no sense of direction, even getting lost sometimes if I had to carry a message from one classroom to another.

He always said I was 'away with the fairies' when he was talking and I probably was. My mind was on other things when he gave his classes, like Sorcha Connolly or some of the other girls from the convent that we used to see walking down by the church in their gymslips or their gabardine coats. I could never answer his questions about silage or fishing, his favourite hobby, or a dockyard in Cork run by a man called Verolme that he seemed to be obsessed about. I wrote down what he said about all of these things in a little notebook I had but sometimes I couldn't even read my own handwriting. He compared it to a spider walking across a page one day. Everyone laughed when he said that.

You always had to laugh when Punk made a joke or you'd get slapped, even if the joke was in Irish and you didn't understand it. He was our Irish teacher as well. His nephew was in the class too. He was from a Gaeltacht area in Donegal and was a fluent speaker. He was set up as our model but one of us could ever come close to him.

Every day when I came home from school I'd have a long face on me. 'Have you done something wrong?' my parents would ask me, 'Are you in some kind of trouble?' I never told them about Punk. School and home were like parts of two totally different worlds. The days were hell and the nights were heaven.

On Mondays we had a double dose of Punk, Geography being followed by Irish. That was my worst morning. Going over the bridge was like walking a gangplank.

Some of the other teachers were all right. Spud Murphy taught us science. He had an easy manner. His jokes were easier to understand than Punk's. 'If it was raining soup,' he said to me once, 'You'd be out with a fork.' He used to let us play with little bits of mercury, running them up and down between cracks of the wood on our benches as if they were ball bearings.

In the recreation hall afterwards (we called it The Wreck) we'd play push penny or read the papers that were strewn on the floor under the table tennis table. We never played table tennis because there was no net on it.

One day Gerry found a photograph of an African woman in a magazine. It was called *National Geographic*. She was naked from the waist up. It was the first time I'd ever seen a woman's breasts. Up until then I never even knew they had nipples on them. Gerry told me he had other pictures like that if I wanted to see them. I didn't know if I did. Pictures like that gave me bad thoughts. Sometimes I had those kinds of thoughts about Sorcha Connolly or some of the women in the cowboy films I went to in the Estoria with big breasts and plunging necklines. Punk said you could go to hell if you 'entertained' bad thoughts. I never knew what he meant by that. It seemed to me that I couldn't do anything about them.

I went to confession to Punk some Saturday evenings. I was always self-conscious because I knew he'd recognise my voice and give me an extra long penance to do. One time I even had to say the whole rosary. But after telling my sins I always felt clean. It was as if something evil had been driven out of myself. I thought of my soul as a physical thing inside my body like a box with the bad thoughts like little devils running around inside it.

After school most days I used to play snooker with Damien Connolly. He was Sorcha's younger brother. We used to swap comics and bubblegum cards with soccer players on them. I was always looking for Jimmy Greaves and he was always looking for Danny Blanchflower. Sometimes he came up to our house and we recorded our voices on a tape recorder our aunt gave us. It had huge big spools on it. We used to imitate Punk's voice and then play it back, laughing uproariously.

Other times I'd go down to Damien's house and listen to him playing the guitar. He liked Gilbert O'Sullivan and a band called Fairport Convention. He was really good on it. Going down to Damien was also an excuse to see Sorcha. She was always knitting and saying 'Fizz it!' when she missed a stitch. If you were lucky she'd sing 'Doonaree' for you in that haunting voice.

When I was in my fourth year at school my father retired. 'There are too many solicitors in the town,' he said to me, 'Anyway I'm getting on.' He was only 58 at the time. One night soon afterwards my mother told me I was being taken out of school. 'Why is that?' I asked her. 'Because we're moving to Dublin,' she said. I thought she was joking but when I looked into her eyes and saw how worried they were I knew it was true. 'I have to go to hospital,' she said then. She said there was something wrong with her chest and that she had to have some X-rays to see what it was.

After that everything moved fast. I never got to do the Leaving Cert or even say goodbye to the people in my class. An auction was held for our furniture in the Town Hall and everything was flogged for a fraction of its value. I felt sad looking at all my father's thriller books, the ones with the orange covers. They were stacked up on a cabinet we had and sold for a few pence to anyone who wanted them. Our furniture went too, and a carpet I liked even though it had a hole in it.

I went home crying that night. I couldn't sleep when I went to bed. I left the window of my room open and looked out at the stars. You could get out onto the roof of the house from it and I did that in the middle of the night, sitting on one of the slates just above the evrun where you could see Gary Rooney's orchard. I knew it would be the last time I'd see it. We used to rob apples from it when we were children. One day he chased after us with a pop gun, threatening to kill us.

The next day my mother called me at dawn. My eyes were falling out of my head from the lack of sleep but I knew I had to get up. She gave me tea and toast and told me not to worry about anything.

Upstairs I heard my father snoring. Neither of them had been at the auction. Instead they'd gone down to my cousins who lived across the river to discuss where we were going to be living in Dublin. They were going up there together on the train the next day. It was close to the hospital my mother was being admitted to.

A few hours later a station wagon pulled up outside our door and a man with red hair got out. He gave a look at my mother and then shook my hand. 'I'm Seamus,' he said, 'I'll be bringing you to Dublin.' He was related to my cousins. My mother told me they were buying our house and the money was going to get another one in Glasnevin where we were going to be living from now on. It was smaller than the one we were in but that was because everything was more expensive in the city.

Seamus took a bag I'd packed and put it in the boot of the car. My mother was crying. She was so emotional she couldn't even say goodbye to me. She just closed the door and went back inside to wake my father.

I don't remember much about the journey to Dublin. The leather in the car smelt hot. Seamus drove fast. The towns whizzed by us almost as if they didn't exist. We didn't stop to eat but he had a flask of tea and some sandwiches that he gave us.

There were two other people in the car besides me and Seamus. One of them was a woman with a hard face who didn't speak for the whole journey. The other was a man who'd lost his wife to cancer. I didn't know anything about cancer except that it was a terrifying disease that had claimed the life of Damien's uncle in Croydon in the 1950s. Hearing this man talk about it made the journey even more miserable for me than it might otherwise have been. It made me worry about my mother and what might be wrong with her chest.

When we got to Glasnevin it was getting on to evening. A strong wind was blowing. The clouds in the sky looked ominous to me. We pulled up in a cul-de-sac outside a house that had a palm tree in the garden. I saw a man in a tracksuit listening to a Walkman. A woman walking behind him was pushing a pram. A dog with one eye barked as we got out of the car. All the buildings around us looked the same. In the distance a factory belched smoke into the air.

'Welcome to Dublin,' Seamus said, smiling again. I knew he was trying to make me feel good but it didn't work. Everything I knew had disappeared from my life, all the things from the house and all the people I knew as well. There would be no more free passes to the Estoria from Mr Mulligan, no more football games in Belleek, no Sorcha Connolly to look at across the street, no music to listen to from the Town Hall as I was trying to sleep at night.

My father said I'd be going to a good school but I didn't care about things like that. All I could think of was my mother's X-rays and having to face strangers in a school I knew I'd hate and wonder what to say to them because I'd be a misfit and a blow-in.

Seamus got out of the car. He told the other people he'd be back in a minute. He walked me up the drive to the house. He turned the key in the door and led me in, taking my bag. As I was walking down the hall I banged my head off a lampshade that was hanging off one of the walls. He laughed as I tried to rub away the pain.

'Do you like the house?' he asked me. I said it looked all right.

'Don't worry about a thing,' he said, 'You'll be fine.' 'Thanks for bringing me up,' I said. 'I can't stay long,' he said then, 'I have to drop the other two off at Chapelizod.' He pronounced it as 'Chapelizard.'

After he was gone I went into the kitchen. It had an Aga cooker in it. There was a glasshouse to the side. I sat down and made myself a cup of tea. All there was in the fridge was a packet of Marietta biscuits so I had one of those. I drank the tea as I started to think about what the future held for me.

Outside I heard some people speaking in Dublin accents, accents I'd heard only on television programmes before. They were rough and guttural and I didn't like them. I knew I'd be hearing nothing else from now on.

I looked out at a little garden beyond the glasshouse. I thought of Gary Rooney's orchard and the day he chased after Damien and myself with his pop gun. The sun was gone down and the night closing in.

After a while the phone rang. When I picked it up I heard my father's voice. 'I got her into a ward at last,' he said, 'I'll be over to you in a while to tell you all the news.'

Death of a Mother

Life was taken from her
without warning, absurdly
snatched from this woman
who was so perfect
she couldn't be mortal.
She was the Blessed Virgin,
Immaculate and impervious,
but cancer took her down
to where the rest of us live
and die.

I visited her in a hospital
 that smelt of cleaning agents.
I asked her to forgive me
for past transgressions
but she saw none.

I thought back to talks we'd had,
mainly about myself.
What could she tell me?
Nothing very much
because I knew it all.

And yet I kept running to her
like an acolyte with a lover
or a reluctant idol.
And then her life ended,
dismally, like a bad movie.

 She had no right to leave me
without sorting out my madness.
She'd promised me this.
Why had she reneged?

At the funeral
everyone was a friend.
They pressed the flesh,
bearhugged hollowly
in the frozen silence.

I sidled up to a drunk
who was blessedly removed
from this incestuous frenzy.
His indifference relaxed me.
I drank so much
I blanked out.
Afterwards I had a vision
of white walls, charcoal voices.
I bowed to stasis,
sunk into a shell.

After three days
I came out of my room
to re-connect with the universe.
I got a bus to town
on the advice of people
who said they cared for me.
I did the normal things.
Everyone said,
'He's let go. '
That night I had a nightmare.
She became my guardian angel,
my terror.
Now she owns me.

A Life at the Bar

He grows up in Ballina. Some people see him as arrogant, an image he doesn't do much to contradict.

'There are two kinds of people in the world,' he likes to say, 'The man who walks down Bond Street like he owns it and the man who walks down Bond Street as if he doesn't care who owns it.' He can't make up his mind which one he is himself.

His father he hero-worships. A self-made man who becomes a mini-legend in the town, his presence hovers over him all his through his youth. He's a Poor Law Guardian and a Justice of the Peace. He's also a businessman, owning a sawmills and a drapery business.

He wants to emulate him and drives himself hard to do that. He's educated at Blackrock College and Castleknock. When he reaches the age of seventeen he enrols in Trinity College Dublin to study law. He has to get a dispensation from the church to go there because he's Catholic.

He has his own room, Number 9. He says his ambition is to break down religious barriers. Some of his best friends are Protestants. One of them even wakes him for Mass every Sunday.

As he starts going to the law lectures he forms the idea that one day he'll become a High Court judge. The only thing that could divert him from his goal is the fact that he might have to actually study to attain it. He doesn't like studying.

His early years at the university are comprised of an eternity of fun times. There are picnics, Treasure Hunts, parties that end only with the dawn, His days he spends lolling on the grass in College Green, chatting up the women who pass by with his great charm. Sometimes he invites them to the coffee houses nearby. Here he beguiles them with exciting anecdotes about his past - most of which are made up.

The years pass by in a daze. His house exams he continues to fails spectacularly, something which doesn't bother him at all.

'You're down again,' his friends tell him as he approaches the results board, after which he usually goes off with them to some pub or other. To 'celebrate.'

News of his exploits eventually reaches his father. One summer when he goes home on holiday he says to him, 'If some of the stories I hear about you are true, I'd prefer to see your skeleton walk through that door than you.'

The next time he comes home there's a silence in the house. It's as if some unspeakable felony has been committed. He waits for the unleashing of his father's temper on him, an unleashing he almost hopes for so he'll know where he stands with him, but it doesn't come. The silence is worse:

Then one day as he's making himself up at the mirror his father insults him, telling him he'll never be anything more than a tailor's dummy in life. Afterwards the distance between them grows. He goes back to Dublin not having healed the breach between them.

A couple of month afterwards a telegram arrives to say his father has died. When he hears the news he wants to die himself as well. When he goes home to see the body it's in in a familiar pose, his hands intertwined across his stomach as if in prayer. He died, he learns, saying the rosary.

There follows a breakdown of sorts, or what the doctor he attends terms a breakdown. He drifts restlessly through his days with some inexplicable fear lodged inside him. At night he gets tremors.

They stop when he meets the woman he's going to marry, a self-effacing girl who's the daughter of a gentleman farmer from a county family in Roscommon. She rides to the hounds.

The pair of them meet on a boat trip organised by her sister. It's a blustery day and the sea is choppy. He becomes nervous as the boat starts to rock. She has no nerves at all. She's amused by his fear that it might capsize on them. He talks compulsively to hide the fear but each time a wave rises up and threatens to knock it over he hurtles backwards. He hugs the sides of the boat nervously as she laughs heartily at the whole escapade.

In the following weeks he becomes obsessed with the idea of seeing her again, infatuated with her serenity, her sense of peace. He harangues her with phone calls and letters entreating her to see him again. In time she agrees. She likes him but he has come on too heavy, chasing her all over Connacht.

When he asks her to marry him she laughs as if he's joking but in time she becomes hypnotised by him. She gets tired saying no to his proposals of marriage. One day she changes it to yes. 'I wore her down,' he says. The fact that she's landed gentry increases her allure for him.

They tie the knot one Sunday morning at dawn against the wishes of her father. He has doubts about his ability to knuckle down to work and leave the good life behind.

But he proves him wrong in this. They move to Greystones where he studies heavy tomes by the light of a blow-lamp in a cottage surrounded by fuchsias. One day, miraculously, he graduates. 'The exams weren't getting any easier,' he explains, 'and I wasn't getting any smarter. I realised the writing was on the wall.'

He moves back to Ballina and sets up a legal practice there. Every now and then he starts quoting phrases from his exam: '*Caveat emptor.*' 'Every man is entitled to the presumption of innocence.' 'He who comes to Equity must come with clean hands.'

He buys a house in Arthur Street. It used to be a convent. It commands the street. 'Norfolk' is the name he puts on it.

He names it after the Duke of Norfolk, the only man in England who doesn't have to stand when the Queen enters a room. The outside is painted in black and yellow, his wife's riding colours. He puts a plate outside his door and has cards made with his details on them: 'Solicitor and Commissioner for Oaths. Ring Ballina 143.'

Children arrive soon afterwards like the steps of a stairs. Most of them are just a year or two apart in age. He calls them 'Irish twins.' He dotes on them, spoiling them with treats every day when he comes home from the office, or from court.

Most of his cases are small time. A man is arrested for poaching salmon. Another one is drunk and disorderly after the pubs close. Two farmers fall out over the ownership of a plot of land.

The cases he hates most are those involving practical data – the skid marks of a car, details a forensic scientist might feel comfortable with. He's at his best where there's a personal element involved. But he still feels frustrated.

He wears a monocle sometimes. 'The doctor told me I have a lazy eye,' he says, but it's really for the image he puts it on. He looks like a German count with it. It sits well with his Trinity college garb. 'I want to look like I come from Oxford,' he says, 'not Foxford.'

He lives beyond his means, carrying about him an air of fallen grandeur even as a young man. And he likes a drink, continuing on the party lifestyle of TCD.

His house is full of books. He reads voraciously, gobbling up thrillers by people like Nelson Blake and Arthur Conan Doyle. He writes verse that he sends to *The Western People*. 'When the situation clamours for a pardonable lie, please begin your observations with "As no one will deny".' He types these because his handwriting is almost illegible. 'If you can read a solicitor's writing,' he says, 'It means he's no good. The same principle applies to doctors.'

When he says things like that it's hard to know if he's serious or not. He tells jokes that are corny. He laughs so much at them, people laugh at him laughing more than they laugh at the jokes.

He struggles to make ends meet.

'I need £6000 to feel comfortable,' he says. It's never any other figure. It's like he's plucked it out of the air. It's the sum that will solve all his problems. 'Money talks,' he jokes, 'Mine said goodbye.'

He knows he's good at what he does but there are too many other solicitors competing for too few clients and the rewards are small. 'Is this what all the slaving was for?' he says to his wife exasperatedly, 'these insulting fees?' But he loves being in court, loves playing to the gallery. That's where he shines.

He charms the witnesses with his personality and his command of words. He even charms guards, addressing them as 'Sergeant.' When they tell him they're 'only' guards he says, 'A slight anticipation on my part.'

'You could get Jack the Ripper off with a warning,' she tells him in acknowledgement of his persuasive powers with judges.

The performer in him takes over in court. It's his stage. Outside it he's quieter. Like most performers he's shy at base. In church he sits in the back pew, going out for a smoke during the sermon.

He's nervous too. He takes a tranquilliser going to court sometimes. In the Estoria he gets a panic attack one night, feeling he could throw himself off the balcony.

The bar is another kind of stage for him. With drink he becomes omnipotent. He tells people that one day he'll become a State Solicitor. At other times, egged on by his audience, he acts out the role of a mission priest on a pulpit, a conductor waving a baton at an imaginary orchestra.

He becomes more mellow as the years go on, a veneer of domesticity enwreathing him. More and more children arrive. There are also two miscarriages and two stillbirths. Those that survive he spoils as his own father once spoiled him. His dishes out money to them, emptying out whatever coins he has in his pockets when they come home from school. If they say they're not well enough to go to school he believes them even when they're putting it on because he's such a soft touch. They get to stay in bed for the day and he brings them comics when he comes home from the office. 'The sick one is always the favourite in this family,' he tells them.

He entertains them with stories. They gather themselves around him like the Von Trapp family as they listen to them. If they have a bad day at school they can't tell him for fear he'll go down to their teacher and complain. It upsets him too much to see them given out to.

He brings them on walks around the town – down by Aunt Nellie's house on the Killala Road, past Marian Crescent to St. Patrick's Well, to Leigue cemetery to see the family vault.

Every night they say the rosary. The children kneel on the stone floor of the kitchen with cushions under them, their elbows on chairs. When they're tired they rest their bottoms on their heels. He stays standing, walking between the chairs as he gives it out. He keeps his hands clasped behind his back with the rosary beads in them. His voice is as dramatic as ever as he begins: 'Lord, open my lips and my tongue shall announce thy praise.' At the end he prays for 'special intentions.'

Sometimes he goes up to the Convent of Mercy to collect his daughters, walking up Convent Hill in his pin-striped suit. The nuns flutter around him excitedly when he does so. They're not used to seeing men. They offer him tea and he starts talking to them, embellishing his past. He commands his audience like a hypnotist.

He doesn't see himself as a snob but someone who wins his spurs and wears them.

He'd like to own a limousine. He cycles a bicycle sometimes but he doesn't want anyone to hear about it. He feels it would lower his standing.

One day he's cycling along the road with his daughter on the carrier when she gets her foot stuck in a spoke. He manages to free it without crashing the bike, avoiding danger to himself. This surprises his wife. She's never seen him as someone good with his hands. He doesn't want the incident publicised, not because he objects to having saved his daughter from harm but because he doesn't want people to know he has a bicycle. To his mind this is *infra dig*.

He often writes essays for his children that are read out at school the following day. If he's feeling playful he might act out the circumstances of a trial for them, putting on the pretend wig of a judge as he gives the order that someone is to be hanged, drawn and quartered.

'I'd like to have been a doomsday preacher,' he tells his wife. He pounds his fist on a pulpit as he delegates defendants to the eternal fires of hell. She laughs at this because she knows how soft he is at heart. He cries at sentimental films as much as if the events in them were happening in his own life.

His children grow up. In 1955, two of his sons leave home after doing the Leaving Cert. He's devastated with loneliness. A few years later two daughters follow them to Dublin. Will the nest be completely empty one day? He wants to keep them as little ducks in his pond. His wife is even more lonely. When one of her sons enters the church she's inconsolable. It's every mother's dream at the time but she can't see it that way for now.

To get his mind off the cruel present he romanticises the distant past. He tells a story about his father having owned one of the first cars in Ballina. It was such an apparition that one day a man looking for a lift asked him to drive him the wrong way purely for the pleasure of sitting into it. Such stories don't go down well with some of the people he tells them to in the bars. They see them as big-headed.

He becomes a kind of eccentric around the town. He carries an umbrella even when it isn't raining. He wears a grey waistcoat with a pocket watch. Sometimes he puts on his pin-striped suit when he goes to the beach.

'I think I'll go down the street and give everyone a thrill,' he jokes. He tells a story about a man who used to wear a bowler hat in the bath 'in case anyone called.'

He's a larger-than-life figure, so large that his anecdotes reduce rooms to silence. His children, in contrast, grow up quiet. How can they compete with him? To some people they come across as stand-offish as a result, an effect accentuated by their double-barrelled name.

He's always impeccably turned out. He swaggers up to court like Lord Knock'em Stiff. Or Burlington Bertie.

When he's had a drink the mask slips. The fun part of him takes over and he forgets his image. At times like this he's back in Trinity again. He's the gadabout, the partygoer rather than the respectable solicitor.

His habit of carrying an umbrella in dry weather leads to a lampoon of him in the *Western People*. It's written in the form of a poem called 'The Brolly Brigade' and signed by someone who calls himself Sean Bocht, a made-up name. What hurts him most is the fact that it's anonymous.

'It's the coward's way of doing it,' he says. So who is Sean Bocht? He becomes obsessed with the idea of the man's identity. Obviously it's someone with a grudge against him, someone who sees him as pretentious.

'I'm not a snob,' he insists, 'A snob is someone who pretends he's something he isn't. I'm not that. I have the background.'

Some people refer to his father a member of the 'rag trade' because he made his money in clothing. The jibe causes him no end of pain.

For a while he stops carrying the umbrella but then he starts again.

Why should he compromise? He has to be himself, even in a town inhabited by people like Sean Bocht.

He continues to obsess about the writer's identity. Is he someone he knows well? Might he even drink with him? Julius Caesar was stabbed by an ally. Et tu, Sean.

A part of him appreciates Sean Bocht's point. Maybe a part of him wants to throw the umbrella away and replace it with a stick, the kind of stick farmers use to drive cows.

The part of him that wants to be the State Solicitor has to subjugate that to the part that likes drinking with farmers and labouring men rather than his colleagues. He's two people and that's the problem.

As he gets older he starts to work from home. Some days he doesn't even dress, seeing clients in a smoking jacket. When they call to the house to have documents signed he spends so much time telling them funny stories he almost forgets why they called. As he reaches the punchline he laughs. The monocle usually pops out of his eye then.

Some of them live out the country and he has to get a taxi-man to drive out to them if they can't get in to see him. He employs a man who drives so slowly, people joke that he stopped on the street one day to give a friend a lift and the friend said, 'It's okay, I'm in a hurry, I'll walk.'

As the years gain on him his energy level dips. He has nine children now and it's difficult to feed and clothe them. His moods grow dark if a bill is large but then he gets a good case, the sale if a house maybe, and everything is fine again.

Life is never dull with him. His mind is always on fire. He writes letters to the newspaper about everything that strikes his fancy, from the corruption of political parties to the local teddy boys – a breed he mistakenly refers to as 'teddy bears.'

He hates watching programmes on the television that feature courtroom scenes. 'They never do it right!' he says, shaking his fingers at the screen, 'It's just Hollywood melodrama.'

His temper becomes short if a file goes missing. Nobody is allowed leave the house until it's found. His family have a joke about anything that can't be found: 'It's in Nellie's room behind the wallpaper.' Nellie is his sister. She lives down the road across from the school. She doesn't marry. She has what seems like a million cats.

If the file is found he's fine again. Or something else might happen to prop up his spirits – a windfall from the sale of a house maybe. These are always the best-paying cases, the easy ones. They relax him. When he's relaxed he acts as if he hasn't a care in the world. His personality becomes jocose; he's the Trinity student again.

People are amused at his colourful personality in court and he becomes elated at their praise. When he wins a case he isn't satisfied until he's bought everyone a round of drinks afterwards in the local bar. That night he might bring his children to the pictures to celebrate. When it's over he sits them all around him like vassals around a king as he embarks upon some other elaborate tale. In his rendition it becomes even more dramatic than the one they've just seen on the cinema screen.

If he's going out of the house for the evening he always wears his Trinity suit and white scarf. And of course his monocle.

He likes to do recitations – *Lasca, Dangerous Dan McGrew, The Green Eye of the Little Yellow God.*

The Green Eye is his favourite. He imbues it with a lot of drama any time he does it, as much drama as any Victorian

153

actor on a stage. Rooms always come to a standstill as he says the opening words in a ponderous voice:

There's a one-eyed yellow idol
To the north of Kathmandu
There's a little marble cross beneath the town
And a broken-hearted woman
Tends the grave of Mad Carew
And the little God forever gazes down.

His expressions grow even more dramatic as he gets to the climax, 'It was the *vengeance* of the God!' When he says this his eyes widen. He becomes the character.

In the pubs people watch him with fascination. They make bets about what story he'll tell next, at what stage of the night take out the photographs of his wife from his wallet. He tells them all she's the most beautiful woman that's ever been born, the most dignified.

If he's drinking whiskey he might become cross with her when he comes home. He always apologises to her afterwards and she always forgives him. 'I wouldn't give your toe for the world,' he says.

His life takes on a pattern. He becomes resigned to being a big fish in a small pond. Or even a small fish in a small pond.

He sees himself as a disillusioned romantic. Life has failed to live up to his expectations and he has to fill the gap somehow. Sometimes he does this with drink. His appetite for life makes him do everything too much: loving, laughing, crying, drinking, even eating. When he orders a block of ice cream from a nearby shop he knocks it all back in a sitting. Other times he'll go for days without food.

He doesn't drink when he's working, consumed as he is by the job in hand. He often gives it up for Lent, going to a priest he knows to take the pledge. 'I've taken more pledges in my life than drink,' he jokes.

Some men become physical with drink, unleashing a violence within themselves. He's different. He becomes sentimental with it, unleashing his vulnerability. It's like a time machine for him, transporting him back to his childhood, to Trinity, to the days when he ran away from his father.

He tells people he still idolises his father but it's probably truer to say that he was intimidated by him. His mother was a bigger love for him even though he doesn't talk much about her. All he'll say is that she spoiled him. His wife continues that pattern.

As he reaches middle age he becomes resigned to the fact that he never became a State Solicitor. He tells himself it was probably an impossible dream.

His wife says he would have been too highly-strung for it, that the job would most likely have driven him to an early grave with the tension of it.

The challenge now isn't to become a State Solicitor but just to continue as he's going, to feed nine mouths and keep the ship afloat.

When his sister gets cancer in the mid-1960s he goes through one of the darkest periods of his life. A saintly woman, she's married to a wealthy man in Bunree on the far side of the Moy. Each night he walks down to see her and hold her hand, pray by her bed. When she dies he's distraught. Her husband follows her to the grave six months later from heartbreak.

He feels he could go through a breakdown himself but his children revive him. They take his mind off himself. He pampers them, reassures them when they express the insecurities he had himself at their age, insecurities he couldn't reveal to his father because of his distance from him.

But he still won't hear a word said against him.

'I should have died when he did,' he says sometimes when the drink goes down the wrong way, 'when the world was still a decent place.' He beats himself up for bringing nine children into the world, a world that's corrupt and heading for disaster.

Many of his contemporaries have died by now as well, the bosom friends – or rather boozing ones. He spends more and more time in bed, trying to shut out the world. He puts bets on horses to pass the time, a shilling each day on any old nag that takes his fancy. They rarely win. He might as well close his eyes and put a pin on the page.

'I put a bet on a horse last week,' he says one day, 'and he's still running.' The fun is in the names they have. He picks them for this rather than their form. But such bets get them through the day. They help him deal with the passing of better days.

'Memory is the only friend that grief can call its own,' he says as he thinks about them, or about himself when he knew them, when the world was young.

'Authority forgets a dying king' is another favourite expression of his. He has a set of quotations that he trots out like his recitations, dragging on cigarettes as he loses himself in his reveries. He smokes a hundred cigarettes a day. Or at least he lights a hundred. Often he lights them and forgets to smoke them. When his doctor tells him they're bad for him he substitutes them with a pipe.

He rhapsodises on the memory of his father, on his tall hat and frock coat and the crease on his trousers that you could cut yourself on. 'He was a magistrate as well as a Poor Law Guardian,' he tells his children over and over again like a mantra, 'and a daily communicant.'

In more solemn moods he says, 'I betrayed him when he needed me, betrayed him for the fair weather friends that went on to betray me when my money ran out.'

With his electric personality he's capable of entertaining

a roomful of people for hours on end. As the night goes on he'll tell the stories everyone loves hearing over and over again because of the way he tells them. Sometimes he'll launch into a rendition of *The Green Eye* or *Babette* or *Lasca,* giving most drama to the last of these, especially at the end where the lover of the narrator is killed in a stampede of cattle.

'And I often wonder why I do not care,' he'll say, rocking himself on the balls of his feet as he draws himself up to his full height and a tear appears in his eye, 'for the things that are like the things that were, for all my life lies buried there, in Texas down by the Rio Grande.'

The room will be reduced to silence at the drama he creates. But if he hasn't done it well in his own mind he'll be disconsolate. No matter how much you praise him he'll say, 'No, it wasn't good, I didn't do it well. ' He'll be like a stage actor disappointed with his performance.

In 1966 the name of the street he lives on is changed from Arthur Street to Teeling Street as part of the 50th anniversary of the 1916 Rising. The one where his office was is changed from Knox Street to Pearse Street. Such changes refuse to impress him. He's never had nationalist feelings. He continues to call them by their old names.

He reads newspapers throughout the night, becomes depressed about the state of the world, the upsurge of violence, murder, subterfuge. If the mood takes him he'll write a letter to the *Irish Times* about such things. He fulminates about the onset of communism, the megalomania of trade unions. He'll tell you his father sacked any man that failed to measure up to his high standards but that he always gave everyone 'twenty shillings to the pound.'

'You're letting the practice slip,' his wife tells him. To relieve her stress she goes out to the front room to play the piano. It always relaxes her. She sings 'Ave Maria' and it brings her peace.

He now spends more time philosophising than dealing with his clients. Sometimes when they call to the house he spends so much time telling them stories he forgets what they called for.

'We'll be in the Poor House yet,' he says, but he's too far gone to stop the slide, too much immersed in his grandiose ideas of himself, in his private world of solipsism and distaste.

He looks at another world become born, a generation or indifference unfolding before him. Such a world seems to exclude his Edwardian finesse.

'Once upon a time I was distinguished,' he jokes, 'now I'm extinguished.' And then, reaching for the glass of gin that dulls the pain, that weans him into the ether of old age, 'I started off studying for one bar and ended up at another one.'

When the practice finally trails off he feels his days in Ballina are numbered. He starts to think about moving away from it. Many of his family are living in Dublin now and he says he'd like to be near them. All he wants is a room, he says. And £6000. That's still the magic figure to solve all his problems.

So he moves to Dublin. Everything has been arranged for him, including the purchase of a house. When he sees it he says, 'Do we own the whole row?'

It's located in Iona Villas, around the corner from the church where he was married in 1935. His life has come full circle.

In Dublin he continues to be the Philosopher King, continues to sound off about anything and everything from his bed. He involves himself in the life of his children once again and they're still afraid to tell him too much about these lives. If they give out about a boss, they fear he'll ring the person up and give him a piece of his mind. It's a re-run of the situation in school all those years ago when they were afraid to say they got bad treatment from a teacher.

Time drags in retirement. He starts to ask the big questions: Why are we here? Where did we come from? Is there life after death?

When he gets into his seventies he starts to talk about having reached the Biblical span. He talks about his need to 'settle accounts' with his creator.

'It must have been an evil God that created a world like this,' he says sometimes. How could a benevolent one allow diseases, earthquakes, wars. His wife says, 'It's a mystery. Eye hath not seen nor ear heard.' Her simple faith contrasts with his tortuous doubts.

'I'll put him in the witness box when I meet him,' he announces, a rueful grin crossing his face. Just this once he'll be the prosecutor instead of the defence counsel. He tells people he'll bully his way into heaven but in other moods he says he'd prefer to spend eternity in hell 'where all my friends are.' Heaven for the climate, hell for the company.

Priests call to the house occasionally to hear his confession. 'They all tell me I'm pure,' he says to his wife scornfully, 'even though I know I'm not. That's what's wrong with the world today. We've lost our sense of responsibility. I fall three times a day, likes Jesus under the cross. I need to be reminded of that.'

They usually give him three Hail Marys to say no matter what sin he confesses

'I could murder someone and I'd get three Hail Marys,' he says to the priest, 'It's a farce.'

'You're a good man,' the priest replies, 'God loves you.'

'According to that thinking,' he says, 'Lucifer would be in heaven.'

He disapproves of the new religion, of ecumenism, of guitars on the altar and nuns tumbling the wildcat up and down the church aisles. 'It's all kindness to the cat today,' he says. 'There was a time Rome roared, now it's afraid to whisper.'

Whenever he sees a priest in mufti he emits a grim chuckle. 'They're ashamed to be seen in their collars,' he scoffs, 'afraid of their position in life. Why did they enter if they weren't proud of who they were? The tail is wagging the dog.' When they go on about grey areas in theology he loses his patience altogether.

'What we need is a dictator in this world, someone to put the fear of God into people.'

All the people who believed in themselves are gone now. Only the lily-livered are left. Even in questions of crime the notion of punishment seems to be gone out the window.

'Every time I read a newspaper,' he says, 'I see murderers getting off scot free. Even if they're convicted we're afraid to hang them. That little piece of rope dangling in the air kept a lot of us alive but where is it now? They get community service instead. Or a few months in a psychiatric institution. Their solicitor tells the judge they hit their head off a stone when they haven't been right since. So they serve a few months in a mental home. They suddenly decide they're sane again and they're let out to murder someone else.'

In his final years he's a mixture of comedy and tragedy, or maybe both in one. He feels the world has passed him by. Or maybe he's passed *it* by. Does it matter which? He's an anachronism now.

He dies suddenly at the age of 72. His wife is distraught but relieved that he hasn't suffered, that he has died as he lived, dramatically. At the hospital she asks for his wrists to be cut because he's always had a phobia about waking up in a coffin after a film he saw once where that happened. His body he donates to medical research. 'Come in to TCD sometime and see me,' he used to say to his wife, 'I'll be in the lab swinging about.'

She cries for him in the following weeks, missing his love and devotion, the way he used to relax her in company. She still feels his presence around her but as time goes on she grows to accept his passing as she's accepted everything else life ever threw at her: her miscarriages, her stillbirths, her underactive thyroid, her mastectomy, the pressures of living with a man who wasn't even aware of the way he hurt her for much of the time.

Maybe he was more of a son than a husband to her in some ways, she thinks, remembering the way he'd be contrite after an outburst. And maybe her mission in life was to be a mother to him as much as a wife.

But she was privileged to have married him, she knows, privileged to have known a man so much larger than life, privileged to have witnessed his inestimable grandeur. Like an oriental mystic she spends her days now, wondering at the magic of time, saying prayers to the Little Flower, her childhood saint, for his release from purgatory.

She thinks of him calling out the rosary when he was in his prime, more drama in it than religion maybe as his voice echoed through the house. She thinks of him in churches or in the convent visiting the nuns, the reverence he had for them and how they'd gather themselves around him as he pontificated.

In her mind sometimes she sees him in performance, a raconteur who captivated great numbers of people with his stories and recitations, his figure small but commanding as he thrust his chest outwards like a peacock, gesticulating to the four corners of the room as he discoursed.

She thinks of him as he sat in his bed looking into space in his later years with a lost look in his eyes, a man who felt he'd outlived his welcome in life, whose great lust for excitement could never entirely be satisfied.

In the weeks following the funeral she watches life becoming stale around her, watches everything take on the pallor of the prosaic. People tell her he was a lovable rogue but she can only think about the lovable part. In the end his only sin was existing out of his time, she tells herself.

It was his vulnerability that made him larger than life, she knows, his vulnerability that made her love him more than anything else.

A broken-hearted woman tends the grave of Mad Carew. In her dreams he'll visit her to soothe her furrowed brow.

Absence

Someone else is with her
 tonight.
Outside a cat disturbs a bin.
Cars wheeze through the tunnels
of desire, linked like vague roadmaps
as my eyes are lifted up
to nests of crows
getting ready to sink their claws
into the Mayo night.

When the sky is empty of light
I take a train to my younger self,
brag about my new freedom
to anyone who'll listen.
Suddenly relief floods over me
like a river.
I can do things now, see things.
Memories dissolve like old clothes
or a photograph album missing a page.
I introduce myself to myself
make plans for Part 2 of a narrative
I'm crafting from inside.

I imagine her with a friend
or stranger, soaking herself
in those moments
where the sky opens up
to reveal different lights,
sounds, poisons.
In a basement flat like we had
I turn the key,
trapped into the dim light

of my self-styled
eternity.

What has been has been.
Tomorrow she'll smile
at her immaturity,
transforming it into something
that worked for a while.
She'll sell herself to him,
advertising the things
I took for granted
when we were like bad habits
of each other, cowardly settlings.
As the nights fly in
I'll relish the next best thing
that happens,
designing her
as a ghost that's calcified
into a non-existent past.

Bunree Playground

They were in the playground at Bunree.

Tommy went to the highest bar of the climbing frame. He flexed his muscles.

'Jesus,' Catherine cried out, 'Come down this second, you'll kill yourself.'

'Leave him alone,' Alex said, 'It's good for him.'

'Are you mad? If he slips he'll be a goner.'

'It's only a pebble surface,' Alex said, 'The worst he'd get is a graze.'

Catherine ran over to him and took him down.

'Don't do that again,' she said, 'You'll give Mammy a bad fright. Would you like an ice cream?'

'We have to go,' said Alex.

'I want to do a wee-wee,' said Tommy.

'Get into the car,' said Alex, 'We have no time for that now.'

Catherine looked at him pleadingly.

'The toilet is only round the corner,' she said, 'He'll wet the car if you don't let him go.'

'He's only looking for attention. Let him wet it if he wants. I don't. care.'

Catherine carried Tommy to the car.

'Why don't you let him walk?' Alex said, 'You'll make a cissy out of him.'

'I'm afraid he'll wet his pants.'

'If he did it wouldn't be the end of the world.'

They got to the car park.

'I want to do a wee-wee,' Tommy said again.

'Let me bring him behind a hedge,' said Catherine.

'No time,' said Alex, 'Everyone in.'

They sat in the car. Alex drove off.

Tommy put his hand over his trousers. He kept saying he wanted to do a wee-wee.

'If you don't stop that lark,' said Alex, 'I'll put you out of the car. Then you'll have to walk home. How would you like that?'

Tommy started to cry.

·'Stop the car,' said Catherine.

Alex pulled up and Catherine got out. She grabbed Tommy from the baby-seat and started swinging him up and down.

'Hickory Dickory Dock,' she said, 'The mouse ran up the clock.'

Tommy laughed.

'Stop shaking him,' said Alex, 'If we hit a bump he'll go through the roof.'

She put him on her lap. Alex lit up a cigarette. He put on the radio and started tapping his foot to the music.

As they approached the hospital Catherine asked Alex if there was any chance they could stop at it briefly. A few days ago her father had fallen off a ladder and broken his leg.

'I wouldn't have time for that,' Alex said.

'Not even for a few minutes?'

'No can do.'

They drove past the hospital. Catherine blessed herself and said a prayer. Tommy watched her fervently as she joined her hands.

'Can I say a prayer too, Mammy?' he said.

'That's a good boy,' said Catherine.

Tommy clasped his hands together. He tried to say the 'Bless me God' prayer but got stuck after the first line. Catherine smiled. Alex yawned.

They reached the house. Alex parked. He turned off the radio.

'Okay,' he said, 'Last one out's a rotten egg. And bring all your mess with you.'

Catherine grabbed the bottles and sandwich boxes from the back seat. They walked to the door.

'Go to the bathroom now, Tommy,' said Alex.

Tommy looked confused.

'It's gone off me,' he said.

Alex grimaced.

'See what I mean?' he said to Catherine, 'He makes it all up just to annoy us.'

They went in the door.

'What time do you have to be at work?' Catherine asked him.

'In about half an hour.'

'Can I come with you? You could drop me off at the hospital on your way.'

'I don't think that would be a good idea.'

'Why not?'

'Because there'd be nobody to collect you. And who'd mind Tommy? I'll bring you in tomorrow if I can.'

'I suppose there's no chance you'll be home tonight.'

'Hardly. They've booked a room for me in Jury's. These things always run on.' He was going to a conference in Galway after work.

'Will Rosanna Houghton be there?'

He gave her a strange look. Rosanna was his secretary.

'I don't know. I suppose so. So what if she is?'

'I'm just asking. How is she getting down to it?'

'How would I know? I'm not psychic. Probably on the train. Anyway I have to go now.'

'Have you time for a cup of tea?'

'Just about. Put it on, will you? I'm going upstairs to sort out a few things.'

Catherine went into the kitchen while he went upstairs. Tommy followed him up. He watched him packing.

'Where are you going?' he asked, his big eyes staring up at him.

'Daddy has to work late.'

'When will you be back?'

'Tomorrow. Do you know when that is?'

Tommy thought hard.

'I do. It's the day after today.'

'Exactly. Now you be a good boy now and help Mammy around the house while I'm gone.'

'But I have to go to school.'

'No, you're getting the day off as a treat. Isn't Tommy a lucky boy?'

He nodded again.

'Can I go to work with you?'

'No. Work isn't for little boys. Only big men. Now go downstairs and help Mammy with the tea.'

Tommy ran downstairs. Alex finished packing. He changed into his suit. The kettle boiled.

'Your tea is ready,' Catherine called up, 'Would you like a Kit-Kat with it?'

'Great,' said Alex.

His mobile phone rang. He answered it. There was a pause before he spoke.

'I can't talk now,' he said.

He hung up.

'Who was that?' Catherine said.

'A wrong number.'

He sent a text. Then he went downstairs. He was carrying his brief case and wearing his suit.

'You look very spruce,' said Catherine, 'It's a pity you wouldn't dress up like that for me.'

'What's that supposed to mean?'

'It seems like you always put on your best bib and tucker for that Rosanna one.'

'In case you didn't know, I'm going to a conference. I have to give a presentation. What do you want me to wear - an anorak?'

'Relax. I'm joking. Drink your tea, it's getting cold.'

He sat down. The tea was cold so he didn't bother with it. He turned on the television. There was a rugby match on. He munched the Kit-Kat and turned up the volume. Leinster had just got a try. Tommy came over to him. He high-fived him. Catherine picked up the Kit-Kat wrapper and put it in the bin.

'I suppose there's no chance you could cancel the trip to Galway,' she said.

'Sorry?'

'I mean because of Daddy.'

'Are you joking yourself? This is a big one. If it goes well I'll get promoted. That means we could afford the trip to Doolin at Halloween. Hamilton told me he'd give me a bonus if it went well.' Hamilton was his boss.

Catherine nodded vaguely.

'All right, but maybe you could drop me off to see Daddy on your way. I could get a taxi home.'

'We can't afford taxis,' he grunted. 'Anyway he probably wouldn't be able to talk to you with all the painkillers he's on. Didn't you say he spent most of his time asleep?'

'That's not the point. I just want to see him.'

'You see him nearly every day. You spend more time in that hospital than the bloody nurses.'

He went into the sitting-room. There were files all over the place. He checked them out. Then he wrote something down in a jotter. Catherine took his tea-cup from the table. She put it in the sink.

'Can I have a Kit-Kat?' Tommy asked her.

'I'm afraid we have none left,' she told him.

Tommy went over to his toy box. There was a train in it. He started playing with it. Alex smiled at him.

'Choo-choo,' he said.

'Choo-choo,' Tommy repeated. He loved repeating things Alex said.

Alex slapped some After-Shave on his face. He started rubbing it in. Catherine saw a piece of dust on his jacket. She brushed it off.

'Stop fussing,' he said, 'I have to go now.'

'I'll miss you tonight,' she said, 'Do you know what time you'll be back?'

'Not really. There'll probably be more stuff tomorrow morning as well. I have to interview that new guy I told you about. He's a right tosser but someone has to do it.'

'I might ask Breege to bring me in to see Daddy.'

'Breege? Christ, are you that bad? I wouldn't advise it in that banger she goes round in.'

'I'll see. Anyway mind yourself. Don't eat any of that junk food they usually give you at these things. If you get a minute you might ring me from the hotel.'

'I'll try, but you never know the way these conferences go. It'll probably drag on till all hours.'

'I could ring you instead if you like.'

He shook his head.

'That's probably not a good idea. I could be anywhere. Anyway I usually turn off my phone when I 'm at work, as you know. It's a pity you don't know how to text.'

'I hate those bloody texts. All they do is waste time.'

'It's just as well you don't work where I do then.'

'I'll miss you,' she said.

'And me you.'

She looked at him worriedly.

'Will there be drink at it?'

'This is Ireland, Catherine. What do you think? We can't function without the stuff. That and potatoes.'

'Don't have too much. You know what it does to you.'

'I'll have Fanta all night,' he said, 'How does that sound?'

'There's no need to be sarcastic. I'm just concerned about your health.'

'I appreciate that but you can't be a dog in the manger.'

'I know.'

'Look, sweetheart, I better go now. Otherwise I'll miss the blasted thing altogether.'

'Okay. Did you say goodbye to Tommy?'

He winked.

'Bye, son,' he said.

Tommy ran over to him. Alex lifted him up in his arms. He gave him a big kiss.

'I'll give you your goodbye kiss too,' said Catherine.

He turned his cheek towards her.

'Only the cheek? You'd think we were on a first date.'

She made him kiss her on the mouth.

'Now,' she said, 'That's better.'

He put on a funny face.

'Come here to me,' he said.

'What's wrong?'

He started sniffing her.

'Your breath smells,' he said.

'What?'

'It's okay. Don't worry about it.'

'Jeepers. You can't just say things like that.'

She ran out to the kitchen for some mouth freshener. She sprayed it on herself. A few seconds later she came back in.

'There,' she said, breathing it out at him, 'How's that?'

'Perfect.'

'You're probably just saying that.'

'No, honestly, you're anyone's fancy now. Listen, I have to go. I'll be sacked.'

She looked glum.

'Are you all right?' he said.

'You have me worried about my bad breath.'

'It was nothing. It's fine now. You smell like a queen.'

'Go away out of that. Flattery will get you nowhere.'

He walked towards the door. He was going out without his files.

'Aren't you forgetting something?' she said. She ran towards the hall table and got them for him.

'Oh my God. I can't believe I was going to leave those behind me. You're a lifesaver. My head is like a sieve these days.'

He put them in his brief case. She reached her face up to him again.

'Am I good enough to kiss this time?' she said teasingly.

He gave an awkward laugh.

'Don't talk to any strange women at the conference,' she said.

'All women are strange,' he said, walking towards the door.

She gave herself another spray of the mouthwash for good measure. She blew a kiss at him. Tommy ran to her side holding his train.

'Okay folks,' he said, 'I guess that's it.'

'I hate you going,' she said.

Someone has to earn a living. See y'all tomorrow.'

He walked out to the car. Catherine and Tommy went out to the door to see him off. He started the engine. The car rolled slowly down the driveway. He turned out onto the road. Catherine and Tommy waved at him as he drove off. He beeped the horn as he got down the road a bit. They waved again until he turned the corner. Then they went back inside.

Tommy went back to his train.

'Choo-choo,' he said.

Catherine rang her friend Breege.

'Alex can't bring me in to see Daddy,' she said, 'Any chance you could do the honours?'

'Don't say he's working again.'

'He's gone to that conference thing in Galway.'

'Again? That man lives at these bloody things. You should divorce him. He's useless.'

'I know. They all are.'

'The car is bunched at the moment but Johnny is working on it. I hear some noises from the garage. If he gets it going I'll give you a shout.' Johnny was her husband. He was great at things like that.

'You're a peach,' she said.

She hung up the phone.

Everything seemed quiet. She turned on the radio. The weather forecast came on. A woman said Ballina was going to be wet for the day.

'Feck it,' she said.

'What did you say, Mammy?' Tommy asked.

'I said "Flip it."'

'Why?'

'I was hoping to go for a walk.'

The house was empty without him. It was empty a lot of times these days. It bothered her but she had to learn to live with it. That was what marriage was about. Sacrifice. Being on your own. Men were different than women. They needed to be out. It wasn't just about earning a living.

'Isn't that right, Tommy,' she said, 'Aren't men different than women?'

'Grnugg,' said Tommy. He was sucking on a sweet. Catherine laughed.

She decided she'd have a glass of wine to relax herself. She went over to the fridge to get it. She looked around but couldn't see it.

'That's strange,' she said.

'What's strange?' Tommy said.

'I was sure I got a bottle of Beaujolais at Tescos.'

Tommy looked up at her with his big eyes.

'Daddy took it,' he said.

'What?'

'Daddy put it in his car.'

'He couldn't have. He'd have told me.'

'I want to do a wee-wee,' said Tommy.

Catherine sighed. She brought him up the stairs and into the bathroom. He still had the train in his hands.

'You better leave that down,' she said.

He put it down. She sat him on the toilet seat.

What would Alex be doing with the wine, she wondered. She thought Tommy must have been imagining things.

The day dragged on. Rain fell over Bunree, over Bridge Street, over Corcoran Terrace where they lived with all the other newly-weds. It was down for the day and she didn't even have her wine to console her.

She went over to the biscuit tin where she kept her coins. Every time she came back from Centra she threw a few of them in there. She counted them out. Unfortunately, there weren't enough to pay for a taxi to the hospital.

'Shit,' she said to herself. It was down to Johnny now.

Alex drove back down towards Bunree. He turned left onto the Quay Road, where the new apartments had been built. He stopped the car and took out his phone. He checked it for messages but there were none.

He got out of the car and put his brief-case in the boot. He had the bottle of wine there as well. He took it out and put it on the back seat.

He drove to Rosanna's apartment. When he got there he pressed the bell that had her name on it.

She looked out of an upstairs window.

'Sorry I'm late,' he called up, 'We got delayed at the playground.'

'No problem,' she said, 'As long as we beat the traffic we'll be laughing.'

She closed the window. A few minutes later he saw her making her way down the stairs. She opened the door. She was in an evening dress.

'That won't look right at the conference,' he said.

'I have a trouser suit in my case.'

'Brilliant. Put that on instead.'

She lifted up the case from behind the door and handed it to him. He took it from her. He brought it out to the car.

'How are we for time?' she asked.

'Not great. She was fussing as usual.'

'We might be able to have a jar before things get going.'

'With a bit of luck.'

He gestured towards the bottle of wine in the back seat.

'Oh you brought it,' she said, 'You think of everything.'

'I know. That's why I'm going to be the next MD.'

'What about a glass now?' she suggested.

'At the wheel? Do you want to kill the pair of us? Curtail your sinful passions.'

'All right Mr Sensible.'

The day brightened. He started the engine. As they got on the road for Galway she reached for the bottle of wine.

'Do you mind if I have a glass?' she asked.

'If you must.'

There were two glasses in the glove compartment. She took one of them out and poured the wine into it. It made her giggly.

'What are you laughing at?' he said.

'I don't know. Nothing.'

She put her arms round him. She started kissing him.

'Not now,' he said.

'You're turning me on in that suit.'

'Stop. You'll make us crash.'

He put his foot on the floor and accelerated.

'Hey,' she said, 'Easy on there. I'll spill my drink.'

'Look Rosanna,' he said, 'You know I love you and all that but you have to start using your head a bit.'

'What do you mean?'

'It's not just the wine, it's the way you go on. I thought I told you not to ring me at home. She heard it.'

'Sorry,' she said, 'I was just wondering about the room.'"

'I told you I'd take care of it. You know I never forget stuff like that.'

'I won't do it again.'

'Good. She's not stupid. I don't want her asking too many questions.'

'I know that.'

'She checks my phones sometimes. If she finds your number on it, that's the end of us.'

'I won't do it again. Don't get a heart attack.'

'Just texts from now on, okay?'

'Okay. So when are you going to leave her for me?'

'Tomorrow. Now shut up while I get out of the traffic. This is the part where it gets tricky.'

They were on the motorway now. He overtook a truck that was ahead of him and got into the fast lane. Everything looked clear ahead of him.

Rosanna opened the sun roof. The sun glinted down through it.

'Tough luck on the poor bastards back in Ballina,' she said, 'being showered out of it.'

'What else is new?'

He looked at the needle. He was going about 85 miles an hour. He tried to hit 90.

'All we want now is to get done for speeding,' she said.

'The sooner we get there the more time we'll have to ourselves.'

He was starting to feel excited. She nuzzled against him again. This time he let her.

'You're a real little tiger, aren't you?' he said.

'Is it only now you're learning that?'

He gave her a hard look.

'By the way, don't talk to me at the conference unless you have to.'

'Am I allowed look at you? I mean I *am* your secretary, right?'

'You know what I mean.'

'Why are you always giving me these instructions as if I'm a five year old?'

'Because sometimes you act like a five year old. And because I don't want to get kicked out of my job.'

'This is 2019, darling. Most of the people you work with are playing away from home. Get with the programme.'

'I don't care if it's 3019. I just don't want Hamilton to know what's going on.'

'Why?'

'Because he likes her. They're friends. He probably wouldn't give me the promotion if he found out. He's like that. A family man.'

'You're not a bore. Do you know that?'

She started laughing. He laughed too.

'How am I going to keep away from you at this thing?' she said.

'Take a cold shower,' he advised.

They drove on as the sun streamed in on them. The car picked up speed. Before he knew it, they reached the toll.

As they got close to Galway he found himself relaxing. All the pressures suddenly went away from him. all the fears about being found out, about Catherine getting hysterical and going into one of her nervous breakdowns. It seemed to him as if they were always this way, as if he had no other life to worry about or be upset by, as if there was no past and no problem. There was only Rosanna in her purple dress kissing him and promising him everything.

'What time do we have to leave in the morning?' she asked as they got into Galway.

'Earlyish,' he told her, 'I have to bring her to the hospital when we get back. The old lad is still knocked up with the gammy leg.'

Sunday

On Sundays the death of the spirit appears.
People loll on footpaths
at Moyletts corner
chewing gum
and measuring their spits
or making smart comments
at the well-endowed girls
from Convent Hill
who stare at the ground
before crossing the bridge
To dubious nirvanas
in Muredachs
where they're reminded
of their eternal end
by a sad-eyed priest
in purple.

They pretend they're happy
as they whistle in graveyards
or pray to Dominic Savio
and Gerard Majella
at St. Patrick's Well
or leave relics
at the holy tree across the road
where discarded ragcloths
fly in the wind.

Sunday, they think,
this journey to the centre
of themselves,
a day when suffering is offered up
and they wonder where their life has gone
or if they have one.

I have devised a calendar
where no Sunday exists,
where Saturday immediately segues into Monday,
thereby doing away with this
limbo of procrastination
where everyone prepares notes
for redemptive tomorrows
and an unanswered child
cries brokenly
in the night.

St. Muredach's

St. Muredach's probably wasn't any better or worse than any other college from the past, or even now, but it seemed that way when I was growing up. Children didn't really have a voice then and the world of an adult was law. Things went the other way in the following decades, which made me feel doubly hard done by when I became a teacher. When, I wondered, was my own day in the sun going to come?

My brothers walked me to school every day like jailers because I never wanted to go. The teachers called me Rip Van Winkle. I was always falling asleep in class or answering questions to the wrong things, like questions in Irish when it was sums time or maybe the other way round. I don't know why I did that. Maybe it was from nerves. I used to get beaten for this until my hands burned but my father would make everything all right when I came home. He used to pull out his false teeth and comb his hair down over his forehead and make funny faces. Sometimes he put a torch under it in the darkness, making him look like a vampire. All of this made me forget about the pain of the beatings, at least until the next time.

Television came to the town, black and white at first and then colour. We stopped swapping comics and playing taws and watched it all the time. I hated the serious programmes but I liked *Kit Carson* and *The Cisco Kid*. *The Virginian* was all right but there was too much talking in it and not even any Indians.

In Muredach's I continued to give the wrong answers and the priests continued to make fun of me. They told me I'd never amount to anything in life. They advised me to go down to Tim West's hardware shop on Garden Street and get measured up for a shovel because that's the only kind of job I'd ever manage to get. I used to wish someone would kidnap them or something so that I could sleep easily in my bed once again.

My brothers got jobs in other towns after they left school. I was glad for them but lonely too even though I wouldn't admit it. After they were gone my sisters rounded on me, forcing me to play with them. I did that grudgingly because there was nobody else around now but I didn't like to be seen with them on the street. If you were spotted playing girl games people would call you a wimp.

Dennis came to the college from a small school in the country. He was a ruffian but an irresistible one. He was always getting himself suspended and then worming his way back into the class. 'I'm teacher's pet,' he joked, 'that's why he keeps me in a cage at the back of the room.'

We sparked off one another immediately. He saw me as one of his protégés, somebody he found it easy to entertain. Or as the priests saw it, corrupt. He made it his ambition to drive me off the straight and narrow. By now I had a lot of wild oats to sow, having come from such a quiet family. My parents warned me away from him but that only increased his spell.

One night my father said that if I kept going out with him I was finished in the house. I couldn't promise him that I'd stop so he sent me to my room. A few hours later I shinnied down the drainpipe and went on a midnight fishing spree with my new dangerous friend.

That was the beginning of the end of my stability at home. Afterwards I was 'in' as far as Dennis was concerned. I became an unofficial member of his club of reprobates with all the knock-on effects that implied. I was expected to emulate his own rebelliousness and I did that in my own tinpot way.

Instead of just being dumb at school now I became cheeky as well.

'It's natural to that bucko,' the priests said, referring to

Dennis, 'but not to you.'

They punished me more severely than him. 'Don't get too big for your boots,' they warned me, 'you might fall on your arse.' There were letters home complaining about me which my parents couldn't understand. It had never happened to any of my brothers.

Why was I destroying the family name? I felt sorry for them but I had to do what I was doing. I was going to be beaten in class anyway so what did the reason matter.

Dennis brought me to places I hadn't even known existed in the town before. I met people as reckless as himself, people who didn't fear consequences. He became my role model. I even copied his chat-up lines to girls.

'The more you treat them like dirt,' he advised me, 'the more they chase you.' He was going with a Leaving Cert student called Annette by this stage but for some reason she fastened on to me instead when she met me. I was slow to react but Dennis told me I'd be mad to let the opportunity slip. He'd had his pick of them and she was just another notch on his bedpost.

Annette dressed in shiny disco jeans and tight jumpers that exaggerated her figure. She smoked cigarettes like a chimney, blowing out the smoke in rings. When I asked her how she did that she just threw her eyes up to heaven and told me not to annoy her. 'You're such a child, aren't you?' she'd say, looking bored. She wore make-up that looked like flour and enough perfume to satisfy the entire population of Connacht.

'How much does she charge you for a bit of how's-your-father?' Dennis asked me once. Whenever we went to the pictures it was always her that took the initiative, drawing my hand up under her jumper to feel her breasts. She gave me kisses that almost suffocated me. So did the smell of her perfume.

In class Dennis went from bad to worse. One day he told

Mr. Forbes, our history teacher, to go fuck himself after he gave out to him for not having an exercise done. The president threatened to expel him when they heard about it, which amused Dennis. If he did that, he said, he'd burn the college down.

Instead he was bundled off to a corrective centre in Kerry as punishment. His parents didn't object. In some ways I think they were glad to get him out of the house. He'd been terrorising the neighbours as well and there were calls to the door. 'Well. 'I guess it's adios to my best amigo,' he said to me when he got the news. I should have been flattered but I felt he'd have someone else to take my place within the week.

After he was gone I got down to my studies as if he never existed. Annette disappeared out of my life, telling everyone in the local cafeteria that I wasn't up for mischief anymore and therefore no good. Before the Leaving Cert she left town. A rumour went around that she was pregnant and being sent to another county by the nuns to have the child secretly. In Dennis' absence, the authorities were sorting us all out.

At home things started to happen as well. My father got into debt and his moods grew black. Then my mother developed a back problem. She was in agony with it. There was a question they might operate for a while but then they ruled against it. She got some physiotherapy but it didn't do much good. All she had were painkillers then, and their effect wore off after a while.

When I visited her in the hospital she tried not to complain but I could see the pain in her face. The main thing that concerned her was whether my father was minding himself. I told her he was but I knew he couldn't cope with the loneliness. After a while he took up a second job and was out most of the time. He said the reason was money but I thought he was just doing it for therapy. At home he had too much time to brood.

After I did the Leaving Cert I made a snap decision to go to university. Nobody could believe it, least of all myself. I wasn't sure of the reason. It was the last place I thought I'd end up. Maybe I was trying to prove something to myself about not being as dumb as the teachers always claimed I was.

I read books from morning to night. It was easy in one way because I had all the time in the world available to me now that I wasn't raising Cain with Dennis. Or 'swimming with the women' as the president put it.

For the next few months I drowned myself in a labyrinth of obscure facts. I was glad of the distraction they provided from worrying about my mother.

My Leaving Cert results were good enough for me to qualify for a grant. My father was over the moon when they came in the post. My mother tried to feign enthusiasm but she was really too weak to care. She was in and out of hospital all the time now. I felt the situation would continue like that until her condition became chronic. I had a conscience about leaving her when it came time to go to Dublin but she told me I deserved what I worked for and that she'd be fine.

Leaving Ballina was like having a limb wrenched from me. I gave out about it but when push came to shove it was all I knew. I had a love-hate relationship to it. It was like Catholicism. You gave out about it but you couldn't escape it.

Over the following months I mixed with people more privileged than myself in the university, articulate sons and daughters of the well-to-do from all corners of Ireland. Milky-faced teenagers who spoke in booming voices and solved the problems of the world over coffee in the campus bar. I said what was expected of me in their presence but I knew I could never belong to their world.

I lived in a bedsit hardly bigger than a bathroom and took the bus to the campus every morning in a daze. I was working without purpose to satisfy some obscure ambition to get the best out of myself, whatever that meant. On automatic pilot I regurgitated platitudes from dusty tomes to satisfy my tutors in the corridors of a converted horse show stadium in the early months of summer.

When I went back to Ballina during the holidays I pretended to everyone that I was happy. One of my brothers was in insurance now. Another had set up a carpentry shop down by the Humbert Monument. Whenever we met we were falsely polite to one another, a contrast to all the years of bickering. One of my sisters got an office job in Claremorris. The other one was teaching in Gortnor Abbey. The house was so bereft of atmosphere I felt almost nostalgic for the old hostilities. When I enquired about Dennis there was a palpable tension. Someone who knew him said he wasn't the same man he'd been when I knew him, that he'd crumbled under the strict regime of the place in Kerry. 'The system always gets you sooner or later,' he said witheringly.

My mother came home from hospital in a wheelchair. She'd had an operation after all but it was only partly successful. Even so, she didn't let the pain get to her. Her main problem was being out of control. She couldn't do things for us now that she used to take for granted and that depressed her. My father waited on her hand and foot but she didn't want that. She resented him for her dependence on him. Up to now it had been the other way round.

She enquired vacantly about my studies and I answered her equally vacantly. The world of books was as anathema to her as it had once been to me. We might as well have been taking about outer space. Whenever I asked her about her health she gave a rueful sigh.

'It's no good,' she said once, 'I'm finished.'

My father's eyes misted over whenever she went on like this. 'She'll be fine,' he kept saying, 'She's just confused. It must be all the tablets she's on.' But in the middle of the night I'd hear him sobbing gently to himself in the kitchen after she'd gone to sleep.

I started to look up old classmates to keep my mind off her but it didn't work. We weren't easy in one another's company. Either they'd changed or I had; I wasn't totally sure. Whichever it was, I had few people to communicate with now. I called on Annette once and she was uncharacteristically quiet. She'd had her child by now and it mellowed her. She had no wish to marry, she told me, no wish to have any truck with men at all.

When I asked her about Dennis she said he'd got married. I was shocked. I felt I had to pinch myself to believe it. She said he was living in a snazzy bungalow outside the town. I thought I'd heard everything now.

'He must have had a brain transplant or something,' she said casually, 'One of these days he'll be in the Resident's Association.'

When I visited him he looked weather-beaten. The spirit seemed to have gone out of him. His hair was short and his clothes uncharacteristically tidy.

He gave me a friendly hug when we met but when we sat down to talk he was guarded with me. I felt he was ashamed of what he called 'going straight'. His wife was a girl I half knew, a demure type he'd have taken great delight in jeering as a Holy Mary a few years before. I gathered from the atmosphere between them that they didn't know one another that well. Or maybe it was my presence that was creating the tension.

'Meet Helena,' he announced, 'the eighth wonder of the world.' I wasn't sure if he was being sarcastic or not. She gave me a limp handshake, looking at me oddly.

'Dennis told me all about you,' she said flatly.

'I could take that two ways,' I said, but she didn't laugh. I felt I represented an intangible threat to her. Maybe Dennis painted me as the ringleader for our shenanigans in order to increase his credibility as marriage material.

'I believe the pair of you raised some hell in your day,' she said with a leer.

'It was all his fault.'

'I bet you say that to all the girls.'

Dennis tried to lighten the atmosphere by telling me some of his old jokes but they fell on stony ground. I found myself shifting uncomfortably in my seat, wanting the visit to be over. What in God's name had they done to him in Kerry? It was as if someone had removed the batteries from a wind-up toy.

Instead of being offered beer I was given a cup of tea. He made hand signals to me about a secret stash of booze he seemed to have somewhere nearby but he didn't follow up on it. He was obviously terrified of Helena. Was this the same man who nearly burned down the school?

'I can see he's the model husband now,' I said to her, half in jest.

'I haven't house-trained him fully yet,' she said, 'but at least he knows how to use the bathroom now. And he doesn't eat his food with his fingers. At least not much anyway.'

'That's a development,' I said.

'What about yourself?' she asked, 'is there any sign of you to get hitched? I heard you used to go out with that Annette one. She's a bit of a hausey, I believe.'

'Not any more. She must be on the same pills Dennis is taking.'

'What's that supposed to mean?' Helena asked.

'Fuck off,' Dennis said to me through gritted teeth.

'Language, please,' said Helena, slapping him playfully on the wrist. Dennis winced, pretending to be in great pain.

188

'Do you see her at all now?' she asked me.

'Never would be too soon for that, I'm afraid.'

'I hear tell she's more kindly disposed to you these days.'

'If she is she keeps it well hidden.'

When Helena went out to make tea, Dennis took a bottle of whiskey out of his pocket and had a quick swig of it. He asked me if I'd like to go down to the pub for a pint with him but I wasn't really sure he wanted to. I said we'd leave it for the moment and he looked relieved.

She came back with the tea and we drank it. The conversation dried up before I had two sips taken. It was also cold and too milky. I wanted to be away so I made up some excuse about having to be at a meeting somewhere. I felt they both knew I was making it up but they didn't care. I was doing us all a favour.

Dennis and myself hugged awkwardly at the doorstep, promising to hook up again soon.

'I don't know whether to be relieved or disappointed at how you've turned out,' Helena said to me as she shook my hand.

'What do you mean by that?' I asked her.

'You're so civilised.'

'Don't believe everything you see,' I said, 'I'm just a good actor.' She forced a laugh at that. Dennis tried to force one too. I waved goodbye to the pair of them. As I shut the gate I looked back at them and waved again. They seemed like a very old couple suddenly, a pair far beyond their years.

I couldn't get the pair of them out of my mind after I left. I knew they looked all wrong together but sometimes those were the kinds of relationships that lasted. Who was I to judge anyway. I felt my own life was a car crash.

The summer came to an end and I started to worry about going back to the university. Now that I'd got a break from it I wasn't sure if it was what I wanted any more. I asked myself if I could be happy in Ballina or would it get in on me over the years running into the same people over and over again. Was Dublin any better? Maybe I'd always be chasing shadows.

My mother seemed to be withering before my eyes. I knew if anything happened to her, my father's resolve would crumble. I tried to be cheery when I was around them but I wasn't as good an actor as I pretended to Helena and they saw through me.

'This is no place for someone of your age,' my father said one night when I was loafing around the house, 'You should be out carousing.' Maybe he was right, but who was there to carouse with?

To get away from him, or from my thoughts, I went walking through the outskirts of the town. Almost overnight it seemed to have been taken over by video parlours and fast-food joints. I watched people moping around the streets and wondered if I'd end up like that too if I stayed. Now and then I ran into some of the priests from the college. They were always nicer to you after you left Muredach's, as if they had no right to tell you what to do anymore. That was such a relief. I saw them as people now, not forces of authority. I felt sorry for some of them. They looked faintly irrelevant outside the security of their fortifications.

I remembered the power they had over me, the fear they could give rise to, how they'd milked it constantly. They were more like toothless dogs now as they hugged their cassocks against the wind, getting their constitutional on Enniscrone beach before heading home to an evening alone or with their housekeepers. I knew a lot of them would have preferred to be on the missions. A life of teaching, I felt, was ultimately unfulfilling. You were trying to live other people's lives for them without having one of your own.

I remembered the way they used to tell me I was a disaster at my lessons, how they used to warn Dennis and myself away from 'the sins of the flesh.' The expression had always made me think of huge, voluptuous women with white skin - the kind you saw in films by people like Fellini. The emphasis on sex was ultimately what did the church in, I knew now. If it could sort out its attitude to that, maybe we could be a good Catholic country again. As things stood, the only people who seemed to be still practising their religion were the old people and the foreigners who came here. Everyone else seemed to have dropped into a black hole. Or discovered that strange phenomenon called Life.

At the beginning of October I got a flyer from the university about registering for the new year.

'I know you don't want to leave us,' my father said, 'but there's nothing here for you now. A blind man could see that.' Maybe a blind man could, but I couldn't. I was still attached to the place.

'Am I such poor company that you want to get rid of me that badly?' I joked. He gave an awkward laugh.

I decided to give the Uni a bash. If it didn't work out I could always come back. That was the way about small towns. They were always there for you – like parents.

My mother was upstairs in bed on the morning I left. She did her best to ask me practical questions about what I was studying but she couldn't hide the pain she was in.

'I'm going to teach here eventually if I can arrange it,' I said to try and make her feel a bit better, 'I'll apply to Muredach's if a position becomes available. That way I'll be able to get my revenge on a whole new generation. I'll be a right tyrant, beating the lard out of them every time they look sideways at me.'

'It would be great if you came back here to live,' she said, trying to put on a happy face. I wasn't sure if she meant it or not. A few years ago she'd have been over the moon about the prospect of having me around all the time but now she was probably too sick to care.

My father drove me to the train in his old jalopy. I felt like someone in a time warp, a traveller out of his era. I wondered what I was going back to: a building of plate glass where scholars tried to look important, impressing one another with phrases other people created. There was a hobo at the train station when we got there. I'd trade places with him in a heartbeat, I thought, anything to relieve the chilling anonymity of it all.

When I suggested as much to my father he thought I was having him on. He couldn't understand that anyone who had the opportunities I did could be so casual about them, so dismissive.

'You're right,' I said, 'I'm an ungrateful brat. Hopefully I'll get sense when I'm your age.' He wasn't sure if I was serious or not. Neither was I.

We parked the car and walked towards the train. I asked him if my mother would be all right and he nodded uncertainly. He got on the train with me before it started. He told me to mind myself. The engine started and he got out of the carriage. Suddenly, standing there on the platform, he looked like a very old man. I told him to keep his strength up for my mother's sake. He said he would.

'We'll see you at Christmas,' he said. I should have been looking forward to that but I wasn't. I felt worse now than if I hadn't come home at all. There was too much happening, both inside and outside myself. Would my mother be worse? Would I be able to take it? Would he?

As the train inched forward it seemed to me as if I'd lost any ambition about what I wanted to do with my life, or not do. My father told me I was a real man now but inside I felt I was dying. I felt everything we'd been told at school about life opening up opportunities and happiness was a lie, a trap. I'd always be a searcher after some vague magic that I wouldn't be capable of recognising even if I was presented with it on a plate.

When I got to Dublin there was a letter waiting there for me from Dennis. It was written in his familiar scratchy scrawl, the last remnant of the person he used to be. He said he'd up in town sometime in the autumn and he'd like it if we could 'touch base' to make up for that bad visit I'd had with him when we were both hamstrung by Helena. As I read his words, for some reason I had to laugh. 'The little lady won't be with me,' he added at the end. I had an image of a child getting up to harmless mischief while his mother wasn't looking.

He scrawled 'From One Survivor To Another' on the back of the envelope. Maybe, I thought, 'From One Sell-out Merchant to Another' would have been more appropriate.

I wrote back to him telling him that that would be great, that we'd really let it rip together like in the old days. I was making out as if marriage, or all the soul-destroying years of conformity had never happened, that we could still be the Likely Lads on the tear once again.

As I posted him his reply I imagined him in the Shelbourne Bar with his toothy grin and his ready one-liners, cracking lewd jokes with all and sundry as he stood them drinks, retreating back to his bungalow in Foxford afterwards to do Helena's bidding, a buck-lepping day out with an old renegade like myself so much ballast to shore against the ruins of his pallid, reinvented self.

Belmullet Feud

A band is striking up in the half-light, going through their playlist with some concern. In front of them the dancers take their partners, circling around each other stealthily.

He moves through the undulating bodies looking for a man he fought not half an hour ago, a man who has nothing to lose now no matter what damage he caused. The music booms around him as he searches for him in the sea of bodies.

Was it masochism or hatred that caused him to come here tonight? A part of him wants to forget anything happened between them but there's also a voice inside him that says this would be suicide, that it would be playing into his hands.

He remembers the night he found him with the syringe in his hand, only the voice of Eily stopping him from killing him as the cattle coughed up their death-breaths onto the parched grass. 'Let him go,' she screamed. As he looked at her he wondered if she hadn't still some tenderness in her heart for him, this man who'd once been his rival for her.

He expects to see him every time he turns a corner but when he gets to the bar it's not Mulrooney that stands in front of him but Anna Kelleher, this beauty in place of the ruggedness he envisaged.

'Well,' she says, grinning. She knows his mind is light years away from her, as it usually is whenever they meet.

'Anna,' he says. She stands up from her stool and gives him a hug. Her jumper is clinging tightly to her, already firing his desire for her.

'You look nervous,' she says, reaching out to touch him. 'Am I that off-putting?'

'What are you doing here?' he asks.

'Roughly the same thing as the other 200 people, I think. As far as I know it's not a breach of the peace to attend a dance.'

'I thought you had to mind your mother tonight,' he says, screwing up his eyebrows.

'Well I must say you're delighted to see me. Would you like me to go back to her?'

'I'm sorry,' he says, 'You caught me by surprise. I'm not myself tonight.'

'I know what you need,' she says, elbowing up against him, 'a nice big glass of whiskey. Walk this way and I'll procure your medicine for you.'

He watches the easy movement of her body as she leads him to the bar and sits him down, giving into her mothering for the relief it affords him, listening without interruption as she launches into a diatribe about her life over the past two months, becoming entranced once again by her spell as if she's a blanket to pull over the world.

She brings him a drink and starts to speak of her life as a mother's nurse, of the death in life that's a secretary's career in the sticks, the even greater death that's the night-life of a single woman abroad in a world of bachelor farmers. She speaks of relationships she's had since they last met, mere trivia to the experience she's had with him.

'Why don't we go out to the car?' he says. Her eyes light up like a child who's just been offered a present. But then the disillusion comes into them again. She frowns.

'We can't, John. You know we can't so why do you ask me?'

'I ask you because I want you to.'

'It wouldn't be fair. You know that. Not fair to you or to Eily and most of all not fair to me.'

'We don't need to do anything except drive.'

'Maybe that would work for you .You have a life to go back to. She's about to have a baby. Have you forgotten that?'

'I need to talk to you,' he says, 'I love you.'

For a moment she sees something turbulent in his eyes, an insecurity she hasn't known before.

He leads her across the dance floor, past the multitude of dancing shapes, a couple like any other, and suddenly she doesn't care about consequences anymore, doesn't care about the remorse tomorrow will bring.

Sean Redmond is at the door when they get to it. He knows he won't approve of them going off together.

'Well Sean,' he says, 'How is life treating you?'

'Not too bad.'

'We're going out to the car. If you see Mulrooney, come out and tell me.'

'I will if I can find you.'

'We won't be far away. And you might drop in on Eily on the way home. Tell her to lock all the doors in case he goes out that direction.'

'Can you not do that yourself?'

'I'm tied up,' he says, indicating Anna.

'I can't keep covering for you.'

'I know that. I won't ask you anything else after tonight. I really appreciate this.'

They go outside and sit in the car. He puts his arm around her. They kiss.

'Well,' she says, 'When are you going to murder Eily for me?'

'Will tonight when I get home be time enough?'

'I'll think about it. We can use strychnine or arsenic. I know all the leading suppliers.'

The wind comes up and shuffles the branches of the trees. He turns on the radio. The weather report comes on. A storm is brewing, the announcer says. There are warnings of fallen trees and other dangers. He releases himself from her embrace and lights a cigarette.

'Why are you so tense tonight?' she says, 'What's wrong?'

'I'm permanently tense. You should know that.'

'Don't be. There's no reason for it.'

'I'll try.'

He starts to ask her questions about her life but she tells him to say nothing, to just let the moment be. As he takes in the wonder of her features he tells himself he has to be with this woman all the time, that he has to leave his wife for her. But equally he knows that tomorrow will bring deliberation again, prevarication, the postponing he's famous for.

'How is Eily?' she asks, 'It must be near the time now.' She's referring to the baby they're about to have, a subject he always shies away from when they meet.

'Let's not talk about that.'

'Why? Because it makes you feel guilty?'

'We should go back in, Anna. We're attracting attention sitting here.'

Now that the threat of losing him appears, she wants him more.

'Let's just drive,' she says, 'I don't think I could face a crowd of people now.'

'Where do you want to go?'

'To the end of the earth.'

He starts the engine and they drive into the night. Some of the roads are impassable because of the uprooted trees. He suggests turning back but she makes him go onwards, rolling down the window and sticking her head out as he spins round the bends, the wind whirling her hair into a frizz. He feels his eyes drooping but she continues to press him further, deeper and deeper into the hinterland as if you can solve a problem by driving far enough away from it.

'You really love me more than her, don't you?' she says and he has to reassure her, though inwardly knowing the waste of it all. He tries to think of something to say to take her down from her elation but each time he talks she reverts back to this comfortable hobbyhorse.

Eventually he stops the car. He puts his head in his hands.

'What's wrong?' she asks.

'I don't know. You worry me when you say things like that.'

'Is that because they're true? You'd prefer me if I was a one-night stand, wouldn't you? That way there'd be no complications.'

'Why are you doing this to me?'

'Because it's gone on too long, John, and because I'm starting to suddenly realise you're like every other man I've ever met.'

'All right, maybe I am. So are you telling me it's over?'

'I didn't say that.'

He listens to a bird squawking in a tree, puncturing the tension between them.

'You'd prefer me if I was a cold fish, wouldn't you?' she says then, jumping up in her seat, 'Like Eily.'

'I wouldn't like you any other way than how you are. But sometimes you scare me.'

'Why?'

'Because if things don't work out between us you'll take it too badly.'

'Maybe you'd like me to go off with someone else.'

'How could you think that?'

'It would make it easy for you. You could walk away from me with your hands clean.'

'Why are you saying things like that? Are you trying to make fun of me?'

'You know something I realised about you recently, John? Do you know why you won't leave Eily for me?'

'Tell me,' he says dutifully, 'Tell me why I won't leave Eily for you.'

'Because I give you an exhilaration you feel you have no right to,' she says. 'Because at the back of it all you're in love with your dead life.'

He smiles disparagingly.

'You're right of course,' he says.

Sometimes in the last few months he's found himself praying that she'd stop seeing him if it would make living with Eily easier. Sometimes it seems to him that the death of his desire would make him happier than its fulfilment.

She looks at his long, hard face, trying to remember the first time she saw him. He was unloading milk crates at the time and she couldn't take her eyes off him. There was a kind of primitive strength in his movements. She wanted him to talk to her but all he did was stare at her as if she was some kind of inanimate object. Her mother had warned her away from him afterwards, sensing something dangerous about him, something ominous. But she persisted, persisted even after he married Eily.

'Let's go back,' he says, the magic of the night broken as a blankness comes into his mind, the inevitable anti-climax that surfaces at the end of every time they meet, 'Eily will be worried about me.'

'Another half-hour won't kill her.'

'It isn't her, it's me. I have a situation at the moment. A man has been poisoning my cattle. I'm taking him to court next week.'

'I know,' she says, 'It's that Mulrooney man, isn't it? People have been telling me about him. I expected you to bring it up sooner or later.'

'I wasn't going to. There's no point in boring you with my problems.'

'There's nothing boring about it. My mother told me your life was at stake. They say insanity runs in his family.'

'As far as I'm concerned he's the only insane one. He feeds off hatred.'

'Do you think you can handle him?'

'I don't know. His recklessness makes him clumsy but it also makes him dangerous.'

She sees a ponderousness coming into him that she hasn't known before.

'Let Eily fight him,' she says jocosely. 'If, they both snuff it, then we can go off together. They might even fall for one another.'

'They did once. That's half the problem.'

She screws up her eyes at this.

'You mean they went out together?'

'They were nearly married. He thinks I stole her from him.'

'Did you?'

'No. It was over long before I came on the scene. He needed someone to take it out on.'

'You'd say that anyway,' she says, 'you with your self-righteousness,' Her barb makes him laugh. When she talks like this she can make him forget any problem, can make it non-existent.

A gentle snow starts to fall as he drives her home. The flakes sail down onto the landscape like forgotten memories, like wool. In a part of himself he feels remorseful. Another part is blameless, as if the situation has always been out of his hands, as if he's always been its unwilling victim. She rests her head in his lap and he wonders what it is that draws her to him. What is it that draws either her or Eily? He feels he has little to offer them. He'd be content with either one, he thinks, if he didn't know the other. But now that he knows both he's content with neither of them. Such was the irony of his life, maybe the irony of all lives.

When he reaches her house he turns off the engine. They sit in the silence. Then he sees her mother turning on a light in the hallway.

'Oops,' she says, 'She sees me. I better go.'

'Can I see you again?' he says as she starts to get out.

She sighs.

'Is there any point?'

'That's up to you, Anna.'

'No, it's up to you. You can't have the two of us anymore. It has to be one or the other.'

'I can't talk about that tonight. As soon as this cattle business sorts itself out.'

'Then there'll be something else. That's always been the way, hasn't it? Stolen moments in hotel rooms as all your dramas unfold.'

'You make me sound like something from a film.'

'That's how it seems to me a lot of the time.'

'Would you see me tomorrow?' he asks but she shakes her head.

'That would only make it worse. I'd be better off forgetting about you altogether, John Moran. You're only causing me misery.'

'Don't say things like that. It's not true.'

He tries to embrace her but she pushes him away from her, denying him this final seal on the night.

He feels clumsy in the nakedness of his emotion.

'Will your mother give you a hard time for being late?' he says for something to say, trying to hold on to her any way he can.

'Hardly. Once she sees I'm all right she relaxes. She's busy offering up novenas for my soul at the moment. I think she's given up on me at this stage. Maybe I've given up on myself.'

'Don't sell yourself short, Anna. You're the purest spirit I've ever met.'

'Says he as he deserts me.'

'That's not fair. Someday I'll have the strength to leave her for you.'

'And pigs might fly. No, I'll always be just the other woman to you. That's the way you like it. Two for the price of one, right?'

There's a cruelty in her smile but he has no answer for her. She gets out of the car and walks up the avenue to her door. She gives him a small wave and then she's gone in. After a minute he sees a light go on. He hears a conversation beginning, the catalogue of lies she would have prepared for her mother, just as he has his own catalogue for Eily.

As he drives home he tries to forget her and think of his next move. That's the way his life has always been. It's like there have always been two people inside him, each of them living only with the present emergency.

He thinks about Eily, wondering how she'll be with him now that he's been away for an evening, if she'll broach the subject of an affair she's half-known about all along. Or will she be too taken up with her own situation to care much where he spends his spare time now? He imagines her in the bedroom feeling her stomach, wondering how long more it will be, this climax to all the months of expectation. At times they've acted as if the baby will bring them ecstasy and then there are the nights when he has images of it being stillborn, images of it being deformed. Once in a nightmare he had she died giving birth.

The farmyard is quiet when he gets home, all the usual noises quelled. For a moment he thinks he sees the shadow of a man in the stables but he ignores it, imagining it to be one of the horses. He goes into the house and takes off his coat.

He tries to think of an excuse for his lateness as he walks up the stairs to the bedroom. When he reaches the landing he sees her lying sprawled across the bed like someone in a trance. He wonders if Redmond would have told her where he's been, who he's been with.

'You're home,' she says flatly. 'I thought you might have been gone for the night.'

'I told you I'd be back, Eily. Don't be like that. Did Sean call?'

'Yes. He said Mulrooney was on the warpath.'

'He said he'd kill me if I pressed charges. I fought him in O'Mahony's earlier.'

'So I heard. And you also saw Anna Kelleher.'

There were never any secrets with women. It was always thus and it always would be thus. The very walls seemed to have ears.

'I didn't plan for that to happen. I went to the marquee looking for Mulrooney but he wasn't there. '

'What made you think he would be?'

'He knew I...' he starts to say and then stops, catching himself out as he always does the more she probes.

'He knew you were going to see Anna Kelleher. Isn't that what you were going to say?'

He looks away from her.

'It's all right,' she says, 'You don't have to lie to me. I'm not a child. You can go off with her for all I care. There now. Does that make you feel better?'

'Don't say that. You know I love you.'

'Don't tell me any more lies,' she says tiredly, 'At least grant me that.'

'Stop it. It's all in your imagination.'

'Is she good in bed?' she says, 'Does she do imaginative positions?'

He wonders where it will all end. He's paying now as he's always paid for any entanglement he's ever had with another woman, paying with the abuse that will last all this night and all the nights following until it will eventually drive him back to Anna again, the final absurdity.

Do Redmond and the others live different lives than he does, he wonders, these men who seem to approximate to perfect peace when he sees them in O'Mahony's, laughing gaily over some television programme or relaying the story of a sick cow. Or do they too return to quiet desperation each night when the crowds are gone?

He goes over to the window and looks out at the fields. He wonders why he bothers trying to seek a way out of his problem, why he bothers trying to make a living out of land that has meant nothing but misery to him since he came to it. This proliferation of stitchwort and furze he calls his home, he thinks, looking out at the acres of infertility, at the ground that refuses to bend to the blade, even in the summer heat. It had once been important to him, important even in its recalcitrance, the greater the sweat involved in bringing home the harvest the greater the pleasure afterwards. But now he's tired of it all, tired as an old man is tired, tired waiting for the returns that will never come.

'Sometimes I think we should just move away from here,,' he says, an injection of spirit striking him from somewhere, the way he can sometimes get an idea unrelated to anything and it can seem the perfect answer. 'Would you not like to get away from all this, Eily, away from all this. . . muck?'

'That's always been your solution, hasn't it? Run away and we'll all live happily ever after. But we all know there's another Anna Kelleher in the next county, and the next one and the next as well. We can't run away from them all, can we?'

'Anna Kelleher should never have happened. I take full responsibility for her. I've always admitted it but I'm trying to fight it.'

'That's what you said the last time.'

'This time I mean it.'

'You're either a very bad liar or a very foolish man,' she says, turning over in the bed, putting an end to his excuses as she always does, sparing him any further duplicity. He searches her face for tenderness but it's as expressionless as a piece of furniture.

'What did Sean say to you?' he asks.

'Just what you told him to say. He was shaking like a leaf. You'd think it was himself Mulrooney was after.'

Mulrooney. How the very name made him wince.

'Do you think he'll show?'

'How would I know? You're the one who talks about him non-stop.'

'The reason I do is because I'm afraid. For both of us. I sent Sean up to look in on you.'

'I would have fought him better than Sean.'

'I didn't mean that. I sent him to tell you to lock all the doors.'

'Do you think locks on the doors will stop a man like him? Fort Knox would be a doddle to him.'

'Why didn't you go somewhere then? Why didn't you stay at your father's house if that's the way you feel?'

He watches her eyes grow tearful.

'Because I'm a fool. Because somewhere in a crazy part of me I thought you'd put me before her. On this night above any one, the night when our child might arrive.'

He sighs at the absurdity of it all. Each time it happens it seems to get worse, this endless tirade of vindictiveness and recrimination.

'Did Sean tell you I was with her?'

'He didn't want to. I dragged it out of him. I was better off knowing anyway. Mulrooney could have gutted me five times over by the time you got back.'

He's surprised by the fear in her voice. He hasn't seen her like this before.

'That wouldn't happen,' he says, 'He's after nobody but me if that's any consolation to you.'

'I don't agree. He's never forgiven me for leaving him. He told me that one night in a pub. '

'If he did it was the drink talking. He knew it wouldn't have worked out between you two.'

She sits up in the bed, her face contorted in pain from the weight of the child inside her.

'Why don't you let the courts take care of him?' she says, 'He's threatened you in public, hasn't he? Wouldn't there be witnesses?'

'The courts are nothing. I've got advice. The worst they'll do is give him a suspended sentence. He'd be out after a few weeks. If he wasn't, his friends would hunt me down.'

'And if you kill him what do you think they're going to do - drink to your health?'

'It won't come to that. He's only interested in seeing if I scare easy. If you stand up to him he'll fold.'

'I wonder.'

'It's over for tonight anyway. You should sleep now. Don't think about him anymore.'

'I've done all the sleeping I'm going to do.'

She turns in the bed. He watches the pained hugeness of her stomach.

'How are the contractions?' he asks. He wonders if the child will ever be born now, this child that could make or break their future together.

'Does it matter? Maybe if it died on me it would be for the best.'

'Don't think like that or something will go wrong.'

He wonders if it's a pose of hers, this negativity. Or has he driven her to it?

'Did the doctor come this morning?' he asks, seeking some form of sanctuary in the factual.

'He said he wouldn't be bringing me in for a week.'

'That's nonsense. Your time is up. I'm sending you in tomorrow.'

'He won't hear of it. There are no beds.'

'I'll get one for you if I have to break the doors down.'

'That sounds noble' she says, resisting the tenderness the remark nudges in her, 'but it won't do any good.'

'I'll ring him. I won't take no for an answer.'

'There's no point. I've tried him already. He's out. Even the locum is out. Everyone goes out on Friday nights. . . everyone except Eily Moran.'

'What did you ring him for?'

'The pain.'

'Is it still kicking?'

'Up until a while ago it was. It's stopped now. Maybe it's stopped forever. Wouldn't it be nice if it stopped forever? We'd have no burdens then, no complications to our pretty little life.'

'Stop,' he says, clutching his head, 'That's a sick thing to say.'

'That's right,' she says, 'I'm sick. We're all sick, aren't we? Sick of life and sick of marriages and sick of husbands and...'

He's about to roar at her in frustration when he looks through the window. As he does so, he sees a flame curling up from the courtyard.

For a moment he's confused. Then it all becomes clear. It's almost as if the inevitable has happened. A light switch flicks inside him.

'The stables,' he says.

'What?'

'The stables. He's in there.'

'What are you talking about?'

'Look out the window.'

She starts to get out of the bed but winces in pain again.

'Wait,' he says, 'I'm going down.'

'Down to what? What's going on?'

'The stables are on fire.'

'I don't believe you.'

She drags herself across the floor. Before she gets to the window she already sees the light from the flames.

'Oh no,' she says, 'Oh Jesus no.'

'I saw a shadow as I was coming in. I should have guessed.'

'Let me ring the guards.'

'No. Just wait here.'

'Why? What are you going to do?'

'I need to let the horses out. It's only starting. They might be all right.'

He bangs his fist along the wall, cursing himself for his ignorance. He knows now that the whole night has been leading to this.

'Don't go down there,' she says, tugging at him,, 'He'll be waiting for you. I beg you.'

He isn't listening to her now.

'Lock the door after I go out,' he says.

He takes his rifle from the cabinet.

'John,' she cries, 'You're just after saying you love me. Don't kill yourself by doing what he wants. You'll kill me too.'

He tries to move away from her then but she won't let him. She claws at him like a child.

'Don't go down!' she screams again.

He pulls himself away from her. She reels backwards from him, falling onto the bed.

'I'm sorry' he says, 'I didn't mean to hurt you. I have to go down. You know that. I can't let the horses die. sleep with a gun under my pillow for the rest of my life.'

He charges down the stairs and out the door. There's a rage in him now almost as great as the hatred Mulrooney said he felt earlier. He's aware for the first time in his life perhaps that he too is now capable of murder. As he walks through the shadows he keeps his finger on the trigger of the rifle.

He's so nervous he knows he'll shoot at anything that moves, maybe even one of his own horses. Behind every crevice he seems to see Mulrooney's face looking out at him. He wills him into the open, wills him even to take a shot at him if it will expose him. But nobody appears, only the horses galloping hysterically through the conflagration, coming close to trampling one another as they bolt.

He grabs a wet blanket and throws it over his head. Then he runs through the half-door at them, sliding across each blackened bolt as he comes to it, listening to the frenzy of their screeching as they surge around him looking for an exit. Then one of them sees a barricade and hurls itself through it, the others stampeding through the gap after it. He throws himself on the back of one of the horses as it makes its way out, the hot flesh of its mane charring him as it canters through the splinters.

It flings him off when it reaches the courtyard. He tries to get up but can't. He watches the lanterns falling into the straw, intensifying the blaze. He calls the horses to him but they ignore him. They're as obedient as circus animals on a normal day but they run from him now as if he's more to be feared than the fire.

When he gets outside a new fear strikes him. Why did Mulrooney not kill them? Was his mind so unhinged that he couldn't even manage a successful fire?

Eily, he thinks suddenly, the idea turning in his head like a key in a lock. Maybe she's the one he wants. Maybe Eily is right after all.

He runs out of the stables and looks up at her window. He seea a silhouette there. As he runs towards the house a light flicks on. Eily appears at the window for a moment and then disappears. Then he hears her screaming.

He races to the house and runs up the stairs. When he gets to the top he turns the handle of the bedroom door. As it opens, a shaft of light shines on Eily.

She has a gag on her mouth. Her eyes are telling him to go away. He wonders from what corner Mulrooney will erupt. Or has he decided to leave his final play to another night?

He looks around him at the shadows as he waits for the blow that must come, a blow he half invites.

And yet it isn't a blow when it comes. It's something that goes into his back and turns itself round inside him so that he feels his bones being prised apart. His eyes go back in his head and he falls to the ground in a heap, the blood coming out of him like water from a tap. A light comes up from somewhere and in the reflection of a mirror he sees the glint of a dagger encased in blood.

'That wasn't very bright now, was it?' Mulrooney says as he looks down at him, 'Making it so easy for me. I always thought you were such a clever dick. In any case, how would you like it, Mr Moran - in the stomach or between the eyes? They say every man is entitled to a last wish. Even a man like you.'

He wipes the blade clean of blood and replaces it in his belt, gazing at the two of them with his eyes wide.

'You were a big boy in O'Mahony's tonight with all your friends around. Let's see what you're made of now.'

He walks over towards Eily and pats her stomach. 'You realise it's my child she's carrying, don't you?' he says, 'You're not the only one who's been playing around, you know. We did it for old time's sake, didn't we, Eily?'

'Leave her alone,' he says as he tries to stand up, 'Leave her alone and you can have anything you want. 'He wonders if he has enough energy to charge at him but then the pain gets worse and he falls down again.

He looks at Eily huddled in a ball at the other side of the room and suddenly it doesn't seem to matter whether he does anything or not. He feels a sense of peace about it all, as if everything has been orchestrated towards this one moment. Maybe he even feels a tinge of elation, the elation Mulrooney himself must be feeling, the elation they say some murderers feel just before they deliver the *coup de grâce*.

'It will be strange at the court next week without you,' Mulrooney says finally, 'all these charges and no one to press them. I might even miss you.'

He picks up his rifle then, fixing them both in his sights as he squeezes his finger slowly along the trigger, secure suddenly in the knowledge that this time there can be no possibility of a mistake.

.

Downhill Hotel

They sat watching the waves slushing along the rocks at Bunree. A seagull was pecking for fish. A couple kissed on a bench in an alcove. 'Get a room!' shouted a biker.

She looked across at Nephin. It looked hard and still in the cool evening.

'Happy anniversary,' she said.

'Happy anniversary.'

He put his arms around her. They were spending the night at the hotel where they'd honeymooned the year before.

'How do you feel?' she asked him.

'Great,' he said.

'Are you sure?'

'Why would I say it if I wasn't?'

'Because you're a man. Men often say things they don't mean to make women feel well.'

He shrugged. She hated the way he shrugged when he had no answer for her on something.

'Why do you do that?' she said to him.

'Why do I do what?'

'Shrug. I hate it.'

'I can't help it. I'm not even aware I'm doing it. It's a mannerism. Why does it bother you?'

'I don't know. It just does.'

He stood up, shrugging now in a different way. His face looked serious, the face of a stranger.

'Sorry,' she said, 'I shouldn't have had a go at you.'

'You did nothing. Don't worry about it.'

He started to walk.

'Where are you going?'

'Just for a walk. Want to join me?'

'Okay.'

She got up. They walked along the Quay Road.

'You're not worried about anything, are you?' she asked him.

'Of course not. What makes you think that?'

'Just call it woman's intuition.'

'Woman's intuition. That's gas. Well let me tell you, this time your woman's intuition is wrong.'

They looked across at the bar, the bar where they'd first met on the banks of the Moy.

'What would you say to a drink?' he said.

'I'd say yes.'

'Okay. Let's have one.'

They went into the bar. When they sat down she started to get nostalgic. She thought of the day she met him. She was wearing a blue dress she'd just bought. She thought that was the reason he'd noticed her. He was standing at the counter with some of his friends and drew himself away from them to approach her. She went weak at the knees when he started to speak to her. She didn't think she'd ever met a man that handsome before. It was a magical day.

But now the bar seemed different. It looked just like any other bar. Even though it was Saturday night it was practically empty.

She was sitting in the same seat as she'd sat with him that first day.

'What's your poison?' he asked her.

'A glass of Guinness, I think. Is that what you'll have too?'

'No, I'll get a whiskey. It hits the spot quicker.'

He went up to the counter. She watched him tapping his fingers as he waited for the barman to come over.

As he ordered the drinks she looked out the window. She remembered the way she felt the first time she sat in this seat with him. She thought he had all the answers to all the problems of the world then.

She slept with him later that night. She thought he'd go

off her afterwards. 'Men are like that,' her mother said. But he didn't. He was the one that stayed.

He came over with the drinks. He took a large gulp of the whiskey, almost emptying it.

'It's very quiet, isn't it?' he said.

'Yes,' she said, 'not like last year.'

'Last year was manic,' he said, 'Even after the wedding. I don't know where they all came from.'

'They probably saw us having such a good time they wanted to be a part of it.'

'Probably. It seems a long time ago now, doesn't it?'

'Not really.'

'To me it seems like years. Do you remember the day we met?'

'What kind of a question is that?'

'A perfectly normal one. Just answer it.'

'The day we met? Jesus, that's a whole 365 days ago.'

'You really kill me with your romanticism.'

'Men are different than women that way.'

'You can say that again.'

'Okay, let's put it this way. I don't remember the day but I remember the dress you were wearing.'

'You do? I don't believe you.'

'Honest. In fact that was the first thing I fell in love with.'

She felt herself going weak. It always made her stomach flutter when he said something like that. Did he mean it or was he just trying to make her feel good?

'I haven't worn it since.'

'I noticed. Why is that?'

'I don't know. I'm just superstitious about things like that.'

'In what way?'

'Maybe I'm worried the spell won't work twice.'

'What are you talking about? We've been together a

year. It's not like it's our first date or anything.'

'I can't help it. It's just the way I am.'

'You should have worn the dress. It looked really great on you.'

She had a green one on now. She thought it looked dowdy by comparison. Was he disappointed she wasn't wearing the blue one? He wasn't the type to let her know if he was. She had to try and read his mind.

She took a sip of her drink.

'You have Guinness on your chin,' he said.

'Oh my God. Thanks for telling me.'

'I'm surprised you didn't feel it.'

'I never notice things like that. You know me.'

'You're strange.'

She wished he wouldn't say things like that. It put a distance between them. Why did men not notice when they were hurting women's feelings?

'Are you happy?' he said, giving her a little tap. He was starting to get merry on the whiskey.

'Very. And you?'

He nodded. .

They sat looking out at the river, at the bishop's palace across the way. She wondered if she'd been honest with him saying she was happy.

She didn't feel comfortable for some reason. She felt he had his arm around her because it was the expected thing to do rather than because he wanted to. It was like an anniversary gesture on his part.

There was a football match on the television. Mayo were playing Galway. The ball soared high in the sky. Two players jumped for it. One of them seemed to push the other.

When he came down he fell awkwardly. He lay still on the ground.

'Ouch,' she said, 'I felt that.'

'It's an act,' he said, 'He'll be up again in a few seconds.

They do that to get a free. Half of them should be in the Abbey.'

Right enough, the player got up as soon as the referee blew his whistle.

'See? I told you,' he said.

The player who was fouled didn't take the free. Another player did. He put it wide.

'Poetic justice,' she said. 'I hate it when someone gets an advantage from doing something sneaky.'

'You're too idealistic,' he said.

'How can you be *too* idealistic?'

'Trust me. You can.'

She knew he didn't want to pursue the subject. When he said something, that was it. He didn't care if someone agreed with him or not. He just left them to it.

She couldn't think of anything to say to him. Even though she knew him like the back of her hand, she felt she was a million miles away from him at times like this.

'Come on,' he said, 'Let's go. The night is getting on. We have to sign in.'

'Already?'

She was just starting to enjoy her drink. She'd like to have had another one but she knew it wasn't on. Whenever he was like that she had to jump to attention.

They walked out of the bar. The night was crisp and clear. She looked out at the river, at the mountains in the distance.

Everything looked different now that she'd had the drink. It looked three-dimensional, as if it was going to start moving.

She reached up and gave him a kiss.

'What was that in aid of?' he said.

'Just to let you know I love you.'

He laughed nervously.

'You'd think we were in a Hollywood movie or

something,' he said.

She wanted to tell him the last year had been the best of her life but something stopped her. Maybe she felt he wouldn't appreciate it. He was more composed than she was, less prone to impetuous remarks like that.

The kiss seemed to make him distant from her.

'Well, we better make our way to the Downhill,' he said, swigging back the last of his drink.

'I suppose so.'

They stood up and put on their coats. She felt cold as they went out.

'There's a nip in the air,' she said as the night wind hit them.

'That's for sure.'

As they walked towards the hotel she could feel his tension. What was he tense about? She'd sensed it all day. Was it something to do with her?

Whether it was or not, it seemed to transfer itself from him to her. She often felt that way, like an almost clairvoyant connection to him.

'You're very quiet tonight,' she said.

'Am I? So what?'

'Nothing. I was just wondering.'

'I'm always like that. You should know me by now. '

'Is everything at the job all right?'

He nodded.

'Everything at the job is all right and everything outside the job is all right. You need to give your mind a rest. You have an over-active imagination.'

'Okay. It's just that you've been acting strange all day.'

'I have? In what way?'

'Well you didn't eat your breakfast for one thing.'

'Wow, I didn't eat my breakfast. Call the emergency services.'

'And then you made that mysterious phone call.'

He stopped walking.

'What phone call?'

'It wasn't to her, was it?'

'What do you mean *her*?'

'You know who. Aileen O'Donohue.'

He'd had a relationship with Aileen O'Donohue before he met her. She thought he still carried a torch for her. She was the elephant in the room in any discussion they'd had about their relationship in the past year. He seemed to get shifty every time her name came up.

'Don't say we're getting into that again. If I've told you once I've told you a hundred times, there was never anything there. We just spent some time together, that's all. Neither of us was interested in pursuing it. It fizzled out. But you'll never believe that, will you?'

'I don't want to give you a hard time. I just can't stop thinking about her.'

'I know. That's what makes it pointless for me to say anything. So what if it *was* to her. What's the big deal? Is there some kind of police state in our marriage that says I can't talk to any other woman?'

She was afraid of pushing him away with her clinginess.

'You're right. I'm too possessive.'

They got to the hotel. They'd parked the car there earlier. He took the cases out of the boot. They walked to the entrance in silence.

'Look,' he said at the door, 'Are we going to let Aileen destroy our night here? Because if we are there's no point in going in.'

She hated even hearing her name.

'I agree. Let's drop it. I just wish you'd be yourself.'

'I *am* myself. Who else could I be?'

They walked towards the foyer. She tried to act excited but she couldn't. The luxury of it all mocked her. It was like she felt in the bar.

What were they doing here? You couldn't recapture the past, could you? Every time you tried it only made the present that much duller. It made you feel like an idiot for trying.

They checked in at the desk. She was annoyed with herself for bringing Aileen O'Donohue's name up. Why did she do that? There was no reason for it. Now everything was ruined.

She found herself wishing he'd put his arm around her again, even though she hadn't felt comfortable with it before. She felt different now but she knew he wouldn't. Men were like that. They did things when you didn't want them to and didn't do them when you did.

They walked down the corridor to their room. It was the same room as last year. She'd been looking forward to seeing it but now she didn't really care.

She kept blaming herself for creating the bad atmosphere with him. Why did she always do that? Her suspicions had no foundation except for his quietness.

They reached their room. It was 109. They had the design all curly. She remembered the way the brass was screwed into the door.

109. The number had a resonance for her. She'd never forget it.

They stepped inside. Everything looked sparse, banal. Last year they'd been given a bouquet of flowers, a complimentary bottle of champagne. Somebody put a heart-shaped box of chocolates on the pillow of the bed. But there were no flowers or chocolates now. They were just another couple. The carpet even looked frayed.

She looked at his face. She knew he was disappointed too. Somehow she felt responsible. Would things have been better if she'd worn her blue dress? Was that what he expected?

He left down the cases and unpacked his things. He hung

his jacket up in the wardrobe. She put her case on the bed and opened it.

She'd bought a new nightie a few days ago in a moment of madness. It had lots of frills and not too much material. She knew Peter liked revealing underwear. At the moment she was too self-conscious to show it to him. She'd packed her old one as well in case she didn't feel like putting the new one on.

She closed her case without taking anything out.

'What's wrong?' he said, 'Are you not unpacking?'

'I think I'll leave it till later.'

'Why?'

'I don't know.'

He gave her a funny look.

'That's weird.'

He shrugged again, that annoying shrug.

'What do you want to do now?'

'Whatever you like.'

She wanted to ask him to lie on the bed with her but she couldn't get the words out. Even after a year she was shy about things like that.

She knew he wanted to get out of the room. It seemed airless, stifling.

'I suppose we'll have a drink downstairs,' he said.

'That sounds like a good idea. I'd love one.'

'Would you mind if I got a breath of air first?'

'A breath of air? But we've just been outside.'

'I know. I feel stuffy in here for some reason. Maybe you're right, maybe I'm not myself tonight. So what do you say? Is it a stupid idea?'

'No it's not a stupid idea. It's just a bit unusual. Can I come with you?'

'Would you mind terribly if I said I'd like to be on my own for a while?'

Her heart sank. She hated that side of him, the one that

was so independent. Why was it coming out now, now of all times?

'I suppose not. Will you be long?'

'Of course not. How could I be? There's nowhere to go around here. When I come back I'll probably feel better. Then we can have our drink.'

She sat on the bed. He put his arm around her again but it was no good. She felt he was already gone from her. She found herself starting to cry.

'Jesus, you're crying. What's wrong, sweetness?'

'It's nothing. Don't worry about it.'

'There has to be some reason. Are you disappointed with the room?'

'No. I can't explain it. My emotions are all over the place these days.'

He came over to her and sat beside her on the bed.

'We've both been working very hard lately,' he said, 'That's why we came away. It'll be fine, don't worry.'

'Do you want to get away from me? Is that why you want to go out?'

'Don't be crazy. I just feel stuffy. I told you. I can hardly breathe in here. God, you're so insecure. You'd imagine you hardly knew me.'

'We could open some windows. I'm sure there's air conditioning. Why don't you look up the brochure?'

He didn't answer her. He just looked around him. What was he thinking about, she wondered.

'You're disappointed in the room, aren't you?' she said.

'Absolutely not. It just takes a bit of getting used to because it's different than last year. I think it's gorgeous, everything I expected.'

'That's not true. I can see it in your face.'

'Stop it, will you? You're paranoid.'

'I wish you wouldn't say things like that.'

'Look, I just need to clear my head. I'll be back in no

time and then we'll have that drink. Okay?'

She went over to the window and looked out. A young man was pitching golf balls in a field nearby. He reminded her of Peter. Maybe they'd have a game in Enniscrone, she thought. Peter often said he loved playing golf near the sea. He played in Howth every Saturday morning with his colleagues from the consultancy firm he owned. She didn't really know them. They were from a different social circle than her. They talked above her head about politics and things.

. She turned away from the window and looked at him.

'Peter, I wish you'd talk more to me.'

'What's that supposed to mean? Where is this coming from?'

'I don't know, I just do.'

'Jesus, you're something else. I never *stop* talking to you. What's wrong with you?'

'I just feel lonely all of a sudden.'

'You're probably missing Jack.'

Jack was their son. Her mother was minding him.

'It's not just that, it's everything.'

'You'll feel better tomorrow. It always takes us a night to settle in when we go anywhere.'

'You're probably right.'

'Of course I am. So am I allowed to go for my little walk then?'

'Okay, but don't stay out too long.'

'Don't worry.'

He stood there awkwardly in the middle of the floor. She thought he was going to say something but he didn't.

'Do you know where you'll go?'

'I never think about things like that. I'm not like you.'

'Stay away from the river. Someone was swept into the sea there last year.'

'There goes that over-active imagination again.'

She laughed. Maybe he was right. Maybe she *was* paranoid.

She gave him a hug. She wanted him to hold onto her longer but he drew himself away.

He opened the door. Why didn't he want her with him? It gnawed at her. They'd spent so long preparing this trip and now it was nearly worse than being at home.

He blew her a kiss and walked out. She followed him to the door. He started to walk down the corridor and she stayed looking at him.

He looked back when he got to the end of it. He gave her a little wave. She waved back and put on a watery smile. Then he was gone.

She went back into the room. It seemed even more sparse now without him. She looked out the window at the horrible car park. She felt like complaining to the management. Why did they always give the worst rooms to the nice people? Was it because they weren't afraid of them?

She didn't know what to do. She always hated being alone, even for small stretches.

She went over to the window again. He was walking in and out through the cars. Where was he going? He seemed to have some destination in mind. She wanted to be with him, to run after him. Why did she think he was going somewhere special? Was it because he wasn't as showy with his emotions as she was? Was there something deeper behind it?

He turned a corner and disappeared behind some trees. She turned away from the window.

She sat on the bed and opened her case again, unpacking a few things this time. She put them hanging in the wardrobe. Everything except for the nightie. She hid that under the pillow.

She'd bought a novel with her. She took it out and flipped through the pages. It was one of those beach books that are usually trashy. It was written by a woman, someone who'd been in a soap opera on RTE last year. They were all at it nowadays. Didn't they call it chicklit?

She usually brought a trashy novel with her on holiday to fill up the times when there was nothing to do. This wasn't really a holiday but it was a mini-one. She didn't really expect to be reading it. She only threw it in at the last minute as a stopgap. But now it was a comfort to her. She wanted to get her mind away from her boring self.

She sat down on the bed and started reading the back cover. It said it was about an *au pair* girl in France who got kidnapped by Russian terrorists. Oh God, she thought, this is terrible. Why hadn't she checked it beforehand? She'd have preferred some cuddly love story to relax her.

She started into it.

'Dorothea sat in the airport lounge, unaware that a killer with an AK47 was striding in behind her.'

Jesus, she could do better than that herself. The woman should have stayed in the soap.

Every page was more ridiculous than the last but she kept turning them. It can't get any worse, she thought. But it did.

There was a kettle by the bed. She put down the book and turned it on. When it boiled she made a cup of tea for herself.

It was her anniversary night and here she was having tea. She was reading a novel about terrorism instead of being down in the hotel bar sipping cocktails with her husband. Where was he?

She sipped at the tea and skipped on to Chapter Two:

. 'Dorothea hadn't always suffered from *wanderlust*. As a child she was firmly tied to her mother's apron-strings.'

She found her concentration going. She was too much immersed in her own head to give a damn what happened to bloody Dorothea. When she realised she was reading the same page over and over again she put the book down.

She decided to ring her mother. She always calmed her when she was feeling distraught.

She tried to think of the number. She rang it a dozen times a week but now it eluded her. In the end she had to look it up in her little notebook.

She dialled the number. Her mother answered.

'What's wrong?' she said as soon as she heard her voice. She always knew if it sounded different.

'Nothing. Would you believe I forgot your number?'

'Christ almighty. How could that happen?'

'I don't know. If my head wasn't tied on to me these days I'd forget it.'

'I told you to save it on your mobile. Can you not do that?'

'I keep meaning to. How are you anyway?'

'Not too bad. More to the point, how are *you*? You sound funny. Is everything all right?'

'Of course. How is Jack?'

'He's fine. He was a bit colicky earlier but he's all right now. Did you have a nice journey down? It was a lovely day, isn't it?'

'Glorious.'

'What's the room like?'

'It's lovely too.'

'What are you doing at the moment?'

'Reading a book, believe it or not.'

'Are you not having a drink?'

'Just tea. We'll probably have one later.'

'Are you alone?'

She paused. How could she have known?

'Yes.'

'Where's himself?'

'He went out for a breath of air.'

'Without you? On your anniversary night?'

'He had a bit of a headache. He'll be back in a little

while.'

'Is he drinking?'

He used to have a problem that way once.

'No,' she said. There was no point mentioning the whiskey.

'He hasn't been onto *her*, has he?'

Her mother was almost as suspicious of Aileen O'Donohue as she was.

'Don't be crazy. She doesn't even know we're here.'

'Are you sure about that? Doesn't she live down that neck of the woods now?'

'Mammy, I have to go now. You're working me up.'

'I'm sorry, I don't mean to.'

'I'm sorry too. I was hoping we'd have a longer chat but I feel tense.'

'Take a Valium.'

It was her mother's answer to everything. If she was in charge of the HSE she'd have run the whole service on just that one tablet.

'Okay.'

'Have you got some with you?'

'You know me. I never go anywhere without them.'

'Take a yellow one now, that's an order.' She usually split them in half.

'I'll take five of them, Mammy. Or 55.'

'I know I'm annoying you. I'll go now.'

'I'm sorry. I didn't mean to be sharp. It's the tension. I just need to lie down for a minute.'

'If he's not back soon, ring me. I'm worried about you.'

'I will. And give Jack a kiss for me, will you?'

'I'll give him a hundred of them. Now promise to ring me again, okay?'

'Goodbye, Mammy.'

She hung up. The call hadn't gone the way she wanted. If anything it made her feel worse. What was wrong with her?

She had to learn to deal with her feelings without expecting other people to solve things for her. That's what he always said.

She reached into her handbag and took out her little bottle of pills. There were loads of half-yellow valiums under a cotton bud. She took one out and put it under her tongue. It worked quicker that way than with water. So they said anyway.

She thought about the year they'd spent together, the whirlwind romance and then the marriage soon afterwards, maybe too soon. Jack came along almost nine months to the day after the honeymoon. He called him a 'honeymoon baby. ' He always said the phrase with a tinge of sarcasm, as if it tied him down.

Were they really a year married? The twelve months had passed like so many minutes. She wondered if they were happy. What was happiness when you thought about it? You could be content in a terrible relationship and miserable in a good one. Life wasn't always about how you were getting on with someone, it was also about yourself. Was she happy in herself? Reasonably, she thought. At least as happy as anyone had a right to be.

Her mother blamed Peter every time something went wrong. Maybe mothers always did. The disappointing son-in-law. Okay, so he wasn't always full of the joys of spring but what man was?

She knew he loved her even if he didn't say it too often. Men were like that. They weren't expressive with their feelings like women. Besides, she always said she preferred a man who acted the love rather than someone who just mouthed the words.

She looked at the clock on the wall. It ticked away like a question mark, boring a hole in her head. He said he'd be back soon but he was now gone half an hour. Had he gone to the pub? Was he phoning Aileen O'Donohue?

She had to stop thinking like that. It wasn't doing either of them any good. But she couldn't help it.

Sometimes she feared he'd leave her for Ann. He talked about her a lot, almost without realising it. If she pulled him up about it he clammed up, which was almost as bad.

Was he more likely to leave her if she kept needling him about her? Probably. The point was, there was nothing she could do about it either way. If he did she'd have to put up with it. Love died in the world just as suddenly as it blossomed. Whirlwinds erupted and then they petered out. It was in the nature of things.

Petered out. That sounded funny. Peter-ed out.

How much longer would he be gone? She had to stop thinking about him. It wasn't good to be clingy. The best way to keep him was by not invading his space too much.

She felt her eyelids getting heavy. The room became hazy around her. She threw herself across the bed and then felt something under her. She thought it might be a bad spring but it turned out to be the novel. It dug into her ribs. She picked it up and threw it onto the floor. Goodbye Dorothea, goodbye Russian terrorists.

She tried to sleep but she couldn't. It was beyond her. Her head throbbed with tension.

She didn't feel comfortable lying there so she got up. She walked around the room like an animal in a cage, prancing from one end to the other, occasionally taking a look out the window in the hope that she'd catch a glimpse of him coming back through the cars.

She turned on the television. A Japanese woman was jumping up and down on a trampoline. You always saw funny things on the stations of hotel TVs. Stations you never got at home. Sometimes they diverted her for a few minutes because of their novelty value. That was why she was here, for novelty. She told herself to stop expecting everything to be perfect, to stop fretting.

She flicked from channel to channel. There was a Kung Fu movie on one of them. Another had Lady Ga Ga roaring her guts out in get-up that looked like something you'd see in a circus.

Most of the others were just advertising channels. Keep fit equipment for executives on the move. Gym equipment with 87 functions that could fit inside a matchbox.

The sound was blaring at her. She couldn't find the remote to turn it down. She popped a Valium into her mouth, a full yellow one this time.

She looked around her at the clock on the wall. The half-drunk cup of tea. The novel that was dog-eared from her lying on it.

She couldn't stop thinking about him. Had he had an accident? Was he beaten up? Had he gone down to the river even though he'd said he wouldn't?

The clock ticked on like a metronome. Images flashed at her from the television. She heard muffled voices from the other rooms.

Where was he? She convinced herself he was lying somewhere injured badly. That was it. He'd been knocked down by a car and he was bleeding to death in a ditch.

Just as she was starting to panic, she heard footsteps outside the door. She ran to open it. As soon as she did she saw him.

Thank God thank God thank God.

His hair was wild. There was a vague smile on his face. He smelt of whiskey and the sea.

She felt relieved but also confused. What was the smile trying to convey?

'I know I'm going to get given out to. I have no excuse. It was a lovely night. I just kept walking. I ended up somewhere beyond Ardnaree.'

She looked at him as if he was a stranger. The words didn't seem to be coming from his mouth. He seemed far away, like a ventriloquist's dummy.

She tried to talk but her voice was gone. He started shaking her.

'Are you all right? What's wrong with you? Say something.'

She couldn't stop thinking about where he'd been. She thought she smelt perfume off him. Maybe he'd tried to cloud it with the whiskey.

'You put the heart crossways in me. Do you know what time it is?'

'As I said, I have no excuse. You can be as mad with me as you like. I got into a rhythm and just kept ambling along. You know me. Couch potato for a month and then I think I'm Sebastian Coe.'

'Who's Sebastian Coe?'

'Look, we still have time for a drink. Will you forgive me and come down with me?'

'I don't know. I feel a bit woozy.'

'Woozy? Why is that?'

'You were gone so long I lay down on the bed.'

'Did you fall asleep?'

'Not really. I was fighting it.'

'I hate that when it happens to me. You're half one thing and half the other.'

'Exactly.'

Did you do anything else?'

'I watched a bit of TV. Then I rang Mammy.'

He seemed taken aback. He always seemed taken aback whenever she mentioned his mother. It was like a mutual distrust.

'Did you now? So how is she? How is Jack?'

'He had colic.'

'Not again.'

'It's okay. He's all right now.'

'Good. He's a real little fighter, isn't he? There's no way

230

a bit of colic will keep that fellow down.'

He hadn't shown as much love for Jack as she'd hoped. Her mother said that would come with time. The way he was now you'd think Jack was someone else's baby. He asked stiff and starchy questions about him more out of duty than love.

That was also the way her own father had been in the early years of their marriage according to her mother. Men took a while to get interested in babies. That wasn't the way it was with women.

Babies came out of women, that was the difference. Men had to have something to relate to, to talk to. It wasn't enough just to dandle them on their knee. Unless they were New Men of course. She didn't really like New Men. They wanted to be in the kitchen too much.

He took a naggin of whiskey from his pocket.

'Like a nip?' he said.

'Where did you get that?'

'I brought it with me. They charge a fortune for it at the bar. This way we can have a few before we get down there.'

'We can get footless for nothing.'

He laughed. She didn't feel like laughing.

'Is that a yes or a no?'

'I don't know, Peter. Let's say no for the moment.'

He put out his tongue at her.

'Spoilsport.'

'Are we not going downstairs for one? I like the atmosphere of the pub. It's nice to see other people around. I haven't clapped eyes on a soul since we got here.'

'Just let me finish this.'

He drained it back.

'I suppose your mother was giving out about me,' he said.

'She didn't say anything. Maybe she was surprised you weren't with me.'

'I don't blame her. I was bang out of order. I'll make it up to you tomorrow.'

'Don't worry about it. As long as you're all right that's the main thing. I had these visions of you stabbed to death in some back alley.'

He laughed again. He was getting giggly with the whiskey.

Now that he was back she felt flat. A few minutes earlier she'd have given her eyeteeth to see him but now that he was here she was hardly aware of him. He often criticised her for that. 'Separation anxiety' he'd called it.

'You only appreciate me when I'm not there,' he said to her one day. She replied, 'Is that why you play hard to get?' She hadn't thought it would have been like that in marriage. Surely marriage was where people stopped playing games? But maybe some games went on forever.

He took another swig of the whiskey. He held the bottle out towards her but she shook her head. He put it back in his pocket.

'So are we going down for a drink or what?'

'Just lie down beside me for a minute,' she said.

'I know what you're up to. You want to have your wicked way with me between the sheets.'

They lay down together. A year ago they'd slept in this same bed after drinking the champagne and eating the chocolates. Then they made love. She was sure that was the night she conceived Jack.

She was excited then, excited to be making love to the man she loved, excited to be making a baby.

There would be no more babies. She was sure of that. 'We're closing the shop after this one,' he said after Jack was born and she went along with it, went along with it as she'd gone along with all of his decisions over the past year, as she'd probably continue to go along with them for the rest of her life.

She went over to the window. She saw two boats on the Moy. The wind was blowing them this way and that. A set of buoys bobbled up and down on the water.

A year ago she'd looked out at a similar scene from a better room. She remembered seeing a woman with a little girl on her shoulders walking along by the river.

She thought then that she'd have loved a daughter too. She was disappointed when she was told she was going to have a boy but now she loved Jack more than anything.

'What are you doing over there?' he said, 'You ask me into bed and then you're gone from me.'

'Just give me a minute.'

She wanted to stay there just looking out. She didn't want to go back to the bed and she didn't want to go down to the bar. What was wrong with her? She had a husband and a child who loved her, or at least who professed to love her. She had no pressing health or money worries. And yet she was a ball of nerves. There was no explaining it.

She went back to the bed. As she lifted the pillow to lie down he spotted the nightie.

'What's this?' he said.

'Oh yeah,' she said trying to sound casual, 'I forgot all about it. I bought it for our trip.'

'Oo la la. Put it on. I'm already getting excited.'

'In a minute. If I undress I'll only wake myself up. We've had a long day. Should we not try and sleep?'

'In our clothes?'

'Why not.'

'So we've made our mind up not to go down to the bar, is that right?'

'For the moment, if you don't mind.'

He pulled off his trousers and threw them on the floor. She held him close to her. There was a strong smell of whiskey from his breath. Had he brought it with him on the walk? Did he have a drink of it somewhere with Aileen

O'Donohue?

She got out of the bed and undressed. She could see he was starting to get drowsy. She took his trousers off the floor and hung them up on a hanger in the wardrobe. Then she put on the nightie and went back to bed. She wasn't self-conscious about it anymore.

She started to say something to him but he didn't reply. A moment later she realised he was asleep.

He started to snore. She poked him but he didn't stop. How could he be asleep this soon after coming in to bed? Was he just pretending about looking forward to seeing her in the nightie?

She envied him his ability to nod off at a moment's notice. He was so different to her, being able to turn his mind off as soon as his head hit the pillow. 'It's my clear conscience,' he used to say. Her mother didn't agree. 'More like an elastic one,' she said.

She knew she'd probably be tossing and turning all night herself if she didn't take a sleeping pill. Had she brought any? She looked into her handbag. Luckily they were in there beside the Valium. She was turning into a right junkie. It was just as well she brought them. She hadn't intended to. She thought they'd have spent the night drinking. Alcohol always acted as a good sleeping pill for her.

She got a glass of water from the bathroom and took two sleeping pills. Then she got back into bed and lay down. She figured it would be a while before they kicked in, as the phrase went.

She took up her novel again but she couldn't concentrate on it. (Dorothea was now in a Chechnyan torture chamber getting electric shocks as she waited on her lover to rescue her). She turned off the light. The curtains were open but she liked it that way. Even the car park looked well now. The moon was shining on it.

He continued to snore. It irritated her. What could she do

about it? He always told her to turn him on his side to stop him but she didn't like doing that.

Eventually she fell asleep. When she did she dreamt about Peter, about the way he drew himself away from his friends to talk to her that first day. She dreamt about her mother, about Jack, even about Dorothea. Everything was jumbled up the way it usually was in her dreams, without any logic. She always felt dreams were like your mind going to the toilet. They were therapy.

The next thing she knew it was morning. Sunlight streamed through the window, flooding the room.

It woke him as it usually did. (He had thin eyelids). He turned in the bed.

'Jesus,' he said, 'I can't believe it's daylight. I slept right through.'

'I know. You spent most of it snoring.'

'Sorry about that, chief. Why didn't you give me a push?'

'I didn't like to.'

'You're too nice.'

He looked down at his clothes.

'Jesus, I forgot to pack my PJs. How about that?'

He always called his pyjamas his PJs. She thought there was something childish about that. She liked it when he was childish.

'Did you get any shut-eye at all?'

'I got off eventually with the help of two sleeping pills.'

'Don't say you're back on them again.'

'I need them, Peter. As you know, my nerves have been at me these last few days.'

'They always make you feel horrible the next day, don't they?'

'Unfortunately.'

'Oh well, that's the price you pay for your forty winks.'

She hated it when he said things like that. She took it to

be his way of saying she didn't look well. That was another thing she thought would have changed when they got married – her need to always be at her best for him. Sometimes she felt she was still in competition with other women for his attention. Or one woman.

'I'm sorry about last night,' he said, 'It was totally selfish of me. I know how much you've been looking forward to this. Like a true hero I went off and did my own thing. It was unforgiveable denying you a few bevvies in the bar.'

'Maybe we were better off. We'd both have big hangovers now if we went down there.'

'Now that's what I call positive thinking.'

He pulled the covers off himself and went over to the window. He shivered as he looked out.

'Going to be a cold one, Goldilocks.'

He always called her that when he was feeling warm towards her.

'So it said on the news.'

He started to put on his clothes.

'Are you not going to shower?' she said.

'I don't think I'll bother. Suddenly I feel ravenous. I think they stop breakfast early if memory serves.'

'Do you want to go down now?'

'Maybe we should.'

She went into the bathroom. She splashed some water over her face to try and wake herself up.

He went in after her and put his arms around her waist.

'I like the nightie, by the way,' he said.

'I'm surprised you noticed it.'

'That was another disaster from last night – right?'

'It doesn't matter. I'm over it.'

'No, really. I wanted to see you in it. And to see you out of it.'

'Now now.'

She started dressing. She looked at herself in the mirror.

'My hair looks like it had an argument with a lawn-mower,' she said.

'Agreed. And the mower won.'

'Less of the jokes please.'

She tried to comb it but got nowhere. Some days you just had to let it do its own thing.

He rubbed his stomach.

'Are you ready to make an onslaught on a major league fry-up?' he said, 'I'm going to have two rashers, two sausages, an egg and some pudding, with toast on the side, and a skinny latte.'

'Sounds exciting,' she said, 'Is this going to be the high point of the trip?'

'That's as good as it gets for people of our age, I'm afraid.'

'What do you mean, people of our age?'

'Okay, what I should have said is people of *my* age.' He was five years older than her.

'Thank you. Maybe next year you'll really go the hound and have three sausages.'

He laughed.

'You're getting your sense of humour back. You must be feeling better.'

'A bit.'

He had a spring in his step as they went down the stairs. Were his needs really this simple? She'd often heard it said that the way to a man's heart was through his stomach. ('I'd aim a bit lower,' her mother joked).

When they got to the breakfast room it was empty.

'Wow,' he said sitting down, 'Has this place become a victim of the recession?

'We could hardly get a seat last year.'

'Tell me about it. Oh well, this way we get to eat more goodies.'

He filled up a dish with cereal and poured milk over it.

'I miss the crowds,' she said.

'Yeah, but they were all hungry bastards.'

She picked up a glass of orange juice and started drinking it. It was cheap juice like the ones you got in the supermarkets.

'Last year they gave us the natural stuff,' she said.

'Last year they were probably rich. Like all of us.'

'That supermarket fizz makes me sick.'

'Don't drink it so. There's no law that says you have to.'

'I know, but when it's there it's hard to resist.'

A waitress came over to them.

'Full Irish breakfast for you, madam?' she asked.

'If you wouldn't mind.'

Why did hotel people always say that? They were hardly in Finland.

'And for me too,' said Peter.

'Yes sir.'

She went off with the menus. Peter leaned back in his chair. He let out a whistle.

'It's a blast being here isn't it?' he said.

'It was a great idea.'

'We've been talking about it long enough anyway.'

'I hope it didn't knock you back too much. I should have contributed.'

'Don't be ridiculous. You're only working part time.'

She had a job in a delicatessen every second day. That was the way she liked it. Her mother minded Jack on those days.

'I know, but still. It must have been a bit of a drain on you.'

'Oh sure, I broke the bank. Las Vegas wouldn't have been as expensive.'

'That's not the point. You've had a lot of bills lately.'

The breakfast arrived. She felt sick as she looked at the two platefuls of food. All she wanted was a cup of tea.

'Can you believe it,' he said, 'A whole year together. And they said it wouldn't last.'

She tried to laugh but she couldn't. Her stomach felt queasy. The orange juice was lodging in it like glue.

He chopped his rashers up and started making sandwiches with them. Pretty soon they were all gone.

'God bless your appetite,' she said, 'You have the breakfast demolished.'

He looked at her plate. It was still almost full.

'If you're not careful I'll be after your one too. Are you not eating up?'

'I'm afraid I'm not very hungry.'

'You shouldn't waste it. We're paying enough for it.'

'You're welcome to anything you want.'

He clucked his tongue as he surveyed the alternatives.

'Throw over a few sausages so, but only if you're sure.'

'I am. If I took them I'd only throw them up.'

'Ouch. That sounds rather dramatic.'

She put them on his plate. He munched into them.

'I don't know what's making me so hungry,' he said.

He polished everything off in record time.

'You've really made short work of that,' she said.

'Why not? We paid for it, didn't we? I can't believe you're just having the tea.'

'It's all I wanted.'

The waitress came over.

'Is everything all right?' she said.

'Smashing,' Peter told her.

He wiped his face with a napkin.

'Don't let me look at food again for at least a year,' he said as he patted his stomach.

'Wait till tea-time,' she said, 'and Hungry Horace will be off again, making for the leg of the table.'

'That's me,' he laughed.

He looked at his watch.

'What time have we to check out at?' he asked her.

'Noon, I think.'

'That would give us time for a lie-down, wouldn't it?'

'If you want.'

He looked at her plate again. There was an uneaten egg on it and some black pudding.

'You really should make an effort to have some of that.'

'I can't. Even looking at it is making me sick.'

'I hope you're not turning into one of those anorexics.'

'You must be joking. Look at my inch pinch. I feel I'm six months gone.'

She put her hand onto her waist and squeezed it.

'What do you think of that?'

'It's nothing. If you're six months I'm six years.'

He looked at his watch again.

'Ready?' he said.

She nodded.

They stood up. Peter adjusted the belt on his trousers.

'I can hardly walk,' he said.

'I'm the same,' she said, 'but for a different reason.'

They went out of the dining-room and out to the foyer. There was a handful of people there. They were checking out. Two of them were wrapped around each other.

'Honeymooners,' he said drily, 'Little do they know what they have in store for them.'

He looked at her to see her reaction.

'It's her I feel sorry for,' she said, 'Women are so much nicer than men.'

'Yeah, ever since Eve did a job on Adam.'

They went up the stairs to their room. A part of her wanted to be home and a part to stay on here an extra day. She knew she hadn't made the best use of her time.

They walked up the stairs. She felt a hollow in her stomach. They went down the corridor to their room. As soon as they got inside he jumped onto the bed.

'It's chilly,' he said, 'I don't think the air con is on.'

'Probably a credit squeeze,' she said.

'Jesus, they've really done it on the cheap this year, haven't they? It's a wonder there's even two pillows on the bed. They might have stuck us with one.'

He pulled the covers up around him.

'I'm surprised you want to lie down considering you slept so well,' she said.

'I always feel dozy after a meal,' he explained.

She lay down beside him. As soon as her head hit the pillow she felt the tears coming again. She tried to hide them from him but he spotted them.

'What's wrong, little girl?' he asked.

'I have that sinking feeling inside me again. It just happens.'

He wiped her cheek with his hand.

'You're working too hard. You're probably burned out.'

She sat up.

'It's not that.'

'What is it then?'

'I don't know. Do you love me, Peter?'

'Of course I do, stupo. Is that all that's bothering you? Lie down beside me and I'll take your tension away. Dr Peter can perform miracles on his patients.'

She remembered him saying something like that the first night. It sounded like a seduction line. Could a husband seduce his wife?

'I don't really want to.'

'Come on. You could put on that nightie again, the one I didn't get enough of a look at last night.'

'I'm sorry, Peter, I'm just not in the mood. You were sleepy a minute ago. Now it's happening to me. If I lie down I'll be out for the count in ten seconds.'

'So what? We should get the use out of the room, especially since we missed out on last night. When are we going to get the chance to get away again? The cleaners won't be here till noon. We have over an hour.'

'I know. It's just that –'

'Shut up and kiss me.'

He gave her a smooch.

'I'm going to undress now,' he said. 'You're under orders to do the same.'

He took off his clothes and got in under the duvet.

She took off her blouse.

'That's all. I'm not putting on the nightie. I'm too tense. '

His face fell.

'Have it your own way.'

He tried to kiss her but she moved away from him.

'What's wrong?'

'I need time to collect my thoughts.'

'Your thoughts? What kind of thoughts? Are you not attracted to me anymore?'

'You know I am.'

'What's the problem then?'

'I told you. My stomach is at me.'

'I'm not surprised. You should be in one of those prisons where they go on hunger strikes. You'll be telling me you have a headache next.'

She felt she was going to throw up.

'Would you mind if I went to the toilet?'

'Here we go. Okay, if you have to. But don't be too long in there. I know what you're like. Time is running on. They're going to kick us out of here at noon.'

She went into the bathroom. She didn't need to go to the toilet. She just wanted a few minutes on her own.

She sat on the toilet seat without taking the lid up. She started to breathe deeply. That always helped. She tried to keep her mind blank.

'All right in there?' he called, 'how long more are you going to be?'

'I'll be out in a minute.'

'I hope so. Otherwise I might do an Oscar Pistorius on you.'

She flushed the toilet. It made a muffled sound because of the lid being down. Would he notice?

She stood up. Her pulse was racing. She looked at herself in the mirror. Her face seemed wrinkled, wan. In the year that passed since she'd been here before she felt she'd got much more than a year older. Would he agree? Would he admit it if he did?

'Marriage ages you,' her mother had once said to her. She was surprised at her attitude. Her one had been difficult too. Both of their husbands were drinkers. Was that what was behind it? But then what Irish husband wasn't?

She washed her face and then put some cream on. She'd been wearing perfume on the journey down. He hadn't noticed it. It was an expensive one. She sometimes splurged out on things like that. She felt he'd like her more if she was wearing expensive perfume. He'd be more inclined to want to kiss her. But now she didn't care. She wanted to get rid of the smell of it.

She went back to the bedroom.

'Feeling better?' he said, 'you smell funny. Is that cream you have on?'

'I don't feel like getting into bed if you don't mind.'

'Here we go again. I get the message.'

'It's nothing to do with you.'

'I believe you but millions wouldn't. It's probably my beer belly that turns you off.'

'You don't have a beer belly.'

He pulled up his shirt and stuck out his stomach.

'What would you call that – a six-pack?'

'I see nothing unusual.'

He pulled his shirt off and started punching himself.

'What are you doing?' she said.

'Maybe if I slap it enough it'll go down. Then you'll come to bed with me.'

'Don't be stupid.'

'I have to do something to get you interested in me that way again.'

'I *am* interested. Just try and bear with me until I get over this.'

'How much time do you need? They charge for rooms by the hour.'

'I appreciate the fact that you paid for the trip. I know I'm not doing what you want. I'm sorry.'

'Don't say sorry. That only makes it worse.'

'Are you annoyed?'

'No.'

'You look annoyed.'

He got out of the bed. She watched him putting his clothes on. The anger was spilling out of him. He did it so fiercely he almost put his feet through the floor.

'Come back in,' she said, 'I'll do what you want if it means that much to you.'

He let out a screech.

'Why do you always make these kinds of offers when it's too late? The mood has gone off me now.'

He put on his vest and shirt without looking at her. He sat down on the bed. She looked at him guiltily as he put on his socks and shoes.

He always spent ages tying the laces, trying to get the two sides to match exactly, but now he just stuffed his feet into them. She kept watching him to see if there was any trace of him cooling down.

He threw the rest of his things into his case and slammed it shut.

'Well,' he said, 'Are you proud of yourself now?'

'Are you?'

She got out of the bed. It looked like he was going to be

in bad form for the day. She started dressing.

She put her clothes into her case. The nightie was the last thing to go in. She stuffed it in in a ball.

She looked at him. He was looking away.

'I suppose we'll go, so,' she said.

'An excellent idea.'

Her stomach still felt queasy. She pinched it to see if it pained her.

'What are you doing?' he said sharply.

'My stomach still hurts.'

'It seems to be the day for stomachs, doesn't it? First my six-pack and now your sick one.'

'I'm worried there might be something wrong with me.'

'Maybe you're pregnant. You'll make history if you are, considering you were in the bathroom while I was in the bed. Or else it's the fact that you don't eat. I read a medical report recently that said if people don't eat, it can affect their stomachs. Very strange.'

She bundled up the sheets and threw them into a heap.

'Got everything?' he asked.

'Yes.'

She looked around her at the wardrobe, the curtains, the little table in the corner. Suddenly the room looked almost cute. She'd been wrong to think of it as sparse or banal. Now that they were leaving it was as if she was seeing it for the first time. It was always the way with her. Maybe he was right. Maybe she always saw things too late.

They walked out to the landing. She heard two people laughing in the room across from them. She found herself envying them. Were they a honeymoon couple too? Would they come back next year and find things different? Maybe it wouldn't be the things that were different; maybe it would be them.

She'd like to have turned the clock back, to be the person she was twelve months ago. She wanted Peter to be the person he was twelve months ago. There was just the two of them then.

They'd been better with each other before Jack came along. Was it Jack that caused the change in him? Did he feel elbowed out of her attentions by the new arrival in the house? People often said men did. Sometimes she didn't see the obvious. Sometimes you didn't see it till you got away from it.

They went down the stairs without talking. He didn't carry her case this time.

They got to the desk. A pretty girl appeared as they left their cases down.

'Was everything all right?' she asked.

'Couldn't have been better,' Peter told her. He was always nice to pretty girls. He turned on his charm for them.

She'd been pretty herself once. She didn't think she was any more. *Marriage ages you.*

He took out his credit card and put it into a machine that was on the counter. It made a ping when he punched in his numbers.

It didn't go through the first time so he tried again.

'These bloody things are great when they work,' he said with mock-gruffness. The pretty girl smiled.

He tried again and this time it clicked in.

'Brilliant,' said the pretty girl.

'For this relief much thanks,' he said.

They reached down for their cases.

Well,' he said, 'See you again sometime.'

'I hope so. Thank you so much for your custom.'

'It was our pleasure.'

She flashed a smile at him. They walked outside to the car. She could see it was going to be a dull day. The morning air bit into her. She looked across at the Moy, the mountains, the steeple of St. Muredach's Cathedral. Everything seemed hazy.

She smelt dilisk. Someone must have collected it from Enniscrone for sale.

'Sorry about not going back to bed with you,' she said.

'And I'm sorry about being out so late last night. Now are we all done with the apologies?'

She felt she was about to cry again. He copped it. He seemed to have cooled down.

'Don't,' he said, 'Everything will be fine when we get back to Dublin.'

'Do you think so?'

'I know so.'

'I hope Jack is all right,' she said.

'He'll be okay. He's in capable hands.'

'I miss him so much.'

'Me too.'

They drove out of the grounds. The avenue swung around a horseshoe bend. She looked back. For a moment, the car was facing the hotel again for a moment. She looked up at their room. It seemed strangely insignificant now. The window was open. A cleaner lady was singing as she bundled the sheets away. She sounded foreign

They drove through the town. There were a lot of shoppers in King Street. He accelerated up the hill and turned right into Bury Street. The lights went red when he got to the end of it. He liked looking at the crazy paving beside the font at the top of Teeling Street. As he turned left for the road to Foxford his phone rang. He looked at it for a moment as if he wasn't going to answer it but then he did.

'Hello?' he said.

She could hear a woman's voice on the other end.

He listened for a few seconds. Then he said, 'Thanks for that. Bye.'

He pressed a button and it went dead. He left it on the dashboard.

'Who was it?' she said.

'Just someone from work. It wasn't important.'

She wanted to grab the phone to see if it was Aileen O'Donohue's number but she didn't. She knew he'd go mad if she tried anything like that.

He drove on. She was already lonely for the town, the hotel, the river.

'How long do you think it'll take us to get home?' she said.

'I don't know. What does it matter? We never do anything on Sundays, do we?'

'Or any other day either,' she said.

He gave a strangled laugh.

'What's that supposed to mean?'

'I don't know.'

He started to pick up speed, overtaking some of the other vehicles.

'What's your hurry?' she asked.

'There's no hurry, I just like going fast.'

She knew he was trying to appear casual even though he was probably still furious with her. She'd have preferred the anger.

He turned on the radio. A pop song blared out, one that was in the charts. He tapped his fingers to the beat on the steering wheel. She thought of him tapping the counter in the bar the previous day when he was waiting for the barman to bring the drinks.

She wondered if they'd come back again next year. Jack would be over a year old then. Would they still be together? Would he be gone off with Aileen O'Donohue?

She looked at him as if she was trying to read his mind. and he looked back at her the same way. Of all the people in the world, they had chosen one another a year ago to walk up an aisle ain a church and say to a priest that they would stay together forever and ever, and yet she felt he was more removed from her than anyone they'd met in the hotel, even the people shed only exchanged a few words with.

'You're very quiet,' he said.

'That's my line.'

'Is everything all right?'

'Yes. Are you sorry we came?'

'If you say that again I'll scream.'

'You probably are, only you won't admit it.'

'All right. I am. Are you happy now?'

She gave him a hard look.

'You haven't been the same since we got married, have you?' she said.

'Do you really believe that?'

'Yes.'

'What do you put it down to?'

'Probably the fact that you were happier with me before we had Jack.'

'That's a new one, I'll give you that much.'

'A lot of Irish women think like that.'

'Really? I wouldn't know. I only married one of them.'

'Do you think they're right?'

'No. It's an urban myth. It helps them explain everything that goes wrong with their happy little formula for married life.'

'Well said. You have it all worked out.'

'Thank you.'

He stopped the car, pulling into a hard shoulder.

'Are we going to be like this all the way home?'

'I'm sorry,' she said, 'I didn't mean to upset you.'

He put his head in his hands.

'Don't be. I'd prefer you to say things than to think them.

'Sometimes I say things I don't mean.'

'But you meant it about me being happier before we had Jack, didn't you?'

'I don't know. I'm raw at the moment. Maybe I was just looking for attention.'

'Is that because I don't give you enough?'

'Maybe.'

'Okay. I'll work on it. Now can we just enjoy the journey before we strangle one another?'

'Please don't talk to me like that.'

'You make me.'

'I can't help it.'

'You're probably sad the anniversary is over. I know you were building yourself up for this.'

He started the car again. She looked up at the sky. Clouds were gathering. She thought she heard thunder rumbling in the distance. She felt her mind leaving her body as the engine hummed.

As they sped towards Swinford the fields and trees seemed to merge into one another, to lift themselves off the ground and into the sky. She felt herself being lifted up with them, sailing away from everything she knew, everything she felt. All her worries disappeared as she closed her eyes and lay back on the head-rest. The sojourn at the hotel seemed like it never happened as they inched closer and closer to their house back in Lusk.

Castlebar Will Sort You Out

On Gabriel Sinnott's fifty-second birthday he came in from his office, went upstairs and locked the door of his bedroom. Fifteen minutes later Mrs. Sinnott heard the sound of a bullet and then a thud. She screamed and ran to the room, succeeding in opening it only after ten minutes with the aid of a hammer. When she went inside she saw Mr. Sinnott splayed out on the floor with blood dripping from his temple and a rifle by his side.

When Colm came home she told him a terrible accident had occurred. Colm would probably have believed her if he hadn't suddenly remembered a conversation he heard one night between his mother and father as he happened to be passing by their room. Mr. Sinnott had been saying to his mother that he couldn't go on anymore and Mrs. Sinnott said that was nonsense. Then the voices got louder. Colm creaked a floorboard and Mrs. Sinnott came rushing out the door with a shocked look on her face, surprised that he'd arrived in from playing with his friends so early.

The conversation had run through Colm's mind all through the next day as he stood in the corner of his class, having been put there by his teacher for not knowing the Conditional Tense of the verb 'ceannaigh' for two days in a row and failing to put a margin on his History copy.

For days afterwards, walking home in that aimless way he had that his mother and Mr. Hanley had both tried to train him out of, telling him that it would eventually result in his getting a hump, Colm had wondered what not being able to go on meant and whether he'd ever feel like that when he grew up and got into a job that would perhaps be repetitive as his father's had been, or fall out of love with his wife.

He thought the grown-up world was a strange one when a man who had a wife and son and a comfortable house and a sandblasting business in Easkey which employed eighteen people as swell as a secretary should go to the lengths of putting the barrel of a rifle down his throat and squeezing the trigger.

Over the next few years Mrs. Sinnott began to take the same red and black capsules that Mr. Sinnott had always taken after his meals upon the advice of his doctor to help his nerves. Sometimes when she was looking extra tired she made a journey to a hospital in Castlebar. When she came back, Colm would notice that her cheeks had regained that sheen he generally associated with them.

He talked to her often about the stresses that life brought to us all, imagining himself somehow to be more equipped to discuss such things than those who out-stripped him in their schoolwork now that he was the victim of a family tragedy, but she usually just told him he was too young to be asking such serious questions and that he would be better advised to just live day to day and play things by ear until life took a pattern to itself. Worry was a bad idea in any case, she told him, because you had to live with what you were given and anyway most of it was preordained for you by your genes and your hormones.

Mrs. Sinnott felt Colm thought too seriously about life. She'd like him to have had a girlfriend to help make it a bit easier for him. Colm never had much time for girlfriends, not that he could have had them anyway, the girls of Easkey not being very likely, he thought, to take an interest in someone who failed to knuckle down to work or who was plain-looking like Colm. Also, the girls of Easkey would have liked a talker, Colm imagined, which he clearly was not, as his aunts liked to remind him each time they called to the house to visit his mother, asking him at every available opportunity if the cat had bitten his tongue and then tittering

252

back and forth with a sound like a violin made before it was tuned.

Now and then they suggested to Mrs. Sinnott that he should be brought somewhere. The 'somewhere' usually referred to the hospital in Castlebar that had improved Mrs Sinnott's cheeks. Aunt Rina in particular felt his silences were highly unnatural for a boy in the prime of his life. For her they were indicative of a kind of mental disturbance she'd witnessed once in a friend of her sister-in-law from Carrick-on-Shannon, a woman who kept putting her hand in and out of her jacket coat for no discernible reason.

Aunt Elsie agreed with the viewpoint, remarking that she never thought Colm to be the full shilling since the day he'd let Popeye the cat, his pet, loose on his hamster, another pet, resulting in the hamster's (rather horrific, she thought) death. Mrs. Sinnott laughed off these grievances with a shrug of the head, however, assuring both Aunt Rina and Aunt Elsie that Colm was quite a happy chap really and just not into smalltalk.

Colm didn't know what smalltalk was. He imagined it to be the sort of thing Madge Conroy went on with when he brought her to the Estoria on Tuesday nights, particularly when the Intermissions came and she took out her banana sandwiches and went on about Peadar Farrelly's new Datsun or her favourite Rolf Harris song or the cold she got without reason last Christmas which made her use up a whole packet of tissues a day every day since.

Mrs. Sinnott strongly approved of Colm's liaison with Madge Conroy. When she came to the house after visiting the Estoria on Tuesday nights she sat her down and served her tea and ham sandwiches, which were her favourites, and talked to her about her father, who had arthritis, and her mother, who was a bingo enthusiast, before filling her a hot water bottle and a glass of Horlicks and ushering her to the visitor's room. It had a Super Ser and a sunset by Turner and a copy both of the *Reader's Digest* and *Women's Own* by the bedside.

'Madge, of course, isn't Colm's girlfriend,' she liked to say to people she met, 'well not yet anyway.'

But Colm found himself getting increasingly involved with Madge the more he saw her. Sometimes, in fact, the tone of her conversation, innocent and all as it was, led him to believe a certain presumptuousness making itself felt in her attitude towards him. Put simply, she wanted him to marry her. He was, after all, what was seen in the town as a 'good catch.' He may not have been Einstein in the brains department but he'd managed to scrape through the Leaving Cert and was now working in Ryan's shoe shop and saving so hard from his overtime earnings that there was a fighting chance sometime in the future that he might one day put up a bid to buy it, or at least a share in it, when Mr Ryan, the elderly proprietor, retired.

Colm was surprised at how Madge liked to introduce him to her friends. Sometimes on Fridays they'd go on a foursome to Gilligan's and consume Harvey Wallbangers with ice and get merry running down Joseph Heatherly, the supervisor at the social welfare office where Madge and her friends worked, and Mr. Hegarty, the shop steward who was suspected of being a queer. Colm often imbibed a glass of Guinness with Madge's friends to be sociable and one night it made him so tipsy he told them all a joke, something he'd never done in company before, which made them all sit up and take note. It wasn't a very good joke, and Larry Dillon, who was Madge's friend's escort for the evening, had even heard the punchline before, but the fact that it was Colm that was telling it made him laugh hysterically, even taking the trouble to say 'Damn good' three times in a row when it reached the end.

Madge was delighted with herself that Colm was, as she put it, 'coming out of himself.' The following Tuesday night on the balcony in the Estoria as she watched Joan Crawford kissing Robert Taylor in Cinemascope she sneaked her hand into his. As she did so she imagined herself married to him in one of the fancy neo-Georgian houses that were going up on the outskirts of Bohola with a patio and an American style kitchenette. Later that night, sitting on the beach at Rosses Point and listening to an *a capella* version of Rolf Harris' 'Two Little Boys' on Colm's Japanese transistor, Madge became so elated that she took Colm's hand and placed it on her thigh, rolling up her skirt a little bit for good measure and then gazing meaningfully into his eyes.

Colm was startled at this, having grown up believing it was men who took the initiative in such matters. But he felt quite pleased at having his hand on Madge's thigh, even though it wasn't the thinnest of thighs. Later that night when he invited her back to his house to listen to Buddy Holly records he found himself dancing close to her with the lights off and his chest pressing against her breasts. He even pulled up her skirt around her waist at one stage though this, he told himself later, was more out of experimentation than desire. Colm had never seen himself as the sort of person to exploit girls in dark lighting conditions when no one else was around but when he did it to Madge Conroy it seemed to him that he might get to like this sort of thing. Dammit, he might even have sex with her someday, and perhaps even conceive a child as a result.

Colm had once seen two people having sex together. It was in Eyre Square in Galway when he was on a shopping trip with his mother some years ago. He'd become separated from her for some reason and had wandered into the square, eventually happening upon a negro and a slim-legged girl who seemed to be pushing one another up against a wall. On closer examination the girl was revealed to be Ann Hallinan, Fr. Gilman's house-keeper, who'd been let down twice in love. Colm had thought she looked comical being pinned against a tree by a black man who grunted. So comical, in fact, that he had to hold his mouth to keep from laughing out loud.

But when Colm pushed Madge Conroy's dress up as Buddy Holly was singing 'Everyday' in the background and Madge looked much more enticing than usual in the dim light, everything changed. Now sex and kissing and all that kind of stuff seemed quite natural to him.

Six months after this incident, Colm put a ring on Madge's finger and they began saving to get married. They also began house-hunting, which became like a hobby for both of them and gave them many hours of pleasure. They had their eye on a particular one that was off the main road but still not too far from the shops. It had lovely duck egg wallpaper and fitted carpets in all the rooms. Colm had left Ryan's at this stage, Mr Ryan having done the dirty on him by selling the shop to his cousin in Templemore, but he'd got an even better post as an orderly in Easkey Hospital by this stage and Madge was doing overtime in the Department of Social Welfare at the rate of time and a half on Saturdays and double time on Sundays.

On the following Whit Sunday they were married in a quiet ceremony attended mainly by Madge's relations, Colm never having got along well with his own ones (especially aunts Rina and Elsie) and feeling also that he didn't want to attract too much attention to his marriage in case it didn't work out. Not that there was any reason it wouldn't but you never knew, did you? The way his father's life ended proved that.

Madge was a different kettle of fish to her mother. Her temperament was more balanced and she was an excellent cook and housekeeper.

She was also able to let her hair down when the occasion called for it, and she had a reputation for being able to think 'outside the box' when tricky situations arose. Colm was a bit nervous on the wedding night, for instance, but Madge knew exactly what to do. She got him to take a few glasses of whiskey, which made him giddy, and then he was fine. Afterwards he got his confidence going and didn't need help from anyone, or any glass of whiskey either.

Over the next few years their marriage became really strong. Madge spoiled Colm with little treats and always had him turned out to perfection when he was going to work or to a do. She also had his breakfast on the table each morning as he rose. His clothes were pressed promptly when he wanted them and Madge's meals were as good as you got in any of the best Easkey hotels. She kept the house like a new pin and whenever she had a spare minute she was out with the duster attacking every bit of dirt visible.

Madge and Colm also knocked out a good time socially. They weren't that big into entertaining but Colm joined a musical society one year and developed a certain reputation around Mayo and Sligo as a baritone. 'I'm no Caruso,' he admitted, but you could get away with certain things when others did you the courtesy of drowning you out. 'It beats sitting in looking at the four walls,' he told his mother, who was delighted to see him coming out of his shell.

Madge's guilty pleasure was the cinema. She dragged Colm along to anything even half-decent that was showing, tearjerkers especially. Every Tuesday she made a point of looking up the *Sligo Champion* to see was there any chance *The Day They Gave Babies Away*, her favourite film, would ever come back to the Estoria. If it did, she felt sure she'd go through a whole set of tissues before it even reached the halfway stage.

Colm often found himself thinking back to his childhood belief that he would end up a bachelor. How silly that seemed now! With the passage of time he cultivated a Van Dyke. He also bought a Hillman Imp to drive to work. When he got to forty he became a clerk for a Management

Consultancy Firm and in the evenings he allowed Madge to advise him on the importance of being promoted.

In the summers they visited Madge's mother and father, an aging couple who were glad to see Madge set up with such a refined husband. Her father was a sensitive man with a limp who entertained Colm for hours telling him about his gardening expertise. Her mother was more severe. She spent most of her time complaining about the irregularity of her pulses when she wasn't watching the latest instalment of *The Brothers* on the BBC.

Madge improved her appearance over the years, at one stage cultivating a fetish for a face cream called Ether which she applied four times daily, at another adorning her neck and wrists with a perfume which smelt too strongly and cost too much, as Colm liked to remind her.

She frequented a hairdresser and a masseur once a week and took to smoking cigarettes called *More* from a filter and getting herself and Colm invited to cocktail parties thrown by the Chamber of Commerce. Colm's mother usually went to these as well. If she had enough sherry she'd pontificate on the declining standard of morality among the youth and the decay of family life. Colm would be irritated with her over these displays. He would keep silent as she spoke, spending his time gazing into the bottom of a glass of Fanta waiting for her to finish. To take the attention off her, Madge sometimes did a karaoke number of a Philomena Begley song.

Colm and Madge didn't have any children. Nobody knew the reason for this but it was Colm who was usually blamed for this. He himself said it was a mutual decision between them not to reproduce. 'I'd feel guilty bringing a child into the world in its present state,' he said one night to a man in the musical society, which led to a rather robust debate. When he told Madge about it she said she thought it was a strange thing for him to say. As far as she was concerned the world hadn't changed very much since she was a child, and even if it had she still thought it was a pretty good place to be.

When he got into his forties, Colm started sleeping in a separate room from Madge. The reason, he explained, was that he slept better on his own and he needed his rest to be able to perform at his best at work the next day. The real reason, however, was that he simply didn't love Madge any more. Her body was an increasing source of irritation to him as the years went on, as was her voice, which tended to rasp when she became excited about something, which seemed to Colm to be a very frequent occurrence.

Sometimes he woke up in the middle of the night and strange thoughts came into his head about his father and his heart would pump for no reason. When this happened he ran into Madge's room in a state, clutching at her without being able to tell her exactly what was wrong with him. Madge would always calm him at such times, popping one of her capsules into his mouth and telling him it would pass, which it generally did.

Colm eventually conquered his problems, to everyone's delight. It was important, he realised, not to think too much about life, as his mother liked to tell him, because when he did the things that came into his mind were jobs that were more interesting than the one he had, or women somewhat prettier than Madge, or a house bigger than the one he had, and a family of three.

Mrs Sinnott got more and more scatty in her old age and eventually she had to be put into the place in Castlebar that dealt with people who couldn't cope in the outside world. Here she spent most of her time asking the carers when her husband would be home from his audit, or how Colm was getting on at school, or if they thought he would ever take a serious shine to Madge Conroy, a rather plain but amiable girl from the Social Security office whom she knew would take good care of him when he started to worry, as Colm unfortunately tended to do.

She would die soon, Colm thought sometimes as he gazed at her pale eyes and the yellowness of her face, which would of course mean taking a day or two off work for the funeral, if he decided to go.

Enniscrone Idyll

Nobody knew his name. He'd been at the beach a month now but he spent most of his time indoors. Sometimes you'd see him out with his dog. He was injured fighting in Libya and had a scar running down his cheek as a result. He rented a cottage overlooking the beach. It was filled with pictures of soldiers. Sometimes children peered in his window to get a look at them. If he saw them he chased them away with a rod.

He drove a car that was on its last legs. It only started when he pushed it down the hill. Afterwards he jumped in to engage the clutch. He always drove to the same place, a war memorial where he sat for a few minutes without speaking. Afterwards he went to a cemetery where he laid flowers on a grave. .

When people passed him on the street he looked through them as if they didn't exist. Eventually they stopped saying hello to him. In the evenings his cottage was always dark. There were no signs of life inside except for the radio that crackled faintly in the background.

If the weather was fine he went down to Rachel's Coffee Shop or bought an ice cream from the van that parked on the beach. Rachel was a local. She started off the shop after her father died to give herself somewhere to go in the morning. She'd been close to her father. She'd given up her job as a district nurse to mind him after he contracted lung cancer. Then he got too bad and he had to be brought to the hospital. When he died people thought she'd go back to that but she didn't.

'The Man', as she called him, had been coming in for coffee for over a month now. He was more polite to her than he was to anyone else but they hadn't had a conversation longer than it took for her to take his order and drop it over to his table.

He reminded her of a ship on the ocean, a ship looking to anchor.

'I can't understand his effect on you,' her friend Jasmine said to her.

One day he dropped a photograph out of his wallet.

'Is this yours?' she said. She picked it up and handed it to him. He grunted a thank you.

He began to come in more in the next few days. He still didn't speak to her but there was something in his expression that seemed to change.

Jasmine still complained about his rudeness.

'He brushed by me at the door yesterday,' she said, 'as if I didn't exist.'

'That's just his way. I wouldn't read anything into it.'

'There's no excuse for bad manners.'

'Maybe he's just awkward.'

'You can't keep making allowances for him. Why do you do that? Are you interested in him romantically?'

'He's unusual,' she said, 'I'd like to know more about him.'

'I can't understand why,' Jasmine said, 'I find him threatening.'

'He reminds me of my father,' she said.

'That's a dangerous comparison to make. He's an odd bod. Anyone with half an eye could see that. I think he'll use you if you show an interest in him. He could even be violent.'

'I don't think so. He's wounded.'

'We all know that.'

'I don't just mean in his body.'

'Don't be too interested in him. Someone saw a gun in the back seat of his car.'

'He's a soldier. He probably has a licence for it.'

'I don't care. I don't trust him.'

Over the next few weeks she saw him walking down the pier in the evenings. He often took his dog for a walk on the beach, throwing a ball ahead of him for him to fetch. Other times he just sat by his car smoking. If people were playing golf in the pitch and putt course across the way he looked across at them. After a while he usually walked down the pier and sat there for a few minutes before turning back. Did he know she was watching him?

She wanted to leave the café sometimes and run out to him to get to know more about him. She wanted to ask him who was the woman in the photograph.

He continued to come in to the café. He'd have his cup of coffee and then leave. Now and again she found herself holding his cup after he was gone.

One day when he came in he didn't order anything at all. He just walked up to her and said, 'It was my wife.'

She said she didn't know what he meant.

'It was my wife,' he repeated, 'the photograph you picked up.'

'Oh,' she said, 'She's a very beautiful woman.'

He stiffened.

'You mean *was*,' he said.

'Was?'

'She died.'

'I'm sorry. I didn't know.'

'How could you have?' he said, 'I never told you.'

She found herself blurting out 'I lost my father,' but he didn't hear her. She was glad. It was a stupid thing to say.

He went out the door and walked down towards the beach. She wanted to follow him but thought better of it.

As she turned back to the counter she noticed he'd left his wallet on it. She ran out of the café to give it to him but he was too far down the pier to follow him.

She decided to bring it up to his cottage that evening. She didn't tell Jasmine because she knew what she'd say.

When she went home she found herself making herself up as if she was going on some kind of date. She wondered if he'd talk to her when she saw him. Would he just take the wallet the same way he'd taken the photograph?

She expected nothing as she walked to his house an hour later. She felt nervous She started to shiver.

She saw a leaf falling from a tree. Autumn is here, she thought. She was glad. You could have too much sun.

She took a deep breath as she knocked on the door. Would he answer it? She wasn't sure.

There was a shuffling sound and then he appeared, squeaking the door open a fraction. He looked her up and down as if he didn't know who she was.

'You forgot this,' she said, handing the wallet to him, 'You left in on the counter.'

His face seemed to register surprise for the first time.

'I seem to make a habit of leaving things at your café,' he said.

He thanked her. She blushed.

'You're welcome. I wouldn't want it to fall into the wrong hands, especially if it has money in it.'

'Only a veteran's pension,' he said, 'Nobody would get far on that.'

She didn't see him for the next few days but she wasn't able to stop thinking about him. Every day since her father died she'd woken up with a knot in her stomach. That was gone now, replaced by a different kind of tension.

She knew she was thinking about him too much. She hardly knew him so it didn't really make any sense. He might be gone next week or even tomorrow. Jasmine told her she was mad.

'How could you think of him in a romantic way?' she said, 'He's obviously obsessed with his wife.'

Maybe she was right. How could anyone live up to a memory?

'I haven't let myself get close to anyone since my father died,' she said.

'Maybe that's the problem,' Jasmine said, 'Maybe you have some crazy idea of turning him into him.'

The days crawled by. Her concentration was bad and the customers became demanding as a result. Work was like drudgery. But then the tourist season ended and business slackened off. There were less people in the café, less on the beach. The ice cream van disappeared. The pitch and putt course closed down.

She watched him walking the pier under the unrelenting sun. In the evenings when everyone was gone home she sat on the wall of the café looking down at him. She felt a strange energy in herself that she half feared. The lights on the beach glinted like an invitation.

The next time he appeared he had his uniform on him. Was that some kind of statement, she wondered? He looked official. He was carrying a bunch of flowers in his hand.

'I picked these off the road for you,' he said, handing them to her.

She found it hard to believe he would do something like that. It seemed out of character. Her hands shook as she took them.

'I'm very grateful,' she muttered.

He looked awkward. She asked him if he'd let her give him a cup of coffee and he said he'd like that.

He sat down and she brought over one for herself as well. They were the only two people in the restaurant. They sat listening to the waves pounding the shore. For the first time she felt relaxed with him. Time wasn't beating down on them. It sat still in the deep of the evening.

A customer rapped at the window but she shook her head at her, miming the word 'Closed.'

He stared at her intently.

'Have you ever been married?' he asked her.

She was surprised that he would ask such a question, that he would ask any question at all. It was a while before she answered.

'I came close once,' she said, 'but we wouldn't have been right for each other. ' It was only because he brought the subject up that she remembered that time of her life. It was a long time ago. Up to now she'd blotted it out.

'Sometimes it's better to walk away from a situation than to make a mistake,' he said.

Was he speaking from experience? She wanted to ask him about himself. How had he got the scar on his face? Where had he fought? She couldn't put the words together so she continued to just sit there watching time pass.

'You gave me a cup of coffee on the house,' he said then, 'Why don't you let me return the compliment?'

She was excited by the offer but tried not to let it show.

'That would be nice,' she said, 'When were you thinking of?'

'What's wrong with now?' he said.

'I'd have to shut down the café.'

'What's the problem about that? I don't see many people here.'

He was right. She stood up and took off her apron. She'd never closed early. After so long doing things the same way she became flustered even at this slight break of routine. She started dropping plates as she put them away.

He seemed amused by her, which made her drop even more things.

'I have palpitations,' she said by way of an excuse, 'the coffee always does that to me.'

'Maybe that's why people drink it,' he said.

The wind was getting up. Down at the beach there was some commotion. It looked like something was washed up, maybe a small whale. A lot of people had gathered to see what was going on. Some of them were filming it on their camcorders.

She locked the door and they looked down. Children were jumping up and down excitedly.

'That's some crowd,' he said, 'I haven't seen so many people in one place since I got here.'

'It's because so little happens,' she said. 'Everything is magnified.'

The wind knifed through them. She pulled her collar up around her. He only had his uniform but he didn't seem bothered by the cold. .

She hadn't been out with a man since before her father died. It was something you had to get used to. She didn't know what to say. The simplest sentences became suffused with tension, even comments about the weather.

'That wind would cut you in half,' she said. He nodded.

She wondered if he was nervous too. Maybe he was just quiet. It wasn't the same thing.

Their footsteps crunched through the gravel. When they got to the cottage he stopped. For a second she thought he was going to kiss her but he didn't. He bowed and said, 'My humble abode.'

He opened the door and looked in. He asked her to stay outside for a moment while he tidied something up. As she waited she looked around at the back of the cottage. His car was there, looking like a wounded animal with all the scratches on it, and the rust. His dog was sitting beside it.

He came out and made a clucking noise. The dog wagged its tail.

He flicked his fingers.

'Shed,' he said and the dog waddled over to the shed.

He went back into the house. He was gone for a few minutes. When he was ready he called her in.

She was surprised at its tidiness. Everything seemed to be in its place. It didn't look lived in.

'You have it like a little palace,' she said.

'It's a pigsty in comparison to your coffee-house.'

She looked around. It was clearly the home of a bachelor. Everything smelled of disinfectant.

He told her to take a seat while he put the kettle on. There was a Nat King Cole record playing on a turntable. She looked around her. There were pictures of battles on the wall, figurines of soldiers on a side table.

A few minutes later he came out with the coffee.

She sipped at it, wondering what they'd talk about. She thought it would be easier than in the café but maybe it was going to be just the same.

'I don't think your friend thinks too much of me,' he said. She hadn't known he was even aware of Jasmine.

'Why – has she said anything?'

'She doesn't have to. Her face says it all.'

'I wish she wouldn't be like that. She has no right to adopt an attitude. She doesn't know you from Adam.'

'Maybe I don't know myself,' he said.

She thought he might say something more but he didn't.

'It's a small town,' she said, 'Most strangers get that treatment. After twenty years here you're still a blow-in.'

He smiled.

'How did you get your scar?' she said suddenly.

'It's a long story.'

'I bet you were very brave,' she said.

'I never felt brave, 'he said, 'just unlucky.'

'How are you adjusting to ordinary life?'

'Not very well,' he said, 'but then you know that.'

She was going to ask him about his wife but she stopped herself.

'Do people keep nagging you about where you fought?' she asked instead.

'Not really. Nobody really cares and they're right not to care. It's over. At least for them.'

'Is it for you?' she asked but he didn't say anything to that.

He got up and walked around the room. Then he stopped.

'Why did she die and not me?' he said. She wasn't sure if he was talking to himself or to her.

'What do you mean?' she said.

'I'm sorry. I shouldn't have said that. Forget it. Can I get you another drink?'

'No thanks.'

'Do you think I'm odd?'

'I understand you.'

'That's some achievement.'

'I suppose when you've seen the things you have, you don't have much interest in trivial chit-chat.'

'I'm afraid I was never much good at that anyway,' he said smiling. When he smiled his scar seemed to go away..

The record finished. She listened to the needle scratching on the turntable. He turned it off. Then he came over and sat down beside her.

'He's very unlucky,' he said, looking down at the ground.

'How do you mean?'

'The man you didn't marry. He's very unlucky not to have got you.'

Her heart started to beat faster as he spoke. She wanted to kiss him, to feel his breath on her. She wanted him to bring her down to the sea, to swim with him in the ocean. The nurse in her wanted to bathe his scar.

The moon outside the window was clear and full. As she looked out at it she had a memory of a day long ago when she walked through a wood with her father. That was before his illness ruined everything.

He pulled up his sleeves as he was pouring the coffee and she saw more scars on his arms. As she looked at them she felt herself becoming weak. Then she burst out crying.

She tried to drink the coffee but the cup was shaking so much in her hand it started to spill on the floor. He took it and put it on the mantel-piece.

'I don't know what's up with me,' she said. 'Maybe it's my father. I don't know what to think. I can't concentrate. Tonight when I came up here to you I didn't know what I was doing. I still don't. I haven't been myself for a long time now. I don't even know how I feel. When I walked in here I felt it all coming back to me. The smell of disinfectant reminded me of the hospital. I started to think of sickness, of suffering, of all the things I –'

He put his hand over her mouth.

'Don't talk,' he said.

He sat down beside her and looked into her eyes.

Everything was quiet suddenly, even the waves.

She smelt the leather of his uniform.

A Convent with no Mercy

She sat beside her suitcase in the kitchen. Her mother was across from her in her wheelchair.

'I suppose you'll be gone from us forever now,' she said.

Forever. What did that mean? The past was another kind of forever for her. It had moulded her beyond her wishes.

Joe Danaher had moulded her too. Was he a reaction to this? A denial of her true self?

Her mother wanted to know if Danaher could provide for her. Fr Dineen wanted to know if he would one day marry her. Everyone else wanted to know everything about the girl who was once supposed to become a nun and was now tarnished.

They'd groomed her all those years in the convent. She was the prize pupil, the one who always put her hand up first at catechism, who was never sloppy or disobedient. Someone from what was called a 'good' family. Someone who never looked at a man. But the quiet ones were always the most unpredictable. Everyone knew that. They had a tendency to from one extreme to another.

Simon Creedon called. He'd been her boyfriend since as long as she could remember. After she got pregnant with Danaher's child he'd offered to 'do the decent' by her. To accept another man's child as his own.

Was this touching or desperate? Maybe it was both. She'd spent over a decade dating Simon, seeing him more like a brother than anything else. After she met Joe she broke with him almost overnight.

'It's still not too late to change your mind,' he said now, the words out of him even before he'd properly crossed the threshold. He was standing in an old anorak looking forlorn. The lost child he'd always be.

'I know that,' she said. But she knew she wouldn't.

She didn't know whether to ask him in or not. If she did it could get awkward. Up to this she'd managed to keep him at arm's length but now, on her last night in the village, he felt he had a kind of legitimacy to call.

And of course he also knew her mother preferred him to Joe. That was another bargaining chip.

'If there's anything you need you have only to ask,' he said, 'You know that.'

'I do, Simon, and I will. Believe me.'

She stood up and gave him a hug. He tried to kiss her but she drew away. She was glad when she heard her mother's voice from the kitchen.

'I'm off now,' she said, 'I'll call you from the airport.'

'So that's all I get,' he said, 'A lousy three-minute phone call. After everything we shared.'

'We've been through this before, Simon. I'm not able for it tonight.'

'You're making a mistake, you know. Everyone says that.'

'Probably,' she said, to stop him saying more.

He put on the sad look again.

'Well okay, I'll leave it at that. It's your funeral. But don't come running back to me if it doesn't work out. Or should I say when it doesn't work out.'

'I won't. Goodbye, Simon.'

He looked as if he was going to try and kiss her again but in the end he didn't. He zipped up his anorak and lurched out.

'Goodbye, Mrs Ferriter,' he called from the doorstep but she didn't hear him.

She shut the door and moved over to the window. She watched him walking down the lane.

Her mother wheeled herself in.

'You'll not find anyone else like him,' she said, 'He'd have stood by you through thick and thin. Not like the other article.'

She remembered the night things changed. She'd carefully resisted Joe's advances any time they went out before, even when she felt her heart pounding inside her at seeing him. But that night she gave herself to him. She didn't really know why. They were just sitting quietly in the car and she felt herself weakening.

He said he loved her. She didn't believe it but it was enough. It was the first time he said it. And the last. Two weeks later she learned she was pregnant.

He was casual when she gave him the news. That made her think it wasn't the first time he'd heard it from one of his paramours.

'Have you thought about having something done with it?' was his first reaction. She wasn't surprised. She hadn't gone to him expecting him to propose marriage to her, or to propose anything at all, even a prolonging of their relationship. The words were spoken in the tone of voice you might use for getting a new hat.

'No, I'll have it,' she said bluntly. She didn't think she had much of a maternal instinct but she couldn't consider anything else.

'That's what I expected you to say,' he said. She didn't know if he was glad or upset. Maybe he was just neutral. Maybe it didn't matter.

'I'm going to London,' he said, 'you're welcome to tag along if you want. No plans, no promises.'

Her heart started to pace as he spoke. No plans and no promises. In a way that attracted her. It was so different to everything she'd known up to this.

'I'll tag along,' she said. He smiled a rare Joe Danaher smile. Did that mean he wanted her? It had to. He wasn't the type of man to make an offer from duty, that much she knew.

She didn't know if they'd last together but somehow that didn't seem to matter either. After all the years with Simon she almost wanted change just for the sake of it. Did he love her? Maybe love was too grandiose a term for what they had. No plans and no promises. These were the reasons she was going with him. When you didn't make promises you couldn't break them. It was that simple.

In some ways she was enjoying her rebelliousness. 'A Convent of Mercy girl gone off the straight and narrow.' That was the way her mother put it. She hadn't defended herself, the last few weeks characterised by sullen silences more than anything else. After a decade of nursing her she was starting to think of her own needs for once.

She wasn't nostalgic about leaving. Not guilty either. Her mother was partly responsible for that. She rarely thanked her for anything she did for her. It was almost as if she expected it. Children took care of their mothers in old age because mothers took care of their children in youth. That was the way it worked.

But what if you didn't get on with your mother? What if she exaggerated her symptoms? She often exaggerated her symptoms. That made her harder to nurse.

She'd always had a tendency to dramatise things. Were her aches and pains a part of that drama? Did she drive her husband away because of it all those years ago?

He was gone almost a decade now. His absence had thrown them too much together for too long, casting them almost like a married couple. Or was it too easy to blame their problems on him? Her mother's afflictions, her own blunted life, her alliance with Simon.

'You've inherited your father's badness,' she said to her the previous week. And then, 'If you leave me I'll die.' It wasn't the first time she'd used emotional bribery.

Maybe it was what kept her under her influence all the years. If it had, it was gone now. The hand had been over-played. In her mind she was already gone from Ireland. Maybe that was the way she'd been for years. Maybe she'd been waiting for a Joe Danaher to come into her life.

She saw the taxi coming up the driveway. She looked at her mother. There was no response. She kept her head down. She was knitting, not even dropping stitches. She was going to last out the stubbornness.

When the taxi-man knocked on the door she collected her bags quietly.

'Dr Nolan said he'd look in on you later,' she said. Her mother nodded.

She bent down to hug her. She wanted to tell her she loved her but she couldn't. Her mother looked up at her helplessly, her arms hanging like cement by her sides.

'I'll call you,' was all she could think to say.

'I'll pray for you,' her mother said.

She answered the door. It was an elderly man, a man she knew slightly.

'I'll be with you in a minute,' she said, handing him her bags.

She went over to her mother and put her arms around her. She was crying. She gripped her tightly, dropping the knitting. . She had to pull herself away.

She looked back as she went out the door but her mother was looking away. She went into the taxi. She started to cry.

'Are you all right, ma'am?' the taxi-man asked her.

'I'll be fine.'

The engine revved. She looked back at the house as they drove off. It seemed frozen in stone. For a moment she was tempted to run back, to cancel all her plans, but she resisted it. In some ways it was harder to go than stay.

The taxi-man asked her about her mother, about Simon, about her forthcoming baby. She was polite but

275

non-committal with him. Maybe she sensed his disapproval of her actions even though he did his best to conceal it.

He dropped her at the train station and she went into a waiting-room to sit down. She felt heavy and breathless. She still had seven months to go.

What would the English hospitals be like? What if Joe deserted her before the birth?

She couldn't let herself think about things like that. Go with the flow, she kept telling herself. *Que sera sera.*

The train arrived. She got on. She saw some familiar faces but ignored them, digging her head into a magazine. Seven months to go. Twenty-eight weeks of worry.

Don't think. Don't think.

The landscape sped by. She had two cups of coffee and felt her heart palpitating. She thought of Simon, what he would be doing now. Probably taking in the cows. Taking in the cows and brooding about a woman who walked out on him after pledging her loyalty to him for ten years.

Women, the gentle sex. The betraying sex.

'I don't love him,' she'd said to her mother when she tried to get her to change her mind about him.

'What's love?' her mother had snapped at her, 'Love is Hollywood. Love is broken promises, men who want you for the night. Don't marry him if you don't love him but for God's sake don't go from the frying pan into the fire.'

Joe was the fire. Fire sounded interesting. But fire didn't last. It burned itself up.

She could take that. Even if it lasted only a year, or even if it lasted less than a year. She'd have given the ten years with Simon for one with Joe. It was shallow but what was wrong with shallowness? What was right for a day was as good as what was right for forever.

'You're infatuated with him,' her mother had said, 'He'll be gone from you before you touch down at Heathrow.' Maybe she was but she'd deal with that too. If she didn't go she'd have spent her life wondering about what she was missing, even if that was worse than the life she knew with Simon.

It was raining when she reached Connolly Station. She walked across Amiens Street and waited for a bus. She checked her phone for messages but Joe hadn't rung. Before that would have fazed her but now it didn't.

Alone or with him she'd survive. There was something exhilarating about the uncertainty. It wasn't a frying pan or a fire. It was just change.

She got on a bus for the airport. There were hardly any seats on it but she managed to get one at the back. Nobody was talking to each other, just staring blankly ahead. It was so different to the country, so strange and cold. And yet a part of her welcomed this coldness. It was what she was looking forward to about London, in such contrast to where she was coming from.

When she got to the airport she didn't see any sign of Joe. He'd promised to be there before her but he was always late for everything so she wasn't surprised. Whether he did it deliberately or not she didn't know. He always had some excuse, each more elaborate than the last. She didn't really hear them anymore. Or care. When he arrived he probably wouldn't refer to his unpunctuality or apologise for it. That was all right too. They'd have a meal and he'd tell her not to fuss, as if women left their mothers every day of the week. Or had babies every day of the week.

She had another coffee as she waited for him. Something about airports had always entranced her: the exaggerated emotions, the pairings and the partings, the long silences followed by the chaos of a plane landing. She listened to the sounds of farewell, of laughter and tears. She saw herself in the people going away and the people coming home. She was like all these people, she was inside their heads.

She wondered if her life was beginning or ending. She didn't think she was burning her bridges. If it didn't work out she could always go back to her mother. After a time away from her she might have better feelings towards her; she mightn't judge her so much. Most anger, they said, was anger against oneself. What she was breaking away from wasn't another person. It was her own inhibitions.

What would London be like? Most of her friends had been there a number of times but she'd never been outside Ireland, not even for a weekend. She'd only been in Dublin a handful of times as well. When she told people that they looked at her as if she had two heads. 'What planet have you been living on, girl?' they said. But it wasn't as if she hadn't had opportunities. Up to now she simply hadn't wanted to travel, she didn't need it. She never went anywhere just for the sake of it.

She wondered if Joe would be different in London than he was here. 'Could he be worse?' her mother had said when she put that thought to her. She could understand why she said it. He'd always been rude to her any time he called to the house.

He might be attentive or he might be cruel. She'd heard rumours about him getting other girls pregnant and then abandoning them. He might even have one in London. She ruled nothing out.

The important thing was not to come back humiliated if he left her. The important thing was not to come back to her mother begging for forgiveness or agreeing with her that she'd misjudged the situation.

Her mother would say something like, 'The poison is gone from you, thank God.' She could almost hear her voice mouthing the words.

'You'll miss your hot baths and your colour TV,' she'd said to her last week. Which was true.

278

She'd miss Simon too, despite herself. He was like a blanket she pulled over her head for so long. She imagined him in the years to come, popping the question to another woman when the loneliness got to him, making a big splash for the wedding, raising a barrel-load of children with the Old Values.

Joe appeared before her as she was lost in her thoughts He had no luggage with him, just the clothes on his back. She hadn't expected more. He was going to create a new life for himself in London just as she was.

'How's the going?' he said, as casual as ever, as if he was joining her for a day's picnic. She didn't dare ask him if he'd brought his passport, knowing how much he hated questions like that.

'Did the old lady put up a fight?' he said.

'Yes,' she said, 'but I beat her on points.'

He laughed. Now that he was beside her, all her doubts about him subsided. Any that remained she pushed to the back of her mind. He's here tonight, she told herself, even if he won't be tomorrow.

He bought her another coffee and they laughed about nothing.

The words of old love songs went through her mind: songs of Connie Francis, Petula Clark, Brenda Lee.

'Come fly with me?' he said as the number of their flight was read out over the tannoy.

They walked towards the departure gates. She felt afraid and confused. The night bit into her as they walked towards the plane.

He had his hands in his pockets. As they boarded it she felt a rush of excitement. Her baby kicked inside her as she sat down and he seemed to sense it, putting his hand on her belly.

Her knees shook as the plane took off.

She looked down at the fields below. They spread out like so many handkerchiefs, a mosaic of green. She thought back to the way she'd been the night she first met him, her heart beating with a mixture of excitement and fear, a virgin ripe for the plucking at his crude and rustic hand.

Diaspora

I waited for her in the torrents of rain, my ears buzzing with the whoops of Arsenal supporters, jeers sent out over the balustrades as the own goal went in during extra time. There was a stampede outwards after the whistle went and in the thunder of feet I felt a sense of panic that proved almost clairvoyant. An ambulance wheeled past a few minutes later. I tried to ignore it but when it stopped outside her house I seemed to know. She was lying outside the door with a white cover over her. A sea of bodies surrounded her and I elbowed through them, telling everyone I knew her. 'There was nothing I could do, guv, honest,' a man said to me, the man who must have been driving the car that mowed her down. Beside him a policeman was putting a blanket over her.

'Did you know her?' he asked me after I'd pushed my way to the top of the queue. I found myself saying, 'I'm not sure.' He thought I was trying to be clever but I wasn't. We'd only been going out for a month.

I became involved with another woman, either to prevent myself brooding too much or to pretend I didn't care. She was a supermarket cashier with a cockney accent. She'd reminded me of those women you saw in black and white films on UTV. She hadn't much interest in me nor I in her. We just came along at the right time for each other. There was almost a sense of liberation in expecting so little from a relationship. Both of us believed we'd seen it all. Maybe we had.

In the first few weeks she was a novelty to me. She told me of a deprived upbringing in the Black District and it held a kind of fascination for me. We spent most of our time getting drunk together, feeling undressed without our whiskey. Sometimes she flirted openly with acquaintances from her job but it hardly bothered me. We threw parties attended by her navvy friends, huge Geordies with Kawasaki 900s parked outside the door. 'You're not such a stick-in-the-mud after all,' she said to me one night as I did a dance on the table for her. It was probably the closest to a compliment she'd ever get.

She spent most of her time doing courses – in self-development, creative writing, how to be assertive. Why, I thought, did assertive people always feel they needed to be more assertive?

The days passed in a haze of abandonment. We talked seldom, which seemed to work. Then one night I came home to find a man with her. She was sprawled on the sofa and he was on top of her. It looked like they were involved in some kind of athletic exercise.

'So this is what we've come to,' I said.

'It's not what it looks like. Or maybe it is.'

I decided to go home to Ireland. It had always been my escape route when things became too much. My father had a farm outside Ballina. It wouldn't be the first time I'd used it as a psychiatrist's couch.

He met me at the train station, whether out of curiosity or concern I didn't know. I communicated with him so seldom maybe he was relieved to know I was still alive. He never made any secret about the fact that I was dubbed the black sheep of the family. I never knew what it was that I'd done to deserve this tag. Maybe it was what I hadn't done. My brothers had all been high achievers. Maybe I was just a grey sheep instead of a black one. In my own mind I was simply colourless. This was the way I liked it. It gave me less responsibility.

My mother, like most Irish mothers, still regarded me as a child of ten years old. England, of course, was the pagan country to her. She thought I wouldn't be able to resist its various temptations. (Of course she was right). I could sense her trying to burrow her way through to my soul as she bombarded me with questions: 'Have you had relations with other women? Are you keeping bad company? Are you still going to Mass?'

Both of them looked older than I would have expected. When I mentioned this, my father told me it was my fault: I was worrying them into early graves.

They gave me my old room. Memories of my youth nudged as I entered it. How many hours of misery had I spent here being beaten by him before I had the courage to leave. No wonder England appeared as a promised land to me all those years ago. Anywhere would have.

My father put me working on the farm, imagining every problem of the mind could be solved by a dollop of fresh air. Maybe he was right. When you were working you had no time to think. I fell into bed every night like a child, my head singing with exhaustion.

They kept asking me why I came home from London. I told them a woman I knew had died. At first they suspected I might have had something to do with it. I was always sorry whenever I told them anything because it usually led to dark questions. You were better to say nothing, though that led to other kinds of suspicions.

I felt myself getting itchy feet but I wasn't sure if I had anything to go back to. I'd left my job and wasn't sure it would be kept for me. When I suggested I might be going off again, my mother grew distressed. She tried to guilt-trip me.

'Your father won't live forever,' she said.

'He probably will,' I replied.

Maybe she relayed that comment back to him. The next time I saw him he was different. He'd reverted back to the cruel man I grew up hating.

'Where did we go wrong with you?' he said, 'Everyone in the family got the same upbringing.'

And the same beatings?

'What does it matter now anyway?' I said, 'I'm going off. It's always the same. After a week or two we argue. It's always going to be like that.'

'Could we not give it another try?'

'What's the point? I'm not sure you even want me here.'

'Your mother does.' Well at least he was honest enough to admit that.

I told her he was the main reason for my leaving.

'I know he's heavy weather,' she said, 'but he loves you. He just doesn't know how to express his feelings.'

I felt like saying he expressed them well enough with his fists when I was a child but I didn't.

Instead I just said, 'I have no bitterness towards him but I need to go away now.'

'I get that,' she said, 'Just don't make it forever.'

A few days later I sat with him at the railway station. He was wearing his one and only suit, the one that was trotted out for weddings and funerals. It was showing its age as much as he was. And as much as I was.

'There's no need for this,' he said, 'Maybe we'll start to get on if you stay. 'It was almost amusing to listen to this latest strategy he was using now that I was slipping out of his net again.

'We can probably love each other better from a distance,' I said. I slipped him a few quid as the train came and it took the edge off my guilt, my awkwardness. His eyes lit up as he saw it, making the goodbye easier for me. I was glad my mother wasn't there; she wouldn't have allowed herself to be bought off like this.

'I'll write to you,' I said to him as I got on the train.

'I hope you will,' he said. It wasn't much to ask but then I'd never offered him much. I watched him getting smaller as the train drove off. He looked like a sad little boy in his crumpled suit, all dressed up for a non-event.

When I got on the train I felt strange. The people around me looked unreal; I thought I was seeing them through a daze. I reclined in my seat and listened to the clack of the wheels, the chatter of people around me. Now and then they tried to engage me in conversation but I had nothing to say to them. A man came around with sandwiches. I bought one but it tasted like leather. I felt my stomach retching so I went to the toilet. I thought I was going to throw up but I didn't. Everything was locked down inside me, waiting to explode.

I thought of my father and his little life. Was my own one any better? One of us was isolated in a field, the other in a block of concrete. Neither of us had a plan or an ambition; we kept ourselves going by the reiteration of platitudes. He was looking for peace and me for love but it didn't look like either of us would be successful in our searches.

When I got to Heuston it was raining. I didn't bother to pull up the hood of my anorak because I wanted to feel it on me. Maybe, I thought, it would wash away all my pain. I got on a bus for the airport and booked into a hotel there. I conked out as soon as I hit the pillow. The next morning as I boarded the plane I felt strangely cleansed.

In London I found my job was gone. In the old days I would have screamed blue murder but I didn't care now. A part of me was almost glad. I wandered the streets trying to decide what to do with my future but in the end I decided on nothing. A decision not to make a decision is still a decision, maybe the most important one of all.

The sun was a sickly yellow, there was a kind of ash overlaying everything. I hung around my apartment playing old fifties records, trying to ignite some flame of nostalgia in me. I had nightmares about the accident, about her lying there. Was I trying to block it out? I told myself she meant nothing to me, that I hardly knew her, but the nightmares kept coming.

One night I rang my father even though I had no news. It was the first time I'd ever contacted him from London. He said he missed me. I said I missed him too. We were softer towards each other than ever before but I knew it wouldn't last if I was home. I needed the control of distance to feel warm towards him.

When I got bored with being bored I started going to dances. At one of them I met a girl who was a professional dancer, a 25-year-old who saw in me a father figure, a man with all the answers. Because she thought it, I acted like it and eventually I came to believe it. There was something wonderful in the inconsequentiality of it all.

We didn't go out after the first few weeks of getting to know each other. Sometimes we just went walking in the park or played records in the apartment, doing little but letting time pass. She was too young to have had a past but in that emptiness there was purity. Freedom from the past was freedom from its sins as well.

It was ludicrous to attempt anything permanent with her, ludicrous even to ask her to give up her career. I wondered at what stage my age would become an issue. Sometimes I told her about my mad Irish parents and she laughed. 'At least you *have* parents,' she said. She didn't follow up on the remark and I didn't ask her to. I didn't want to know too much about her for fear of spoiling what we had.

We never intended to spend our lives together. We told each other we'd know when it was over and then one day it was. There was no need to say anything. One night when she was dancing at a concert I put some things in a case and just walked away from it all. I didn't feel I was doing anything she'd disapprove of or even be surprised by. I tried to picture her coming home to the empty rooms, going up to bed and waking up the next morning without me, wiping the sleep from her eyes like the child she was.

I got another job and threw myself into it, working hard to murder my need of her. One time she wrote me a letter but I burned it without reading it.

The new year came in and I did my best to forget, forget casual departures as I'd once forgotten a final one. I started to fear memory for the weight it put on me, a weight that did away with my freedom. I became quiet, quiet with self-sufficiency.

On a dreamscape pure as birth she came back to me, the world became flesh once again, illusion a new tenet.

I hald a stranglehold on time.

Leaving Leigue

The sky is calm. Clouds like pregnant women hover over her. She stands beneath them with her shoulders drooped, the words of the priest echoing dimly in her ears. People come over and sympathise with her. Her expression remains implacable. There's, a calmness inside her she hasn't known before, the calmness of seawater stilled. 'At last I'm free,' she says to herself, 'Emotion has been the lie.'

She listens to the dribbling of clay on dull ash and thinks: I have become woman again.

The priest closes his missal and the mourners walk to their cars. Most of them look guilty to her. It's as if they feel there's something to be apologised for in being able to walk away.

Engines wheeze to life like before a rally. Then the sky opens and she listens to the drumming of rain on their roofs. There are nods and gesticulations, embarrassed: farewells, dutiful offers to visit them when she feels up to it. She thanks them but inside herself she's laughing at their bland politeness, at the artificiality of their gestures. As they drive out of the graveyard she feels a kind of pity for them. She feels they're dead inside themselves.

After they've gone she stands alone in the silence, the rain like a balm to her. Today my life has begun, she tells herself, my imprisonment has ended. Now I will be like a child in the spring.

At home she removes all memories of him. There's a fishing rod, a photo of him in a duffle coat, a prize he once won for basketball. In some ways it doesn't seem as if he's dead. He seems to have just flitted off to some strange place, a place she can visit anytime she wants.

In the next few days she changes her hairstyle, the way she dresses. She meets people socially, acts jaunty with them. She's accused of not being properly bereaved, and later of being hysterical. Those who think they know her well say, 'It's her way of dealing with it.' They think she's in denial, having a kind of breakdown.

She collects a new set of friends around her, people who don't annoy her with interrogations, with character analyses. She decides to create a new identity for herself, to move bull-headed towards whatever destinations she decides on.

The weeks glide by and her plan seems to work for her. 'I'm not grieving,' she says, 'I'm celebrating.' 'It's as if he held her back in some way, as if she wasn't properly herself with him.

There are countries to be visited, she tells herself, men to be encountered. Her life up to now has been compromised; she's one of the few blessed with a second chance.

She reminds herself of a woman trying on a new coat, the coat of a different personality, one she half fears for its strangeness.

She starts socialising at fashionable restaurants. Men come up to her and tell her she's sophisticated. If they ask her to go to bed with them she's more amused than anything else. She consents sometimes but only if there are no strings attached. If they ask to see her again she refuses. Some of them pursue her, pursue her more the more she runs away from them, as is always the case. Sometimes she's flirtatious with them and sometimes nonchalant. She plays them like a violin.

She buys expensive dresses, running up bills in exotic boutiques. From youth she always craved predictability. Now she cultivates change for the sake of it.

On many evenings she sits by her window just looking out at the night. When people call she's polite but distant. 'A widow melting into her situation,' a friend remarks.

'Involve yourself in things,' he tells her, and she smiles. 'I'm already involved,' she says, though in what she's not quite sure.

Winter arrives. It's a brutal one but she's immune to it, immune even as it saws at her bones. When the new year comes in she watches the shoots come up, the frost dying into an explosion of colour in the park outside her door.

She plays with children, becomes a curiosity in the neighbourhood, a strange old woman who seems to have no roots.

She starts to cultivate the attentions of people who ask little of her, who respond to her much as you would to an item of furniture.

She sits in lounges sipping wine with acquaintances, her finger crooked on the edges of liqueur glasses. She speaks of opera, the theatre, escapism. But to her it's not escape; it's a new reality.

Her life is a game now, a glorious, decadent game. She plays it with a new-found gaiety, the gaiety of a child. The only thing she fears is that one day somebody will come to know her as she is, one day invade her mind and in so doing deprive her of it.

She misses appointments, forgets even to eat. There are moments in life, she tells herself, when nothing appears to be happening and only when they're past do you realise they've been the seminal points.

Flyers come in the door advertising evening classes. She signs on for some of them, hardly looking at the details. She sits in lecture-halls taking notes on European literature, reads books by authors she never heard of before.

He comes back to her in sleep sometimes, appearing more real in death than he was in life. He flickers before her cowed and submissive. She remembers what he was like in the early days, the days before they really knew each other, before they started taking each other for granted. She thinks of her lack of concern for him, the excess of his concern for her. She said to him one day, 'I wish I could be injected with some of your passion.' He replied, 'I have enough for both of us.'

He's now moved into a part of her that nobody can touch. He's like a domestic animal, something thing to be taken out and patted when the need arises, something to be consoled and flattered.

A solicitor calls her to come in and listen to the details of his will. When the probate is wound up, his money comes through to her. 'What will you do with it?' the solicitor asks her. She says, 'Spend it, of course. 'What else could one do with money?

She visits a casino one night expecting to get a thrill from it but nothing happens. It can only be exciting, she realises, when one has a fear of losing, when one can't afford to lose. One night she makes an outrageous bet and wins. She's amused. It seems to be always the way with life – you win when you don't care if you do or not.

Her money brings her a new kind of attention from men. They try to seduce her in such transparent ways she's almost insulted. For a while she goes along with it.

She creates new identities for herself, forms fantasies she discards almost as soon, turning her back on them when more enticing ones become available.

Summer arrives, the sky a royal blue, the heat almost equatorial. She wallows in it for a while and then runs away from it to the shadows. Indoors she draws the curtains and meditates. She falls in love with the night.

She goes on a holiday to Spain, becomes an object of fascination to people bewildered by this strange woman in colourful clothes who bothers with nobody.

What's her secret, they wonder, that she seems to have no need of anyone?

She walks through the streets without looking where she's going. There are near-accidents, the swear-words of drivers who swerve to avoid her. Each step she takes is a potential hazard. At home she reads endlessly into the night, forgotten texts of sixteenth-century mystics, the print swimming before her eyes. Sometimes she stays awake all night gazing out at the metamorphosis of traffic lights, the apparent idiocy of them when there are no cars around to obey them. At dawn, with gold ringing the edges of the trees, she watches all the busy people rushing to work, their faces gritted against the wind as they hug their brief-cases. She sees them as people who mistakenly think they're going somewhere in life, people like she once was herself.

She enters a cinema, watches images tumble in upon one another in the half-light. The screen is watery for a while and then blank, blank like her mind, an area of empty space. The projector starts to whirl, the celluloid getting caught in the spools.

When the film ends the projector continues to run on its own, the confused blotches of footage like kaleidoscopes along the wall. She becomes dizzy as she looks at it.

But then it stops and a new image takes shape. She sees him as he was that first day along the promenade, a freckle-faced boy in wellingtons running up to her beside a beach, his profile fringed with the sun. He calls out her name and she answers him. Then she begins to run as well, the wind blowing her hair so wildly she's blinded by it.

She feels a longing for the sea.

Handyman

It's winter and you're standing there in front of me like a part of the landscape, your eyes glaring at me as if suddenly I'm something to be feared.

You smile at me sometimes and I smile back at you or grimace, depending on how old you make me feel, or how irrelevant. You're boring me with theories about Proust and I'm boring you with theories about Karl Marx. The evening is still around us, the river flowing free in the channels. The leaves are stripped from the trees and the hills are bare but the sky is blue above us in the twilight, bluer even than the royal blue of your eyes.

Your expression becomes seductive as you tell me you want to take me to your room. I wonder for a moment if I'll accede to the temptation but then I look around me at all the work I have to do and I call on my inner reserves and tell you I'm going to soldier on until the light fails. You register surprise at this, as if I'm guilty of some great sin in putting you second, but I tell you it's only for a time. Afterwards I continue cutting wood and you continue driving me insane with your shapeliness. The wind is ruffling your hair in the way you hate but I tell you nothing could interfere with your beauty and a naive gaiety lights up your eyes.

Your father arrives, a volatile man in a Porsche. He pays me my money as he does every Friday at the same time, the money we've been putting away for our future together, though he isn't to know this yet because I'm just a worker to him, not someone he should expect to engage his daughter's affections.

He shakes my hand as he enters but I find it difficult to be natural with him. When he holds you close to him I'm jealous. I'm even more jealous as he kisses you, as though he has some kind of ownership of you. As you lift yourself up to him I see you suddenly as the baby daughter you'll

293

always be to him, the little girl who used to play in the attic with rag-dolls or make up stories about being married to princes in medieval castles. I've never claimed to be the prince to meet your dreams but I've told you I'm a pauper often enough. So often maybe you've become immune to it by now, which might be the reason you smile at me behind his back as he gives me my cheque.

When he speaks to me I'm shy with him and this you smile at too. You're amused at the contrast in me because you can hardly shut me up when I'm alone with you as I rant on about my latest pseudo-intellectual thesis. When he asks me if the work will be finished on time I mumble some half-excuse to him about the bad weather, or some half-excuse about the quality of the paint I'm using, and again you fall apart laughing at my lies. As I watch you making faces at me from behind his back I think I deserve an award for staying serious with him.

He exits eventually. I tell you you're a very naughty girl to be carrying on like this and still not too old to be put over my knee. You turn on me when I say this, asking me why our feelings for each other should all be a secret anyway. Why am I not shouting about you from the rooftops, like any man sure of his love? But I tell you I'm not the shouting kind. And that your father would strangle me with his bare hands if he knew the truth about us. Anyway, what man was ever sure of his love, or what woman either? You grow quiet at this. As I take in your vulnerability I can't help wondering if you wouldn't be better off with one of those accountants he has in mind for you instead of this futureless interior decorator who treats you so badly.

The night comes down. You talk to me more solemnly now, asking me when are we going to be committed to each other forever.

'When will we see the end of all these guilty weekends away from him?' you ask me.

Tomorrow would be too long to wait if I had my choice, I tell you, but as things stand I have no fortune or house or connections or pedigree or wedding cake or monkey suit or ring. Apart from these minor considerations, however, I'm welded to you like the wood I cut to your father's specifications.

I drive away from you soon afterwards, from the tension and confusion of you, heading off down the driveway in a pick-up truck that's been on life-support for many years now. When you overtake me in your Alfa-Sud you all but ram me into the ditch. Is this is your little revenge on my vacillations?

'Are we going out tonight?' you scream at me above the din of the traffic as you pass. I tell you that's up to you, that you've always been the organiser of our going out together even if you haven't been the organiser of our future. You seem pleased at this. In fact you always seem pleased at any sliver of power I confer on you.

You name a place and a time. As I watch you careening down the motorway in your familiarly suicidal fashion I'm already lonely for you. I wonder what it is in me that holds me away from you, whether it's a fear of what you represent or the terror of what I might become myself if I was with you 24 hours a day.

Later in the night you call to my bedsit. You're dressed tantalisingly in a pinafore that shows far too many of your curves for the good of my heart, but when I try to kiss you you fend me off like an interloper, like someone who has no right to your charms. Afterwards you go into one of your famous silences again, one of those silences that make me wonder at the ineradicable contrast between us, the contrast between your sensitivity and my dull world of facts.

Maybe it's because of something I've said, I think, or something I haven't said. Or maybe it's due to nothing at all. I don't enquire about the reason now because you've always been a mysterious creature to me. Maybe it's this more than anything else that I worship in you.

You sit before the television with your head buried in a book by Proust. I wonder if you're reading him to annoy me or because you really are fond of such bilge. When I can't take it any more I slam your book shut. I put a record of Tom Waits on the turntable instead and you scowl at me, telling me he's raucous and incoherent. I tell you that's why I like him and you scowl some more. I realise how different we are from one another, how bourgeois you are at the back of it al, or maybe even the front of it all. But I say nothing to you about that. I'm terrified of your temper when I criticise you, a temper almost as relentless as your love.

As the night drifts towards midnight we lie together without speaking, your eyes sad again with our evanescence. I'm sad too as I look at you though the reason is less clear to me. I find my mind drifting away from me as I hypnotise myself with you, drifting into a fantasy that either includes you or some woman who looks like you.

I begin to be afraid of the waywardness of my mind. I read my love poems to you and you cry as you always do when I try these pretentious ditties on you. Most of them end sadly in one way or another and this you take to be my way of saying something disastrous to you about us. I smile at you when you say this, telling you it's not true, that all poems are sad, or at least all good ones. You ask me if I see myself as a good poet then, and I say yes, but a better lover. I hold you to me and you're like a beautiful flower as you lie beside me looking as defenceless as a hunted animal.

'Are you always this possessive with your women?' you ask me then, the curiosity lighting up your face, but I tell you there's only you, that it's always been you and you alone. By the way you look at me I think you believe me even if I don't believe myself.

I don't know why I spend so much time telling lies to you, being the maverick I am where women are concerned. It's probably a result of cowardice. If I didn't maybe you'd walk out on me, seeing me for what I am, or am not. Maybe they're part of my survival kit, my ticket to a temporary Eden.

In the morning, sober, you head off for your philosophy lecture to contemplate the meaning of life and I head off to your father's house to contemplate centimetres. We become distant again in our society roles, our early-day irrelevance to one another. It's as if last night has never really happened to us, or any of the nights.

When we meet again you're full of the parties you've been at, the classmates you've listened to in buzzy university corridors, the prosperous young men from North Mayo who've asked you to accompany them to the more fashionable dinner parties in the suburbs. When I ask you why you haven't taken them up on their offers you frown at me, not appreciating my joke. I have to apologise for it afterwards but in a part of myself I think it would be good for you to see these people, if only to avoid my claustrophobia. You become enraged when I say that to you, telling me they're only children, that if we belonged fully to one another there'd be no need to suffer their juvenile overtures.

'But you're a child too, 'I say then. You frown at this, telling me this is my famous three-year-old excuse for not marrying you. As I look at you now I see the maturity of a woman twice your age in your features and wonder for a moment if it isn't me who's the child after all.

The day you tell me you're carrying my child I laugh at you, thinking it's one of your little jokes, but then I see the intensity in your eyes, the mixture of fear and anticipation that makes them iridescent, and I know it's true. I'm stunned until I realise how long we've been together without this threat of progeny and suddenly it all seems inevitable and right.

I ask you if you're trying to bribe me into marrying you and you smile. There's a kind of insecurity in you now, or is it relief?

You imagine I'm going to be annoyed and in a way I am. You always told me you didn't want children. You ask me what we're going to do with it and I shrug my shoulders, telling you I'm not quite sure, that we could either flush it down the nearest toilet bowl or love it to death, whichever you want. You're amused at this. You laugh at my joke but what you don't see is my tension. You don't realise I've never had this kind of complication in my life before.

We're married soon afterwards in a ceremony that has two witnesses, a priest and (I think) ourselves. This is to keep your father happy. You know I'm not the marrying type, even if I adore someone as much as I adore you.

When everything is over we adjourn to the poshest fifth-class restaurant in the area for a meal that does away with my life's savings in one fell swoop. As we get up from the table you ask me if we'll have to wash the dishes to pay for it. You seem to be joking I tell you it's uncomfortably close to the truth.

Your trousseau is a hand-me-down bolero, your bridal suite a boarding house in Tubercurry that's falling apart but both of us become too drunk to worry about such details. At the end of the night we fall into each other's arms like a pair of children. You tell me this is all you ever wanted in life and I say the same. I feel like someone out of a continental movie. All we're missing is a trip to the local fleapit in a battered-up car with the windshield wipers going back and forward frantically as it lashes rain and we made mad love inside.

We move into a one-up, one-down flat your father buys to house his beloved daughter and his indigent son-in-law.

Our first few months together are uneventful, despite what I expected. We don't seem to argue any more than the other couples on the estate judging by the breaking glass we hear nightly around us, and the roaring voices. I'm still unable to provide for you as you should be provided for and I tell you I feel ashamed of this but you order me to shut up when I say this, telling me it's always been an ambition for you to be poor, that it's a novelty to you no matter what way your father feels about it.

He condescends to visit us occasionally now that I've made an honest woman out of you, having made your bump legitimate. Any time he visits us he thrusts some money into my hands before he leaves because otherwise we'll have nothing to buy food with. I apply for whatever carpentry jobs I can find but they're few and far between now, as I always expected would happen if I ever tied the knot with anyone. We spend the nights looking at the four walls rather than going out together to those bars we kept in business before we were married and I wonder if the dream is dying for you as it is for me now that we're together all the time and not secret lovers anymore.

One night a kind of rage grows up inside me and I throw a cheque he gave me into the fire. You cry as you watch me doing this and I apologise afterwards, knowing pride has always been my greatest fault. We don't see him after he hears about this and you try to conceal your frustration at this fact.

The gap between us widens. I don't work at all now and argue with you most of the time.

'You've changed,' you say, and it's true, but I always told you I would if you tried to move me into your stable life. You tell me I have a chip on my shoulder then and I'm almost too lethargic to deny it, almost too lethargic to deny the fact that this is why I give you such a hard time. A part of me has always resented the fact that you were born on a higher social scale than me even though I sublimated such resentment into my passion for you.

I'm around the flat all the time now, criticising you whenever I can find anything to pick on, and sometimes even when I can't. Some nights I hear you crying upstairs as you talk to your father on the phone. I try to guess what he's saying to you as he tries to calm you, imagining he's telling you that you should never have thrown in your lot with a loser like me.

When I meet him afterwards he looks at me with the kind of hatred that says, 'You've ruined my daughter's life.' He doesn't need to speak to me for me to realise he'd murder me on the spot were it not for the fact that such a daughter still seems to care for me in some insanely foolish part of herself. Later in the night I tell you maybe you'd be better off to go back to him because he probably loves you more than I can ever do, or at least love you in the way you want to be loved, with concern rather than passion.

But you aren't really listening to me now. As I speak I see in your eyes that childish sense of hope that we could one day be an irresponsible young couple again, the couple we were when it was all new to us, when we were in the fool's paradise of discovery.

Our baby is born only a month premature. This mean we manage to preserve our respectability with those upstanding relations of yours who've been busy computing dates on their fingertips ever since you began to swell.

When it arrives I'm jealous of it in the way chauvinists are always jealous when their wives have babies. They know they're only going to be second best in their affections now.

The flat becomes insufferable to me as the days go on, yourself and your equally beautiful daughter making my shallowness all the more apparent. I spend most of my nights away from you now, either wandering the streets in some vague confusion or meeting the kind of women you always hated to see me with in the old days, the coarse-tongued breed I used to know before you tried to refine me. At the end of these nights I usually end up sleeping with them. One night I even bring one of them to the flat, stumbling in through the door sometime after midnight, so out of my mind with drink I've almost forgotten where I am. I'm in a merry mood and expect you to be likewise, expect you to indulge me as you've always indulged me, no matter how reprehensible my behaviour. But you're a different woman now that you've had your baby and grown tired of me. You grow sullen instead, sullen with your rage as you retreat into the escape-hatch of our daughter.

I hit you sometime afterwards, a new low even for me. I don't know why I do this and neither of us can believe it when it happens. It's the one thing I promised never to do to you the day we married and I truly believed I never would. But now that it's happened I know it would only be too easy for it to happen again, not only once but maybe a great many times.

'It's the drink that makes you act so cruel,' you tell me afterwards, trying to protect the last reserves of my dignity, but I tell you it's life that does it to me, life and failure and the whole sickly mess of it all.

The reason you don't know this is because you've always romanticised me, as the affluent often romanticise the poor, never having experienced poverty themselves at first hand and seeing it as a kind of magic novelty.

Tonight I took at you curled up beside me in sleep, your beauty merging in to the sepia of old photographs. It's clear to me that I must leave you soon because you're too tender ever to do that to me, though I see a remoteness in you sometimes when I talk to you that suggests you've already done so in your mind.

As I look at you weaving restlessly before me I feel the old desire for other women, women less tolerant than you perhaps, but more desirable to me despite these reasons, or even because of them.

I wonder what your reaction will be if I leave you, whether you'll be angry or indifferent as the months go by, whether you'll try to come after me or be glad I've gone, whether you'll look for someone new to take care of you or slot yourself calmly into the role of a woman anxious to get on with Part Two of her life.

I wonder too what I'll find out there, or even what I'm looking for, or if there's anything to be found in the first place, if it isn't all at the end of the day an illusion created by my wanderlust.

You turn now as if sensing my anxiety, drawing me to you as you whisper from your half-sleep the uncomplicated syllables of your love. I stay in your embrace for a moment and then I release myself from you and stand at the window. I drink in the fragrance of the night as I listen to the wind whistling through the trees.

I look at you without seeing you for the first time and the last time as I edge myself towards the bitterness and empty passion of the road that lies before me in the night.

Going Forward

They were sitting at home in their house in Morrison Terrace watching television. There was a cookery programme showing.

'Do you mind if I turn that off?' he said.

'No,' she said, 'I wasn't really watching it.' She was knitting a jumper for their daughter Sheila.

He started pressing buttons. Eventually he found one of the movie channels. A science fiction film was showing. A robot was trying to take over the planet.

He turned up the volume.

'Jesus,' she said, 'Turn that bloody thing down, will you? I can't hear myself think.'

'Sorry,' he said. He turned it down.

Her hands seemed to be travelling at a hundred miles an hour as she twirled the knitting needles.

'I'm hungry,' he said.

'Not again. You're just after eating.'

'Maybe it's the tablets I'm on. Is there any of that pavlova left?'

'What pavlova?'

'The one I got last week.'

'I can't believe you're saying that. It's probably getting ready to walk out of the fridge by now.'

'I'll chance it.'

'It's your funeral.'

She went out to the kitchen. The cat wandered in from the back room. It started to miaow.

'Here, kitty,' he said. He took it up and started to stroke it. It purred.

The robot was mowing down everything in sight with his big claws. A space capsule was waiting to take him back to his planet.

She came in with the cake.

'It's a week past its sell-by date,' she said, 'but have it if you want it. I'm not going to say anything else. You never listen anyway.'

He started to eat it. The robot continued to gobble up everything in sight. She seemed disturbed by it.

'If you're watching that I don't mind,' she said, 'but *True Stories* is coming on in a minute. Would you mind if I recorded it? It's going to be about this woman who gets pregnant and she's told the baby is going to be deformed but she wants it anyway.'

'Watch it if you want,' he said, 'I'm not interested in the robot. He has nobody left to kill so it's getting boring. In fact I was thinking of going for a walk.'

He put down the cake. The cat jumped down off his lap.

'At this hour?'

'It'll probably do me good. I have a bit of a headache. Walking clears the cobwebs away.'

'I'll give you a Panadol if you like.'

'It's all right. Those lads do you more harm than good. I need to get out. I've been cooped up all day.'

'Don't forget your coat,' she said, 'That wind would skin you.'

'I don't need it,' he said brazenly.

She turned on *True Stories*. A woman was having an ultrasound. A doctor with a grim face was standing beside her.

'Mrs Crenshaw,' he said, 'I'm afraid I have some bad news for you.' Mrs Crenshaw looked up at the doctor pleadingly.

He went out to the hall and put on his coat.

'Don't be too long,' she said, following him out, 'There's nothing good on the streets at this time of night.'

'Don't worry. I'm a big boy now.'

He went out to the car and sat in. She didn't like him driving at night, especially with drink on him. He'd had a few glasses of Guinness earlier.

'There are a lot of maniacs out there,' she always said, 'No matter how careful you are you have to look out for the other fellow.'

He released the handbrake and let the car roll down the hill. That way he knew she wouldn't hear him. When he got to the road he turned on the ignition. He wondered if she'd look out the window. It was unlikely. Mrs Crenshaw was probably in labour by now.

He didn't know where he wanted to go. Anywhere was better than nowhere. He thought of driving to a pub but that would have taken too much time. She'd have blown a fuse. He could call her and say he'd got a puncture but she'd know he was lying. She always knew. Women had that sense about them. And of course he was never a good liar.

He drove down the road without a destination in mind. Almost without intending to, he stopped at an off-licence. The bright lights seemed to be inviting him in. That was his excuse anyway.

He bought a half-bottle of whiskey. When he got back to the car he put it in the glove compartment. He wasn't sure if he was going to drink it or not. Sometimes just having it there was enough. Sometimes he was more inclined to want it when it wasn't there. It was nice to have the choice.

He drove past the river, the church, the Londis at Ardnareee. He saw a courting couple, an old woman wheeling a pram. As he was passing the shopping centre the lights went red and he accelerated through them. When he looked in the rear view mirror a man crossing the road gave him the fingers. He made a gesture back at him over his shoulder. That always made him feel good.

Driving relaxed him. It blotted out his thoughts. If he could have driven all through the night he wouldn't have complained. He'd done that once when they were going on a dawn sailing from Rosslare to Le Havre. That was when

Sheila was a baby. They hadn't been out of the country since.

Before he knew where he was, he found himself at the factory where he worked. When he wasn't thinking, that was where he always ended up. It was as if the car had a memory of its own, as if it knew every crack in the road from home to here.

There were still some lights on inside. He heard the whirring of machinery but couldn't see any people. He parked in the spot that had allotted to him for the past 27 years: 5E.

He turned off the engine and sat listening to the clanking of the machinery. It sounded strange. It felt pleasant to him now that he didn't *have* to listen to it, that it was his choice. During the day it was just like white noise, like an explosion inside his head. Now it was almost pleasant.

Maybe I should wear ear-muffs from nine to five, he told himself, chuckling. That would sort out everything. It would be worth it just to see Toffler's face. Toffler was his boss. He was a bastard.

He turned the radio on. A newsreader was talking about a drug addict who'd raped a child in Newport. He sounded bored. Maybe the whole country was reaching scandal fatigue. Sometimes you didn't even take it in anymore. You listened to horrific reports and put on a cup of tea. We were all turning into robots, just like in the movie. Maybe one day the movie would become real. We'd gobble each other up. The world would end. Everyone would be gone. Except maybe Toffler. Toffler would outlast us all. Bastards always did.

The night grew still. What would he do now? Suddenly he felt adventurous.

He opened up the glove compartment and looked at the bottle of whiskey. It was inviting. Would he leave it there or take it? He was tempted. The forbidden fruit. Drink always tasted sweeter when she wasn't around to see him knocking it back. But would it give him a bad reaction? A worse-than-usual hangover?

He tried not to drink when he was depressed. He was feeling a bit high now. Why was that? It couldn't have been anything a simple as having gone out for a drive, could it? And yet he couldn't remember having done that for months. It wasn't as if she actively stopped him doing it, or pleaded with him not to. He just knew she didn't approve of it. She had that way of conveying such disapproval with an expression. Women didn't need words. They could kill you with a look.

He took a swig from the bottle. It burned into him and made him feel good. He loved drinking whiskey neat, loved the way it hurt you as it went down your throat.

A music programme came on the radio. He started tapping his foot to it. Lights flickered on and off in the factory. Was somebody looking at him? He kept drinking. Dammit, this was good. His headache was going away.

In no time at all, the bottle was half finished. How could he have got through it that fast? 'You're a guzzler rather than a drinker,' she'd said to him once. It was probably true. He didn't know how to pace himself. Maybe that was what was wrong with him, trying to do everything too fast and falling on his face as a result. Not only with the booze – with *everything*.

Imagine, he thought, if he kept drinking and slept in the car all night. Imagine if he wandered into the office at dawn with this massive hangover and sat at his desk with a casual expression on his face.

'Morning, Toffler, how's the crack?' he'd say, or something like that. Toffler would probably be carried off on the spot. Into hospital suffering from shock. After 27 years the mouse had finally roared.

They'd probably sack him on the spot. Or maybe they

wouldn't notice. People were funny like that. Sometimes you thought you were making a horse's ass of yourself and people reacted as if there was nothing at all awry. Of course the more normal situation would be imagining you were being perfectly logical when the truth of it was you were three sheets in the wind.

He finished the bottle and threw it out the window. He felt confused and pleasantly drowsy. What now? Forty winks on the back seat? A breath of fresh air? Back to the off-licence for another bottle, down it in one big slug and then drive the car off a cliff?

Steady on, there. A joke is a joke and all that. Don't lose the run of yourself.

Probably just go home, he decided. He'd had his little bit of diversion. Got the old Dutch courage going. He was ready for her now.

He turned on the ignition and put the car into reverse. Before he knew what was happening it zoomed backwards halfway across the car park. Holy shit. Just as well there was no one around. Especially Toffler.

He was obviously drunker than he thought. Always felt he was a better driver with a few tiddleys in him than stone sober but his friends didn't agree. Neither did the forces of law and order. Nor their damned breathalysers.

Maybe he should leave the car and walk home. The house was about a mile away. Would do him good to get some exercise. The doctor told him he needed that. People his age were dropping like flies from coronaries. Bad lifestyles was usually the reason. Junk food and too much gargle. Too bloody lazy even to walk to the pub. But what good was exercise when you'd polluted your insides with a half bottle of whiskey?

Decisions, decisions. He kept turning the alternatives around in his mind. Drive or walk? What would happen if he got pulled by the fuzz at some checkpoint? Was it worth risking his licence for a half hour's walk?

I'll chance it, he thought. They'd hardly be around at this hour.

He started the ignition again. This time, instead of putting the car into reverse, it went into first gear and lurched forward. He heard a little tinkle as he bumped off something. It was probably the little steel pillar Toffler had built for him way back when to designate his parking area. One of the perks of being a Very Important Nobody.

He tried again. This time he managed to get it into reverse without going 100 miles an hour. Sharp sigh of relief.

He started to drive home. He turned the radio off because he didn't want anything to interfere with his concentration. He wanted his mind to be clear if the guards were around.

The night was cold but he rolled the window down all the same. They said that was a good idea if you didn't want your breath to smell too much of booze if you were stopped by the cops. If they pulled you over and you rolled it down to talk to them, the smell tended to hit them full whack.

When he was stopped at the lights he found a half-eaten packet of polo mints in the glove compartment. That was good for the breath too. He stuffed two into his mouth.

He drove slowly all the way home. That was the thing about being drunk: You were probably a lot safer than sober drivers because you were so terrified of being breathalysed. Maybe that's why he always thought he was a safer driver when he was blotto. Must remember to add that bit in for his friends the next time the subject came up.

He passed the shopping centre, the church, the school - all the landmarks that were so godawfully boring in the morning but which looked warm and welcoming now. Was it the booze that had caused the change? Or his new-found adventurous spirit?

He reached the house and pulled into the driveway. How

long had he been gone? He didn't know. He wondered if she'd give out to him, what he'd say back to her if she did. He checked himself in the mirror and straightened his hair. He felt faintly ridiculous doing this for his wife. It was as if she was like a date, not the woman he'd been married to for 21 years.

He started to shiver with the cold as he got out of the car. As he got near the door he belched. He always did that after he had a few drinks. He was hoping he didn't get the hiccups. That often happened with alcohol. She used to make him throw salt over his shoulder to get rid of it.

How would she receive him? If she gave out to him, he decided, he was going to let her have it. A confrontation was long overdue. It was time for him to be a man. You couldn't spend all your life being pussy-whipped. It just wasn't right.

He turned the key in the door and opened it. She came out to him in her dressing-gown.

'Jesus,' she roared at him, 'I was about to collapse with worry. Where were you, in God's name?'

'I went for a drive. It seemed like a nice night for it.'

'A nice night for it? Are you mad or something? I bet you've been drinking. Here, let me smell you.'

She put her face into his.

'You're maggoty. Did you drive home in that condition? If you did you're even stupider than I thought. I give up. Don't blame me if you lose your licence. That would be the end of your job, the end of everything.'

He closed his eyes in frustration. He should have stayed at the factory, he thought. The best-laid schemes of mice and men...

He stood up to his full height and rocked on the balls of his feet.

'I was going at snail's pace,' he declared.

She raised her eyes to heaven.

'That's even worse. The guards know a slow driver is

that way for a reason, especially at this hour of the night. They pounce on people for stuff like that. I bet you can't even walk, never mind drive. Let me see you take a few steps.'

He walked past her into the sitting-room. The television was on. *True Stories* was over. She was now watching the late movie, one about an orphan who adopted a pony. A woman was crying. Her daughter was being handed over her child to Social Services after she'd been deemed to be an unfit parent.

'Jesus,' she gasped, 'I didn't think they'd go that far.'

He didn't know what she was on about.

'Is there any of that pavlova left?' he asked.

'I know the pavlova I'll give you,' she snapped. 'I threw it in the bin. Maybe I should put you in there too.'

'I feel peckish.'

'That's the drink talking. You've eaten enough for an army today. How could you fit any more in there?'

'It's the tablets I'm on. For the stress.'

'Don't blame everything on the tablets. You're just greedy, that's all. One of these days your belly is going to go on for a career of its own.'

He went into the kitchen. He fished a soggy piece of cake out of the bin. She looked at him with a shocked expression on her face.

'If you survive that I'll take off my hat to you,' she said. 'You'll probably get some disease out of it. But of course you don't care about things like that, do you? No, that would be too much like common sense.'

'I'll take my chances,' he said.

'Don't be so childish. I know the way you get with drink. You just want to be awkward. You won't be happy just losing your licence. You'll want to get yourself banged up in hospital with food poisoning as well.'

'Shut your trap,' he said, 'You'd give a headache to an

aspirin.'

She put her hands on her hips and looked at him. 'What did you say?'

'I said shut up. For once in your life put a fucking sock in it. Now give me some of that pavlova.'

She stood there looking at him. He'd never raised his voice to her before. What had he been drinking? She shrugged her shoulders. Men. You just never knew with them.

He felt quite good about it all. She stood staring at him for a moment and then walked out of the room.

He looked in the bin for some more pieces of the pudding. It was mixed in with tea-bags and vegetables from yesterday's dinner but he didn't mind. He was going to eat it if it choked him.

He put it on a plate and brought it into the living-room. The cat cocked its ears at him as if it knew something was up.

The film about the orphan ended. A political programme came on, one of those ones where they discuss 57 situations in three minutes – and solve them all. He watched it with the sound down.

She came back into the room.

He continued eating.

'Are you enjoying that?' she said.

'Yes,' he said, 'It's scrumptious.'

Hs stomach rumbled. He felt as if he was eating the inside of a sofa.

'Sorry if I shouted at you,' he said casually.

'Don't worry about it,' she replied, 'I know you're going through a rough time.'

He looked puzzled.

'I am?'

'You know, with Toffler and all.'

'Oh Toffler I wouldn't worry about him. You have to

have a boss. Most of them are nightmares.'

Now it was her turn to look puzzled.

'It's not like you to be so philosophical.'

He took another bite of the pavlova.

'Welcome to the new me,' he chirped.

He gave the last piece of cake to the cat. The room was swimming around him. The political programme was still on. A man with a two-toned shirt and a check jumper was getting agitated about the Middle East.

She sat down at the table and started knitting. Whenever she missed a stitch he thought he heard her swearing under her breath.

He turned off the television.

'Look,' he said, 'I don't want to fight with you. I probably shouldn't have gone out.'

'No, you shouldn't,' she agreed. 'Was it because of me?'

'Don't ever think that. You're not really a bully.'

'Thanks.'

'You're right. Things have just been. ganging up on me. And the weather is getting us all down, isn't it?'

'Now you said it.' She looked at him quizzically. What was he going to come out with next?

'Once the spring comes in and the hour goes forward the evenings will be brighter. That should make us both feel better.'

'I'm sure it will,' she said.

He saw a can of beer on the side-table. He stood up to get it. There seemed to be about half of it left. He started to drink.

'Would you not be better off with a cup of tea?' she said.

'If I have any more tea I'll explode.'

'I understand that but more beer at this hour won't do you any good.

'I don't drink it for health reasons, my dear, I drink it because I like it.'

313

'You need to get a better lifestyle,' she said.

'Change the record, Agatha. That one is a bit rusty.'

She put down her knitting.

'Have you thought of going to the doctor?' she said.

'For what - more tablets? If I take any more of them I'll rattle when I walk.'

'No. just for a chat.'

'About what – the weather? 'The doctor knows nothing. I'm just a number to him. The answer isn't out there. It's in here.' He tapped his head.

She took up her knitting again. He finished the beer. The headache was starting to come back.

'Maybe I'll take some of those Panadol after all,' he said.

She went out to the kitchen. She came back with two tablets and a glass of water. He swallowed them.

Suddenly he didn't know what to say. He was sorry he came home. In the car he was his own boss. It was like his office and bar combined. It was the only place she didn't own him. But he always came back to her. He needed her but he hated the need. It was a no-win situation.

'Sheila will be home soon,' she said, packing her knitting away in a plastic bag with masking tape on it. She'd been in Belgium for the past few weeks, working as an *au pair*.

'That's right. The end of the month, isn't it?'

'So she said.'

'Sheila always gives us a lift, doesn't she?'

'She certainly does.'

They sat in the silence. Neither of them knew what to say to each other. They looked at the television. There was some footage of war. She turned it off.

'Why did you do that?' he said, 'I was watching it.'

'I don't like war,' she said. 'We were talking about Sheila.'

'I thought we'd finished on that subject.'

'She's not a subject. She's a person.'

'Sorry.'

He expression brightened suddenly.

'Hey, I was just thinking – could we bring her to Aran with us this year?'

'Aran? That's a bit off the beaten track, isn't it?'

'I know, but what's wrong with that? It'd be a change for us.'

'I'll think about it. Just let me watch my programme now, will you?'

She turned it on. A tank exploded. Two bodies were thrown from it.

'Goodnight,' she said, 'I'll leave you to that depravity.'

'It's not depravity, Agatha, it's life. Whether you like it or not, these things happen. We may not like it but they happen. It's not like your programmes where everyone plays Happy Families.'

She shook her head.

'Listen,' she said, 'I'm having a cup of tea before I go to bed. Will I put your name on the pot?'

'All right. I give in, says he. Finally. Maybe you'd put on a slice of toast as well.'

'At this hour? Would that be a good idea after all that pavlova?'

'The cat got most of it.'

'All right but you're going to be sick in the morning.'

'Let me worry about that. '

She went out to the kitchen and put on the kettle. He picked μp the paper. He started reading an article about mortgage arrears. The Panadol was making him feel dizzy.

The kettle boiled. He heard the toast popping up. She came in with two cups of tea and two slices of toast.

'I gave you Flora for your cholesterol, ' she said, 'I'm having butter myself. Make sure you don't eat my slices.'

'I'll watch out for that. It would be disastrous. A state of national emergency would have to be called.'

She banged it down on the table.

'Just show a bit of gratitude, all right?'

'Keep your hair on. It was a joke.'

'Just eat it,' she said.

He crunched on the toast. The cat looked at him greedily. He cut off an edge and gave it a bit.

'You'd want to be careful,' she said, 'it could choke on that.'

'Careful, careful, careful,' he said. 'You live in a world of careful. But sometimes people enjoy not being careful, Agatha. People sometimes die of being too careful.'

'They do? That's a new one on me.'

'I'm not joking. This geezer I heard about last week overdosed on diet pills.'

'That's different.'

'I don't think so.'

They sat eating their toast. Agatha had a puss on her. He hated it when she put on a puss. She'd probably go into the spare room tonight. He hated it when she went into the spare room too.

He remembered his mother saying to him before he got married, 'Never let the sun go down on an argument.' It was good advice.

'This is like breakfast at midnight,' she said, trying ro sound jolly.

'Uh-huh.' he said.

The cat yawned. It stretched its paws out.

'What date is Sheila coming?' he asked.

'The 18th. She said she'd ring to confirm it. You'll bring me out to meet her, won't you?'

'I can't. I have bowls that night.'

'Bowls? Could you not forget your bloody bowls for one night?'

'They get snotty if you miss it. You told me you like me going to it. For my nerves. I mean, it relaxes me.'

'Forget about it. I'll get a taxi.'

'Well if you're going to be like that…'

'I said forget about it.'

She went upstairs. A minute later she came down with her night clothes.

'I'm going to undress here,' she said, 'Because of the heat. Don't look.'

They were married for 27 years and she was telling him not to look.

'I think I've seen most of your bits by this stage,' he said drily.

'If you're going to look I'll go upstairs.'

'All right, I won't.'

He turned around. He heard the rustle of garments.

'I can cut the bowls short if you want,' he said.

She let out a sigh.

'At this stage I couldn't care less one way or the other. Stay at your bowls. I can get Deirdre to drive me.' Deirdre used to babysit for Sheila years ago. Agatha still met her at the shops.

'No. I'll bring you. No problemo. I want to make a bit of a fuss of her. Maybe we'll even put on a little spread. You know how she is about things like that.'

'Whatever.'

Agatha suddenly looked sad.

'I hope she stays this time,' she said.

'Is there a possibility she might?'

'Do you not remember? There's a chance of her getting a job in Hanleys.'

'Oh yes, I remember something about that. I think she's getting a bit fed up of the travelling.'

'As you do. At a certain age.'

'It happens to all of us.'

'We wouldn't push her, of course.'

'God no. That'd be the last thing I'd do. It's the quickest

way to lose them.'

'On our way to the airport we might buy a few candles in Spar. I'm baking a cake for her. I'd like to dress it up a bit.'

'It's not her birthday, is it?'

'I don't mean that. It's just to make it special. They have candles for everything now. I was thinking of the ones that say "Welcome Home".'

'I'd be amazed if Spar has one of those.'

'Don't make a gangster movie out of it. Any kind will do. It's just the gesture. It's not the be-all and end-all if we can't get them.'

'We'll get them. Don't you worry your pretty little head about that.'

She smiled. He loved it when she smiled. She looked as if she was 21 again.

'If Spar don't have them we'll try somewhere else. It'll make all the difference. Scanlons have a party section now. They might have them there.'

'We'll see. Anyway, don't lose any sleep over it. Anyway, speaking of sleep I'm off to the *leaba* now.'

She gave him a kiss. That surprised him. Was he forgiven?

'Will you set the clock when you come up?' she said, 'If I was you I'd put it on for a bit earlier than usual. You'll probably have a head on you.'

'That's a good idea,' he said, 'I'm glad tomorrow is Friday.'

'Crunchie day. Maybe we'll go out on the town.'

She gave a dry laugh.

'That'll be the day. I'd hardly know what it looks like.'

She went up the stairs. He listened to her brushing her teeth. Afterwards she went into the bedroom and turned on the radio. She always listened to the Lyric Music channel. It relaxed her.

He looked at his watch. It was 12.27. That would give

him about six hours sleep – at least if he managed to sleep. Most nights recently he hadn't. With a bit of luck the whiskey might help tonight.

He imagined himself tossing and turning for a few hours and then suddenly it would be morning. That was the way it was every night, insomnia giving way to sudden sleep.

He'd drag himself out of bed and then shower and shave. He'd have a black coffee to keep his head clear for the company reports he had to do every Friday.

He'd drive to spot 5E and look around for the whiskey bottle he 'd thrown out the window. He'd look for the dent in the steel pillar that he'd made when he went into first gear instead of reverse. Then he'd do his eight hours work for Toffler and wonder if the old man noticed his hangover.

On the way home he might try to get the candles for Sheila's little bash. It was good, as Agatha said, to have something to look forward to.

In actual fact he had two things: Sheila's homecoming and the long spring evenings after the clocks were changed.

The Old Stomping Ground

I live in Dublin now but a few years ago I went back to Ballina. I thought it might be an idea to try and revive some memories. It was Halloween and my wife Mary was with me.

We drove to Enniscrone first, at her behest. I was always telling her about the great times I had there as a child. The highlight was climbing 'The Valley of Diamonds', a sandhill with so many seashells at the bottom of it that when the sun was shining they seemed like diamonds.

The thing about Enniscrone, like most beach towns, is that if you go there out of season it can seem very dead. It's also on the internet now, which means that all the magic places we thought were ours and ours alone now have to be shared with the whole world. That takes some of the magic away.

The first thing we did when we got there was go into a pub. One of the tables had a brochure listing the town's main attractions. I was sad to see that Enniscrone was now on the tourist map. It had 'amenities.' The seaweed baths were mentioned. We were told how many metres it was from the pub to the beach.

All the points of interest were tabulated. Everything but the Valley of Diamonds was described in painstaking detail. No doubt, I thought, that day would come too.

We walked up the empty streets. How many days had I gone up these same streets with a surge of excitement as I waited for the summer to begin? It was our private kingdom then. A paradise eight miles from home. We felt we had a kind of ownership of it by going there so much.

We decided to walk the beach. Mary was well used to me boring her with stories about the old days here too. We walked across the little bridge and down the shore as I told her about the games of hide-and-seek we played, how we had our own taxi driver to bring us there, how the days seemed endless as we postponed returning to the everyday routines of Ballina.

The walk made me feel ten years younger. No matter how extravagant some of the Dublin beaches were, there was nothing like the Atlantic Ocean to give you a sense of exhilaration you couldn't get elsewhere. On the way back to the car I watched the sun going down behind the dunes in the cool afternoon haze. As I did so I felt suddenly lonely – for my parents, my friends, my past self. I was lonely for all the experiences I took for granted while they were going on, the passing nature of all childish things.

We went back to the car. On the way towards Ballina I pointed out landmarks to Mary as I always did. 'You should write a history of the town,' she said jokingly, 'You never stop talking about it.' Somehow I didn't want to do that. I thought of Nietzsche's statement, 'We only speak about that for which we have lost respect in our hearts.'

As with speech, so it is with writing. I even felt that way about taking a photograph. People said a photograph could capture a scene but why would we want to capture it? Isn't it better to let it be free?

I often wondered if I would have felt as sentimental about anywhere I grew up as I did about Ballina. Was it the town I was nostalgic for or the memories it called up? When an elderly man falls in love with a young woman, people say, it's his own youth he's searching for rather than hers. Maybe it was the same with me and Ballina. I was searching for my childhood, an impossible goal. The places I harped on about meant so much to me mainly because of the events I associated with them.

As we got to the outskirts of the town, Mary said, 'Let's go to some lively bar instead of the usual haunts.'

On previous trips I'd brought her to landmark places that were drenched with the aforementioned memories. The problem with this was that it seemed as if I was trying to suck her into my own time warp. By agreeing to her plan, I thought, I might be making the first step towards killing my old self. In some ways I was afraid of turning into my father, a man who on his own admission lived in the past.

We parked the car near St. Muredach's Cathedral, a building that had dominated my life growing up in every possible way - architecturally, spiritually, psychologically, even socially.

We then walked to a pub in the centre of town, one of the trendy new ones that had opened up to capitalise on the roar of the Celtic Tiger. A delegation of people from Scotland were having a sing-a-long in it and we joined in.

As we did so, I felt we could have been in any town in Ireland. I wasn't sure if this made me feel happy or sad. I still carried the scar of nostalgia inside me, the 'backward glance' that infused almost every Irish writer since Yeats, or even before him.

Mary got talking to a soccer player from Dundee. After a few minutes he asked her out onto the floor. They did the twist. She started to get merry and I was glad for her. I was l aware I'd inherited two left feet from my father. When she sat down she said, 'You should have come out on the floor with me.' I told her I didn't want to cramp her style.

As I looked around the pub I couldn't help wondering if I might see some old photographs of the town, the sepia ones I loved that had been taken in my father's time or even my grandfather's. Mary spotted this. She told me she thought it might be a better idea to forget my family tree and just live in the moment.

I had a whiskey to try and get my mind off myself. The reason I kept coming back to Ballina, I knew, was to try to burn a bit more of it out of myself each time I came to it, so that in time the wound of departure from it would finally be cauterised. I'd never really got over the feeling that I'd been taken from the town against my wishes, being the youngest of the family.

If I'd been the eldest, I always told myself I would have been happy to live there and continue the rich vein of memory that made my youth so romantic. I'm not so sure I would now. The world is a big place. I might have felt hemmed in, even claustrophobic, if other options hadn't been available. You can only be bored by the outer world after you've seen it, not before. If I romanticised those who never stepped outside the county, maybe it was because I myself had. Distance lends enchantment to the eye. In my case it was combined with premature departure. I was a bit like Orson Welles pining for Rosebud, his childhood sled in *Citizen Kane*.

These were the thoughts I was having in the pub as Mary danced the feet off herself with the Dundee supporter. 'The whiskey was a good idea, I told her after she came off the floor, 'Already I feel cured of the past.'

'Good,' she said, 'Does that mean no more anecdotes?'

I said it did. She had often said to me, 'Listening to other people's memories is a bit like listening to them telling you their dreams. You can never sound as interested as you're supposed to.'

After we left the bar we booked into a B&B behind the cathedral. I suggested it because we'd never been there on previous visits to the town so I felt I wouldn't be known there.

It was run by a Dublin woman. That struck us as being ironic. We felt we could now wear our Connacht colours without having to go into too much detail about who we were. I always hated the 'Oh, so you're Hugh Dillon-Malone's son' speech I often got from hoteliers over the years, followed by stories I'd heard a hundred times before. All this woman cared about was that we were quiet, and wouldn't hare off tomorrow morning without paying the bill. I even gave her a false name. Since the eighties, I always introduced myself to people as someone called Peter. It gave me the anonymity I craved.

After we unpacked our stuff I decided to go for a walk around the town. 'You can go on your own if you want,' Mary said to me, 'I'll do my hair and watch some TV.' She knew if she came with me I'd re-cycle the anecdotes I'd firmly promised not to in the bar.

I stepped out onto the street and smelt the night air. I sat on a wall and listened to the church bell tolling with that doleful sound it always had, as if somebody had just died.

After it stopped I walked over the bridge and up the town. Despite my promise to be a man of the moment, I couldn't resist visiting my old home from home, the snooker hall we called The Hibs. I'd spent half my youth there but had only been back to it once or twice over the years, maybe fearing that it would draw me into its web and make it hard for me to settle back to my Dublin life afterwards. I'd avoided it on previous visits to the town. In fact I wasn't even sure if was still in existence.

The building was standing all right but it was boarded up. When I looked through the window, all I could see were cobwebs. I stood up on the sill to have a better look. When I did that I saw that both of the tables that had always been in it were gone. It was just an empty room now. On the wall hung a dog-eared 'Rules of the Game' picture that probably went back to the turn of the century. It was the one thing I recognised apart from the card table. This was in bits. There were no cards on it, just some matchsticks and a mouldy-looking ashtray. I felt I was looking into the bowels of a dilapidated theatre with only the ghosts of the departed actors for company.

After a few minutes I went round the back. I pushed a door open and went inside. There was a musty smell everywhere but it looked same as I remembered it. Things always looked smaller as you grew older but that sense was cancelled out by the removal of the tables.

How many stories could these walls tell, I wondered, as I walked through the room where I'd spent the lion's share of my youth. How many people had nurtured dreams like mine as they bent over the snooker table to line up their shots? The world was simpler then. Life was a treasure trove of dreams. How many of them had wound up to nought? Had mine?

I thought of the days I used to chase players round this room as we argued with one another about the score of a long-forgotten game, or swung our cues around like swords after coming out of some swashbuckling film in the Estoria or the Savoy. It was a hive of activity then, the focal point of the town for those of us who were hooked on the idea of putting round crystalate objects into holes with sticks.

I felt a lump in my throat as I stood there. Its sad state made me fear anywhere else I might visit from that time – the college, the church, even my own house. I'd stayed away from these places too on previous visits, and for the same reasons. I didn't want them to have power over me when they weren't the places they used to be, just like I wasn't the same person who was haunted by them.

Outside the hall I listened to the chitter-chatter of a few old men moaning about the weather. Some of them looked at me as if they knew me. This always happened in small towns. You could be gone from them for decades but after five minutes a hint of recognition dawned.

I passed the shops of grocers with the same enamel signs that had also formed an indelible part of my youth. Equally indelible were the cracked names on shop-fronts, the display windows withering into anachronism, the side alleys that reminded me of the Stone Ages. The streets were as empty as the streets of Enniscrone had been and I was also glad of that. I didn't want to run into anyone I might know, not that there was any danger of that as my family had been gone from the town for nearly half a century now.

I was glad most of the people I grew up with had moved away, either to the outlying counties or the bright lights of Dublin. If they'd stopped in front of me I would have had nothing to say to them. Nor, I imagined, would they to me. Much as I hated to admit it, I knew a part of me had become urbanised, whatever that meant.

I went into a shop and bought the *Western People*, our local newspaper. In a café on King Street over coffee I read stories of drunken men kicking in doors after one too many, or being confined to the peace after altercations in bars. These were the kind of cases my father had dealt with when he was a solicitor there, smalltown tales of smalltown lives. In Dublin the headlines were of murders and the like; here it seemed to be news if somebody caught a salmon bigger than his neighbour's one. Maybe I needed to get back to that simplicity.

After finishing my coffee I walked up Bury Street. I went past the old offices of Bourke, Carrig and Loftus, a legal firm my father had dealt with. I went up towards the font, where horses had slaked their thirst long before I was a gleam in his eye.

When I turned into Teeling Street I saw the Estoria was gone, a faded poster of Robert Young and Myrna Loy in a glass frame outside it the only clue as to the fantasies this visual factory had for me as I held my breath going to the matinees there all those centuries ago.

I walked down past Norfolk, our old house, which was just across the road from it. It was a community centre now. I resisted knocking on the door not because I was afraid I wouldn't be allowed in but because I was afraid I might be. I knew the house had been refurbished significantly when it was bought by the local council. It would have been too painful to witness the changes at first hand. Instead I just walked by it, pretending to myself that it was just another house.

What used to be the Town Hall, two doors away from us, was now converted into apartments. At the end of the road I paused to look across at where Geraghty's grocery shop had been. It had doubled as a pub, which meant one could do one's shopping there and then get drunk, thereby fulfilling the two main functions of many people's week in one fell swoop. The offices of the *Western People* now stood on its spot. My aunt's house on the nearby Killala Road was also gone. A petrol station stood there now.

I turned left towards Convent Hill. My sisters had been educated in the Convent of Mercy, a building almost as grim to them as Muredach's College had been to me. Across from the convent stood a multiplex cinema, the replacement for the Estoria. It looked like all the other multiplexes.

I expected the town would also have other big chains in it, the Spars and Centras that had sprung up in most places now, making everywhere resemble everywhere else. The similarity of such 'developments' filled me with sadness, not so much for myself as the generation growing up. How could they know anything of diversity? At least I had, the loss of what had preceded them being the price you had to pay for witnessing them in the first place.

Some young people passed by me carrying mobile phones. They were dressed in Adidas tracksuits and wore Nike runners. I imagined them playing songs by people like Beyonce and Justin Timberlake on their iPods. Or were these singers already *passé* now? The only thing that made them different to Dublin children was their accents. It was refreshing to hear the brogue, one of the few links to the past that seemed to be left.

I felt the town wore the insecure aura of a child trying to grow up too fast, unaware of what it represented, trying to conceal its insecurity with a kind of slickness that didn't suit it. That was probably a prejudice I would have harboured for any town I grew up in no matter where it was.

I resented it the way any older person resents the latest technology, particularly if they aren't able to master it. The Celtic Tiger had brought the boom to Ballina as it did to most other reasonably sized towns in Ireland, though not as obviously as to the cities. Despite all the fancy goods shops and the designer gear I felt that not too much had changed at all.

As I came back down Convent Hill I thought I might see if Norfolk was open after all. Maybe my courage had been bolstered by the whiskey Mary encouraged me to have. I knew she'd have wanted me to go in, knowing I'd regret not doing so on the way back to Dublin if I didn't. 'You're lucky that you can walk in anytime you like,' she often said to me, which wasn't the case with most people who moved house, including herself. She was just as attached to her old family home in Salthill as much as I was to my one but it had been sold privately rather than to a council. That meant she could only view it from outside anytime she was in Galway.

When I got to the door I gave it a push. As was the case with the Hibernian Hall, it surprised me by opening. I walked inside and stood in the hall. The staircase was much the same, as were the doors to the left and right of it, our old sitting room and dining room. There was a prayer meeting going on upstairs. I listened to the gentle purring of the voices in unison. Downstairs was empty. I went into the room that had been my father's office. I expected it to look smaller but it didn't, anymore than the Hibs. There were easy chairs round the walls, making it look like a room in an old folk's home. The carpet was threadbare. Everything was different except for the old skirting boards. I closed my eyes and tried to inhale the sensation of the days, when I thought it would be my permanent home.

This was the room where I used to play a game with matchboxes that my father gave me. Every time he finished a box of matches he gave it to me to keep. He was a chainsmoker. That meant he went through a lot of them. When I had enough of them collected I used to stand them on their sides and put them in a weaving pattern. When you tipped one over, they all fell like dominoes.

Whenever my mother saw all the matchboxes it brought home to her just how much my father was smoking. He told her he didn't smoke all the cigarettes he lit. Sometimes he could have three lighting in three separate rooms. He lit one and then forgot about it. Then he lit another one up in some other room. They were smaller than the usual cigarettes. He smoked a brand called *Boston* which didn't stay long on the market. His fingers were always brown because he held them upside down in his hands and let the smoke blow into them. You could always smell the nicotine off him from way off.

I pulled back the curtains to let the sun in. The dust danced in its light. I looked out at the sky, at the narrow street. I remembered how cars used to stop and start as they made way for one another at a time when there were few enough of them in existence. I used to look out at them as a child as they sped up the road to Foxford and Swinford, wondering what places lay elsewhere in Mayo and what they might look like.

I didn't go upstairs, feeling I'd seen enough for one visit. Despite what I'd said to Mary, I knew I'd probably never be able to conquer my feelings of loss any more than any sensitive adolescent taken away from his comfort zone.

A mass of memories crowded into my head as I walked back up Teeling Street. I thought of all the summers cycling down to Enniscrone by the Quay Road, looking out at the massive old ship that lay marooned in the middle of the Moy since the war. I thought of measuring my cycling time against the last journey like in a race, of the way my heart used to beat with excitement as the first dunes came into sight at Skermore House, the old mansion near Bartra that had no roof on it.

I remembered the games of soccer we played in Belleek with the Courells, the bottle of lemonade that was passed around at half-time with a piece of newspaper stuffed into it instead of a cork, the day Dessie Callaghan took a penalty and ended up kicking his boot into the goal instead of the ball. I remembered my two brothers going down to Byron's record shop for the latest hits by Elvis or Cliff Richard or Tommy Sands. We listened to the Everly Brothers singing 'Cathy's Clown' on Radio Luxembourg on Sunday nights when we were supposed to be in bed, sucking the last few minutes of ecstacy out of the weekend before the dreaded odyssey to Muredach's the following day.

In some ways I was back in that time again. I felt I was still the child that walked these streets and thought these thoughts, even if they were still only available to me now at a remove. If I tried to grasp them too hard they'd disappear, like Lot's wife turning into a pillar of salt. If they did, would I be better off? I might be able to move on with my life then. I would be content in my new station, content to wear the suit of the present. I wouldn't fantasise about moving down here for keeps any more, realising that it was just the pipe dream of a homesick child.

I walked down Bridge Street where my father's office used to be. I went down past the Ridge Pool and up past the house of Aubrey Bourke, the doctor who delivered me, who thought I was named after him instead of the poet Aubrey de Vere, whose biography my father was reading the night I was born. Bourke's daughter, Mary Robinson, went on to become president of Ireland in 1991. My own achievements in life resounded slightly less dramatically.

I walked across the Moy and stepped inside the cathedral. It was one of the biggest I'd ever seen in my life – and I'd been in the Vatican. That hugeness had to have been part of its allure, the allure of a time when even walking into it made you feel humble. I looked at the crumbling stucco of the pulpit, the statue of St. Francis perched behind it like some form of apocalypse. I used to sit in these same pews as a child, looking at my sisters transfixed in some obscure bond with the almighty. I always envied them their devotion to something so pure and so intangible.

This too had disappeared with the brave new world of modern Ireland. The sun used to filter through the designs of the stained glass windows. It gave me a strange elation as it did so. I got a similar elation after confession on Saturday nights, my soul spring-cleaned to new heights as the sins I was told would damn me to hell were airbrushed out of my life by the gentle whispers of the old man on the other side of the grill who seemed more like a Thomist monk than a Vincentian.

After leaving the cathedral I walked down to Muredach's. I was intent now on visiting all the old haunts for no better reason than that I'd started. It was like a drug addict upping his dosage in search of the ultimate fix.

It stood like a mute colossus in the dying night, its gothic structure filling me with almost as much dread now as when I was a child. As I walked up the pathway to its doors I wondered how often my stomach lurched as I made this journey before, seeing the priests as dictators in a regime of knowledge instilled into you without your wishes, knowledge you had no choice but to bow to, even though you knew that 99% of it bore no relation to anything you would use in life afterwards.

The brickwork was cracked and some of the windows were broken. These simple details seemed to relax me. Like the dwindling number of priests who lived within its walls it seemed to have lost its capacity to inspire fear. I saw it as little more than a run-down building now, surrounded by wasteland.

In various articles on it that I'd read over the years I'd learned that it was no longer a boarding school and that its priests were mostly gone, either to outlying parishes or to their eternal reward. I didn't know why this should make me feel good. I doubted any of them had gone out of their way to make my childhood unhappy. In many ways they were as much victims of their time as I was. When I was growing up they were like gods but now that the world had turned against them they were as likely to be spat at on the street as knelt to.

In a few years I could see the college being sold to make way for the latest multi-national looking for a tax break or to pay off some sexual debt. This would be ironic because sex sins seemed to be the only ones imaginable to the men who taught me when I was a pupil there.

I felt strange as I walked down the main corridor, an age-old kick of guilt making me expect a clip on the ear from some soutaned figure for being late, or not having my copy with me, or having some inane line of poetry misquoted. The very smell of the walls seemed to bring back this sense of expectation, this pathetic fear of the next lash of the canes with the ends stippled to give them extra force.

There were no bamboo canes now, and no priests either. A deathly silence enwreathed the place. All I could hear were my footsteps and the squeak of any door I opened. The woodwormed benches where we'd scrawled our names for perpetuity, as were the stained inkwells, sitting to attention as if waiting for new ghosts to inhabit them.

I walked outside. A group of young boys were playing football over by the handball alley. They were decked out in the familiar red and white, the Muredach's colours. There was a training session coming to an end, a clutter of voices raised over some trivial indiscretion by a forward on a back. The coach smiled at me as a curse rent the air, throwing his eyes to heaven in mock-frustration.

I told him I'd been a past pupil there and he said he was one too. He knew of my family, in particular my father.

'I hear he was quite a character,' he said. We fell into conversation as the game ground to a halt. We exchanged stories about canes being stolen and beatings administered, the petty mythologies of days most adults had forgotten about or pushed into some subconscious part of their brain. He was a few years younger than me so he would have been part of a more relaxed time, one where pupils were allowed to wear their hair longer. And maybe even have minds.

'Are you going to the parade?' he said then. I told him I hadn't known about it. 'They're going to a bit of trouble this year,' he said, 'You should check it out.' I told him I would. As we parted we exchanged phone numbers. We promised to keep in touch but I felt it was unlikely that we would have much in common except for this brief exchange of school stories. He didn't have any of the angst I had. After I left him I found myself envying once again the fact that he'd grown up at a time when the draconian excesses of my own generation had more or less all been exorcised.

When I got back to the B&B, Mary was sitting on the bed. She was watching *Coronation Street* on a television set that hung on the wall. 'So the prodigal son returns,' she said. 'How was the Hibs? I suppose you had a few frames with Jimmy White.' (He'd become another obsession of mine by now, one of the few who didn't hail from this neck of the woods). 'I beat him ten-nil,' I joked, 'but then most people can nowadays.'

We sat talking about what I'd seen in Norfolk and the college. After a few minutes, as we wondered whether we should go for another drink or not, we heard some noise coming from the street outside.

When I looked out the window I saw that the parade was already starting. People in weird costumes were streaming up and down in droves, some of them chanting in rhythm as they pounded on drums with wooden spoons.

'What's going on?' Mary asked me.

'It's a parade for Halloween,' I said, 'I heard about it down at the college. I forgot to tell you.'

We put on our coats and went outside. As we got close to the church our paths were blocked by throngs of people chattering. The ones who were dressed in modern clothes looked almost like the oddities as a pageant of medieval dresses appeared before us. As I looked at the mass of them swaying back and forth I thought I'd never seen as many people in one place, not even in a summer I'd spent in New York. It looked like the whole population of Mayo had come to the town for this one night.

On the bridge there were travellers selling cowboy hats with flashing lights perched on the tops of them. I bought one of them, as well as a pair of psychedelic sunglasses. 'If you put those on,' Mary warned me, 'I'm going home.'

Just then a belly-dancer from Brazil passed us by, dressed in a leopard-skin bikini. She had little objects strapped around her ankles that jingled as she danced. I felt like pinching myself to make sure I was really in my home town. The only processions I'd ever witnessed in my youth were religious ones.

The parade proper started then. It was close to midnight but there were dozens of children there. The streets were lit up as brightly as if it were mid-day. We got a viewing spot on Garden Street behind a barrier. A horde of dancers came towards us with painted faces. They swirled back and forth to the sound of jungle music being beaten out on little drums by men and women whose expressions remained impassive. Some of the dancers were like whirling dervishes. Others looked as if they were just happy to be dressed up, making the occasional movement as they waved to relatives in the crowd. In the upstairs windows of surrounding buildings people drank beer as they looked out, having their own makeshift party indoors.

Every few minutes the people in the florid colours moved away from the main parade and a new act made its way into the vacant spot. Dancers were followed by fire-eaters, by jugglers, acrobats, twenty-foot high men on stilts who shook hands with you with artificial limbs that clicked open and shut by means of hidden switches. There were also a horde of strange modes of transport on display – boats shaped like little arks which were carried along on wheels, three-wheeled motorcycles and five-wheeled bicycles. Children watched open-mouthed, locked between confusion and awe, unsure whether to laugh or scream in fright.

When the last man on stilts finally passed us by, the crowd began to dissipate. I told Mary I'd never seen anything like it in my life. She said she hadn't either.

We started to walk back towards the car when suddenly someone shouted, 'Fireworks!' I looked down across the bridge and the sky lit up with a multi-coloured array of sparks like an electric flower opening in outer space.

For the next half hour we stood entranced as crackers exploded over the Moy. Many of them were sent up parallel with the spire of the church, as if they were exploding that too. It seemed like a symbol to me, a changing of the guard, a replacement of one world with another.

Would it be better or worse? Who knew? 'Paganism has come to Ballina!' Mary chortled. I told her she'd have got a clip on the ear if she said that in Muredach's – or even the Convent of Mercy.

We were both lost in the frenzy of activity. Beside us a young man jumped up on the bonnet of a moving car. He started chanting something, refusing to allow it across the bridge.

Two members of the gardai leapt on him within moments and carted him off. Somehow that little incident seemed to break the spell of the night. The fireworks were still going on but people now started to disperse.

I watched a lone straggler in a tattered clown's outfit making his way home up towards Bachelor's Walk. He looked like something out of a Fellini film as he carried his wig in his hands. I suddenly felt surreal, as if I was a part of a dream that had just ended.

Suddenly I felt I'd got rid of all my demons. Because the town had ridded itself of its origins, I was now free to rid myself of them too.

I didn't want the day to end.

'Let's go back to Enniscrone,' I said to Mary.

'At this hour?' You're mad. But if that's what you want I won't stand in your way.'

We went back to the car. My head was dizzy with a kind of weird excitement as we drove to Enniscrone. We hugged the river as the last slivers of light disappeared from the sky.

A fox crossed our path at one stage, slinking through a crevice in a wall. These were the sights I missed in Dublin, the sights I wasn't even aware of missing until I saw them. I kept thinking of the parade. It was just over and yet it seemed as if it hadn't happened, as if it was all a figment of my imagination.

When we got to Enniscrone I took a can of beer out of the boot of the car. I walked onto the beach without putting to put on my overcoat. The waves were thrashing the shore as they usually did at this time of night, my favourite time. I sat on the sand watching the waves ebb and flow around me. Mary looked at me and said, 'You do realise you're going to catch pneumonia, don't you?'

She went back to the car to get a blanket. We sat under it and shared the beer as the waves got closer. I listened to their slushing and thought of the line of Baudelaire, '*Homme – toujours tu cheriras la mer.*'

Why was I always drawn to it when it looked exactly the same each day? Maybe for that reason. It was an oasis of permanence in a world of flux. And yet it was also a part of that flux.

I nodded off eventually. When I woke up it was morning. The blanket was still around me but Mary was nowhere to be seen. The sea seemed to be miles away as a raw dawn bit through me. The air was clean, the houses of Enniscrone like toy buildings in the distance.

Eventually Mary appeared. She seemed to be coming from the Valley of Diamonds.

'Well,' she said, 'You didn't get pneumonia after all. I was wrong. How do you feel?'

'I feel cured of something,' I said, 'but I'm not sure what.'

'Maybe now you can get on with your life and forget this place.'

'Maybe,' I said. But in another part of me I felt more a part of it than ever before. It was as if a new self had been born into me, or me into it. I felt I'd become transmogrified into another identity, a reincarnation of my old one without the scars.

We drove back to Ballina without talking as the sun burst through the sky. I tried to process what I'd seen the previous night but I couldn't. It was as if it had happened to someone else, as if I wasn't really a part of it, not even a witness. Even now the car seemed to be driving itself without me moving it. I travelled along roads that showed the same landmarks but in a way I didn't recognise. They also seemed to have changed, to have morphed into new constructs.

Another day was beginning as we reached the B&B. We parked the car and walked up to the door. The streets were full of streamers, party hats, the detritus of the night before.

A man from the council picked them up with a stick that had a clip on the bottom of it and put them into a bag.

'That was some hooley last night,' he said as he passed. 'Thanks be to Jesus we're free of it for another year.'

Across from us we watched an early morning angler throwing his fishing rod onto the gently sweeping current of the Moy.

L - #0152 - 110119 - C0 - 229/152/19 - PB - DID2411830